NICOLE TSOPO

Gamuchirai Receiver

Copyright © 2024 by Nicole Tsopo

All rights reserved. No part of this publication may be reproduced, stored or transmitted in any form or by any means, electronic, mechanical, photocopying, recording, scanning, or otherwise without written permission from the publisher. It is illegal to copy this book, post it to a website, or distribute it by any other means without permission.

This novel is entirely a work of fiction. The names, characters and incidents portrayed in it are the work of the author's imagination. Any resemblance to actual persons, living or dead, events or localities is entirely coincidental.

First edition

This book was professionally typeset on Reedsy. Find out more at reedsy.com

My mother, who inspired Gamuchirai and named her.

*To the black girl: Look behind you. Millions stand with you.
You cannot afford to stop. Forge the path forward.*

"Chinokanganwa idemo, asi muti haukanganwi."—"The axe forgets, but the tree stump does not."

A Shona Proverb

Contents

Chapter 1	1
Chapter 2	8
Chapter 3	25
Chapter 4	42
Chapter 5	51
Chapter 6	56
Chapter 7	67
Chapter 8	86
Chapter 9	94
Chapter 10	100
Chapter 11	112
Chapter 12	125
Chapter 13	135
Chapter 14	143
Chapter 15	151
Chapter 16	162
Chapter 17	171
Chapter 18	189
Chapter 19	197
Chapter 20	208
Chapter 21	214
Chapter 22	223
Chapter 23	241
Chapter 24	249

Chapter 25	255
Chapter 26	263
Chapter 27	271
Chapter 28	280
Chapter 29	289
Chapter 30	293
Chapter 31	303
Chapter 32	311
Chapter 33	313
Chapter 34	347
Chapter 35	362
Chapter 36	374
Chapter 37	379
Chapter 38	385
Chapter 39	397
Chapter 40	409
Chapter 41	415
Chapter 42	423
Chapter 43	441
Chapter 44	446
Chapter 45	453
Chapter 46	460
Chapter 47	466
Chapter 48	475
Chapter 49	483
Chapter 50	502
Chapter 51	512
Six Years Later	520

Chapter 1

Part One.

The square fills steadily, a slow tide of humanity pressing forward, drawn together by a wordless, shared fear. Anxiety ripples silently through the crowd, a chill whisper that curls around their bones, leaving breath shallow and uncertain. Bodies crowd tightly, shoulder to shoulder, seeking comfort in proximity, as though their closeness might ward off the darkness they all sense approaching. Each hesitant shuffle stirs the dry earth beneath, sending faint clouds of dust upward to settle on damp skin.

Little wide eyes with dread glance skyward, scanning the grim, shadowed faces for a glimmer of hope, but finding only muted despair and quiet resignation. Mothers clutch their children fiercely, their fingers white-knuckled, trembling from fatigue and worry. Soft, urgent whispers ripple through the air: "Vanza maziso ako, pfukidza nzeve dzako"—*"Hide your eyes, cover your ears."* These words hang heavily, fragile yet charged with meaning, spoken by voices burdened by memories of past terrors, voices bracing themselves for whatever comes next.

Even the young men—those who would normally scowl in defiance—stand silent today, their bravado swallowed by the crushing atmosphere. Fists clench, jaws tighten, and their bodies tremble as they struggle to maintain some semblance of control. *Ndambira Nyembe* has long known better than to recruit these young men from Nakuru as soldiers. Instead, he ensnares them through more insidious means, assigning them to hazardous, grueling tasks that keep them far from their families, ensuring that their visits are so rare that any whispers of rebellion are silenced before they can take root.

But today, all of that is forgotten. *Today is a lesson for all.*

And still, the crowd waits, the inevitable drawing nearer, a shadow darkening the edges of their world. There is nothing left but to stand and face it.

Aisha stands tall at the center of it all, her angular features as sharp as the authority she wields. She is a figure carved from steel and cold resolve, her eyes gleaming with pride. Her boots are caked in mud from endless days spent overseeing the extraction of the village's most precious resources. This land, teeming with the materials Ndambira covets, is hers to command, to dominate. She ensures a relentless flow of wealth and is ruthlessly efficient in her role as overseer. Her gaze sweeps over the gathered crowd, a slight smile tugging at her lips as she drinks in their fear; the horror about to unfold lies squarely at her command.

CHAPTER 1

At last, Ndambira strides into the square, *a predator* whose mere presence sends shivers through the crowd, forcing them into submission before he even speaks. The crowd cowers but he doesn't notice, he doesn't care. Ndambira's contempt is so effortless it borders on indifference. He doesn't so much as glance at the gathered villagers. To him, they are less than the dust beneath his feet, not even worth the effort of a glance. His soldiers, mirroring their leader's disdain, keep their eyes forward, weapons held with lazy confidence.

At the center of the square, he doesn't so much as glance Aisha's way. For all her ruthlessness, for all her efficiency, Aisha is nothing more than another tool in Ndambira's hand—a tool not even worthy of his attention. The slight is subtle, but it cuts deep. She forces herself to stand tall, her head held high, her posture rigid, trying to convince everyone around her—and perhaps herself—that the indifference doesn't sting.

The voice is as deep and commanding as the call of the hornbill at dusk, resonant and final. "To defy me," he begins, "is to defy the very marrow of order itself. When order fractures, so does everything you cling to—your families, your homes, your lives." He pauses, allowing the tension to coil tighter. "There will be no mercy for those who dare to question me. Disobedience is a rot festering in this village, and I will carve it out like a cancer, root and stem."

The words are a creeping poison, seeping into every crack of the crowd's fragile resolve. *"Your fear* will be the fuel for this new world, your obedience the bricks that build it. You believe you can conceal yourselves, that your whispers and feeble acts of defiance slip by unnoticed in the shadows. But shadows are my domain. I see everything. I hear everything. And when you stand against me, I will grind you to dust beneath my heel."

He gestures to his soldiers, who seize Tenda and Abu—Aisha's mining laborers—and force them to their knees. The crowd holds its breath, horror etched into every face, as the executioner steps forward. Clad in camouflage fatigues, his presence is as cold and menacing as the large, gleaming axe he wields.

Tenda's face is a mask of defiance, every line etched with fierce determination. Even as he kneels, he refuses to bow his head. His gaze locks onto Ndambira's with unwavering resolve. In a final act of defiance, he spits, the saliva landing squarely on Ndambira's polished shoe, now marred by the dust of Nakuru. It's a small rebellion, but it sends a ripple through the crowd—a brief moment of resistance in the face of overwhelming power.

Ndambira, standing tall and immaculate in his pristine suit, untouched by the grime of the island, embodies everything that makes him an outsider. His eyes flicker, a hint of amusement playing at the corners of his mouth as if Tenda's defiance is nothing more than a fleeting distraction. With a subtle gesture, almost dismissive, he signals the executioner to proceed.

CHAPTER 1

As the executioner steps forward, raising the axe high above his head, the crowd recoils in unison. No one dares to close their eyes—such an act would only mark them as the next in line. The blade catches the harsh sunlight, a blinding flash before the inevitable strike. With a single, swift stroke, the axe descends, cleaving through the thick, oppressive silence.

The sickening thud of steel meeting flesh and bone is met with a collective gasp, the sound echoing in the still air. Blood spatters the earth, a stark crimson against the muted browns of the dirt. Tenda's head rolls to the edge of the crowd, his lifeless eyes reflecting the cloudless sky above as if seeking a mercy that will never come. The crowd is frozen, horror etched into every face, but the executioner does not pause.

The axe rises again, its edge gleaming with fresh blood, and falls with brutal finality. The silence is shattered once more, another sickening thud resounding through the square. Abu's body—no older than seventeen—collapses forward, lifeless and limp. His blood weaves into Tenda's, soaking into the earth as the last traces of defiance are wiped away.

Aisha allows herself a small, satisfied smirk, and I can't help but think how easily I could end her right here and now—with a brain seizure, or by watching her claw her throat in a frantic, senseless panic as blood fills her lungs. They'd never suspect me—just another "tragic" accident in this harsh world. The thought lingers, but then, something almost amusing dawns on me: how absurdly fragile her sense of power is. Here she is, basking in her fleeting triumph, unaware that a greater force could snuff her out without a second thought. The illusion of power is *laughable*, really. And from where I stand, she's not pathetic because she's weak—no, she's pathetic because she actually believes in that power, believes in that pitiful smirk of hers, like the way chickens peck at shit, thinking they've found something valuable. The real joke is on her, thinking she holds any real control in a world that could swallow her whole without even pausing to chew.

Ndambira turns sharply, his expression indifferent, as if what just transpired is nothing more than routine. His soldiers follow in his wake, exuding a sense of superiority. As they depart, the final message hangs in the air: treason will not be tolerated. Obey, and you may live in peace. Defy, and you will share the same fate.

If I were to seize the opportunity to kill, it would be him I'd target. Yet, I'm aware of my ignorance about the system here—how can I be certain that I wouldn't be exchanging one tyrant for a worse one? And is it truly my place to plunge into the maelstrom of power? I know from experience that power is undermined by haste and recklessness. Besides, I've long accepted that I am not meant to be a hero. I am not meant to pretend to be anything more than a mere shadow in the background—*a nobody.*

The crowd lingers, and the image of the executions seared into their minds. Mothers clutch their children tightly, desperate to shield them from a world devoid of mercy. The children who didn't heed their warnings stand frozen,

CHAPTER 1

wide-eyed, their innocence shattered by the horror they've just witnessed. Even those who hid their eyes grasp the grim reality. The men avoid each other's gaze, shame and helplessness settling in their hearts like a dark cloud that refuses to lift.

Chapter 2

Nakuru nestles between fertile lands, encircled by rolling hills and dense forests—a place that should be a sanctuary. Yet under the iron grip of Administrator Ndambira, it has become a prison. His rule poisons the village like venom creeping through its veins, choking its lifeblood with enforced labor and stifling its once-thriving culture. And still, I remain.

The square feels muted, its pulse faint and irregular, still reeling from the recent execution that left a shadow hanging over everything. Market stalls stand subdued beneath that lingering cloud. I move through the space, careful and quiet, my feet carrying me toward the edge of the square and into the solace of the woods, where the river winds like a silver thread through the dense greenery.

The market itself is bleak—a scattering of threadbare cloth and paltry offerings. Wilted vegetables and hastily carved trinkets lie atop weathered stalls. The villagers shuffle between them like ghosts, their voices barely more than murmurs, eyes darting from soldier to soldier as if every breath might give away their secrets. Ndambira's men patrol constantly, their presence a heavy reminder of submission. They carry short, curved swords, weapons made for quick strikes in the tight alleyways or dense underbrush, and barbed spears designed to keep the villagers from daring even the smallest hint of rebellion. They are clumsy in their movements and loud with their conversation, but it isn't their skill that inspires fear—it's the cold certainty of violence, the eager willingness to inflict pain on anyone who steps out of line.

I feel eyes on me—some curious, others familiar. To many here, I am the healer who mends their broken bones, who cools their fevered brows with steady hands. They trust me and confide in me. But they do not know the truth that lurks beneath this guise of comfort—the truth that would freeze their blood if they knew. I deal in shadows, bartering pieces of my soul for the dark power that hides within me. Every time I call on this magic, it takes more of me—draining, weakening—but the power it gives me is worth the sacrifice.

I notice a pair of eyes lingering on me for too long, watching me with a scrutiny that unsettles me. A soldier. His gaze is too sharp, as though trying to see past my healer's face to what lies beneath. Without breaking stride, I veer toward a nearby stall, letting the herbs and spices on display form a barrier between us. I keep my face composed, but inside, my pulse quickens.

The air here stings with the scent of cinnamon and cloves. The merchant, an old man, offers no greeting—only a wary glance before turning to the task of gathering my herbs. His hands tremble as he wraps them in a cloth, and I feel the weight of the soldier's gaze still pressing down on me, an unwanted shadow. I hand over a few coins, murmuring, "Mazvita,"—*"Thank you."* before turning away, the herbs tucked securely beneath my cloak. The soldier remains fixed on me, his suspicion like a cold hand on my shoulder.

I move with purpose, slipping into the narrow alley flanked by stalls draped in vibrant fabrics. My heart races, but I force myself to breathe slowly, crouching low as if examining a sack of grain. I use the clutter of rotting barrels and discarded wood as cover, edging further from the soldier's sightline. Yet, as I glance back, I see him at the alley's entrance, his gaze sweeping over the area with cold intent. My pulse quickens, but I keep my movements steady, pulling my hood lower to obscure my face.

As the soldier questions the nearby merchant, I seize my chance. With a quiet, deliberate step, I slip deeper into the alley, the soft leather of my sandals barely whispering against the packed dirt. A group of women passes by, their lively chatter like a protective veil that wraps around me. I weave into their midst, letting their voices cloak my movements, and use their presence as a shield to mask my escape. Just ahead, a line of bright linens dances in the breeze, their colors vivid against the gray backdrop of the village. I duck beneath the fluttering cloth, the scent of fresh soap washing over me as I vanish into the shifting folds. Hidden among the billowing fabrics, I become one with the shadows, slipping through them like smoke, silent and unseen, before the soldier can close in.

CHAPTER 2

Finally.

"Hei! Usafamba imwe nhanho!"—*"Hey! Don't take another step."*

The sharp bark slices through the stillness, striking me like a cold slap and freezing me in place. His accent is strange—unfamiliar, like it belongs neither to Nakuru nor Mvure, but to some forgotten place in between. The words sound almost out of place on his tongue, clipped and foreign.

"Hongu, ndirikutaura newe,"—*"Yes, I'm talking to you."*

My heart lodges in my throat, blood pounding in my ears as another soldier steps closer to me. He strides toward me with grim purpose, suspicion carved into the harsh lines of his face.

His camouflaged uniform blends into the foliage, a ghost among the trees. A battered helmet casts his eyes in shadow, but I feel them on me—sharp, calculating. Mud clings to his boots, a well-worn machete hanging within easy reach, its handle worn smooth from years of deadly use. Over his shoulder, a rifle glints dully in the fading light, a silent promise of violence.

"What brings you here?" His voice is cold and authoritative—leaving no space for defiance. His hand drifts toward the machete, fingers brushing the blade in a way that feels almost idle—but the threat is unmistakable.

My pulse races, hammering against my ribs, but I force myself to meet his gaze with a mask of calm. The weight of my power stirs within me, dark and restless, pressing against the corners of my mind. I have to hold it back, keep it chained. "Makadii, sahwira,"—*"How are you, friend?"* I keep my voice steady despite the roiling beneath the surface. "I'm headed to the river." The words tumble from my mouth like stones falling into deep water, each one sinking into the depths of his scrutiny.

His eyes narrow, suspicion flickering in their depths as he assesses me. His gaze sweeps over my form, noting the absence of any container, no bucket or jug to justify a trip to the river. The question lingers between us, unspoken but heavy—what kind of woman ventures to the river alone at this hour, and with empty hands?

"Unoenda kurwizi pasina tsime kana chirongo?" His voice is low, calculating. *"Are you going to the river without a water container or bucket?"*

"I go to collect herbs and tend to a sick woman," I reply, the lie slipping easily off my tongue. Simple, believable, and *true.*

For a moment, he says nothing, only studies me, his gaze searching for the cracks in my composure. "If you venture beyond the river, you may not return, especially after dark," he finally speaks.

Not all of them are cruel, some maintain a distant, almost

CHAPTER 2

nonchalant vigilance, their harshness kept in check until their leaders demand otherwise. "Ndinoziviva,"—"I know," I say softly, my tone gentle yet firm. "But it's urgent—the elders need help."

He hesitates, then nods curtly, dismissing me with a wave of his hand. But as I move past him, I can still feel his eyes boring into my back, like a blade poised to strike—*you never know.*

The path to the river winds like a secret, barely visible beneath the thick underbrush that tangles and creeps along the ground. The forest closes in on me, the air heavy with damp earth and the sharp tang of rotting wood, as though the trees themselves are conspiring to smother me in their silence. My muscles coil with tension, each step tightening the knot in my chest until my breath comes in shallow, ragged bursts by the time I reach the river.

The water flows with deceptive calm, its surface rippling softly under the fading light. For a fleeting moment, I allow myself to believe in the peace it offers, in the quiet escape that feels so close, so real. But as I kneel to drink, the whispers return. They begin as they always do—soft, insinuating, coiling at the edges of my mind like tendrils of smoke. But they don't stay quiet for long. They rise, insistent, gnawing away at my thoughts, until they become a constant, cloying presence I can no longer ignore. I fight them back with sheer force of will, pressing them into the corners of my mind, but the effort is exhausting, and it only holds them at bay for so long.

I move along the riverbank, fingers trailing over the leaves of plants as I search for the herbs I need. Each plant hums beneath my touch, vibrating with a subtle energy that sends a shiver up my spine. But the whispers grow louder, feeding off that same energy, rising into a roar that drowns out the sounds of the forest, the gentle babble of the river—everything. They swallow me whole, suffocating me in their demands until I fall to my knees. Desperation grips me as I crawl back to the water's edge, the herbs clenched tightly in my hands like a lifeline. I close my eyes, squeezing them shut against the rising tide of power that threatens to pull me under.

The prayer that slips from my lips is more plea than devotion, each word trembling with the fragile hope of someone teetering on the edge of oblivion. It's a plea for control, a desperate grasp at the last remnants of who I am before the darkness swallows me whole. The power inside me is relentless, surging forward like a black wave, seeping into every crevice of my mind, filling it with a dread that has no name. It's a force I can no longer contain, a storm that grows stronger with each passing day, and I know—deep in my bones—that one day it will consume me entirely. When that day comes, I will be nothing but a hollow shell, a shadow of the person I once was, lost to the very darkness I once thought I could control.

The urges that plague me, the violent compulsions twisting against everything I once was, have become a relentless curse—a war raging deep within. For so long, I held firm, my will strong enough to resist the dark whispers that slithered at the edges of my mind, clawing at my sanity. But now, something far more sinister has sunk its teeth into me. It tightens its grip with every breath I draw, no longer a subtle influence but a brutal assault, ripping at my soul with a beast's savage claws. The pain that follows is sharp and unyielding, as though my very essence is being torn apart, fiber by fiber. It seeps into the core of me like poison, curling through every thought, spreading a torment so profound that it leaves me gasping, vision blurring into a storm of dark shadows and burning flashes of light.

I force the words of my prayer through trembling lips. They continue to spill out like an incantation, each syllable trembling with fear yet laced with defiance, a battle cry against the encroaching darkness. I call upon the spirits of the air, the water, the earth, and the sky—beings I do not fully comprehend but have come to revere for the power they have bestowed upon me. Whoever or whatever has reached out to intervene in my life, I demand that they reveal themselves. They must show their face, state their terms—anything—before this power consumes me whole—before I am ripped apart piece by piece.

The world around me begins to distort, reality slipping like water through my fingers. The familiar sounds of the forest—the rustling leaves, the steady hum of the river—recede, fading into an unnatural silence that presses in on all sides. My breathing slows, syncing with the heartbeat of the earth beneath me, each exhale dragging me deeper into a trance-like state. The edges of the world soften, and I feel myself drifting, weightless, untethered, slipping into a vast and unknowable space where time and sense no longer exist.

I'm lost in the stillness, floating between moments when suddenly, it shatters. The peace I clung to is ripped apart by a scream—high, desperate, fragile yet raw with terror. The sound slices through the quiet like a blade, reverberating through the forest and yanking me violently from my trance. My heart lurches, ice flooding my veins as I try to make sense of it. A young girl's voice—shaking with fear—echoes through the dense trees, pulling me into the sharp reality where the shadows around me have deepened.

I surge to my feet, still trembling, the dark whispers that haunted me moments ago lingering at the edges of my mind like a sickness that won't fade. My prayers hang in the air like delicate threads, thin and fragile, threatening to snap under the weight of what's to come. But that scream has ignited something inside me—something fierce and unyielding. I must find her.

I push through the underbrush, my heart pounding in my chest, but I barely make it a few steps before pain lances through my skull—a searing, white-hot agony that brings me to my knees. I clutch my head, my fingers digging into my braids as I fight to stay upright. The whispers return with a vengeance, louder now, a chaotic storm of voices that drowns out the world around me. They swirl through my mind, a twisted chorus of disjointed words that scrape at the edges of my sanity, heavy with this dark intent that I can't comprehend.

CHAPTER 2

"I don't understand," I whisper, my voice trembling, barely holding back the fear that's clawing its way to the surface. The forest around me spins in a dizzying blur of darkness and shadow, the world twisting in on itself. I stumble to my feet, my breath ragged. "What do you want from me?" I shout into the blackness, desperation thick in my throat. Each word is tinged with terror, the terror of not knowing—of being at the mercy of forces I can't see, can't fight.

The whispers swell, stretching into something almost tangible—words on the edge of forming before they twist into something monstrous. The shriek that follows is inhuman, and dreadful, tearing through me like a clawed hand. It rips at the fabric of my soul, a sound so unnatural it feels as though it's unraveling me from the inside out. My entire being quakes beneath the onslaught. I press my palms to my ears, desperate to block out the noise, but it's useless.

The girl's screams cut through the night, sharp and frantic, each cry stabbing at my heart. She's out there—somewhere in the darkness—so close yet agonizingly beyond my reach. The sound of her fear wraps around me like chains, tightening with every second that passes. I can't get to her. "Please," I whisper at first, my voice trembling, ragged with the weight of my plea. "Please," I beg again, louder now, my throat raw, the words tearing from me in gasps. "Let me help her... release me. Please, please."

The hissing in my ears rises to an unbearable pitch, a sharp dissonance that seems to tear at the edges of my mind. Just when I think I'll scream, it stops—cut off so abruptly that the silence that follows rings in my head like a bell. I gasp for breath, my chest heaving, my heart slamming against my ribs. But there's no time to recover. The girl's scream lingers in my mind, a haunting reminder of what's at stake, fueling a volatile mix of fear and fury deep inside me. My legs tremble, but I force them to move, pushing myself forward, and stumbling through the underbrush. The forest looms dark and oppressive, but I press on, driven by the desperate need to reach her, to prove to myself that I still have some control—that I haven't surrendered to the darkness just yet.

Her cries grow louder, and more frantic, leading me deeper into the heart of the forest. My breath is sharp and uneven as I weave through the thick tangle of branches and roots, each frantic step pulling me closer to her terror. The weight of the night presses in around me, but I don't stop, don't slow. Not until I burst into a small clearing, my heart lurching as my eyes take in the scene before me.

There she is—a young girl, no more than seven, pinned to the ground by two soldiers. Their faces twist with sadistic pleasure as they hold her down, one of them laughing cruelly as she struggles beneath them. A third soldier looms over them, a whip coiled in his hand, poised to strike again. The girl's face contorts in an attempt to mask her fear, but I see it there, flickering in her wide, tear-filled eyes. Her cries have gone raw, hoarse from the relentless screams.

"Stop!" The word rips from my throat, trembling with fury as it echoes through the clearing.

CHAPTER 2

The soldiers turn, their heads snapping in my direction. For a brief moment, surprise flashes in their eyes, but it quickly fades, replaced by something darker, more insidious. Amusement curls their lips into cruel smirks, and the air thickens with malice.

"Nu fari mi kesi pa nu, re ke lamaniwa seke lo re fas para," one of them sneers, his voice thick with contempt. His eyes gleam with mockery as they sweep over me, sizing me up like prey.

"I su ma i las?" another taunts, his words dripping with lewd anticipation.

Their language is foreign, a twisted dialect that slips through my understanding, but the meaning is unmistakable.

Two of them have already shifted their attention to me, their eyes gleaming with vile hunger as they trade crude remarks. They speak of me as if I'm nothing more than a piece of fruit, ripe for the taking, their voices laced with twisted humor. Each word is venomous and degrading, as they discuss who will claim me first, their laughter filling the air with sickening glee.

This is their sick game—reducing women and girls to nothing more than objects for their depraved amusement. Later, they'll gather like vultures, laughing over the *"fruit"* they've consumed, their twisted jokes filling the air with the stench of cruelty. These soldiers thrive on their power, taking pleasure in stripping away every last shred of humanity from their victims. The word "fruit" is a weapon, a way to dehumanize us, reducing lives to nothing more than another indulgence in their grotesque feast. Disgust twists in my stomach, churning into something harder, something fierce. A seething resolve settles in my bones.

I clench my fists until my nails dig into my palms, the sharp pain grounding me. Every step I take forward is deliberate, my body trembling—not with fear, but with a rage so deep it feels like it might consume me. I fix my gaze on them, steady and unblinking, daring them to look away. *"You are filth,"* I spit, my voice low, thick with venom. I let my contempt seep into every syllable, let them feel the weight of my fury. I drop my gaze for the briefest second and spit onto the earth between us, the sound harsh in the tense silence. Then I look up again, my eyes locked on theirs, daring them to take another step, daring them to cross that final line.

They laugh, their voices thick with derision. "She's like a ripe mango, eh? If you don't bite, you cut it in half, *na?*" Their mockery is laced with crude amusement, but I refuse to let the words penetrate. I turn inward, away from their taunts, toward the raw power coursing through my veins. The air around me thickens, heavy with the dark energy I summon from deep within. I feel the shift—the moment when my will sharpens into a lethal blade.

The first soldier falters, his cocky grin crumbling as a strangled cry escapes his throat. I've taken hold of his blood, feeling it pulse and writhe beneath his skin as it rebels against him. With a whispered command, I force his blood to congeal, to fight against its natural flow. His knees buckle, collapsing beneath him. His eyes bulge in terror, veins straining against his skin, a grotesque web of dark lines as his lifeblood obeys my will, not his. He gurgles, choking on the thickened mass within him, and then collapses—a lifeless heap at my feet.

The second soldier fumbles for his weapon, but fear has made him slow and clumsy. It's too late. I seize control of his blood with a single thought, sending it rushing into his limbs until his muscles lock into place. His eyes go wide with terror, lips trembling as he stands frozen, paralyzed by the force inside him, his every instinct to flee overridden by the crimson power I now command.

Behind him, the soldier with the whip stumbles back, his bravado dissolving into raw panic as he watches his comrades fall. "Witch!" he screams, the word cracking with fear. "Rarha!"—"*Demon!*" He stumbles, trying to retreat, but I am already advancing, my voice a deadly whisper, the darkness in me spilling out with every word. With a flick of my wrist, I send his blood surging violently to his head. Vessels burst in an instant, crimson spilling from his eyes, nose, and mouth. He crumples with a wet thud, his life draining out of him, his body twitching briefly before falling still.

A suffocating silence falls over the clearing, broken only by the girl's ragged sobs. I stand there, their blood pooling around me, my heart still pounding with the fury. The magic leaves me cold, and hollow, draining the last warmth from my body as I struggle to hold on to what remains of myself.

I turn toward the girl, my chest heaving, teeth clenched against the tide of emotions threatening to break free. She looks at me with wide, terrified eyes, her small frame trembling, her breath coming in short, panicked bursts. In her gaze, I see it—a reflection of the monster I've become. The fear in her eyes cuts deeper than any blade, but this is my reality now. A reality I've shaped with my own hands, one I can no longer escape.

I struggle to regain control, but the magic surges like a relentless tide, an unchecked flood of power and fury that I can barely contain. Kneeling beside the trembling girl, I force myself to breathe, willing the shadows to retreat, to release their grip on me. "It's all right," I murmur softly, my voice a strained whisper as I extend a trembling hand to her. "You're safe now."

Her wide, tear-filled eyes meet mine. She hesitates, her small body flinching ever so slightly from my touch. I try to smile, to offer some measure of reassurance, but I can see it in her eyes—she's still afraid. Not just of what's happened, but of me. Her gaze darts to the fallen soldiers, then back to me, torn between her desperation for safety and the terror of not knowing whether I am her savior or another threat lurking in the shadows.

"Usatya,"—*"Don't be afraid,"* I say again, but the words ring hollow, even to my own ears. The darkness I wield, the cost of the power I've embraced, it's all laid bare before her. There's no hiding from it now. "Ndiri pano kuzokubatsira,"—*"I'm here to help you."*

The fear still clings to her, tangible and thick. Her body trembles as she edges back from me, mistrust woven into every movement. "What are you?" she finally whispers, her voice so small and fragile, as though she fears the answer will shatter whatever fragile hope remains.

I swallow the lump in my throat, feeling the weight of her question and the truth that clings to me like a shadow. Her dress is torn, her skin marred with bruises and streaks of blood. My heart aches for her, for this place, for all the lives crushed beneath the heel of Ndambira's regime. These men—these soldiers—deserved far worse than the mercy of death I gave them. But in this moment, I know my power, for all its darkness, can't be the answer. It's not enough. Not yet. Perhaps not ever.

I offer her a small, sad smile, though it barely reaches my eyes. "I'm a friend," I say softly, the words weighed down by a weariness I can't shake. "Let's get you back to your village."

She studies me for a moment, her eyes still wide with lingering fear, her body trembling from all she's endured. The hesitation that hangs between us like a thread stretched too thin. I wonder if she'll ever be able to see me as anything other than the monster I've become. Yet, in that moment, something shifts. Slowly, she edges closer, her small frame trembling as she steps into my arms. She buries her face against my chest, and I hold her gently, cradling her as though she might break. The tension in her body begins to ease, and I can feel her trust, tentative and fragile, settling between us.

I glance down at the soldiers' bodies, feeling a cold chill sweep through me. I was lucky this time. Their numbers were few, and only one had a firearm. It could have gone differently, disastrously so.

Chapter 3

"Can you tell me where you live?" I ask her gently.

She nods, her voice barely more than a whisper. "Down the path, near the old baobab tree. My mother will be worried."

We walk together through the deepening twilight, the golden light fading like the last embers of a dying fire. The air is cool and still, fragrant with the earthy scent of moss and ferns, grounding us in the moment—a peaceful interlude that feels fragile, too brief to last. We walk slowly, her small frame resting lightly against me, yet her unspoken trauma feels like a heavy, invisible weight that neither of us can truly carry alone. She leads me through the winding paths and tangled underbrush, her eyes darting with quick, furtive glances—attempts to conceal her fear, but I see it all the same.

"Are you a witch?" Her voice trembles, so soft I almost don't hear it. "A *Rarha?*"

"Yes," I reply without hesitation. There is no point in lying.

"But a good witch?" she asks, her voice quivering with uncertainty.

I hesitate, feeling the weight of her innocent question settle over me like a shadow I can't escape. The truth tastes bitter on my tongue. "No," I finally say, quietly, the admission heavy between us. "Good people don't kill others."

She falls silent for a moment, considering my words. Then, with the quiet bravery only a child can muster, she speaks again: "But you saved me. They wanted to hurt me." Her voice is tentative but hopeful, reaching for something to hold onto. "I don't think you're evil... just scary." She glances up at me, her eyes wide, then quickly adds, "But not now. Now you are beautiful. Only before."

I can't help the smile that tugs at my lips, though it carries a sadness that lingers. "You're beautiful, too." She smiles back—a small, gentle smile that softens the air between us, a flicker of light.

"You have brown eyes, like my uncle," she says suddenly, her voice carrying a note of quiet wonder. She reaches out to touch a strand of my hair, her fingers gentle and curious. "He is kind."

Her innocent observation slips past the armor I've built around myself, cutting through the layers of darkness I carry like a second skin. I'm struck by the purity of her perspective—how, despite the horrors she has faced, she still holds onto the possibility of kindness. It's a fragile, delicate thing, this child's hope, but it shines bright even in all this suffering. And for a brief moment, I marvel at her resilience, at her ability to see beauty where I can only see shadows.

As we approach her home, a modest hut tucked beside an ancient baobab tree, the village is bathed in the warm, flickering glow of fires pushing back the encroaching darkness. The flames dance and sway, casting long shadows across the thatched roofs, creating an atmosphere that feels both eerie and comforting. The soft clucking of chickens settling in for the night mingles with the distant murmur of villagers winding down their evening routines, a sense of normalcy in the face of all that has happened. The huts, arranged in a semi-circle, give the village an intimate, protective feel, as though the very earth has drawn them close to shield them from the outside world.

A woman rushes forward, her face a portrait of raw emotion—etched with worry, lined with relief. "Mama!" The girl's voice trembles as she breaks away from me and throws herself into her mother's arms.

Tears fall freely down her mother's cheeks as she pulls her daughter close, her hands fluttering over her as if needing to touch every inch to believe she's truly there. "Yoweh! Makanaka chaizvo Mwari!"—*"You are so good God!"* She sobs, sinking to her knees to be level with her daughter, enveloping her in a protective embrace. She murmurs soft, soothing words, her voice a quiet lullaby of comfort and love. She peppers her with kisses.

The village's tranquility is fragile, a thin veil that shivers beneath the presence of soldiers lingering nearby. They sit in small clusters around their own fires, their uniforms blending into the shadows, the flicker of flames barely touching their faces. Their postures are relaxed, and at ease, their laughter and banter disturbingly lighthearted in contrast to the tension that hangs in the air.

The mother glances nervously at the soldiers, her dark, almond-shaped eyes wide with a mix of fear and relief, the tattered edges of her headscarf clinging loosely to her tear-streaked face. She turns to me, gratitude shining through the exhaustion that weighs on her. "Thank you, thank you for bringing her back," she says again, her voice trembling with emotion. "I am so grateful."

I nod, offering a simple, quiet response. "It was the right thing to do."

Her tears fall again, streaming down her face as she turns back to her daughter, brushing strands of hair from the girl's face with trembling hands. She presses a fierce kiss to her forehead, her love battling with her panic."Uri right here? Chii chakaitika kwauri—ah, tarisa! Vakukuvadza here?"—"*Are you alright? What happened to you—ah, look! Are you hurt?*" Her voice quivers as she checks her daughter's bruised arms, her fingers searching frantically for deeper wounds, for any sign of lingering pain.

The girl clings to her mother, whispering, her small hands gripping the fabric of her mother's dress like a lifeline. The relief in the mother's eyes is palpable—a rush of raw emotion flooding her gaze—but behind it, the terror lingers, deep and gnawing, the kind of fear that will not easily fade.

Suddenly, her mother's demeanor shifts. The relief twists into anger, sharp and biting. "Wanga uchitsvagei musango?"—"*What were you doing in the forest?*" She snarls, her voice trembling with fury. "I have warned you, Chinai!" Her hand lashes out, striking the girl hard across the face. The girl stumbles, her cheek flushed with pain. "Uchaenda unotsvaka tsvimbo uyo. Ndichakurova manheru ano!"—"*You will find a stick and bring it to me. I will beat you tonight!*" She grabs the girl by the ear, yanking it taut, and a cry of pain escapes the child's lips.

I turn to leave, hoping to return to the river and find some semblance of solace in its waters. But before I can take more than a few steps, the woman's voice rises behind me. "Mirai, mirai,"—"*wait, wait,*" she calls, rising quickly, her tear-streaked face desperate. She halts me in my tracks, wiping at her eyes as her daughter clings to her legs, seeking refuge. "What's happening to our daughters?" Her voice cracks, her sobs shaking her body. "Every day, every night, I live in fear—wondering if my child will be next."

I turn to her, the weight of her pain sinking into me. "We must continue to pray," I say quietly, hoping the words offer her some measure of comfort, though they feel thin in my mouth. I add softly, signaling my intent to leave.

But her voice trembles again. "Please," she calls after me,

"stay for dinner. It's the least I can offer for what you've done."

I shake my head gently. "No, no. It is alright. I will be on my way."

She nods, reluctantly, but as I turn once more, she suddenly shouts, "Sei, please… you are the healer, aren't you? Is it not so?"

I stop, the weight of her plea pulling me back toward her. I meet her eyes, and for a brief moment, I see the flicker of desperate hope, clinging to the possibility of salvation. But I shake my head again. "No," I reply softly, the truth heavy between us. "I am sorry. I am not."

Her face falls, and though I can feel the sorrow in the air between us, I force myself to turn away. The darkness of the forest calls me back.

"Please!" Her voice trembles, raw with desperation. "I can sense it in you. There is power… my mother, she's very sick. You are difficult to find, but isn't this the hand of *Mwari* guiding you here?" Her eyes search mine, pleading. "I have prayed and prayed for you. Please."

I am unsettled by her awareness of the power that simmers beneath my skin. The way she sees through me, her intuition cutting past my defenses—it makes me uneasy, my pulse quickening with caution. She senses it. The dark magic that still hums through my veins, its presence nearly tangible.

CHAPTER 3

I should turn away. I should leave her to her prayers and escape back into the forest, to the quiet solitude that shelters me from these entanglements. But the tears in her eyes, the raw emotion pulling at her voice—it keeps me rooted in place.

"Please," she begs again, the tears flowing once more, her body trembling.

A dark dread fills me. The magic inside me is restless, and I know the pain will seize me again soon, clawing at the edges of my mind. It always does. But despite the mounting tension, I nod. Something compels me forward—whether it's duty, guilt, or the fleeting urge to quiet the storm raging within me, I cannot say. "Take me to her."

Her breath catches in relief, and for a moment, hope flickers to life in her eyes. She wipes her tears hastily, grasping her daughter's hand as she leads me to her shelter. With each step, the weight of the dark magic presses heavier against my skin, pulsing like a restless heartbeat in the back of my mind, whispering things I try not to hear.

We step inside the hut. The space is simple but cozy, with walls lined with woven mats, shelves crowded with clay pots, and bundles of dried herbs hanging from the beams above. Earth and spices, a small quiet haven. "Eat first," she insists, her voice firm but respectful. "I serve you first."

I shake my head gently, trying to decline. "No, that won't be necessary. Take me to your mother, and I will do what I can."

Her eyes widen, desperation flaring in them. Her voice trembles as she pleads, *"Please. Do not refuse me this. Allow me to honor you."*

Her words stop me. I see the emotion in her gaze and hear the raw need in her voice. This isn't about food—it's about dignity, about gratitude. It's her way of offering something back to the god she believes brought me here, of honoring what she sees as a blessing. To refuse would be to strip her of this small ritual of hope.

"Zvakanaka," I say softly, relenting. *"Alright."*

Her face lights up with relief, her shoulders finally easing. She moves with quiet reverence as she prepares the meal, the careful movements of her hands full of purpose. The girl, still shaken, sits down slowly, watching her mother with wide eyes. The scent of stewed beans and maize begins to fill the air, earthy and comforting, mingling with the warmth of the hut. The firelight flickers, casting dancing shadows on the woven walls, creating an almost surreal intimacy.

She places the meal before me—a simple offering of stewed beans and maize, humble yet full of meaning. I accept it, and as I do, I feel the weight of her gaze on me, full of gratitude and something else—something like hope.

"Thank you again," she says, her voice steadier now, though a faint tremor of admiration lingers. "You are brave."

CHAPTER 3

I pause, glancing at the little girl beside her. "It is your daughter who is brave," I say softly. "She did not shed a single tear, even when they tried to break her."

Her gaze shifts to her daughter, her expression softening into something profoundly sad. "Yes," she whispers, almost to herself. "She is strong. But tears... tears are beautiful. They help us bloom, help us transform. It is tragic that we have had to harden ourselves in defiance, to force strength when we should allow fear and horror to show themselves." Her voice lowers, heavy with sorrow. "It is not fair—especially for little girls."

I lower my gaze and continue eating, feeling the heaviness of her words settle inside me. The simple meal grounds me at the moment, but her sadness lingers in the air.

"We need to teach them to heal," she continues softly, her fingers gently combing through her daughter's hair. "To let them know it is okay to cry when they are hurt. That there is strength in their tears, not weakness."

I listen in silence, the crackle of the fire and the sounds of the night filling the space between us. Outside, nocturnal creatures stir, their calls mingling with the distant hum of quiet conversations from the village. It's a fragile bubble of peace that surrounds us, but I feel like an outsider in it—unable to offer more than my presence, my power distant and alien to this tender moment.

As we finish the meal, she guides me silently to a smaller

shelter tucked away at the back of the hut. The air feels heavier here with a dim light from a single lamp. In the center of the room lies an elderly woman on a simple bed, her breaths shallow and labored, each one a fragile struggle. Her once thick, coiled hair has thinned into sparse gray wisps that escape from beneath a loosely wrapped scarf. She radiates a delicate dignity despite her frailty, her features etched by time and illness.

The little girl's mother kneels beside this elderly woman, her hands tender as she brushes those loose strands of hair back from her mother's forehead. Her touch is gentle, yet in her eyes, there is an unmistakable weight—a profound sadness that seems to anchor her in place, even as hope flickers faintly beneath it. "Please, help her," she whispers, her voice trembling, full of emotion that she can barely contain.

I nod slowly. "I need to understand what is happening to her first," I reply, my voice soft, reassuring.

She watches me closely. "I will touch her now," I murmur, lowering myself to the floor beside the bed. "May I have your permission?"

Her nod is eager. A single tear slips down her cheek as she gives her silent consent.

I reach out carefully, placing my hands on the elderly woman's forehead. Her skin is cool to the touch, fragile like the paper-thin petals of a withered flower. I close my eyes, sinking deeper into my senses, letting the world around us fade away. All I hear is her shallow breathing and the faint, distant pulse of life within her, struggling against the tide of her illness. Beneath my fingertips, the currents of energy begin to stir. I follow them, tracing the delicate threads that connect her body and spirit.

The essence of her blood begins to reveal itself, and with it come flickers of images—memories, sensations, the fragments of a life lived. Each drop of blood carries pieces of her soul: moments of joy and loss, of resilience and pain. But beneath it all, I feel something else—a deep weariness that extends beyond her body, a spiritual fatigue that weighs heavily on her soul. "She carries a burden. It is not only her body that is suffering."

She looks up at me, her expression full of confusion and desperation. "I don't understand," she murmurs, her voice breaking. "Ndapota,"—*"Please*, what do you mean?"

I keep my eyes closed, allowing the sensations to guide me. "In our world," I begin, my voice steady but distant, "a person's spirit is not just an abstract thing—it is tied to their blood, to the very essence that sustains them. Each drop of blood carries not just our physical markers but a powerful imprint of who we are spiritually. It holds echoes of our ancestors, fragments of past lives, and the vibrations that shape our soul."

I pause for a moment, feeling the pulse beneath my fingers grow weaker, the exhaustion of the woman's spirit seeping through. "Illness isn't always about the body," I continue. "It often reflects something deeper—an emotional wound, a spiritual imbalance. When there is unrest within the spirit, it ripples through the blood, and from the blood, it touches the body."

Her eyes fill with tears again as she processes my words. She looks at her mother, fragile and worn, and then back at me, her expression one of helplessness. "What can be done?" she asks, her voice barely more than a whisper.

I open my eyes, feeling the weight of her question hang between us like a lingering shadow. "I will do what I can," I say softly. "But this is no simple ailment of the body. Her pain runs deeper than what I alone can heal."

She nods, her eyes brimming with unshed tears. "She has seen much hardship," she whispers. "But her spirit... her spirit is strong."

Closing my eyes again, I reach into the depths of my power, letting the rhythm of her life force pulse beneath my fingertips. Slowly, I let the dark magic that flows within me merge with hers, sensing the spiritual disruptions that have manifested into her physical suffering. The ritual begins and I draw a small blade from my belt, its edge catching the dim light.

She gasps, a reflex of fear, but I meet her eyes with a steady, reassuring smile. "It's part of the process," I explain, my voice calm but firm. "I must offer my own blood to help heal her."

CHAPTER 3

She hesitates but nods, trusting in what she doesn't fully understand.

I know that this act is both symbolic and practical. My blood represents sacrifice and a deep commitment to the healing. But it's also the medium through which the energies will work—my power, infused into her blood, will seek out the roots of her pain and begin to mend what has been broken. This is not just physical healing—it is a merging of the physical and spiritual, a restoration of the delicate balance that illness has disturbed.

I make a small cut on my palm. The blood wells up, dark and rich with power. I carefully open the elderly woman's mouth, its edges caked with a thick, white residue of sickness. I squeeze my palm, allowing the drops of blood to fall onto her tongue, feeling the surge of magic flow through me like a current. As her body absorbs the blood, I sense the connection deepening, the magic within me channeling into her. I become the conduit, my energy bridging the gap between her weariness and the restorative power of the ritual.

With reverence, I begin to chant ancient incantations, the words spilling from my lips instinctively, as if they've always been inside me. Each syllable is heavy with intention, woven into the fabric of the room—a plea for comfort, for the easing of her burdens, for the weariness to leave her spirit. The air grows full of energy, the incantations swirling around us like a soft wind. I feel the subtle shifts in the room, the weight of the spiritual realm responding to my call. The woman's energy stirs—slowly at first, then stronger, like the rising of a tide. A gentle calm washes over the space, and her breathing begins to steady, her body relaxing as the pain loosens its grip.

I continue, whispering the words with intention until I feel the worst of her suffering ebb away. Her face softens, the deep lines of strain relaxing as peace settles over her. I pull back, knowing the ritual has done what it could. The woman's burdens have been eased, and her spirit mending.

"Mai" the little girl's mother whispers, her voice trembling with awe. She cups her mother's face, pressing kisses all over her cheeks, her tears now those of gratitude. "Thank you," she breathes, her voice thick with emotion as she looks up at me, her eyes shimmering with relief. "Thank you so much."

Her fingers tremble with gratitude as she clasps my hands. "Please, let me give you herbs for the wound."

I smile faintly, shaking my head. "No, there's no need. I have herbs of my own," I say softly, the weight of the healing settling over me heavily. "She should rest now," I add gently, slipping my hands from hers and beginning to rise.

But before I can fully stand, a sharp, searing pain pierces through my skull. I gasp, the agony slicing through me with brutal force. I collapse back onto my knees, clutching my head as if trying to contain the chaos raging within. The whispers, once a subtle hum, now rise in a whirlwind of overlapping voices, urgent and relentless, clawing at my mind.

"Eh! What is the matter?" Her voice, though shouting, reaches me as though from a great distance, muffled, like sound traveling underwater.

I grit my teeth, struggling to fight through the pain, but it threatens to consume me, to drag me down into its depths. "Nothing," I manage through ragged breaths, trying once more to rise, though the world spins and darkens at the edges of my vision. "This is my burden," I say, the words strained as sweat beads on my forehead. It feels as though a thousand needles are stabbing into my mind, probing every corner of my consciousness, driving me to the brink of collapse.

"Ndapota!"—*"Please!"* she pleads, her hands supporting me, trying to guide me back to the ground. "Garai pasi zvakare,"—*"Sit down again."*

Her concern grates on me, fraying the edges of my patience. My mind is raw, fatigued by the unrelenting onslaught of pain, the whispers, her *kindness!* I push against her, trying to rise, to escape, to flee the crushing weight of it all. But just as I manage to gain movement, a rough, weathered hand grips my knee firmly, halting me.

"Receive," the elderly woman's voice rings out, low and resonant, her gray eyes wide and luminous as they fix on mine. Her gaze holds me captive, and there is something within it—something ancient, beyond the veil of ordinary

reality. "Wava kure nekumusha,"—*"You have wandered too far from home."*

The whispers in my mind *soften*, becoming a steady murmur, *urging* me to listen. I sink back to my knees, the pain that had gripped me moments before receding into the background. The elderly woman's eyes seem to draw me in, their depth and power pulling me toward a truth I can't yet comprehend.

"Iwe ndiwe," she continues, her voice now filled with a sacred resonance, as though she speaks not just to me but to something beyond me. "Zviri mumaropa ako, saka zvakadai. Ehe, unofamba pakati penyika, uri mutsigiri wezvido uye huchenjeri hwezvisingaoneki. Iwe, zita rako ndiani, mwanangu?"

"You are the one. It is in your blood, and thus it is. Yes, you walk between worlds, a conduit for the will and wisdom of the unseen. You, what is your name, my child?"

The answer comes from somewhere deep within me, slipping from my lips before I even realize it's there as if the name has been waiting all along to be spoken *here*. "Gamuchirai." *Receive.*

"Uye zvakadaro!"—*"And it is so!"* She affirms with a solemn finality, her voice now carrying the weight of a sacred decree. "*Gamuchirai* is a command to your lineage, a call to the very essence of your being. Mugashire mwana uyu! Tarisai zvabuda murima—chiedza chavepo!"—*"Receive her! See what has emerged from the darkness—a light has come forth!"*

CHAPTER 3

Her voice sharpens as if the very earth and sky bend to her words. "They must receive what is theirs, yet you have strayed far from your path," she intones, her gaze unwavering, her words cutting through the air like a blade. "Gamuchirai, you must *yield!*"

There is something in the air, unseen yet undeniable, and I feel the stirrings of power deep within me—a power older than memory, older than time itself. The woman's gaze never wavers; her presence is a living channel of the unseen forces that seem to swirl between worlds.

Chapter 4

"Uri kutambudzika zvakanyanya," — *"You are under great torture."* The old woman's breath shudders with each exhale, a trembling rasp that thins the air in the room, making everything feel smaller, more fragile. Her voice is barely a whisper, frail yet insistent. "The spirits who have chosen you," she gasps, her words thick with urgency, "they are trying to impart something of immense importance. The agony you feel… it is their way of forcing your attention, urging you to decode their message, to seek the relief they promise."

She shudders as she tries to rise, her body slow and unsteady, like a puppet tangled in its own strings. The girl's mother and I rush to her, steadying her frail frame by the arms, bracing against her weight. But despite her weakness, her eyes burn with a fevered intensity that cuts through the dimness, latching onto me as though I were the only soul in the room.

"Who are these spirits?" My voice quivers, caught between fear and defiance. I've drawn on the darkness for so long that its presence is as familiar as my own shadow, yet its true nature has always remained shrouded—something I've never fully understood *or* wanted to.

"Your ancestors," she rasps. The silence between us hums with a weight I can't explain. "You are a Receiver." Her finger trembles as it rises, pointing at me as though her words carry the gravity of the heavens themselves. "Chosen to receive... and to give. Their magic, their power, it is bound to you now, woven into your blood."

My chest tightens, anger bubbling beneath my skin. My pulse hammers against my skull, each beat sharper than the last. *Their magic?* The very thought of it twists something deep inside me. For a long time, I've believed my power was mine—my own. To think it could be shared, stolen, claimed by others... it's intolerable. I swore I'd never again bow to weakness, never again be at the mercy of something I couldn't control. Yet here I am, tethered to forces beyond my grasp. I can't allow it.

"You cannot avoid it any longer," she breathes, her voice a brittle whisper that somehow feels unyielding. "Their light... their power... it is your burden now."

Her words set fire to the embers of my rage. "Why me? What reason do they have to force this on me?" My voice rises, trembling with emotions I can no longer suppress. "I never asked for this."

I am a witch—*that* title is mine. That power, small as it may be, is something I can hold, something I can control. Let others chase after destiny; I would choose peace over the crushing weight of their expectations.

"No one chooses their destiny, Gamuchirai," she presses on, her gaze unrelenting. "Names are more than labels; they are revelations, unfolding as we walk through life. Each one carries a deeper truth—truths we often resist, truths that remain hidden until we are ready to embrace them." Her voice softens, yet the intensity behind her words grows sharper as she leans closer.

"Do you understand this? Our ancestors guide us, and protect us, yes. But sometimes, their influence must be channeled through a vessel, someone strong enough to bear the weight of their power. That is the role of the Receiver—your destiny." Her eyes seem to dig deeper into mine, as though trying to unearth something buried within me. "You were chosen because your spirit is strong enough to carry this burden, to wield the power that others cannot."

"I don't believe it," I hiss, the words slipping through clenched teeth. "Is this what their wisdom demands? Torment without purpose?" The bitterness in my voice is unmistakable.

"Pain is their tool," she retorts, her voice rising with conviction. "It is how they get your attention. It is how they show you the path that lies before you." Her lips tremble, her voice faltering for the first time. "But you are stubborn, child. You've let darkness take root inside you, overshadowing their light."

CHAPTER 4

"You ask me to accept a power I never sought, a burden I never wanted." My voice sharpens, cutting through the thick air between us. "My magic has never depended on anyone but me. I won't be shackled by the whims of the dead."

"You think you can simply walk away from this?" Her voice sharpens, cold and biting. "You'd rather live in the shadows of your own making than face the truth of who you are?"

The little girl's mother, her face lined with worry, places a gentle hand on the old woman's shoulder, trying to calm her. But my anger surges again, threatening to overflow.

"I know what I am," I snap, the bitterness in my voice like venom. "A witch. Not a puppet for powers beyond my control."

The little girl's mother, her face a storm of pleading and frustration, implores softly, "Please, understand. "Amai vangu vari kungoedza kubatsira,"—*"My mother is only trying to help."* Her voice quivers, strained by the weight of witnessing this fraught exchange.

Her gaze weighs heavy on me, and guilt gnaws at the edges of my anger. For a moment, I falter. This is an elderly woman—frail and weathered by years. How could I speak to her like this?

The old woman's *laugh* cuts through my thoughts, low and jagged like a blade twisting deep in my chest. "Do you believe that rejecting this destiny makes you free? No, *little* girl, you are far from free. You are trapped. Trapped by the *fear* of what you could become."

Her words slam into me, sharp and unrelenting, striking a place deep inside I've fought to bury. *Fear?* No. I've lived through horrors that would break most. I've clawed my way out of darkness thicker than any shadow she could conjure. *What could I possibly fear now?*

"You don't know me," I hiss, my voice trembling with barely contained fury. "You don't know what I've endured."

Her eyes gleam, unsettlingly calm. "I know enough," she says softly, each word weighted with certainty. "And I know this: you are afraid—the shadow of fear is clocked around you."

No. I crush the thought before it can take root. I will not be ruled by fear—not of magic, not of fate. My life is my own. *I* will decide what to do with it.

The old woman's voice rises again, sharp as a blade slicing through the air. "You've chosen darkness, I see it!" Her eyes widen, bulging with a terrifying mix of shock and horror, as if she's glimpsed something unspeakable—and her revelation shakes me to the core.

"You think you're special, but you're headed for a reckoning, little girl. Rima rinotisvitsira tose, kunyangwe tichida kana kuti hatidi!"—*"Darkness chooses us all, whether we want it or not!"* Her words pierce my defenses, eerie and hoarse, her lips trembling with the weight of what she knows. "Ramba rima, kana uri wakachenjera." — *"Reject the darkness, if you are wise.'* Choose your path now, for the war within you has already begun. The battle for your soul is not a distant threat — *it's here,* it's now." Her voice softens to a whisper, yet the weight of her final words hangs heavy like a curse foretold.

"You will pay for this, Gamuchirai. One way or another — you *will* pay." She narrows her eyes, her voice dropping to a low, ominous tone. "Pamweya paunosvika mugomba rine rima, unochinja zvachose, nekuti hapana munhu anobata chinhu chacho usina kutakura chikamu charo mukati mako." — *"When the soul reaches into the abyss, it is forever altered, for no one can touch the void without carrying a piece of it within."*

A fierce wave of anger and panic surges within me, twisting tighter with every breath. *Who is she to dictate my choices?* My eyes flicker between the old woman and her daughter, whose pleading gaze grates against my raw nerves. The darkness within me, the one I thought I had tamed, begins to stir, writhing like a living thing. It claws at the edges of my control, demanding release.

Damn her. Damn them both. *I will pay?* Perhaps I will. But I've known this all along — and I don't care.

The old woman gasps, her frail body trembling under the weight of her own words. Her breath comes in shallow, ragged bursts, each one a visible struggle. "There is a terrible darkness upon you," she gasps, her voice trembling with fear, each word a jagged edge of terror. *"Bva pano!—"Leave this place."* She trembles and vibrates violently, as though her heart is racing too fast, threatening to explode. "Bva pano izvozvi,"—*"Leave this place, now!"*

Spit clings to her trembling lip like dew on a dying leaf, while her eyes—wide and frantic like a trapped animal's—dart desperately to her daughter. I watch in mounting horror as the old woman's strength abruptly wanes, her form growing insubstantial as if the very essence of her being is seeping away into the shadows. Her voice, once forceful, now trembles with desperation.

"Bvisa iye kubva pano,"—*"remove her from here."* She quivers, her voice barely holding together. "Anofanira kubva panzvimbo ino uye haafanire kudzoka zvakare,"—*"She must leave this place and never return."*

Finally, she collapses inward, shrinking into herself, becoming frail and fragile, like a flickering candle on the verge of being snuffed out by an unforgiving gust.

Her daughter rushes forward, cradling the old woman's trembling head with desperate tenderness. "Ndapota, mukanganwirei."—*"Please, forgive her,"* she pleads, her voice quivering with urgency. Her wide eyes dart toward me, seeking reassurance, shimmering with fear. "Iye mukadzi akadzvinyirirwa nemanzwi akawandisa."—*"She's a woman overwhelmed by too many voices."*

Too many voices. Voices.

CHAPTER 4

I rise to my feet, every muscle coiled with tension—I've had enough of this.

"Aiwa, usabva—haungamusiye akadaro."—*"No, don't leave— you cannot leave her like this."* The little girl's mother looks at me with eyes filled with silent, pleading hope. "Please, stay. Help us," she implores, her voice trembling with a fragile desperation.

"She has simply overexerted herself," I reply sharply, trying to mask the turmoil roiling beneath my surface. "There is nothing more for me to do."

Her eyes widen, filled with sorrow and the faintest flicker of dread. She senses my resolve and sees that further persuasion will be futile. "Please... do not forget us," she whispers, her voice breaking. "Ndapota,—*"please."* But as she speaks, something shifts. Her eyes linger on me longer, her gaze sharpening as a flicker of recognition passes across her face—a realization that dawns slowly, settling over her like a shadow. She sees it too, now. The darkness clinging to me, the evil force stirring within. Her expression shifts from sorrow to dread.

I turn away, suddenly unable to bear the silent judgment in her eyes. As I hurry toward the door, the little girl peeks from the other room, her wide, frightened eyes tracking my every move. The whispers return, insidious and unrelenting, echoing the old woman's warnings. They coil around my thoughts like serpents, hissing their demands for me to confront the darkness within. To heed the warnings I had dismissed. To understand that this battle is far from over.

The murmurs of the soldiers by their fire become a distant hum as I slip into the night, the cool air wrapping up around me. I fade into the shadows of the huts, leaving behind the flickering warmth of the firelight and the suffocating tension of that cursed house. I plunge into the dense forest, the darkness thick and alive, where each step is muffled by the carpet of damp leaves. My pulse quickens—not from exertion, but from the restless urgency that gnaws at me.

The whispers follow, relentless. The battle, it seems, has only just begun.

Chapter 5

The moonlight filters through the gaps in the canopy, casting a silvery sheen over the river's surface, like scattered shards of light across dark velvet. The river shimmers, its gentle ripples the only sound breaking the profound stillness of the night. I kneel at its edge, letting the cool, clear water lap against my fingers.

The quiet, rhythmic flow of the river mocks me with its tranquility, a sharp contrast to the storm raging within. I am adrift in my thoughts, grappling with the weight of what has been thrust upon me. *Why did I even go out of my way to help them?* The knowledge I've gained feels heavy, like chains dragging me into a mire of regret and frustration.

I clench my fist as a fresh wave of pain surges through me, burning like fire in my veins, twisting and coiling like a serpent. My head throbs, my vision blurs, and for a moment, the world around me becomes a haze of searing heat and dizziness. *Could I truly endure this for the rest of my life?* The thought claws at my sanity, tearing at the edges of my mind.

With a raw, guttural scream, I unleash everything inside me.

"*Leave* me alone!" My voice shreds the stillness of the night, a primal cry that reverberates into the darkness, carried by the relentless pain that wracks my body. "No! I refuse to accept this. Do you hear me?" I shout, my words echoing off the trees. "I will not be your Receiver! I reject all of it!" The declaration rips from my lips, fierce and defiant, hurled at the unseen forces that torment me.

As the final echoes of my scream fade into the vast emptiness, a sudden and unnerving quiet settles over everything. The pain that had been tearing through me vanishes in an instant as if my defiance has severed its hold. The whispers that once filled my head with their insidious murmurings fall silent. The river before me, once shimmering with life, now lies unnervingly still, its surface like glass, mirroring the sudden, eerie calm that envelops the night.

I breathe heavily, my chest rising and falling in ragged gasps, the remnants of tension still clinging to me like a suffocating weight. *Am I truly free?* The question flickers in my mind, but I'm afraid to trust it—afraid to believe in this fleeting calm, knowing that the darkness has a way of creeping back when least expected.

Slowly, as my breath begins to steady, I kneel by the river's edge and peer into the water. My reflection stares back at me, the moonlight casting strange shadows across my face. The terror in my eyes is stark, unfamiliar, a haunted look that feels foreign—like I am looking into the eyes of someone else, someone I do not fully recognize. For a moment, my own gaze unsettles me, revealing the fractures of fear beneath my anger. But I refuse to let that fear take root. I inhale deeply, forcing the tension from my muscles, and slowly, deliberately, I compose myself. I mask the fear with a facade of strength, willing it to recede behind a wall of control. My reflection shifts, the terror replaced by something more resolute, more hardened. Whatever comes next, I will not falter. Not again.

Yet despite the calm surrounding me, the silence feels like a deception, as though the night itself holds its breath—waiting, watching for me to falter. The water remains unnervingly still, its surface too quiet, as if the river too is waiting for something to stir. My chest tightens, a whisper of doubt curling at the edges of my mind, but I shake it off.

I am quickly proven devastatingly right. Peace—*freedom*, it seems—is a cruel illusion, never meant for someone like me.

My heart lurches in my chest as a sinister whisper slithers from the depths of the river, threading and twisting through the rustling leaves and invading my mind instantly. Before I can even react, a flash of vibrant color breaks the water's surface—*a fish*, dazzling in hues of yellow, red, and orange, glistens in the moonlight. The sight jolts me, a strange beauty in the darkness. But the moment of wonder is short-lived. A yellow snake darts from the shadows with lightning speed, its jaws snapping open in a deadly arc. I recoil in horror as the serpent swallows the fish whole, the water churning violently in the brief, chaotic struggle before sinking back into an eerie, oppressive calm.

The voices flood my mind once again, louder and more vicious than before. Their shrieks resonate with a dread so powerful it feels like my skull might split. Desperation tightens around me. I feel exposed, vulnerable, as if the serpent beneath the river's surface could strike at any moment. Its presence stirs something primal in me, a fear so deep it chills me to my core.

My hands fly to my head, fingers tangling in my hair, as a ragged scream rips from my throat. Pain surges through me, each wave sharper, more violent than the last, crashing relentlessly against my resolve. My body shakes uncontrollably, muscles spasming as though trying to escape the torment that claws at my soul. Darkness flutters at the edge of my vision, threatening to pull me under.

Then, as if summoned by my agony, the yellow snake rises again from the murky waters—larger now, more menacing. It glides with predatory grace, its scales shimmering under the moonlight, each movement more calculated, more deliberate. Its eyes, cold and glinting, lock onto me, and in that gaze, I see a promise—dark and deadly. The serpent's hiss slices through the night and my blood turns to ice.

The snake coils, muscles rippling beneath its slick, gleaming skin, preparing to strike. Paralyzing dread roots me in place, my body frozen as it lunges toward me with terrifying speed. Reality blurs and my consciousness plunges into a vortex of shadows and searing pain. The snake's hiss intertwines with the relentless voices in my head, their shrieks merging into a single, overwhelming roar that consumes me whole. The world distorts, twisted into a whirlpool of agony and darkness. My mind fragments as the serpent's strike reverberates through me, and for a moment, everything becomes a cold, numbing void.

And then—nothing.

The roar fades into silence, the pain dissolving into an emptiness that stretches endlessly. I am left adrift, lost in the cold, quiet dark.

Dead?

Chapter 6

I awaken to the comforting crackle of a nearby fire, its warmth slowly seeping into my chilled body. My head throbs with a dull ache, and as I attempt to move, I realize I'm bound. Panic rises in my chest. Straining against the ropes, I glance around and spot a slender figure seated by the fire. Draped in a lightweight brown cloak, her hood is pushed back, revealing long, flowing white hair that catches the firelight like threads of moonlight. Her skin is pale, almost translucent, as though it might vanish in the flames' glow. She sits quietly, peeling fruit with delicate fingers that seem to glow against her stark complexion.

Sensing my movement, she looks up, her wide eyes filled with a mix of relief and concern. "You're awake," she says softly, her voice carrying a gentle rasp that feels both calming and distant. She sets aside the fruit and knife, her movements graceful but purposeful, and quickly makes her way toward me. "I found you unconscious by the river," she continues, crouching beside me. "You were muttering strange things."

Her earthy-toned tunic, slightly frayed at the edges from

wear, is cinched at her waist with a braided leather belt. A small pouch and dagger hang from it, swaying lightly with her movements. Her green trousers, worn thin in places, are tucked into scuffed boots that have seen better days. Despite her rugged appearance, there's an elegance in the way she moves, as though she belongs more to the ethereal world than to the earth beneath us.

I blink, trying to piece together what happened. Memories of the yellow snake and the excruciating pain flood back, jarring me from my stupor. "Where am I?" I croak, my voice hoarse and weak.

"In the forest, far from the square," she replies, helping me sit up against a nearby log. "I was on my way to the river when I found you. You were in no state to remain there, so I brought you here. It's safer, farther from watchful eyes."

As she draws closer, I study her features more intently. Her pale skin seems to shimmer faintly in the firelight, and her eyes, deep and luminous, are framed by strands of snow-white hair. There's something almost otherworldly about her presence—calming yet sharp, as though she holds secrets just beneath the surface. My mind races with questions, but one in particular gnaws at me, teetering on the edge of impoliteness.

"Oh," she interrupts suddenly, as if reading my discomfort. "I apologize—I'll untie you. I wasn't sure of your intentions." Her eyes widen with sincerity, her hands trembling slightly as she reaches for the knots. "I only wanted to help."

I raise an eyebrow, silently questioning the logic. *With ropes?* I think dryly. If I truly wanted to harm you, I muse to myself, mere ropes would be inadequate. The depths of the ocean wouldn't suffice to keep you from the darkness I could unleash.

"Who are you?" I ask sharply, testing her resolve.

"My name is Sparrow."

"Sparrow?" I repeat incredulously, the name falling from my lips like an absurdity. "Is that your given name?"

She nods solemnly. "It's the only one I have."

I narrow my eyes, sensing there's more to this than she's letting on. I pause, unsure how to approach my next question. "And... are you a boy, Sparrow?"

Sparrow hesitates, searching my gaze for judgment. Her brow furrows slightly, tension creeping into his expression. "Yes," she finally answers, her voice steady but wary, as though bracing for my reaction.

I glance around, absorbing the implications. The government's strict enforcement of gender roles is no secret. "How would you prefer I address you?" I ask gently.

"As you would any boy," Sparrow replies, though uncertainty still lingers in his eyes.

CHAPTER 6

I nod. "Are you alone out here?" I ask, shifting the conversation.

His face darkens, becoming more serious. "I have friends," he replies evasively.

I offer him a thin smile, trying to ease the tension. "Thank you for helping me," I say sincerely. "I appreciate your caution... and your kindness."

Sparrow meets my gaze, a tentative smile tugging at the corner of his lips. He gestures for me to extend my hands, and with ease, he begins to untie the ropes binding them. His fingers work swiftly, the knots loosening one by one until I'm free. I rub my wrists, feeling the blood return, then watch as Sparrow kneels to untie my ankles, his fingers are delicate and warm. The bindings fall away, leaving only red marks where the ropes had bitten into my skin.

"Thank you," I whisper, my voice softer now.

"Come closer to the fire," He says, his voice equally gentle.

I obey but remain uneasy, watching him closely. "You've lit a fire here," I remark cautiously. "Aren't you afraid of being discovered?"

He glances into the shadows, his eyes scanning the darkness just beyond the firelight. "The snakes," he murmurs, almost to himself. "They're everywhere in these woods. The soldiers and anyone else know to avoid this place after dark."

A chill runs down my spine despite the warmth of the fire. "I survived one myself," I say quietly, shuddering at the vivid memory of the yellow serpent.

"You are fortunate," he replies, leaning closer, his expression earnest. "If you don't mind my asking, what happened by the river?" His voice is gentle, almost coaxing. "I heard you muttering strange things."

I hesitate, unsure how much to reveal. The weight of what I've seen, what I've felt, presses down on me like an invisible burden. "I… saw something," I begin cautiously, my voice low. "I thought it was a vision, maybe a warning. But perhaps it was just a snake—a yellow one with black dots."

He listens without flinching, his face calm, as though the revelation isn't surprising. "A yellow snake is not to be taken lightly."

"What do you mean?" I ask, dread already creeping into my chest.

"There are myths surrounding the yellow snake," he says, his voice carrying a gravity that sends a shiver through me. "It's rare to see one; they say it kills without being seen, a spirit of the river. If you see it and survive, that's a sign. A sign that the spirits have chosen you for something… important."

My breath catches in my throat. His words echo what the old woman had said by the river, intertwining with my own fears. "A sign?" I whisper, uncertainty and fear coloring my

CHAPTER 6

voice. "Important as what?"

He shakes his head slowly, his eyes holding mine with a steady, unwavering gaze. "I'm not sure. But those who encounter the yellow snake often go on to do great—or terrible—things."

I stare into the flickering flames, his words pressing down on me like an invisible weight. "Terrible things," I mutter, the words barely audible. It seems far more likely. Ever since I ran from my past, since I abandoned everything, I've only used my power for terrible things.

His expression softens as he continues. "According to legend, the spirits of the river are benevolent if shown respect. But they can also be vengeful when disrespected. People leave offerings to appease them, seeking their favor and protection. Perhaps... perhaps you unknowingly offended them. And now, you're meant to make amends."

I look at him sharply, the surrealness of the situation sinking in. "How do you dwell among snakes, then?" I ask, a slight edge to my voice. "Snakes that even soldiers fear?"

He lowers his gaze momentarily, his white lashes catching the firelight. "To me," he says softly, "they are companions."

A strange thing for someone so peculiar to say. The idea feels wrong and unnatural, but the way he speaks is so calm and so measured, that it makes me wonder. "How can snakes be your companions? They are creatures of darkness—

deceptive, striking from the shadows. They distort the past and future, striking at our very heels," I remark, my voice steady but laced with disdain. "They are aligned with evil."

Sparrow's lips quirk into a faint smile. "Are they?" he asks. "Not all snakes are viewed as evil. Many are revered as symbols of knowledge, rebirth, and protection. They sense disturbances in the natural order, and their presence often signifies something important—a message, a warning. Their connection to the earth makes them conduits between our world and the spiritual one. They shed their skin to renew themselves, just as we must shed our fears to grow."

His words stir something deep within me—a discomfort that coils tighter, like an imagined serpent writhing in my gut. The fear I've held since childhood, deeply rooted, remains untouched by his calm logic. He must see it on my face; the resentment is still there, unshaken.

"But snakes don't shed fear, they instill it—*revel* in it."

He smiles warmly, breaking the tension by offering me a slice of fruit. His eyes linger on mine with a gentle intensity, and I find myself accepting the gesture, surprised by the unexpected closeness it creates.

"I suppose," he says gently.

I glance at the fruit, reassured by the fact that he's eating from the same pile, though I pretend that this act is enough to quell my suspicions.

CHAPTER 6

Despite my wariness, I can't help but feel a pang of self-pity. *Why am I so drawn to him?* There's something magnetic about Sparrow, a pull that I can't quite place. *Is it his aura, his calm certainty? Or is it something within me that's searching for connection in this strange moment?* I *need* to leave, I tell myself, an urgency flooding my thoughts. But my body remains frozen, as though tethered to the ground by an invisible force I cannot break.

After a pause, I speak again, mostly to distract myself. "Is it magic, your connection with them?" I ask cautiously.

Sparrow shakes his head. "No, not magic. It's simply a skill—understanding their ways, learning to read their movements, listening to what they have to say."

I narrow my eyes, still uncertain. "I see," I murmur. But I don't believe him. It's magic. Dark magic.

"You think it's magic because magic shapes your world," he says suddenly, as though reading my thoughts, his curiosity piqued. His tone is soft, not accusing—almost as if he's been waiting for this question to surface all along.

His words catch me off guard—a witch. "Why would you say that?" I ask cautiously. "I know herbs, not spells."

He smiles, almost amused. "You're so quick to separate the two. But herbs... aren't they magical in their own way? When you listen to them, when you understand their properties, isn't that a kind of spellcraft? You say my connection with snakes is magic, yet you dismiss the same process when applied to plants."

I blink, flustered. His insight needles at me, though I try to appear indifferent. "I suppose," I mumble.

"So," Sparrow continues, "you're a healer, then?"

"Yes," I confirm, taking another bite of the fruit, using the pause to steady myself.

He nods slowly and thoughtfully. "And yet, the snake didn't harm you."

"Luck," I mutter, though the gravity in my voice betrays the unease simmering beneath the surface.

"Luck?" He tilts his head, studying me. "Nakuru is full of snakes, and yet they spared you. Perhaps they fear you—or perhaps they see something sacred in you. Either way, it means that magic defines your world, whether you accept it or not."

"You're right," I murmur, almost to myself. "There is magic inside me. But it's not mine to claim." The words weigh heavily on me but I am testing them against myself—*against reality.*

Sparrow gazes at me with a soft, understanding smile. "It takes wisdom to understand that not everything needs to be claimed or controlled. But magic—magic is part of you, part of all of us, whether we choose to embrace it or not. Those who run from their magic often do so because they're afraid."

I swallow hard against the lump forming in my throat and I can barely choke out the words. "Afraid of what?"

Sparrow's voice softens, yet it lands with the weight of certainty. *"Themselves."*

And then he simply goes on, a soft smile playing on his lips as he slices his fruit, *seemingly oblivious* to the fact that his words have just cracked the surface of my world. They settle over me like a cold, creeping fog.

I should feel anger at his insight, a familiar spark of defiance rising within me—a need to retaliate, to shield myself behind the walls I've built. But I don't. *Not this time.* Instead, I make a choice I rarely allow myself: I choose to feel. Just for this moment, I let my walls crumble, testing my resolve against the fear that lurks in the shadows of my mind. Though everything in me screams to leave, to retreat to the safety of solitude, an unseen force keeps me rooted here, an inexplicable longing tugging at my core. It's as if I know that once I return to the isolation that has become my refuge, I won't dare try again. I'll go back to hardening myself, locking away the parts of me that still long to be free. The truth is undeniable now—I am *terrified.* And I allow myself to admit it, if only for a fleeting moment before I retreat back into the safety of my familiar defenses.

He doesn't press further into my fear, nor does he rush to fill the silence.

"You mentioned there are others," I say, my voice breaking the fragile silence between us. The words are calm, but I can feel the vulnerability beneath them, like a thread that could easily unravel.

He nods. "Yes," he replies softly, "there are others."

For a moment, we let the crackling fire and the quiet night speak for us, the weight of unspoken thoughts hanging in the air. Then, without another word, Sparrow rises and offers his hand once more. "Come," he says gently. "I know someone who might be of value to you."

I hesitate, instincts urging me to retreat. But curiosity, coupled with the flicker of trust that has grown between us, pushes me forward. Reluctantly, then with a growing sense of resolve, I take his hand.

Chapter 7

Sparrow halts before a curtain of hanging branches and dense foliage. With quiet determination, he pushes them aside, revealing a hidden passageway shrouded in shadow, a narrow tunnel winding downward into the earth. "Go on," he whispers, his voice carrying both a challenge and a reassurance.

A flicker of uncertainty rises in me. "I'd rather not have someone behind me," I protest, though my words lack conviction. I feel foolish—following Sparrow into an unknown tunnel, one that could very well be a trap. My instincts scream for me to turn back, to retreat into the safety of isolation. But something else, something stronger, tugs me forward—a quiet, inexplicable pull that gnaws at my hesitation, pushing me into the unknown.

Sparrow smiles faintly, his expression calm and knowing. Without a word, he bends low and slips into the tunnel, his movements fluid, as though the dark depths ahead hold no fear for him. Reluctantly, I follow, ducking beneath the low-hanging branches that scrape against my skin like ghostly fingers.

"Who made this choice for you?" he asks, his tone contemplative, almost philosophical as his voice drifts back through the shadows.

"I made it myself," I retort quickly, though a shadow of doubt trails behind the words. I know better than to actually believe that.

The cool, damp air wraps around us as we descend deeper into the passage. The scent of moss and damp earth clings to the air, grounding me in this strange place. My fingers brush against the rough, uneven walls, searching for balance as the light from the entrance fades into nothingness. Darkness closes in around us, thick and oppressive, the kind that presses against your vision and makes you feel small and lost.

"That seems unlikely," Sparrow's voice emerges again, soft yet thoughtful. "Humans are wired for trust; it's what we crave, the foundation of love. A tree doesn't uproot itself. Someone must have pried you away from what's natural, what's essential."

His words strike something inside me, weaving through my mind like a persistent thread.

My breath feels loud in the stillness, and though I cannot see him, I sense Sparrow ahead, moving effortlessly through the dark. His presence, a quiet guide in this strange place, both unnerves and reassures me. My thoughts race with questions, doubts clawing at my resolve. Where is he taking

CHAPTER 7

me? What awaits us at the end of this tunnel?

Ahead, a faint glow begins to materialize, cutting through the darkness like a beacon. My heart quickens as we move toward it, the passage widening into a cavernous chamber. The light grows stronger, revealing more than I anticipated.

We step into an open space where torches, mounted on stone walls, cast long, dancing shadows across the cavern. The chamber, though simple, exudes an air of resilience. Rough-hewn benches are scattered around, woven mats line the ground, and despite the starkness, there's an undeniable sense of comfort—a refuge carved out of the earth itself.

As my eyes adjust, I notice a figure stepping forward from the far side of the chamber. A girl with sharp, angular features and piercing brown eyes, her expression taut with suspicion. "What have you done?" she demands, her voice cutting through the air like a blade. "Who is this? Why have you brought an outsider here?"

Sparrow, ever calm, meets her glare with an air of quiet reassurance. "Six, calm down. She is not a threat."

Six? Sparrow? I think, the names catching me off guard. Rebels—that's the only explanation.

Her eyes narrow as she scrutinizes me, suspicion etched into every line of her face. "If she caught your attention, then she's a snake—and I *despise* snakes."

Standing at about 5'8", *Six* commands attention with a rogue-like presence. Her thick, dark hair is braided tightly against her scalp, adorned with intricate beads that clink softly as she moves. Her deep, rich brown skin glows in the flickering torchlight, her lean, muscular frame accentuated by a pair of pants tied securely at the waist and a fitted green tank top. A distinctive scar cuts across her left cheek, adding to the fierce intensity of her aura.

Behind her, an even more imposing figure looms, his broad shoulders casting long shadows on the walls. He's tall, and powerfully built, with coppery brown skin and a shaved head that emphasizes the sharp lines of his jaw and cheekbones. Despite his formidable appearance, his hazel eyes—flecked with gold—radiate warmth and quiet strength. A series of intricate tribal tattoos snake up his arms and across his chest, and a pendant carved from bone hangs around his neck.

I wonder if his name will also be something as ridiculous as *Sparrow* and *Six*.

"That is exactly why I've brought her," Sparrow says, his voice firm. "A yellow snake came to her."

Six's fierce expression falters, her suspicion giving way to something more measured. "A yellow snake?" she repeats, her tone softer but still guarded. "Are you certain?"

Sparrow nods. "Certain."

CHAPTER 7

Six studies me for a moment longer, her gaze penetrating, as though trying to see beyond the surface. "What's your name?" she asks finally.

"Gamu," I reply, keeping my voice steady despite the tension crackling in the air. I refuse to let them intimidate me.

"Gamu?" Six repeats, frowning slightly. She seems to consider something before speaking again. "I too have been dreaming of a yellow snake."

Her words catch me off guard, and I feel a flicker of unease stir in my chest. "Have you managed to make any sense of your dream?" I ask, my tone cautious.

Six's gaze sharpens, her brow furrowing with a determination that sends a shiver down my spine. "I have now," she replies, her voice heavy with certainty. "And you seem to be a part of it."

Ugh. I've had enough of people trying to pull me into their paths, their prophecies. I've been dragged along for too long, and something inside me sharpens with defiance. "Or perhaps it's a journey that remains separate from mine," I reply, my voice edged with a stubborn resolve.

Her lips twitch into a mocking smile. "The yellow snake doesn't make mistakes," she says, stepping closer, her presence growing more imposing. "And if I thought otherwise for a second, you wouldn't be still standing here. But the spirits aren't to be questioned."

I can't tell if she's threatening me or merely stating a fact. It almost amuses me, this dance of intimidation. *Cute,* I think. I'll play along, for now.

"You're putting a lot of faith in a snake," I say, trying to inject a bit of mockery into my tone.

She doesn't flinch. "It's not just a snake. It's an omen. And I've learned to never ignore them."

"I'm certainly not afraid of omens, snakes, or you," I retort, my words sharp as steel.

"Really?" she raises an eyebrow, eyes narrowing with curiosity. "Then why do you look like someone who's seen a ghost? In fact, why did you feel the need to say it out loud, *Gamu?* Or perhaps..." Her eyes gleam with mischief, her lips curling into a knowing smile. "You're afraid of the truth."

A surge of frustration bubbles up inside me, quickly turning to anger. This whole situation feels too neat, too carefully orchestrated. It's as though I'm a piece on a chessboard, someone else moving me around for their own game. Every word, every glance feels like a calculated step in some plan I can't see. And I hate it. I want to tear it all down, rip apart this web they've spun around me. But something holds me back. If this truly is a trap, I need to learn more. I can't just lash out blindly and walk away, unaware of how deep this goes.

"What truth?" I demand, my voice dripping with mockery.

CHAPTER 7

"Sparrow said himself that Nakuru is teeming with snakes. So what if we both like the color yellow? You hate snakes, and I hate snakes—we both had a nightmare about it. It doesn't mean anything."

"So *defensive* you are. I mean the truth that awaits. I mean the truth that lies ahead. The spirits come to us solely to reveal what we often aren't prepared to face." She steps closer, her presence bearing down on me like a challenge. "So, listen, princess, because the truth will come." she hisses, her voice low and threatening. "You can dismiss it all you want, but you won't be able to ignore it when it arrives."

The word stings—*princess*. Why would she call me that?

Rage flares inside me, igniting something raw and dangerous. *"Don't* call me princess," I snap, my magic rippling through me, crackling like invisible lightning just beneath my skin.

The air around us shifts, charged with energy, and Six's eyes widen in surprise. She instinctively takes a step back, and so do the others, recoiling from the force of my power. It surges out of me, a warning, a threat, hanging in the air like a storm about to break.

"The snake didn't even show itself to me directly," I continue, my words tight with anger. "It was focused on something else—" My words catch in my throat as a sudden, piercing clarity cuts through the haze of frustration. The image of the fish—vivid yellow, red, and orange—floods my mind, its colors burning in my thoughts. *"Fish..."* I whisper, my voice trembling with the weight of realization.

Six's expression shifts, curiosity flickering in her eyes. "Fish?" She asks carefully.

"It wasn't just the snake," I murmur, my thoughts racing as the pieces begin to fit together. "There was a fish." The memory hits me hard—how the snake hadn't been hunting me, but something else. That fish. Bright, beautiful, and out of place. A creature that didn't belong in the waters of Nakuru.

Six raises an eyebrow, her sharp gaze fixed on me. "That's... unexpected."

I swallow hard, the implications sinking in like a stone in my gut. There's more at play here—something I hadn't seen before. *"Mvure,"* I say softly, the word catching in my throat as understanding dawns. "Mvure is the fish," I whisper to myself. It suddenly clicks—a warning I should have understood earlier, but hadn't. "I have to go home," I murmur quickly, the urgency of the situation taking hold, the words slipping out as if I hadn't meant to share them.

Before I can even process the thought, Six steps forward and grabs my arm, her grip firm and unyielding. There's an intensity in her eyes that stops me cold. "You cannot go back there," she says sharply, her voice taut with fear.

I flinch, not liking the sudden sense of danger in her tone.

CHAPTER 7

It feels too personal, too restrictive. "Why not?" I pull my arm free, the defiance rising up inside me like a shield.

"The same evil that threatens your home," she says, her voice tight and urgent, "has roots here as well. You can't go back to Mvure."

"What are you talking about?" I demand, my voice sharpening, anger and confusion swirling inside me. "What do you mean?"

She takes a breath, her gaze locking onto mine, her expression grim. "Nakuru and Mvure are bound by more than just proximity. Ndambira—he's after something hidden in Mvure, something powerful." She pauses, weighing her words. "He intends to harness that power to tighten his grip on both villages… and maybe even more beyond that."

"That's absurd," I snap, though my voice falters slightly. "Do you really believe this? What kind of power could Mvure possibly possess?"

"A legend come true," she replies without hesitation, her conviction poised to cut through my disbelief. Her eyes burn with certainty. "They spoke of a pact with a serpent spirit—one powerful enough to bend reality to its will. We didn't believe it either. But now we know better."

I let out a sharp laugh, though it rings hollow in the heavy air between us. "Rubbish! I'm from Mvure," I say, forcing a veneer of arrogance into my words. "There's no such thing.

We are fishermen, nothing more."

Her gaze darkens, shadows deepening in her eyes as though she's seen things I can't begin to fathom. "It's real, Gamu," she says, her voice low, carrying a weight that settles like a stone in my chest. "You have to accept it. Before it's too late."

I scoff, though the sound feels brittle, insincere. "Alright," I say, waving a hand dismissively, trying to keep my tone mocking, though doubt slithers through my thoughts. "Let's pretend for a moment that this is true—and I assure you, it's not—why hasn't Ndambira struck Mvure? Mvure would've been no match for him—it shouldn't be taking him this long." My words drip with condescension, a final desperate attempt to shake her ridiculous theory.

But she doesn't flinch. Her jaw tightens. "Ndambira's been circling Mvure for a long time—watching, waiting for an opening." Her tone is like a blade cutting through silk. "He's learning, measuring the strength of the forces that protect Mvure. It's not weak, Gamu. The serpents—dark magic—they've kept the village safe for years, hidden behind an illusion of peace." She pauses, her eyes narrowing as though willing me to understand. "But something's changed. The protection is failing, and he knows it. He's preparing for something much larger."

The image of Mvure rises in my mind—its peaceful riverbank, boats gliding across the water, the steady rhythm of nets being cast, and laughter ringing out across the village.

CHAPTER 7

It feels so real, so tangible. Yet for the first time, cracks begin to form in the perfect picture. *Could it all have been a facade? A carefully constructed lie?*

Her voice drags me back to the present. "The spell that's shielded Mvure is breaking. And Ndambira—he's ready now. He's been waiting for this. If you go back, you'll be walking straight into his trap."

I want to dismiss her, to laugh off her words as the ravings of a paranoid mind. But something stirs deep within me, a memory so faint yet so persistent that I can't shake it. Whispers from my childhood bubble up—warnings from the elders about outsiders, veiled in vague terms but always laced with fear. The way they spoke of Mvure as *'blessed,' 'pure,'* and *'untouched,'* as if we were separate from the rest of the world as if venturing out could bring ruin upon us. And I'd believed it all, without question.

Then another memory claws its way to the surface, more personal and more painful. Titan. The strange orphan I found in the forest, with his lighter skin and unfamiliar accent. I had been so determined to protect him, to keep him close, thinking I could be his savior. But instead of welcoming him, the village recoiled as if he carried some invisible plague. They dismissed me, separated us, and told me he would be sent away—back to wherever he came from.

But Titan never left. I found him again in the forest, *hiding*, insisting that our meetings stay secret. He made it seem like a game—something innocent as if he were testing his stealth, learning the ways of the forest. He made me promise to report anyone who spoke of him, and I did it willingly, never questioning why.

Am I so blind? The realization hits me with a force that knocks the breath from my lungs. Titan had always acted like he knew something I didn't. He kept me in the dark, feeding me just enough to keep me loyal, to keep me innocent and naïve. And that magic—his memory-erasing magic—it suddenly makes sense. Who knows how many people he'd manipulated, how long he'd been twisting the village's reality to suit his own needs.

I feel like I'm teetering on the edge of madness, my mind unraveling as the ground beneath me shifts and crumbles. I grasp for something solid to hold onto, but all I have are the fragments of memories that now feel like pieces of a puzzle I never realized I was part of.

I shake my head, trying to regain control, but my voice betrays me. "You're lying," I whisper, though the words lack conviction, sounding hollow even to my own ears. "You don't know anything about Mvure. Mvure is peaceful. It's grounded in love and community. Boats on the river, fishermen pulling in their nets, songs and dancing every evening."

Six's eyes flash with something I can't quite place—pity, perhaps, or exasperation. Her gaze pierces through me as if she can see past all the walls I've built, straight into the fragile core I'm trying so hard to protect. "That's the illusion

CHAPTER 7

they've built," she says, her voice soft but unrelenting. "I thought you were different. I thought that's why you left—that you'd seen through the facade. Mvure may seem like a haven, but beneath the surface, it's cruel. Outsiders are threats, and anything that could disrupt their way of life is kept out—by any means necessary." She steps closer. "I know more than you think, Gamu. And deep down, you know it too. You've seen the signs, felt the undercurrents. It's in your face now, Gamu. You can't deny it." Her voice drops to a whisper that feels like it echoes inside my chest. "We can see the fear in your eyes."

Fear. I want to deny it, to fight against the truth that's staring me in the face. But as her words sink in, I realize that the fear is all around me—everywhere I look I'm made afraid.

"Think about it," Sparrow adds. "Where else have you heard of a place so pure? The people of Mvure are like children, untouched by the world's evils. No hunger, no thirst, no war. Do you honestly believe that? If you are from Mvure and you have magic, does that not imply there is magic there as well?"

I don't want to hear any more of this. My mind races, grasping for a logical explanation, something solid to cling to. I latch onto the only plausible answer: If Sparrow truly has the ability to manipulate snakes, they could have easily staged the entire encounter. It's all part of some broader scheme, a ploy to use me. They're rebels, trying to exploit whatever power they think I possess. I have to focus on that—the likelihood that I'm being drawn into their fight, rather than letting them cloud my judgment with talk of magic and destiny.

"My magic is rooted in herbs," I say firmly, though I can hear the slight tremor in my voice. "And I didn't learn it in Mvure."

Six narrows her eyes, her suspicion growing. "Herbs didn't cause what we just felt," she counters, her voice low, sharp. "That wasn't natural."

The room seems to tighten around me as their eyes bore into me—Six, Sparrow, and the silent man standing against the wall with his arms crossed, a quiet but imposing figure. His presence unnerves me more than I care to admit. Six clearly holds the reins here, but there's a palpable loyalty from the others, a unity I can feel without words being exchanged.

I blink, fighting to steady myself. "I don't know what you're talking about," I reply, trying to sound indifferent, but I can feel the tension building. "And what exactly do you propose? That the three of you—and me—should confront Ndambira? Why this sudden urgency? I've seen no sign of any rebellion before now."

She meets my gaze. "We may be few, but we've been preparing in the shadows, gathering what we can. We don't know everything—how Ndambira discovered the power in Mvure or what his exact plans are—but we know we must act now. If we hesitate, if we lose our conviction, everything we stand for will be crushed. This meeting between us—it wasn't a coincidence. Your knowledge of Mvure and the magic you carry, whether you see it or not, could be what tips the balance in our favor."

A pang of shame twists inside me. How little I know of Mvure, my own home. "Do you even have the means to make a difference?" I ask, my voice quieter now, doubt creeping in. "Is it truly just the three of you?"

For a moment, the room falls into a heavy silence, thick with an unspoken grief. Then, from behind Six, a deep voice speaks. It carries an undeniable authority, cutting through the air like an axe. "There are others," he says. "We have skills, though not all of them are easily seen."

I glance toward the speaker—A fighter, no doubt. But still... what of it?

Six takes over, her tone more measured now. "We're part of a network. Small, yes. But we're not alone. And neither are you. If you rush back to Mvure without a plan, you'll be playing right into Ndambira's hands."

The idea of a handful of rebels standing against Ndambira's regime sounds ridiculous, even laughable, yet their resolve is undeniable. And there's something more—a suggestion of hidden strength, of a resistance ready to be mobilized, if it truly exists.

"But I have nothing to offer you," I insist. "I'm just a healer."

"There's more to you," Sparrow says softly, his eyes filled with quiet certainty. "You know there is."

"There isn't," I reply, my voice hardening with finality. "I'm telling you, there's nothing special about me."

Six's gaze sharpens, her patience thinning. "Fine. We've never relied on magic. So if you truly don't have it, that doesn't change what we're fighting for. But we need to understand why you're here. Why the yellow snake came to you. You can't tell me it means nothing."

She's pressing now, pushing me to acknowledge something I don't want to face. But I can't shake the feeling that there's more at play here, something far beyond a simple rebellion. And though I want to dismiss her talk of omens and serpents, I can feel the weight of it all pressing in on me, forcing me to confront a truth I've been running from for too long.

For a moment, I waver. There's something in the way they look at me, a mixture of hope and desperation as if I'm the key to something bigger than all of us. But I can't allow myself to be swept up in their cause. Not yet. Not without answers. They can't genuinely believe my involvement rests solely on the influence of some serpent. No, they know more than they're letting on, more about me, more about my abilities.

"If what you say is true, then my first duty is to my people. I will lend my strength to them, to warn them. Mvure comes first."

CHAPTER 7

Six scoffs, her words dripping with disdain. "So that's it?" she snaps, her voice sharp enough to cut. "You'll look out for your own and leave us to fend for ourselves? Typical. I can almost hear the arrogance of Mvure in every word you speak."

Her accusation lands like a blow. Anger flickers at the edges of my mind, but before I can respond, the silent figure behind her steps forward. His presence looms large, his powerful frame taut with restrained energy—there's no mistaking the fury in his eyes, directed squarely at me.

Six gives him a sharp glance, enough to stop him in his tracks. "Let it be, Osi," she says, her tone a warning.

Osi—at least his name sounds familiar, a shred of normalcy in this tangled web of strange allegiances. But any comfort I find in that is fleeting.

"All people are your people," Osi declares, his voice steady, resonant with conviction. Each word lands with the weight of an undeniable truth. "We're divided by nothing but self-importance, ingrained fears, and prejudices. These are the barriers that stand between us. Mvure and all its people are cowards."

The truth, wrapped in his accusation, hits harder than I want to admit. I can feel my resolve faltering, a part of me shrinking. I murmur quietly, almost to myself, "And if I choose not to involve myself?"

Osi's response is swift and merciless. "Then, as I said, you are a coward." His voice is flat, resolute, carrying no room for argument.

Six raises her hand, cutting through the tension with a gesture that is both commanding and dismissive. "Then you may leave," she says, her tone final. "The omen binds us all, whether you choose to acknowledge it or not. I can only hope your refusal to act has no greater consequence. That, by dismissing this, you escape the fate it may bring. For your sake, I hope this is nothing more than coincidence."

Sparrow steps closer, placing a gentle hand on my shoulder. His touch is light, almost a plea. "Please, Gamu," he says softly, the sincerity in his voice undeniable. "Help us."

I stand at the crossroads, torn between the urge to cast off this strange chain of events and the growing dread that, if I do, something far worse could be on the horizon. A part of me wants to believe this is all some elaborate ruse, a story spun to manipulate me. But there's another part— a deeper part—that can't shake the feeling that something much larger is at play. *But am I truly willing to upend my life over these bizarre happenings?*

Deep down, I already know the answer. Despite the swirling confusion, a cold detachment has already settled over me, and I realize it. *I already know what my decision is.* "You will find me by the river tomorrow evening."

And with that, I turn away, but the weight of their expecta-

CHAPTER 7

tions follows me, heavy and inescapable.

Chapter 8

I veer off the main paths, slipping into narrow alleys and overgrown footpaths where the darkness swallows me whole. Each shadowed corner harbors the potential for betrayal—an informant ready to barter my location for a few coins or a promise of safety from Ndambira's enforcers. This fear gnaws at me, not just from the danger itself but from the gnawing paranoia that shadows my every step. I've never let my guard down before, and the fickleness of people never fails to make me wary.

The forest envelops me as I slip into its cover. Moonlight filters through the thick canopy, casting ethereal patterns on the ground that shift with every gust of wind. I navigate the dimly lit paths until I reach a small, weather-beaten structure nestled in a clearing. Its low roof and rough-hewn walls blend seamlessly with the natural surroundings, barely noticeable against the backdrop of ancient trees.

Inside, the air is cool and musty, heavy with the earthy scent of dried herbs and a lingering hint of wood smoke. Shelves line the walls, cluttered with jars of herbs, dried flowers, and various arcane trinkets. I reach for a candle, its wax marred by countless uses, and strike a flint against it. The flame bursts forth, its warm, flickering light casting dancing shadows that stretch and recede across the dimly lit room. The flicker of the flame reveals the cluttered yet oddly comforting chaos of my sanctuary.

I sink onto a rough-hewn stool, feeling the solidity of the wood beneath me. The coolness of the air and the dim glow of the candle offer a momentary respite from the chaos. I take a deep breath, letting the musty scent of the hut and the earthy aroma of the herbs calm the storm within me.

As the candle's flame steadies, I turn to my work. I carefully mix the herbs I gathered by the river, their textures rough and earthy against my fingers. Using a mortar and pestle, I grind them into a coarse powder. The subtle crunch of the leaves and the soft, powdery release of the ground herbs mingle with the warm light of the candle, creating an atmosphere of focused serenity amid the clutter of the small hut.

My hands work metholodically, crushing and blending, yet my mind is anything but focused. *Why is this happening?* The question pounds through my thoughts, each repetition louder, more urgent; a relentless drumbeat echoing in the caverns of my mind. I came to Nakuru seeking refuge, a sanctuary from the ghosts of my past. I wanted to escape the suffocating weight of failure, the relentless grip of shame that clung to me like a second skin. The purpose of my flight was clear—forget, move on, sever the ties to the life I had abandoned. I craved release from the tangled web of regret and disappointment that had consumed me.

But to truly escape, I had learned, you must first shrink yourself. You must shed your identity, cast off the pieces of yourself that once stood tall, and slip into the quiet anonymity of insignificance. That was my plan—to become invisible, to dissolve into a life of no consequence. If you are nothing, no one can expect anything from you, and the burden of your past can no longer weigh you down. It was supposed to be that simple. But now, with every twist of fate, it feels like I'm being pulled back into the light, forced to confront the very things I had worked so hard to bury.

Each twist of the pestle feels like an attempt to grind my past into oblivion, but instead, it rises to the surface with every press, every forceful crush of the leaves. My frustration spills over, and I slam the pestle harder than necessary, the vibrant herbs reduced to lifeless powder beneath my relentless grip.

My thoughts tangle and twist like the herbs I crush, memories of the life I once had surging back like a torrent. I had a duty to my people, to my parents, who gave me everything—safety, comfort, a future. And yet, I chose to flee. I abandoned them without a word, leaving behind the honor that was my birthright. I told myself I was destined for something greater than the mundane life of fish and village routine. I believed I was smarter than everyone else, meant for more than the simplicity of Mvure.

But instead of rising to something greater, I surrendered myself to shadows and deceit. I gave myself to a man who manipulated me, stripped me of my dignity, and left me vulnerable to darker forces. I descended into the dark arts—not out of survival, but out of weakness. What began as a desperate longing for love became a twisted pursuit for power, leading me deeper into the abyss. *The prince of Netherus* lured me in with false promises, deception cloaked in grandeur. Blood and sacrifice marked my path, and now, the very magic I once sought for meaning has become a tool for survival—its cost measured in blood still.

Escape and forget. That was supposed to be my salvation. That was supposed to wipe away the sins of the past, to help me carve out a new life untainted by the shadows of Mvure. But now, with the knowledge that Ndambira's pursuit is real, that Mvure—this place that feels more foreign to me now than ever—is in grave danger because of the dark power it harbors, I can no longer ignore the truth. I am the one who must warn them, the one who must face what I left behind.

But I already know my decision. The idea of returning to Mvure churns inside me, violent and terrifying. How could I ever face them again? The shame of my abandonment coils around my chest, tightening with each breath, suffocating me with guilt. If what Six and the others said is true, then my return will only confirm what I've become: tainted by the world. No longer pure, in soul or in body. No longer fit to claim the title I once held. I have lost my place among them.

Yet, a faint glimmer of reclaiming my honor lingers, the prospect of returning to Mvure, confronting my past, and seeking redemption. The thought teases at me. But the fear is paralyzing. The idea of being turned away, branded as impure and unworthy, looms like an impenetrable dark cloud. Panic rises within me, each breath coming faster and more erratic.

I force myself to stop, steadying my breath with deliberate calm. *They are well-prepared,* I remind myself, having defended their realm for centuries—perhaps even longer. My absence might be part of their divine reckoning. If Mvure suffers, it could be a necessary judgment for their past deeds, a reckoning I am not meant to interfere with. Staying here and allowing this new chapter of my life to unfold seems safer and the right course of action.

I continue focusing on the herbs, grinding, and mixing with mechanical precision, trying to drown out the terrifying thoughts swirling in my mind. But the question persists: *What if this power, if I turn my back on my calling, fades away entirely? How can I be sure?* The very notion sends a chill of dread through me. This calling, as that old woman said, is my gateway to the other side—a door that I fear might close behind me forever if I walk away. *How can I be certain it won't lock me out, leaving me stranded and weak?*

If that is the case, if I am to truly forget and move on, then this power must be left in the past. If that is the truth, and I fear it is, I must cease to wield this power now. Perhaps then they won't be able to hold me accountable for my choices. By forsaking it, I might sever their influence over me—the whispers, the terror, the pain. If I distance myself from the magic, might it all finally fade away? Maybe then, I can find peace, and become unburdened by the weight of the past and this pressing responsibility that demands that I confront it.

The vow forms easily in my mind—a solemn promise to sever my ties with the dark magic that has been my crutch, just like I did by the river. But the weight of this vow chokes me. Will I be able to continue without it? The terror of being powerless, of losing a part of my very essence, paralyzes me. I have relied on this power for so long; it feels like tearing a piece of my soul away. The fear of living without it, of facing the unknown, is a chilling prospect

The vow lingers unspoken, a silent promise that may never see the light of day. Instead, I immerse myself in the task at hand, finishing the preparation of the medication with methodical precision. My fingers, stained with the earthy hues of crushed herbs, move with care as I blend the final ingredients, each motion deliberate, each action a step toward closure.

I survey the hut with a critical eye. The simplicity that once brought me solace now feels tainted, a reflection of the rejection and judgment I project onto it. This sanctuary, once a haven of freedom, now feels compromised. I will protect it fiercely—against Mvure, rebels, restless spirits, and the weight of the past, which I am determined to bury and forget. Every step forward is a defiance of that shadow.

With a decisive breath, I rise from my seat, the wooden stool creaking softly beneath me. I begin the meticulous task of packing the crushed and blended herbs into their jars, each container labeled with precise care. The soft clinking of glass against glass punctuates the stillness of the room, a subtle rhythm in the quiet.

I turn my attention to my clothing, untie the cords of my hood, and let the fabric slip from my shoulders. I pull my shirt off and fold it gently before setting it aside. I do the same with my pants, folding them into a soft pile. I slip out of my boots, feeling the tickle of sand on my bare feet as I set them in the corner.

As I extinguish the candle, its flame sputters and fades. I move to my cot with a sense of finality, settling into the thin, worn mattress, I pull the rough blanket over me and let the quiet envelop me, the weight of the day sinking into the darkness around me.

I've made my decision: I am done with Mvure's legacy and any other expectations thrust upon me. I am no longer worthy of their purity or their judgment. I refuse to be dragged back into the past; the very idea of it terrifies me— makes me feel like I'm suffocating. If being called a coward is the price, then so be it. Osi's disdainful glare might haunt me, but I refuse to let it define me.

Though it might often feel like a facade, I hold the reins of power and control now, and I will not relinquish them. I belong to myself for the first time, and that's all I ask.

CHAPTER 8

Yes, I'll stay here, in this sanctuary I've carved out, away from the conflicts and responsibilities others seem eager to thrust upon me. As I close my eyes, the night sounds of the forest gently lull me into sleep. Tomorrow, I'll continue as I always have—silently, in the shadows—a nobody, unburdened by judgment, untouched by fear.

Chapter 9

The first rays of dawn slip through the cracks in the hut, casting delicate patterns of light across the earthen floor. I wake abruptly, my mind still tangled in the shadows of last night's decisions, each one weighing heavier with the breaking day. I push myself up from the cot, feeling the stiffness in my muscles from a night of restless sleep. The cool earth beneath my bare feet grounds me as I move with quiet determination toward the corner where my bathing tools are neatly stored. I gather the small wooden bucket, a bar of soap wrapped in cloth, and a simple washcloth, the textures grounding me in the present.

Stepping outside, the early morning light drapes a soft, golden veil over the clearing. The forest stirs to life, the gentle chirping of birds weaving through the air, and a delicate mist hugs the ground. I approach the wooden container where my stored water rests. Its surface, worn smooth from years of use, feels cool and familiar under my hands. With a lift, I pour the clear, cool water into the bucket, the soothing sound of the liquid filling the vessel echoing in the stillness. The water glistens, catching the morning light and shimmering like liquid crystal.

I make my way to a secluded spot at the edge of the clearing, where the dawn's serenity envelops me. Hidden behind the protective shelter of a towering tree, I bathe with deliberate ease. The cool water cascades over me, washing away the remnants of sleep and sweat, easing the knots of tension that accumulated through the night. The chill is refreshing and invigorating, and with each splash, the weight of yesterday's troubles begins to dissolve.

Back in the hut, I slip into the same clothes from yesterday. They feel familiar and comforting in their simplicity. Stepping outside again, I tend to the hearth, kindling a small fire. The crackling flames gradually dispel the lingering coolness of the morning, their warmth seeping into my bones. As the fire grows, I prepare a simple meal of dried fruits and nuts, the aroma of the warming fire mingling with the earthy scent of the forest.

In this quiet morning ritual, I remind myself of my purpose: seclusion and survival. Here, in this solitary haven, I find a semblance of peace, however fleeting.

Just as I finish eating, a soft rustling outside disrupts the tranquil solitude. Instinctively, my senses sharpen, my magic crackling to attention like a drawn blade. I scan the surroundings with heightened alertness. At the edge of the clearing, a Shiwo stands, her figure half-hidden by the shifting shadows cast by the dappled light filtering through the canopy above. Her stance is rigid, exuding an urgent, almost frantic energy. Our eyes lock briefly before she speaks, her voice trembling with fear.

"Please," she pleads, "it's Kail. Will you come?"

With a resigned sigh, I nod in agreement, signaling my willingness to accompany her. "Stay here," I instruct, as I gather my pouch and dagger. Stepping out into the cool morning air, I motion for her to lead the way. "Show me where he is."

Her steps are quick and driven by worry, and I match her pace with silent resolve. My mind races with unanswered questions about Kail and the urgency of her plea as we follow the narrow path through the village. The path winds past thatched-roof huts and children laughing and playing in the dusty lanes, their carefree voices a stark contrast to the tension I feel.

As we approach, the villagers emerge from their homes, their expressions a mixture of recognition, curiosity, and caution. Chickens wander freely, pecking and clucking with an air of nonchalance, scratching the earth for scraps.

Shiwo pushes open a wooden door, and I step into the dimly lit interior. The room is cloaked in shadows, with only a sliver of light filtering through the gaps in the wooden walls. On a bed of woven reeds, a figure lies half-hidden by the encroaching gloom.

As I step further in, I see Kail's forehead glistening with

beads of sweat, despite the gentle breeze wafting through the open window. Lines of pain are etched deeply into his features. Yet, as he catches sight of me, a weak smile flits across his face, momentarily softening the agony that marks his expression.

"Gamu," he murmurs, his voice a gravelly whisper laced with relief at my presence.

I kneel beside him, my hands instinctively reaching for his wound. His fever radiates a searing heat, and the deep gash on his arm pulses with a vivid red inflammation. My fingers dive into my pouch to retrieve the herbs and salves that I know will ease his pain. His body tenses at the initial touch, but he remains still, his eyes locked on mine with a mix of gratitude and a silent search lingering in his expression.

"You shouldn't have come," he murmurs, his voice barely audible.

"I couldn't ignore Shiwo's plea, or you," I reply softly, focusing on my task.

He opens his mouth to respond, but hesitates, his gaze drifting away before returning to me. "Thank you," he manages, the words a fragile bridge between his discomfort and his appreciation.

Outside, the village is beginning to stir. I finish applying the salve and bandaging his wound, the quiet intimacy of the moment not lost to us.

"Rest now," I urge gently, "Let the herbs work their magic."

He nods, his eyes fluttering closed with a faint, weary sigh. But as I prepare to stand and leave, he coughs, the sound strained and filled with worry. "I've been having troubling dreams," he confesses, his breath coming in ragged gasps. "I can't remember them clearly, but I wake each time with a deep concern for you."

Seeing his distress, I settle back down beside him, a resolve to stay longer taking hold. The weight of his fears mixes with my own. "I'm alright," I assure him softly, my voice lacking conviction. "And you need to be careful too."

Kail is a soldier who often opposes his fellow colleagues to protect the villagers, a selfless devotion that might have led to his current fever. He has once shielded me as well, diverting undue scrutiny and government attention away from my activities. When I later saw that his sister was sick, I returned the favor, and it was soon after that that I began to see the wounded brought to my doorstep by his hand.

The worry deepens the lines on Kail's face, his eyes pleading as he struggles to find the right words. "Please," he whispers, his voice barely audible, "stay a little longer."

I don't hesitate, despite the magnetic pull of his gaze. "You know I can't," I say softly, gently extracting myself from his bedside.

I start to walk out and Shiwo speaks to me softly yet urgently, her voice tinged with concern, "Won't you use your magic? It could heal him faster."

I loathe the implication of her words, the way they reduce me to just my abilities. "No, that won't be necessary," I reply, my voice cold and resolute.

Chapter 10

The villagers, newly awakened, go about their daily tasks with a familiar rhythm. Their movements are purposeful yet unhurried. They scoop fresh water from the stream into clay pots, the liquid sloshing with a soft, soothing sound that blends with the crackle of kindling fires. The air is thick with the smell of wood smoke and freshly turned earth, underscored by the quiet hum of morning rituals. Their eyes occasionally shift toward me, their gazes a blend of quiet recognition and reserved curiosity.

I stand apart, uneasy, as an elderly man shuffles towards me. His movement, though slow, carries an urgency that pierces through the morning calm. His gray hair peeks from under a wide-brimmed hat, every strand neatly in place, except for the stray wisps that escape, fluttering like spider silk in the breeze. As he reaches me, he removes his hat with trembling hands, revealing hair that glints silver in the early light. His eyes, clouded yet intense, hold a reverence that sends a chill down my spine.

"*Munhu akaropafadzwa!*"—*"Blessed one!"* He calls out, his voice crackling like dry leaves, bowing low before me. He extends a piece of bread, its warmth seeping through his fingers, the aroma of yeast and earth mingling in the air. "Ndapota, gamuchirai chibayiro ichi chinyoro,"—*"Please accept this humble offering."*

"Aiwa, zvakanaka,"—*"No, it's alright,"* I whisper, my voice barely louder than the morning breeze. Accepting such a gift, showing even a hint of agreement with his words, could paint me as a revolutionary—or worse, a threat.

The village is already on edge, tension simmering beneath the surface. I can feel it like a current running through the ground. The soldiers I killed in the forest are surely being sought, their bodies discovered by now. There's a hunt for answers, a search for someone to blame, and I can't afford to stand out any more than I already do.

But the old man presses the bread into my hands, his voice rising, insistent. "Ndapota, chitora. Chitora."—*"Please, take it. Take it."*

Reluctantly, I take the bread, nodding my thanks. "May the spirits bless you," I murmur, forcing a tight smile as I press the warm loaf against my side, trying to mask the tremor in my hands. His face brightens with an almost childlike joy, and he shuffles away, leaving me with a gift that feels like a curse.

I hurry along the path, feeling the bread's heat seeping through my clothes, a reminder of the precariousness of my situation. The act of kindness, innocent on the surface, weighs heavy with danger. The old man, his mind perhaps drifting with age, couldn't know what his reverence could cost me.

I quicken my pace, the familiar path beneath my feet suddenly alien, shadows creeping around me. There's a presence behind me, close, like a shadow stretching long and dark across my path. I don't look back but feel it, a chill running down my spine. I'd caught his eyes earlier—sharp, probing, filled with suspicion. Now, he's gone, but the weight of his gaze lingers.

I listen, my senses stretching out. He's good—too good, almost. His footsteps are nearly silent, but not enough to escape my notice. I pretend not to hear, and continue down the path with measured steps. The soldier's approach is cautious, each step carefully placed to avoid detection, but I can feel the tension radiating from him, a coiled spring ready to snap.

At a fork in the path, I slow, feigning uncertainty. The soldier hesitates, just behind me. His steps quicken, a sudden burst of energy closing the distance. My heart pounds, but I'm ready. I whirl around, faster than a blink, my dagger flashing in the sunlight, slicing through the air towards him.

His eyes widen in shock as he stumbles back, his hand jerking toward his weapon. But I am quicker. Instinct takes over, a primal need for survival. I channel the forbidden power I've tried so hard to forget.

CHAPTER 10

"Ndichakuuraya!"—*"I'll kill you!"* My voice is a mix of fear and unyielding resolve. My wrist flicks and his gun is wrenched from his grasp, clattering to the ground with a dull thud.

He gasps, eyes widening as he realizes what's happening, the invisible force tightening around his throat. His hands claw at nothing, desperate for air as he chokes out a strangled plea, *"Nda—"*

I don't wait. I surge forward, my movements sharp and deliberate, plunging my dagger into the soft flesh of his neck. His scream dies in a gurgle, blood spurting from the wound, a dark stream staining the earth beneath us.

I pull the blade free, wiping it clean on his tunic. His body crumples to the ground with a heavy thud, the silence that follows deafening. My hands tremble, not from the sight of death but from the realization of what I've done—again. Another life taken, another burden on my conscience. The cycle of violence seems endless, and each time, the weight grows heavier.

I take a deep breath, forcing down the rising panic. My thoughts whirl, but I know I have to move. Quickly, I drag his body into the tall grass, the blades swaying as if whispering secrets. I kick dirt over the bloodstains, the dust rising in a thin cloud, obscuring the crimson patches. The forest holds its breath, the air thick with the gravity of what's just happened, as if the trees themselves are watching, judging.

I rush down the path, heart pounding, legs moving on instinct. My sanctuary looms ahead, but it no longer feels safe. It's a place tainted by my actions, reflecting back the darkness within me. I stop a few paces away, my chest heaving, tears threatening to spill over. I dig my nails into my palms, grounding myself with the pain, fighting to steady my breathing.

Slowly, I focus, drawing in air and releasing it in controlled breaths. The world sharpens, my panic receding like a tide. Today, I need a routine, a shred of normalcy to cling to—a reminder that I'm still here, still in control, even if it feels like everything around me is falling apart.

I move swiftly, each step carrying me to the back of my shelter, where my herb garden flourishes in quiet defiance of the wilderness around it. The air is filled with the scent of damp earth and fresh greenery, a mixture of sweet and sharp that fills my lungs with every breath. Kneeling down, I press my knees into the cool, wet soil, feeling its texture shift and compress beneath me, a grounding sensation that steadies my racing thoughts.

I begin to tend to each plant. The earth is soft and forgiving under my fingers as I gently pull away weeds, careful not to disturb the delicate roots of the herbs. My hands move, coaxing the tender leaves into place, straightening stems, and brushing away dirt. At first, the task feels like a burden, a mundane chore weighed down by the morning's violence. But slowly, the simple act of nurturing these living things calms me, the repetitive motions soothing my frayed nerves.

CHAPTER 10

Some of the herbs I tend are cultivated for healing, their leaves and stems carefully harvested, dried, and stored for times of need. They have a clean, medicinal scent that reminds me of the old remedies I learned long ago. Others are reserved for rituals and offerings, their vibrant colors and potent aromas essential for sacred practices. Each plant has its place and purpose, each one a small piece of the balance I seek to maintain in this fragile world.

A sudden flutter draws my attention, and I look up to see a familiar visitor—a bird, sleek and striking, with feathers like polished ebony that shimmer with iridescent hues of blue and green in the sunlight. It lands lightly on a nearby branch, watching me with bright, intelligent eyes that seem to miss nothing. There is an uncanny awareness in its gaze, a depth of understanding that always makes me wonder if it sees more than I know.

As I work, the bird flits closer, hopping from branch to branch, its movements quick and purposeful. It chirps softly, a melody that weaves through the rustle of leaves and the whisper of the wind, adding a layer of music to the garden's natural symphony. I can't help but smile at its curiosity, its keen interest in everything I do.

"You come without a gift?" I tease, glancing at the bird with a raised eyebrow. It tilts its head as if considering my words, its beady eyes shining with a hint of mischief.

"Do you not understand a woman's desires?" I continue, my tone playful. "It's quite simple: a bright, unusual feather, a shiny pebble, or a particularly striking flower. These small gestures show you care, that you see the beauty in the little things and want to share it with her."

The bird cocks its head to the other side, its eyes narrowing in a way that seems almost amused. Then, with a sudden flutter of wings, it takes off, leaving me chuckling softly to myself. Its departure leaves a stillness in the garden, but the brief moment of lightheartedness lingers, lifting my spirits just a little.

As the sun climbs higher, casting longer shadows and warming the air, I pull my hood low over my face. I leave the sanctuary of my garden and make my way down the familiar path, the weight of recent events pressing down on me like a shroud. I pass the spot where I hid the man's body, my heart hammering in my chest as I steal a quick glance. There is no sign of disturbance, no hint that he has been discovered, but the faint, metallic tang of blood clings to the air, lingering on my tongue like a bitter memory.

I avoid the bustling square, slipping into the narrow, winding paths that cut through the dense grass and tangled underbrush. The ground beneath my feet is uneven, the yellowing blades whispering against my legs as I move. Every step feels deliberate, each one bringing me closer to the place I seek.

Finally, I reach the hut. Its worn walls are barely visible through the thick foliage, the structure almost swallowed by the wildness around it. Lowering my hood, I step into

CHAPTER 10

the warm, dim interior. The air inside is thick with the earthy scent of clay and the faint hint of smoke, a familiar combination that instantly puts me at ease.

My gaze is immediately drawn to the man at the pottery wheel. His hands move with fluid grace, fingers dancing over the spinning clay, shaping it with an artistry that defies his sightless eyes. The clay bends and curves under his touch, forming intricate shapes and delicate patterns as if the material itself is eager to obey his will. Though he cannot see me, he turns his face toward my presence, a soft smile playing on his lips as if he has sensed my arrival long before I stepped through the door.

I stand silently, watching him work, captivated by the motion of his hands and the quiet strength they convey. The hut is filled with a gentle hum, the wheel's turning, and the soft murmur of the clay being molded.

"Masikati akanaka,"—*"Good afternoon,"* he greets warmly, his voice startling the quiet of the hut.

"Masikati,"—*"Afternoon,"* I reply softly, my own voice barely a whisper in the stillness. "I've come to see your beads."

A gentle smile spreads across his face, and he nods, the movement slow and deliberate. I move carefully through the room, my footsteps soft against the earthen floor as I pass the display of beads, necklaces, and ear hoops meticulously arranged on the shelves. Each piece is a testament to his artistry, a reflection of the care and dedication he pours into his work.

"You've returned," he says softly, his fingers never pausing in their dance on the pottery wheel. "I recognize your scent—the collection of herbs that follow you."

I glance down at the small bundles of herbs tied around my waist, their familiar aromas filling the air around me. "Eya," I reply simply, my eyes still on the vibrant displays that line the walls.

The gentle smile dances on his lips and he continues to work with the clay, his hands moving, molding, and shaping the soft material with a grace that defies his blindness. I clear my throat, settling into the space, and allowing my gaze to wander around the small hut. The shelves are filled with an array of pottery, each piece unique, the intricate patterns and vibrant glazes telling stories of countless hours spent perfecting his craft. Nearby, delicate jewelry crafted from metal and stones catches the light, the designs intricate and precise, reflecting the same meticulous attention to detail that is evident in all his work.

I find myself drawn towards the beads. They are arranged with care, each one a small masterpiece, showcasing a variety of colors and textures. Some are polished smooth, catching the light with a soft sheen, while others are rough and natural, their imperfections telling a story of their origins. I reach out, my fingers brushing lightly over the smooth surface of a crimson bead, feeling a strange pull towards it.

CHAPTER 10

In the silence, his voice breaks through again. "What kind do you seek?"

I hesitate for a moment, the memory of my dreams coming back to me. In them, I wear beads—not the kind I wore in Mvure, but ones of deep crimson and shimmering gold. They are relentless in their appearances, vivid and impossible to forget. I recognize them immediately, and they evoke a deep sense of reverence within me.

"Crimson and gold," I murmur reverently, my fingertips tracing the smooth surface of the beads.

"Yes," he says, his voice thoughtful and measured. He rises with grace, moving towards me with a confidence that comes from years of intimate familiarity with his surroundings. His movements are fluid, each step deliberate as he navigates the room, avoiding obstacles with ease.

As he approaches, he wipes his hands on his trousers, but the clay clings stubbornly to his fingers. I notice a slight tremor in his hands as they reach out to mine, his touch gentle despite the roughness of his skin from countless hours of shaping and molding. He carefully lifts the necklace from the display, his fingers moving with delicate precision.

"These beads are special," he says softly, his voice filled with a quiet intensity. "Your spirit is trying to tell you something. Crimson for the blood of our ancestors, gold for the wisdom they pass down." He holds up the loop of beads, which trembles slightly in his hands. "Dreaming of them may signify a heavy past and a spirit in need of strength and guidance."

I take the beads from him, feeling the weight of their significance, the smooth coolness of the beads against my skin. The words he speaks resonate deeply within me, coming from a man who sees the world without sight yet understands it more deeply than most. I want to reject them, to push away the memories of a past that feels too heavy to bear. But something within me, something much stronger, wants them, needs them.

"Come," he says gently, taking the beads from me once more. "The past can indeed be a burden, but it also holds immense power. Embrace it, and let it guide you." With a careful, reverent touch, he drapes the necklace around my neck. "Wearing these beads symbolizes a deep connection with the strength and wisdom of your ancestors' stories. It signifies your acknowledgment of them and your acceptance of their power as your own."

The beads rest heavily against my chest, their weight a tangible reminder of what I have vowed to reject. But now they feel like a fragile connection to a strength I need. I want to convince myself that their presence on me is not a mark of failure but a sign that there might still be a place for me in this world, despite my doubts. I can allow myself this, right?

"Thank you," I whisper, my voice thick with emotion. Perhaps my fears and pleas have been heard, and maybe, there is still a chance for me to find the strength and

CHAPTER 10

guidance I so desperately need.

Chapter 11

As the sun dips low, I retreat to the sanctuary of my hut. In one hand, a chicken dangles upside down, its frantic fluttering and alarmed clucks a discordant symphony against the quiet of the fading day. Though the body I hid earlier remains undiscovered, the tension of its absence hangs heavily in the air.

I secure the chicken to a wooden post outside, ensuring its safety for the night. The cool air brushes against my skin as I enter the hut, my movements automatic as I slip on my other beads. The familiar weight against my skin grounds me, yet my attention is swiftly drawn to the corner where my drum waits—my conduit to a deeper power. Isolated by choice, my shelter stands apart from others, a sacred space reflecting my innermost self.

Taking a deep breath to center myself, I reach for the drum. The worn hide feels alive under my fingertips, a living connection to the world's *ancient* rhythms. The first touch of my palms against the drum's surface sends a jolt through me, a primal awakening. As I strike it, the sound fills the hut, a resonant call that vibrates through the very walls, summoning the air itself to dance. My eyes close, and I surrender to the rhythm. Each beat is a pulse of the earth, each vibration a whisper of age-old secrets. My body responds instinctively, moving with urgent grace, my spirit syncing with the drum's deep heartbeat. It's more than sound—it's a communion, my very essence entwined with the rhythms that echo through the ages.

The beat intensifies, each thump a declaration of my presence, my desires echoing out into the world. My heart races, my pulse syncing with the drum's escalating tempo. With every beat, the tension within me builds, the drum responding to my touch, drawing out my rawest emotions and highest desires. I strike harder, each thud resonating through my core, a symphony of energy that courses through me, exhilarating and overwhelming. The intensity mounts, each vibration blending into an ecstatic torrent that threatens to sweep me away. I am both the tempest and the calm at its eye, caught in an unrelenting storm of sensation.

As I reach the peak, my strikes become fierce, each one a release of energy that shakes the very air around me. My body trembles with the force of the drum's response, a powerful release that leaves me breathless, my spirit soaring on the waves of unleashed power. Finally, as the last echo fades, I let the drum fall silent. I linger in the aftermath, the vibrations humming through my body, soothing, invigorating. My breathing steadies, and slowly, I rise, the euphoria lingering, my skin flushed with the warmth of the exertion.

With the drum carefully placed back in its corner, I step outside into the evening's cool embrace, the shift from the hut's warmth to the open sky grounding. The fire pit awaits, its stones cold and expectant. Methodically, I build the base with dry twigs and branches, the tactile process a calming counterpoint to the drum's intensity.

Sparks fly as flint strikes steel, catching the kindling. Flames lick upward, their crackle a comforting soundtrack to the evening's rituals. The dancing flames cast playful shadows around me, their light flickering across my face.

Turning to the chicken, I bring it from its post, its body still now in my firm grasp. With a swift motion, I end its fluttering life. The silence that follows is filled only by the soft rustle of feathers as I pluck each one, the repetitive task a meditative act that grounds me after the drum's storm. In Nakuru, I've adapted to many things—none more so than the art of preparing my own meals from scratch. The slick warmth of the chicken's innards, and the resistance of its flesh against my knife, are now familiar, almost comforting in their routine.

As I add the chicken along with fresh herbs, roots, and vegetables to the pot over the fire, the aroma of cooking fills the air, blending with the smoke to create a homely scent. I sit by the fire, allowing its warmth to seep into my bones, the flames a mesmerizing dance that lets my mind wander.

A sudden prickling sensation at the back of my neck alerts

me to an unexpected presence. Someone has approached—silent and unseen. My muscles tense, and my heart pounds against my ribcage as I whirl around to face the intruder. My hands involuntarily clench into fists, quelling the surge of fear and surprise that threatens to betray me. "What are you doing here?" I demand, my voice laced with an accusatory urgency.

"Wow," Six says, "Your senses are sharp."

"How did you find me?" I snap, unable to mask the edge of displeasure that sharpens my words. My gaze narrows, scrutinizing her every move.

"I asked around," she replies simply as if it were the most natural thing in the world.

"Why?" The word slips out, terse and laden with suspicion.

Yet, instead of answering, she ventures a step closer, her next words tinged with a casual revelation. "I haven't told you why they call me *Six*, right?"

My instincts scream to step back, to restore the physical distance between us, but I remain rooted to the spot, refusing to show any signs of intimidation. I've carved my own path through hell. I won't hesitate to carve one through her.

"Honestly, it's quite silly," she continues, her voice holding a calm intensity that somehow fills the space between us. "Nobody really knows my name—they had to give me one.

They find it amusing that whenever someone tries to pester me, I warn them: if I count to six and you're still in my face, you won't like what happens next. It's a merciful threat, really. I could say five, but I value patience in action."

Her explanation hangs in the air, a subtle assertion of her patience and potential for violence. I maintain my composure, my expression unreadable. "Why are you telling me this?" I inquire, deliberately brushing off her attempt to assert dominance in our exchange.

She steps even closer, her gaze piercing, as if trying to peer into my very soul. "Relax. You're not in danger, *Gamu*. I thought that would help us bond, that's all."

"Answering my questions might be more effective," I retort, my tone firm and firm, making it clear I won't be swayed.

She smiles, a sharp, knowing smile that slices through the tension between us. "I thought you might be inclined to return swiftly to Mvure to warn your people—especially since you don't need us, though we need you," she admits, finally addressing my question. "You said you'd come back, but I personally don't believe you were going to. After all, you made it clear that your duty lies solely with your people."

"And you came here to dissuade me?" I challenge, my voice steady, though my heart races with a mix of anger and apprehension.

"No, I'm not here to coerce you into anything you're not

willing to do; otherwise, we'd be no better than Ndambira the oppressor," she counters, her voice soft yet resolute. She exhales softly, a sigh that seems to carry the weight of the world. "What's happening isn't your fault, and therefore not your burden. If you choose not to assist us, at the very least, you could prevent Ndambira from seizing the ultimate power he seeks in Mvure. Your success is crucial—any action you take here or in Mvure will substantially aid our cause. I'm here to ensure you understand the gravity of the situation you're stepping into, so you have the best chance of succeeding. My priority is the cause, and I will support whatever option weakens Ndambira, even if I don't agree that it's the best route of action." She sighs again, the sound tinged with a mix of frustration and resolve. "But again, I won't force you—that's not how we operate."

"Go on," I urge, my voice steadier than I feel.

She pauses, her gaze searching mine, probing deep as if trying to unearth my secrets. "In Mvure, the use of dark magic is a closely guarded secret, especially in safeguarding the village's wellspring of power. The secret is known only by a select few in the royal family, dedicated to this duty through generations."

Her words send a cold shiver down my spine, the implications reverberating in my mind like the distant echoes of something terrible creeping closer.

"Ndambira has taken advantage of the chief's death—Anesu's death—and the rise of his wife—"

A knot of dread twists in my gut, and I cut her off, my voice sharp with disbelief. "Death? What are you talking about?"

"Yes. May his soul find peace; he's been gone for months now."

The heaviness in my stomach deepens, anchoring me in place as if the very ground beneath me has shifted. "What are you saying?" My voice comes out strangled. Grief seeps into every syllable, disbelief tainting the edges.

"You didn't know?" Her tone is soft, almost disbelieving itself as if surprised by my ignorance.

"No," I whisper, shaking my head, the denial already taking root. "That can't be true. You're lying." The words are hollow, lacking the conviction I want them to carry. It's less a statement and more a plea—a desperate attempt to fend off the weight of what I refuse to believe.

"It's true," she says, her voice steady, unyielding in the face of my unraveling. "His wife has taken over leadership, and Mvure thrives under her. I have no reason to lie."

Could it really be true? The idea feels foreign, too brutal to absorb. My father, gone? The thought alone stabs through me like a blade, twisting deeper with every pulse of my heart. But why would she lie? What could she possibly gain from this? The realization settles like a stone in my chest, and I feel my knees threaten to buckle beneath the weight. My hands instinctively press against my stomach, as though I can physically hold myself together in the face of this unbearable truth. The world spins, too vast, too heavy, as I try to find something solid, something real in the storm of my thoughts.

"But that's not why I needed to speak with you privately." Her voice slices through the haze, pulling me back for a moment. "You don't look well—should I continue?"

I'm barely aware of her words, adrift in the suffocating fog of grief. I don't even realize she's been calling my name until I blink, the sound finally reaching me through the thick veil of shock. My throat constricts, tightening around the words that refuse to form. They dissolve before they can leave my lips, lost to the tremors shaking my body. The air feels thin, every breath a battle against the crushing weight of reality pressing in on all sides.

A small, calculating smile creeps across her face. "I might've waited till evening, but I knew you'd disappoint. You've proven to be like your people in every way. If you managed to slip away, I couldn't risk it; our time is already gone, and the march on Mvure is in motion."

"I... I don't understand." The soft crunch of approaching footsteps sends a chill down my spine. They grow louder with each passing second, closing in, tightening the trap around me. My heart pounds, each beat echoing like a drum, mirroring the rhythm of the advancing threat.

The air seems to grow colder, shadows stretching longer

across the ground as twilight creeps in. My breaths come harder, heavier as if even the air itself conspires to suffocate me.

"Gamuchirai." Her voice drips with satisfaction, each syllable a thorn meant to wound. "I have to admit, you look a little different—a shadow of the heir I heard all about. But when I saw you, I recognized something. And now, you've confirmed it for me, Gamu. Do you know you're the reason your father fell ill? I saw it myself—he became depressed, unable to speak or eat. He grieved you, or maybe the idea of you—after all, you left him with nothing."

The words slice through me, leaving me gasping. I left him with nothing. My mind reels, circling the thought like a vulture over carrion. My father's suffering, his decline—it was my doing. The weight of it crushes my chest, unbearable. Please, no. I can't bear this.

Her voice is merciless, each word a hammer blow. "He lost his will to live, Gamu. Every day, I watched him wither away, consumed by the void you left behind. He died with a broken heart, still hoping you'd return."

A sob wrenches from my throat, raw and uncontrollable. Guilt and grief tear through me like knives. Her words paint a vivid picture of my father's decline—once strong and commanding, reduced to a ghost, haunted by my absence. The image is unbearable, too real. My vision blurs with tears as nausea rises, twisting my stomach into knots.

CHAPTER 11

I can almost see him—my father—reaching out from the darkness, pleading for me, and I wasn't there. My hands dig into my torso, gripping the fabric of my clothes, as if I could tear the pain from my body, and force it away before it consumes me.

Four soldiers emerge from the shadows and surround me, their presence as suffocating as the guilt that grips my chest.

Six's gaze remains cold, merciless. "Well, you failed, Gamu. And now, you have to live with that failure."

Before I can react, two soldiers seize my arms, their grips like iron shackles, unyielding and absolute. I'm trapped—paralyzed by their strength and the weight of my own guilt. There's no fight left in me, no words, only the hollow ache of my failure and the terror of what's to come.

Six's voice cuts through the haze, smug and triumphant. "I meant it when I said you weren't in danger—I need you alive. But you and your people will come to embrace your duty while it's still a choice, just as I have. You've given me the greatest opportunity—to change this world. The spirits who guide us have shown me that where all hope might have been lost, the key to Ndambira's ambitions has been placed in my hands instead."

"Please," I struggle against the knot in my throat and the sting of tears clouding my vision. "I will help you; I was wrong. I'll share my magic, and together we can make this right."

"No," she counters coolly. "I am no longer sure if your mother will share anything just because you ask nicely. But she might if your life is on the line." She narrows her eyes, "Everything was really dependent on you, Gamu, and the decision we gave you a chance to make," she says bitterly. "Mvure is selfish. We've suffered, and despite our pleas for help, they've done nothing. They only care about maintaining their safe sanctuary, indifferent to everyone else. I hoped you'd be different, but you proved to me that maybe we do need to learn a little selfishness."

She lifts my chin gently, her expression thoughtful yet resolute. "From analyzing how you dispatched those soldiers, I've deduced that your magic revolves around blood manipulation—including how you heal people," she remarks, her voice even and measured. "That means we can't simply sedate you with substances that enter your bloodstream. Well, I don't know," she ends with a casual tone.

Swiftly, she withdraws something from her pocket—a torn piece of fabric—and moves to cover my face. As the fabric envelops my head, darkness swallows me, stripping away my visual cues and leaving my other senses heightened but disoriented. The cloth carries a pungent chemical scent, overpowering and invasive, an obvious attempt to sever my connection with my abilities.

But she is misguided. Desperation lends me clarity and relying on my heightened hearing to detect the subtle rush of blood, I summon my magic, focusing intently on the soldier nearest to her. With a surge of will, an invisible force wraps tightly around his throat. I hear the strangled gasps as his body convulses, then a heavy thud as he falls limp to the ground. The remaining soldiers recoil in shock and fear. However, their recovery is swift. They tighten their grip on me, their hands pressing into my flesh.

In a frantic bid for escape, I shift my focus to the next target, tuning out everything but the sound of pulsing blood. Suddenly, the sharp report of a gunshot pierces the silence—once to my left, deafening, a sharp echo reverberating in my skull, then another to my right, my ears ringing with the violence of the sound. I barely register the third shot, but the ensuing pain is unmistakable. A searing, burning agony explodes at my side, the impact stealing my breath and buckling my knees.

The pain is blinding and overwhelming, as I struggle to maintain consciousness. My mind races, each thought punctuated by the harsh, ringing echoes of the gunshots and the visceral pain that threatens to consume me. My legs buckle, the strength draining from them as if siphoned by an unseen force. The soldiers adjust their hold.

The ringing in my ears subsides into a dull hum, replaced by the more immediate sensations of being manhandled in the soldiers' unrelenting grip. In my disoriented senses, I feel a sudden shift in movement, more deliberate and controlled than the scuffle before. Strong hands reposition me, and without warning, I am hoisted off the ground. The abruptness of the movement forces a sharp gasp from my lungs, a painful reminder of the gunshot wound searing through my side. The fabric blindfold against my face rubs roughly against my skin as I'm swung upwards and then positioned over a soldier's shoulder.

His shoulder presses into my stomach, exacerbating the nausea and pain, but also anchoring me to the fleeting remnants of reality. Each step he takes jostles me uncomfortably. The motion is disorienting, each movement amplifying the throbbing pain and the dizzying swirl of semi-consciousness that threatens to pull me under completely.

Every thought I try to weave into something tangible slips through my fingers like sand. My mind is succumbing to the inevitable. The darkness behind my blindfold deepens, merging with the blackness of unconsciousness.

Chapter 12

The darkness behind the blindfold seems to pulse with the rhythm of my heartbeat, intensifying the chemical stench that saturates the cloth pressed against my face. Each breath I draw is laced with the sharp tang of whatever substance they've used, deepening my disorientation and fueling a rising nausea that threatens to overwhelm me. Despite the swirling dizziness, an acute awareness of my body's weakened state sharpens my focus. Blood loss has drained my strength, leaving my limbs heavy and unresponsive, my mind struggling to maintain a coherent stream of thought. The edges of my consciousness fray, dipping perilously close to the void of unconsciousness that beckons seductively.

The relentless throbbing of my head and the raw sting of the wound are momentarily eclipsed by a surge of sorrow. Memories of my father, once suppressed by the immediacy of survival, now flood in unbidden. The realization of his death, imparted with such cruel indifference by Six, settles heavily in my chest. He is gone, and the part I played in his final days haunts me with renewed vigor. Tears escape from beneath the blindfold, mingling with the chemical residue that seeps into them. Each breath I draw is tainted with the acrid scent, intensifying the burn in my eyes and the bitterness on my tongue. My sobs are muffled against the fabric, each one a sharp pulse of grief that wracks my weakened body. Each minor shift sends spikes of pain radiating through my body. The chemical sting and the tightness of the bindings around my wrists seem trivial against the backdrop of my loss. I lay there, engulfed in mourning, lost in the depths of despair, as time slips by unmarked.

But as the initial wave of grief subsides, a spark of resolve flickers to life within me. The harsh reality of my situation reasserts itself—*Mvure*. The realization plants a heavy stone of dread in my stomach. I can't go back, not when I am responsible for this—I can't. The fear of facing them all, and the desperation serve as clarity and solidify my resolve to get out of here.

In a defiant push against the encroaching darkness, I summon what remains of my willpower, channeling it into the very fibers of my being. I visualize the wound, the raw, angry flesh that threatens my life, and mentally command the blood to coagulate, to form a barrier against the relentless flow. It's more than mere physical healing; it's a battle of wills against my body's own failing systems, a determined stand to remain anchored in the realm of the living.

This internal fight consumes every shred of energy I possess, drawing on reserves I barely remember having. Each heartbeat, each pulse of blood through my veins becomes a marker of time, counting down the moments as I fight to stabilize my condition and regain some semblance of control over my battered body.

Blinking against the oppressive darkness behind the blindfold, I struggle to anchor myself in this new, disorienting reality. I am experienced enough to recognize the rhythmical creak of a boat, each groan of its timbers a haunting melody that resonates with the gentle lap of water against its hull. I shift my body, each movement eliciting a groan as pain flares across my wounds, a stark reminder of my physical limits.

A wave of claustrophobia washes over me as the full realization of my predicament sinks in—I am trapped beneath the deck, confined within a small, suffocating cage crafted from cold iron.

Straining my ears, I seek out any faint murmur or shift in the boat's steady creak that might hint at our progression. Fear claws at the edges of my consciousness, and panic threatens to overpower my senses. I steel my resolve, painfully aware of the limitations imposed by my senses being shrouded. The darkness and silence wrap around me like a suffocating blanket, making the potent magic at my fingertips feel frustratingly impotent. Escape is not just a priority—it's a necessity. Though my hands are bound tightly behind my back, I push against the unyielding iron bars with all the force I can muster, but they mock my efforts with their rigid, cold indifference.

Time seems to stretch and distort, dragging into what feels like an eternity. Each second ticks by heavily, laden with the weight of my desperate thoughts as I cycle through possible scenarios of escape, of survival. Suddenly, the muffled cadence of voices filters down from above, each word indistinct but unmistakably there, freezing me in place. My breath catches in my throat as I strain to decipher their conversation, to glean any clue about my captors' intentions or my own fate.

Then, a voice cuts through the barrier of wood and iron, clear and chillingly familiar. "Check on her; we're docking." Six's command echoes in the confined space, her tone as cold and commanding as ever, slicing through the heavy air with razor-sharp precision.

A new surge of urgency grips me as I realize that the soldier's impending descent marks my critical chance to break free. Every muscle in my body tenses, coiled like a spring, every nerve firing with heightened alertness as I brace for the inevitable approach. The sound of footsteps on the wooden steps grows louder, each step resonating like a drumbeat in tune with the rapid pounding of my heart. Adrenaline floods my system, sharpening my senses, and readying me for the moment of action.

I steel myself, drawing on every last ounce of determination and resilience left within me. My entire body is like a live wire, tensed and ready to react.

I lie still, feigning unconsciousness, while inside me, a storm

CHAPTER 12

of desperation and calculation rages.

His methodical approach resonates softly on the wooden planks, each footstep a measured echo that fills the cramped space beneath the deck. He pauses just outside the cage, and his presence feels as heavy as the iron bars imprisoning me.

I draw in a shallow breath, concentrating intently on detecting the subtle rhythm of his heartbeat—the vital pulse of blood coursing through his veins. This is the lifeline I can exploit, a thread of life I might twist to my advantage. Yet, most of my will is already taxed, fiercely dedicated to stemming the blood loss from my own wound. Each heartbeat marks not only the passage of time but also escalates my sense of urgency.

A slight shudder passes through him, a tremor too faint for his own senses to register, but not mine. He clears his throat, a subtle note of discomfort coloring the sound—a small victory, indicating my influence seeps into his system. I press on, weaving my intent deeper into his veins, but the boat chooses that moment to sway gently. The motion jolts a sharp pain through my side. The sound of water slapping against the hull momentarily drowns out my focus, scattering my concentration like beads.

But then, as if drawn by the thread of my silent plea, he pauses and turns. There's a moment of silence, heavy with my suspended hope, and then the sound of his steps reverses, descending back toward me. As he pauses outside the cage, the heavy silence stretches between us, fraught with tension.

I sense his gaze upon me, and a cold wave of dread washes over me, distinct and more profound than any fear I've felt before. It's not just the fear of capture or the sting of my wounds—it's the primal, gut-wrenching fear of a violation far worse. Memories of whispered horrors endured by others here in Nakuru claw at my mind, chilling me to the bone. The possibility of rape, of being utterly powerless and violated, is a terror that dwarfs all others.

My breath hitches in my throat, and I struggle against the panic rising like bile. I must not show my fear. I must not let him dominate my will. Clenching my teeth, I summon every shred of resolve, focusing intently on his lifeblood. My magic, though weakened, responds to the urgency of my need, stirring with a raw, visceral power that I channel into the fight for my very soul.

However, the fear does not recede; it intensifies, each heartbeat pounding in my ears like a drum of war, threatening to overwhelm my senses. The jingle of keys becomes the soundtrack to my rising panic as the lock clicks open. "Get a hold of yourself, Gamu!" I command myself silently, stern, and unyielding. In this crucial moment, driven by desperation, I resolve to do something unprecedented: to stop the blood in my own body.

As the pulse throbbing in my ears begins to fade, so does my life force, casting me into an eerie, tranquil silence that feels almost otherworldly. Just as the door swings open, I gather the last vestiges of my willpower and seize control of his circulatory system.

CHAPTER 12

Harnessing the lifeline, I manipulate the flow of his blood with precision and finality. My intent is clear and lethal—halt the movement, and create an immediate and disorienting impact. His steps falter, confusion and shock overtaking him as his body responds to the sudden, unnatural cessation. In that disoriented moment, as he grapples with the abrupt betrayal of his own veins, I find my chance.

He struggles, fighting against the invisible force constricting his life's flow. I maintain the pressure, channeling my focus through the pain that flares like fire in my side, anchoring my resolve through my dwindling strength. His gasps for air grow more frantic, his movements more erratic, until finally, with a sickening gurgle that echoes in the cramped space, his resistance fades. His body goes limp, collapsing heavily to the floor. The thud of his fall resonates against the wooden planks, a grim punctuation to the struggle.

Heaving for breath, the weight of my exertions pressing down like a physical burden, I feel the adrenaline begin to ebb, leaving behind a sharp ache across my body. "Come on, get up," I urge myself, my internal voice commanding harshly. I've survived far worse than this; I cannot allow the pain to claim me now. With a grimace, I channel every last reserve of strength and shift my position, contorting my body to bring my bound hands from behind to the front. The ropes cut cruelly into my wrists, each movement a new slice of pain.

On the wooden planks, the soldier's lifeless body lies a short, desperate crawl away. The possibility of a dagger, a tool for my continued survival, spurs me on. Each labored breath I take is a battle, but necessity drives me forward. The cage bars groan under my weight as I pry them apart, my injured side screaming in protest. I grit my teeth, focusing past the pain, as I inch towards freedom. Collapsing beside the soldier, my knees hit the wood hard, sending jolts of pain shooting through my already battered body. But pain now is merely background noise to the task at hand. My fingers, clumsy and stiff from disuse, search his belt frantically until they close around the familiar shape of a dagger. Clutching the handle, I twist awkwardly to *saw* at the ropes binding my wrists.

After a tense, grueling moment, the ropes give way, loosening their torturous grip. Relief floods through me, sharp and sweet, as I pull my hands free at last. The rush of blood back into my fingers is painful but welcome, a sign of life and action. Quickly, I rip the blindfold from my eyes. The dim light that filters through the cracks of the boat's hold stabs painfully at my retinas, but I blink rapidly, forcing my eyes to adjust. The world that comes into focus is damp and shadowed, the air thick with the scent of the sea and something darker—blood and despair mixed in equal measure.

I peel the stinky cloth from my face, finally free from the chemical assault that clouded my senses. Taking deep, shuddering breaths of the stale, salty air, I prepare myself for what comes next. My heart continues to pound, a relentless drumbeat of exertion and fear, but also determination.

CHAPTER 12

I glance at the fallen soldier, ready to search him for anything useful when a sudden wave of familiarity stops me cold. A crushing tightness grips my chest as recognition dawns, unsettling and profound. Tentatively, I reach out, my hand trembling as I turn his face toward mine. The truth that greets me is like a physical blow, knocking the wind from my lungs. "Kail?" The name escapes my lips in a broken whisper, lost in the deafening pulse in my ears. His eyes, those familiar eyes, stare back with a haunting emptiness, frozen in a final expression of terror.

My breath hitches, caught in the jaws of disbelief and burgeoning sorrow. "No," I murmur, the denial spilling forth involuntarily. "No, no, no... I am sorry, I didn't know. I couldn't have known."

As the initial shock gives way to profound grief that presses down mercilessly on my chest, a seed of doubt takes root, twisting like a thorn in my heart. *Why was Kail here, in this dank, shadowed place, with me? Did he come to assist me, or was he under their orders all along? But* the pain in my side throbs relentlessly. Clenching my teeth against it, I force myself upright, using the cage bars for support. The tears that blur my vision are hastily wiped away with the back of my hand as a fierce resolve takes root within me.

"I can't afford to dwell on this," I mutter to myself, my voice a low growl of determination.

Gritting my teeth further, I steady myself against the sway of the ship. Each step towards the stairs leading up to the deck is a battle, the ship's movements threatening to undermine my shaky progress. The wooden planks creak under my weight, and with each step, my determination hardens into something fierce and cold. The pain becomes a distant concern, secondary to the burning need to confront Six. The thought of facing her, of turning the tables and teaching her a lesson she won't forget, fuels my ascent.

Chapter 13

Ascending the narrow stairs leading to the deck, each step is an exercise in endurance, pain lancing through my side with every movement. I cling to the rusted railing for support, steeling myself as I step into the cool embrace of the night air. My eyes slowly adjust to the dim moonlight that casts long, eerie shadows across the deck, transforming the familiar into something ghostly and unfamiliar. The scent of salt and brine is heavy in the air, mixing with the pervasive dampness that clings to every surface, soaking into the wood and my senses alike. Dark clouds loom overhead, shrouding the stars and adding a sense of foreboding to the night.

With cautious steps, I melt into the shadows, my movements deliberate and soundless as I close the distance between myself and an unsuspecting soldier. Drawing upon the deep reservoirs of my magic, I begin an incantation, channeling the raw power of blood magic. The scent of iron fills my senses, both intoxicating and dangerous, sharpening my focus to a razor's edge. With a swift, calculated movement, I unleash tendrils of magic that curl invisibly around the soldier's throat. The force is relentless, designed to cut off his air supply silently before he can utter a sound. His body crumples noiselessly to the wooden deck, his life extinguished as quickly and quietly as a snuffed candle.

One by one, I vow silently, they will fall. With the threat neutralized, I retreat swiftly back into the enveloping darkness, my senses heightened, nerves strung tight as piano wires. Across the deck, another soldier patrols, blissfully unaware of the dark fate that claimed his comrade. At the opposite end of the deck, Six is engaged in a game with two other soldiers, their voices floating over the night air, punctuated by the clack of wooden jugs and bursts of raucous laughter. Positioning myself behind a stack of coiled ropes, I survey the scene, planning my next move.

Six's voice cuts through the night, sharp and tinged with irritation, as she scans the shadows that pool around the hold's entrance. "What's taking him so long?" Her question hangs heavy in the salty air, charged with a palpable tension.

My heart pounds, a steady drum in my chest as I inch closer, each movement cloaked in the cover of darkness. The deck beneath my feet feels like a precarious stage where every step must be measured and silent.

"Relax, he's probably just having a bit of fun," one of the soldiers chimes in, his voice a careless drawl that dismisses her concerns with a wave of his hand.

But beneath Six's outward calm, a tempest brews. In a swift motion that betrays her simmering anger, she flings her drink directly into the face of the dismissive guard. The liquid arcs through the air, catching the moonlight before splashing violently across his features. He recoils with a sputter, swiping at his eyes as he curses under his breath. Before he can fully grasp the assault, Six's fist connects with his jaw—a swift, punishing strike that echoes softly on the wooden planks.

"Fuck!" He stumbles to his feet, his fists balled in anger and surprise.

Six squares off against him with fierce defiance, her eyes blazing with an intensity that burns in the dim light. "You think it's funny, making light of the horrors they're inflicting on women and girls in our village?" Her voice slices through the air, sharp as a knife. Her disdain is palpable, her anger crackling like a live wire. "Asshole," she spits vehemently onto the deck, her contempt unmistakable. "I won't tolerate such jokes on my boat."

Their confrontation is electric, the space between them crackling with raw energy. They stand inches apart, their eyes locked in a silent, volatile challenge, her fury hot enough to ignite the very air between them.

"If you're going to do something, do it already. Because once I get to six and you're still in my face, *mmmmh*," Six's voice is calm, yet it carries a lethal edge, her threat delivered with chilling precision.

He moves closer, his body language meant to intimidate, but

Six stands resolute, her posture unyielding, her gaze steely.

Suddenly, Six freezes, her attention snapping to the surrounding shadows. Something has shifted—a subtle change in the atmosphere that doesn't escape her keen senses. "Something's changed here," she mutters under her breath, her voice low and laced with suspicion. Her eyes narrow as she scans the deck, every sense heightened, her instincts razor-sharp and ready for whatever lurks in the darkness.

The old wood of the stairs groans under Six's hurried steps and descent, each step echoing like a drumbeat of doom in the tight, shadowed space of the ship's hold. In the darkness, my heart races, pounding against my ribs, fueled by a mix of fear and adrenaline.

With a swift and desperate motion, I grip the nearest soldier by the neck, my fingers finding the vulnerable spots between the sinews and bones. His reaction is immediate and primal; he claws at my hands, his eyes bulging with raw terror. Gasping for breath, he buckles to his knees, a wet, gurgling sound escaping from his constricted throat. Six's footsteps grow louder, urgent, and fast, each echo a grave reminder of her approach. "She's out here! She killed him!" The words reverberate through the damp, cold air.

The soldier who had just moments ago stood defiantly against Six, gazes in horror towards the lifeless form before him. The gravity of the situation renders him momentarily paralyzed. But before he can comprehend fully or react to Six's warning, my magic lashes out, coiling around him with the inexorable force of a riptide. With a desperate surge of strength, I tighten my grip. He struggles against the invisible binds, a futile resistance that fades as his body slackens and he crumples to the deck, another life extinguished by my hand.

Above the chaos, Six's voice cuts through, sharp and commanding, "Gamu don't!" she cries out. "Come out, okay?" Her tone shifts, softening, a surprising gentleness replacing the earlier harshness. "You're bleeding—there's a trail of blood; you've lost too much."

Dizziness sweeps over me like a wave, the edges of my vision darkening. The cold bite of the sea air mixes with the iron tang of blood, my own life force spilling too freely from the wound that throbs with each heartbeat. Every spell cast, every movement, has drained me, leaving my limbs heavy and my head light.

"Let's talk, alright? Can we do that?" Six's voice reaches out again, this time with a hint of pleading. The background noise of the ship—the creak of wood, the slap of waves against the hull—fades into a distant murmur as I lean heavily against the cold metal of the railing, struggling to maintain consciousness.

Six's voice pierces the dissonance, sounding as if it comes from underwater, muffled and distant beneath the layers of ringing in my ears and the surreal detachment from my own labored breathing. The world tilts dangerously on the verge of darkness, each blink a fight against the void that beckons with deceptive serenity. My back presses against the rough, weathered wood of the boat's pillar, the coarse texture grounding me to the moment as each breath becomes more difficult. My eyelids, heavy as lead, flutter in betrayal, each droop a threat to plunge me into darkness. I summon every shred of willpower, clenching my teeth against the overwhelming fatigue that seeks to claim me.

The taste of iron fills my mouth. In desperation, I claw for control over the disarray, reaching inward to tap into the dwindling reservoir of my blood magic. With fierce concentration, I send ethereal tendrils of power coursing through my veins, probing the depths of my being. I'm searching for a lifeline, something, anything, that might anchor me to consciousness and sustain the flickering candle of my life force. My magic, usually so potent and responsive, now feels like grasping at smoke—elusive and intangible in my weakened state.

As my magic delves into the depths of my being, it stirs something profound within me—a sensation so gentle and unexpected that it halts my descent. I sense a subtle shift—a faint stir of life within me. Not a heartbeat, but a gentle pulse, as delicate as the first flutter of a butterfly's wings. The sensation is so unexpected, so profound, that I am utterly transfixed. For a moment, all else fades into insignificance as my senses heighten, fully attuned to the enormity of what this gentle pulse signifies—a new life, barely two months old, fragile and nascent, quietly burgeoning within me.

The weight of my actions crashes down on me with newfound gravity. Every exertion of power, every draw on my magical reserves, now carries a dual threat—the risk of losing not only my own life but also endangering this nascent being that relies wholly on my survival. The stark understanding that my continued use of magic could harm, or even terminate, this fragile life transforms my fear into a protective instinct. Tears breach the barriers of my stoic facade, spilling over as the dual realities of hope and danger converge. The enormity of my situation presses in, squeezing my chest with a jaw-like grip of emotion. Cautiously, I retract my magical energies, pulling them back as one might carefully unwind tangled threads. The world around me, once held at bay by my fierce concentration now rushes in, blurring into soft shadows and light as my strength wanes.

Through the haze, Six's figure materializes, her face etched with lines of concern and urgency. She steps closer.

"I... I'm pregnant," I whisper, the words barely a breath as they leave my lips, laden with fatigue and fear. The revelation hangs between us, delicate and profound.

Shock registers on her face, quickly morphed into a complex tapestry of emotions—concern, urgency, perhaps a hint of understanding. Her eyes search mine, likely reassessing the situation in light of this new, vulnerable truth.

As the ship sways gently beneath us, the world tilts precariously. The edges of my vision darken, every blink heavier than the last. Six's image doubles, then triples, before slipping away as darkness claims me, her voice a distant echo calling me back from the brink.

Chapter 14

Gamu's whispered confession hangs in the air, a heavy, haunting echo that presses down on my chest with its grave implications. Her body, now limp and disturbingly still, slumps against the rough wooden planks of the boat, her lifeblood seeping out and staining the wood a dark, ominous red.

Instinctively, my shock morphs into action. I rush to her side, the urgency of the situation kicking my senses into overdrive. Her skin, unnaturally pale and clammy to the touch, contrasts starkly against the creaking timbers beneath us. Each shallow, labored breath she takes is a stark reminder of how critical the situation is. The sight of the blood pooling around her sends a sharp jolt of panic through my veins—she's losing too much, too quickly.

"Osi!" My voice cracks as I call out, desperation seeping into every syllable. He's already there, though, his presence a sudden comfort. His hands move with efficiency as he assesses Gamu's condition, his actions are swift and sure.

"We need to stop the bleeding," he commands, a calm and

resolute anchor. He swiftly retrieves a small pouch from his satchel, filled with medicinal herbs and emergency supplies we had packed just in case. As he opens the pouch, the earthy, pungent aroma of the herbs cuts through the briny tang of the river.

My mind wrestles with the chaos of emotions and events. I struggle to reconcile the sight of her—vulnerable and broken—with the reality of her actions. Gamu has left a trail of death in her wake, her decisions brutal yet possibly born of desperation rather than malice. A fleeting thought crosses my mind: Is she truly heartless, or is she a cornered survivor, acting out of a primal urge to protect herself and the nascent life within her? I can't help but think back to the moment I shot her, the moment I forced her into that dire situation. Was it my actions that pushed her to this extreme? The realization that she is pregnant adds another layer of complexity to my thoughts. Her fierce determination and her ruthless actions might have stemmed from a deeper, more instinctive drive—a mother's primal urge to protect her offspring. A *good* mother.

"Hold her steady." His brow is furrowed, eyes narrowed in focus as he zeroes in on the task at hand.

I carefully cradle Gamu's head, feeling the full weight of her unconscious state in my arms, and the immense responsibility of the moment. Despite the storm of events that has led us here, her face remains strangely serene, untouched by the turmoil that churns just beneath the surface. It strikes me then, how vulnerable she really is—

stripped of her defenses and her magic, she's just a person, fragile and human, just like me.

As Osi gently lifts the edge of her tunic to expose the wound, he applies a thick, green paste with a tender touch. The paste is cool against her fevered skin, slightly gritty as it spreads over and begins to seep into the wound. Almost immediately, a faint, soothing sensation seems to emanate from the area, signaling the beginning of the healing process. The herbal concoction, a blend of ancient knowledge and natural medicine, starts to work its magic, the potent properties gradually slowing the blood flow and encouraging the wound to close.

"We have to keep her warm and hydrated," he murmurs, his voice low, every word tinged with a quiet urgency. His expression remains concentrated, his hands steady as he works, yet his concern is evident in the slight crease of his brow and the careful way he monitors her responses. The seriousness of the situation hangs between us.

My mind races, ensnared by conflicting thoughts. Tasked with delivering Gamu to Mvure as a bargaining chip against her mother, I now grapple with a profound moral dilemma. The thought of the life growing inside Gamu tugs at something deep within me, awakening a buried part of my conscience I had long suppressed under layers of duty and ambition. Duty demands sacrifice, and I've done whatever it takes to fight for Nakuru without hesitation or doubt, but am I prepared to sacrifice an innocent child—*again?* My whole body trembles at the thought. Seeing Gamu like this—

wounded and carrying new life—everything inside me shifts violently. The clear lines between enemy and ally blur into a chaotic blend of guilt and empathy. I am forced to confront the painful echoes of my past and question the path I've chosen. I realize that right here, right now, I am being given a chance to redefine myself and seek redemption in a way that truly matters.

Gathering my resolve, I turn to Osi, my voice quivering under the gravity of my decision. "Osi," I start, the words heavy on my tongue, "we need to turn back. We can't continue to Mvure with her in this condition. Nakuru is much closer. Now that there's an innocent life involved… everything changes."

I hold his gaze, my eyes pleading for understanding, dreading that he might perceive this shift as a weakness, a betrayal of our hardened resolve. His eyes, a mirror to his thoughts, flicker with a range of emotions. I search for a sign of agreement or rebuke, any indication of his stance.

After a moment that stretches taut with tension, Osi's features soften, the lines of command easing into those of compassion. "You're right," he says, his voice firm yet infused with an unexpected warmth. "Her life, and that of her child, takes precedence. We'll reroute to Nakuru."

The boat shudders and groans beneath us, the aged timbers protesting against the relentless assault of the churning waters. Osi moves with determined precision, manipulating the controls to reroute our course toward Nakuru. The urgency of his movements matches the rapid beat of my own heart, echoing the chaotic churn of my thoughts.

As the boat cuts a determined path through the dark, churning waters, I set about creating a sanctuary of warmth and safety for Gamu within its rugged confines. I move quickly, gathering every available blanket and spare piece of clothing from the storage bins and tucked-away corners of the vessel. Each item is chosen with a single purpose—to cushion Gamu against the unyielding hardness of the wooden floor.

With quick, deliberate movements, I layer the blankets, each one adding a degree of softness to the makeshift bed. The textures vary, from the roughness of old wool to the smoother touch of worn cotton, each layer crafted to offer Gamu a respite from the boat's unforgiving planks. Over the top, I drape my heavy cloak, its fabric thick and designed to retain warmth. It settles over her with a gentle weight, shielding her from the cool bite of the evening air.

Outside, the prow of the boat slices through the water with renewed vigor as we redirect our course toward Nakuru. The hull, once merely contending with the river's currents, now thrusts forward with purpose. Each wave that meets the bow does so with a clash, challenging our progress, yet the boat holds its course, resolute and undeterred. The resulting spray sends droplets glinting through the air, catching the last dying lights of dusk.

As I watch over Gamu, each replay of the day's events in

my mind intensifies the weight upon my conscience—the decisive moment of pulling the trigger, the stark resolution in my actions. My hands betray my internal strife, trembling with a fine, almost imperceptible quiver. Osi approaches, his presence a steadying force, as he places a reassuring hand on my shoulder. His eyes meet mine, conveying a depth of understanding and silent support that anchors me momentarily in the tumult of my thoughts.

"You did the right thing," he murmurs, his voice low, imbued with a quiet conviction. "Turning back."

His words pierce through the fog of my doubts, offering a fleeting solace. He may not fully grasp the extent of their impact, or perhaps he understands more than he lets on. "I hope so," I whisper back, the words escaping me like a sigh. My eyes drift to Gamu, her form still and vulnerable. "I hope it's enough."

In that moment of quiet reflection, a small bird darts into view, cutting gracefully through the river breeze. It circles above us, a fleeting blur of motion, before alighting on the edge of the boat with an elegant flutter of wings. It's a sparrow, unremarkable at first glance, yet there's an uncanny intelligence in its gaze, its beady eyes flickering observantly.

"Sparrow's bird," Osi notes softly, recognition dawning in his tone.

The sparrow cocks its head, as if considering our presence, then hops closer with deliberate, tiny steps, its talons clicking lightly against the wooden surface.

A surge of hope rises against the tide of despair. "We can send a message to Sparrow," I propose, the possibility infusing my voice with a newfound energy. "Let him know we're coming back to Nakuru."

Osi nods, his expression shifting to one of resolve as he grasps the urgency of the situation. He rummages through his satchel quickly, retrieving a small piece of parchment and a stub of charcoal. The simplicity of the materials belies the significance of the message we are about to send, a message that could alter our course yet again.

As Osi scribbles a brief note, the sparrow watches intently, its small body poised on the edge of action.

Sparrow,

Returning to Nakuru. Gamu injured, pregnant. Need safe passage.

Six and Osi

Osi rolls the parchment tightly and ties it securely to the sparrow's leg. I whisper a soft prayer, a blessing for speed and safety, and the bird takes off with a burst of energy, wings cutting through the air as it speeds toward Nakuru. The departure of the bird marks a pivotal moment, leaving us with a silent, anxious wait. The next steps, the outcomes, now rest in the hands of fate and a tiny bird braving the vast sky.

Chapter 15

As the dense foliage of Nakuru's forest looms ahead, a sprawling green expanse unfolds beneath the moonlit canopy. As our boat nears, a rhythmic patter of rain begins to fall, each drop adding a somber note to our cautious return. "We're almost there," I whisper to the unconscious Gamu, her presence a silent weight on my conscience. "Just hold on a little longer."

We navigate the snaking river with precision, the boat cutting through the black waters under the shroud of night. In the distance, the dim glow of patrol fires flickers through the rain-soaked air, casting long, wavering shadows that dance eerily on the forest floor like restless spirits. The flames crackle softly, their smoky tendrils spiraling into the damp night, providing brief flashes of light that illuminate the silhouettes of patrolling soldiers.

The currents beneath us are gentle yet insistent, guiding our boat with a lulling rhythm. Overhead, the dense canopy stretches out like a vast protective shield, catching the relentless downpour. This natural cover muffles the sound of our movement, the chorus of raindrops striking the river's surface blending with the ambient noises of the forest to cloak our presence.

We edge closer to the riverbank and the boat glides to a silent halt against the soft earth. Osi is the first to disembark, his boots sinking slightly into the mud with a soft squelch. He moves with the stealth of a hunter, familiar with the terrain, quickly securing the boat to a sturdy tree trunk. The rope strains with a slight creak under his expert hands, anchoring us to this secluded spot. Turning back, he assists me in maneuvering Gamu's unconscious form from the boat. Her body, though limp and unresponsive, is handled with an unexpected tenderness by Osi. Despite the heft of her frame, he lifts her with the care of cradling a child.

As I step onto the rain-soaked riverbank, the chill of the evening permeates my cloak, the moisture seeping through the fabric and chilling me to the bone. Despite the cold biting into my skin, my focus remains unyielding, locked onto the task at hand. We carefully lift Gamu from the boat, her form limp but safe in our arms, as we navigate through the slick mud to a concealed location beneath the dense canopy of the forest. The relentless downpour seems to cleanse the atmosphere momentarily, washing away the palpable tension with each heavy drop that merges with the murmur of the river.

Our steps leave soft impressions in the mud, each one a muted squelch underfoot. I catch the sound of footsteps—distinct, purposeful—and my hand shoots out to halt Osi, signaling him to quicken our pace. We duck into the thick underbrush, the foliage enveloping us in its damp embrace as we crouch low, our bodies hidden from the passing patrol. The voices of the soldiers are a low hum, blending with the rustle of leaves and the persistent rain. The flicker of their torches pierces the darkness intermittently, sending shadows dancing wildly around our makeshift shelter. I hold my breath, the cool rain trickling down my face, and try to calm the pounding in my ears.

From our concealed vantage point, I survey the well-trodden patrol routes, familiar with each soldier's movement and the scheduled timing of their rounds. Near the landing spot where we left the boat, a group of four soldiers maintains a vigilant watch. They are stationed strategically, rifles at the ready, their eyes scanning the darkness for any signs of disturbance. Two of them occasionally break their vigil to tend to the fire or scan the underbrush, their movements methodical and alert. This orchestrated network of patrols creates a web of surveillance that blankets the riverbank and seeps into the village. But their routine is predictable.

The trees in this part of the riverbank are denser, their sprawling roots reaching into the murky water and forming natural alcoves that provide excellent cover. As we edge closer, I point to a narrow, hidden channel obscured by a curtain of overhanging branches and lush foliage—a secret pathway I've used in the past. It's a narrow vein through the forest, invisible to those who don't know it's there. The soldiers patrolling the bank focus their attention on the more open areas, making this secluded spot an ideal hideaway.

As the patrol's footsteps and voices gradually fade. I let out a slow, measured breath. "We'll wait for the shift change," I whisper to Osi, ensuring my voice is drowned out by the natural soundscape.

Osi nods, his gaze sharp and alert in the shadowy light. The shift change at the soldiers' posts provides a critical opportunity—a brief period when their attention shifts from the perimeter to their colleagues, discussing updates and instructions with their replacements. This slight dip in vigilance, though momentary, is our best chance to move unnoticed. This brief window, when the soldiers are most distracted, is not just our chance to escape—it's the moment we find out if our call for help has reached an ally.

As we hunker down in the shadows, we ready ourselves for the moment of transition. Each minute stretches, filled with the tension of waiting and the hope that Sparrow received our message and understands the urgency of our situation.

As each second ticks by, my doubt swells, testing the edges of my resolve as I question the effectiveness of our plan. It's in this moment of uncertainty that the orchestrated bird sounds begin, masterfully initiated by Sparrow. From the dense canopy above, the calls weave through the rain— a series of clear notes that rise and fall with deliberate precision, expertly mimicking the subtleties of human mimicry. This language of the forest, known only to those intimately familiar with its secrets, carries a message of deception.

CHAPTER 15

The soldiers, deeply conditioned to the nuances of their surveillance network, instinctively react to the auditory cues. They turn their heads toward the source of the sounds, their movements transitioning from idle to purposeful as they fall back on the familiarity of their routines. Their trained minds interpret the complex bird calls as routine signals for a shift change. As a result, their sharp, watchful gazes soften, their focus momentarily shifting away from their immediate surroundings.

This subtle relaxation of their guard, prompted by the clever ruse orchestrated from the treetops, creates a pivotal opening for us. Seizing this moment, we prepare to move, relying on the distraction to cover our stealthy advance through the shadowy underbrush. The rain, persistent and steady, plays its part in our covert operation, masking the sound of our movements and blending our actions with the natural rhythms of the night.

We tread carefully, avoiding the patches of slick mud that threaten to drag us down. My heart thunders in my chest as we draw closer to the edge of a village. But just as fragile hope begins to take root, it's shattered by a voice, sharp and authoritative, cutting through the rain and darkness like a blade.

We freeze in place, the harsh sound jolting me from the comforting lull of familiarity. The rain seems to pause around us as tension snaps the air taut, every drop now an echo of the sharp reality we've been thrust back into.

A figure steps into the dim firelight ahead, his silhouette tall and imposing, a dark shape carved against the backdrop of flickering flames. My pulse quickens, the rhythm erratic as my mind scrambles for a solution. Each beat of my heart feels like a ticking clock, urging me to act before the fragile thread of our escape is severed. I strain to see more clearly through the sheet of rain, willing my racing mind to calm as I assess the threat before us. The figure moves with purpose, his posture one of authority, and I sense he's no mere patrolman.

We're no longer hidden in the shadows—we're exposed, vulnerable, standing at the precipice of disaster. My thoughts race. Run? Fight? Bluff? Time seems to stretch, every option presenting itself and yet feeling impossibly out of reach.

I slip seamlessly into my role as one of Ndambira's soldiers, a familiar mask that slides into place with ease. His eyes widen in fleeting recognition before narrowing, his gaze sharp as he peers past me toward Osi and the unconscious Gamu. Suspicion carves lines into his face, taut with skepticism.

"What's going on here?" His voice is a growl, rough and barely audible over the rain that falls steadily around us.

Damn it. He isn't young—not remotely close to my age. This guy is seasoned, and older, with hard-set lines etched deep into his hard face. Silver beard, dark and piercing eyes that scan me with a gaze that misses nothing, lingering on the scar running down my eye. I can feel the weight of his experience pressing down on me. This isn't someone who'll be easily swayed by words or lies.

"This woman is a prisoner we captured," I reply, forcing my voice to remain steady even as my insides twist in apprehension. My thoughts swirl like a storm behind the façade, calculating and trying to keep this lie intact. I cannot afford for him to probe deeper. "We need to move her discreetly."

His eyes narrow further, suspicion sharpening as he turns his attention to Osi. "Which unit are you with, comrade?" he asks, his authority challenging mine. "You're not familiar."

I cut in quickly, my pulse quickening as I anticipate where this might lead. "He's a new recruit, under my watch," I say, injecting authority into my words.

"A *recruit*," he repeats, disbelief flickering across his face. His doubt lingers in the air between us, thick and oppressive.

"Yes," I reply, allowing a trace of irritation to edge into my tone. I need to control this conversation, to make him believe in the legitimacy of my story. "It's all under control, comrade."

The pause that follows is excruciating, every second a heartbeat closer to exposure. His frown deepens, his scrutiny feeling like a blade poised above us, waiting to fall. "I haven't heard of any such operations," he says, his suspicion deepening, his eyes scanning me for cracks in my story.

I force myself to meet his gaze. "It's above your clearance level," I say, forcing confidence into my words. "If you have a problem with that, feel free to take it up with headquarters."

For a moment, his expression wavers, uncertainty flickering in his eyes. I seize the advantage, stepping closer, my voice lowering with deliberate firmness. "We're all on the same side here. I trust you understand the need for discretion."

A tense silence hangs between us until he nods at last, though the skepticism never fully leaves his gaze. "Alright," he says, a slow grin spreading across his rain-soaked face. But there's no warmth in it, just a veiled challenge. "But surely, this mission doesn't require you to skulk around in the shadows."

"Like I said," I respond, matching his grin with one of my own, though it feels strained, a mask slipping dangerously close to cracking. "It's above your clearance level."

He chuckles, but the humor doesn't reach his eyes. His gaze shifts back to Osi, scrutinizing him with equal suspicion. "You be careful now," he says after another long moment. His words are measured and deliberate. "We found another one of our own dead, hidden in some bushes. A pack of flies gave him away."

I nod curtly, fighting to keep my expression neutral even as my mind races. "I need your name, comrade," I say firmly, trying to reassert my authority. My voice doesn't waver, but inside, the urgency to end this encounter sharpens. "In case any details about this mission need to be reported or reviewed."

The glint in his eyes lingers, his small, knowing smile barely masking his suspicion. "Iman Kesi," he says, offering his name with a casual finality, like an unspoken dare.

I nod, the tension still tightly coiled within me, every nerve on edge. But then, just as he turns to leave, my stomach drops with an icy realization: this man is a risk I can't afford to take.

In that instant, instinct takes over, cold and unforgiving. My resolve tightens like iron. Without a second thought, I make my move. The blade slides free in one fluid motion, the metal cold in my grip. Silent as a whisper, I close the distance between us. My hand clamps over his mouth before he can react, muffling any cry. My blade finds its mark, slicing cleanly through flesh and muscle. The shock in his eyes is immediate, his body jerking violently against mine as he struggles in his final moments. His eyes widen, filled with disbelief and a silent plea, but it's too late. The life drains from him quickly, his gaze glazing over as the light fades from his eyes. His body slumps heavily in my arms, the weight of him dragging me down for a moment as the rain washes away his last breath.

The relentless patter of rain fills the silence left behind. There's no relief, no release—only the cold certainty of what needed to be done. I wipe the blade clean against his uniform and I straighten and turn to Osi. His eyes meet mine, hard and understanding, reflecting the gravity of what just transpired. There's no need for words. And so, without hesitation, we resume our task, moving swiftly and quietly, the urgency of the moment pressing us forward.

As we approach the edge of the village, Sparrow emerges from the shadows like a ghost, his presence almost ethereal in the moonlit gloom. His eyes gleam with satisfaction, a small, knowing smile playing on his lips. "Welcome back," he whispers, his voice a soft breath in the dark, a mixture of approval and pride. The thrill of our successful deception hangs between us like an unspoken victory.

"Thank you," I murmur as I pull him into a tight embrace, feeling the warmth of his body against the cold bite of the night. His timing, as always, had been impeccable. "Your timing was perfect."

Sparrow's gaze softens as he looks at Gamu, still limp in Osi's arms, her form fragile under the dim light. His eyes reflect a quiet concern, his voice barely above a whisper as he asks, "Pregnant?"

"Yes," I respond, my voice subdued but firm.

He offers me a reassuring smile, one that seems to ease the weight on my shoulders. "You did the right thing."

His words hit deeper than I expected, a validation I hadn't realized I needed until now. I nod, unable to fully express how much it meant, but he knows. We share a brief look of mutual understanding, our bond solidified by years of

CHAPTER 15

survival and trust.

"I'll ensure the way is clear. We're not going to be followed."

Chapter 16

The village, soaked by the previous night's downpour, lies cloaked in a veil of mist. Inside the small hut, the silence is broken only by the sound of labored breathing and the occasional drip of water from the thatched roof. Shiwo stands before me, her eyes filled with an unspoken urgency, questions lingering in the depths of her gaze. I hesitate, feeling the weight of the words that hang heavy on my tongue.

"Come in," I murmur, stepping aside to let her pass.

She enters cautiously, her gaze sweeping the shadowed corners of the space before coming to rest on Gamu. The dim morning light filters through the cracks and she walks slowly toward the bed, her steps quiet but laden with the weight of what she's about to confront.

Gamu lies motionless, her face pale and etched with the lines of suffering. Her breath comes in shallow, uneven gasps, her body a delicate shadow of its former strength. Shiwo's breath hitches as she takes in the sight—her face twisting with grief, confusion, and something more difficult to define.

"This is…" her voice falters, her throat constricting around the words that refuse to come.

"You know her?" I ask, trying to keep my tone neutral, though inside, a knot of tension tightens.

"Yes," she whispers, her voice carrying a faint tremor. "She is the healer. It is she who healed Kail twice before."

"Oh, right… right." The truth is a stone in my gut, too heavy to carry much longer.

Shiwo kneels beside the bed, her fingers trembling as they hover above Gamu's hand. Finally, she brushes her fingers against Gamu's skin with the gentleness of a mother cradling a newborn, her touch light and reverent.

"How did this happen?" she whispers, her voice so fragile it threatens to break. "Why is she here?"

"It's complicated," I say, my voice soft yet heavy with the gravity of the situation. I search for the right words, but nothing feels adequate. My mind spins with the implications of telling her everything, the consequences of unveiling the truth. For a moment, I think of sparing her the full weight of it—just for a little while longer—but I know I can't. The truth must come out.

With a sudden burst of resolve, she stands up, her hands

balled into fists, her determination cutting through the grief that had paralyzed her moments before. "My brother, Six... does he know about this?"

Her question jolts me like a slap to the face. My pulse quickens. I shake my head instinctively, the answer coming too quickly, too automatically.

She hesitates, her eyes narrowing as something shifts in her expression—something darker, more urgent. "I know he says to keep me out of it, but Kail... he's missing. Do you know where he is?"

I freeze, the question hitting me like a punch to the gut. Damn it. This is my duty and responsibility, and I know what I have to do. I need to tell her the truth, but the weight of it feels crushing.

"Shiwo," I begin slowly, my voice careful and deliberate. Each word feels like a sharp blade, cutting deeper into the fragile moment. I have to be both firm and compassionate, knowing that what I'm about to reveal will shatter her world. "There's something you need to know about your brother."

Her eyes widen, the anxiety and fear swirling in them like a gathering storm. Her world is poised on the edge of devastation, and I am the one who must tip it over.

I take a deep breath, my chest tightening under the weight of what I must say. "He is—" The words stick in my throat, refusing to come out. I swallow hard, clearing my throat, trying to steady my voice. "He is, uhm," I repeat, struggling to brace myself for the blow I'm about to deliver. "He's dead."

Her face contorts as if struck by an unseen force, her expression twisting with a violent mix of emotions—rage, disbelief, and a profound sense of betrayal. She steps back, her breath coming in quick, shallow gasps as if the very air has been ripped from her lungs. "What?" she whispers, the word barely audible, raw with disbelief.

"I am sorry," I say quietly, holding her gaze with a resolve I'm not sure I can maintain. The truth feels heavy in the air between us, suffocating in its finality.

Her eyes bore into mine, searching desperately for some glimmer of hope, some thread of explanation that might pull her out of this nightmare. Her hands clench tightly at her sides as if she's holding herself together by sheer force of will. *"Why?* Why did this happen?" she demands, her voice trembling with barely contained rage. "How?" Her voice cracks, the anger and sorrow twisting together, splintering like shattered glass. She clutches her stomach, her gaze slipping past me, unfocused as if staring into some unseen void.

My mind spins, caught between the instinct to protect her from the full horror of what has happened and the urge to be truthful. I know the truth will break her, but to lie feels like an even crueler betrayal.

"How did this happen?" she cries, her voice raw and

broken, her grief cutting through the air like a blade. "What happened to my brother, Six?" The words come out jagged. Her eyes burn with an intensity that demands an answer, her whole body trembling with the force of her anguish. She needs to know—needs justice, needs something to cling to in this chaos, something that can make sense of the horror she's been thrust into.

"He—" I begin, but the words falter in my throat. Her eyes are wide, searching mine, clinging to a hope that I know will be destroyed if I reveal everything. My heart twists painfully in my chest, torn between duty and mercy. At this moment, I make a choice, one I hope I can live with.

"I promise," I say softly, my voice barely a whisper. "I promise you, Shiwo—we will find out who did this. But right now, you need to stay strong." My words feel like a betrayal, but I press on, trying to steady myself. Her eyes bore into mine, filled with questions I can't answer, at least not truthfully.

"Will you tell me nothing?" she presses, her voice thick with grief and suspicion.

I hesitate, my mind spinning frantically as I construct a lie, weaving it carefully, ensuring it holds under her scrutiny. "I don't know anything yet," I say, my voice firm, though my heart hammers in my chest.

Shiwo's face shifts, the fierce anger that once burned in her eyes softening into a strange blend of confusion and hopelessness. Her gaze lingers on Gamu, but her expression has become detached, almost vacant, as though she is no longer seeing the woman lying before her but is instead searching for something—anything—to anchor her back to reality. I can almost see her mind working, sifting through the shattered fragments of everything she's just learned. She's grasping for something concrete, some piece of the puzzle that will help her make sense of the chaos swirling around her.

But there's a flicker of recognition in her eyes, something dangerous in its clarity. She looks at Gamu, still and vulnerable, and I see Shiwo connect the dots—perhaps it's a suspicion or perhaps it's just her grief twisting everything together, but it's there. She's beginning to fixate on the idea that Gamu might have been with Kail, that somehow, Gamu's presence here in this state is linked to her brother. What else could explain why Gamu, of all people, is lying here, gravely wounded? The thought seems to root itself in her mind, providing her with a thread to pull on, a way to cope with the overwhelming grief that's threatening to consume her.

"She was with him, wasn't she?" She whispers, her voice trembling, almost breaking. The question hangs in the air, thick with emotion and accusation, the unspoken blame already forming in her mind.

I hesitate, unsure of how to respond. I don't want to feed her fixation, but I also can't deny the connection she's beginning to make. I can see that she needs something to focus on, something to give her a sense of control during her spiraling grief.

"Shiwo, I assure you, if I knew anything, I'd tell you."

Her gaze, filled with raw grief and simmering suspicion, shifts back to me. Her eyes are a haunting mix of heartbreak and desperate hope, clinging to whatever shred of clarity she can find.

"But I promise," I continue, holding her gaze steadily, "we'll find out what really happened. And when we do, we'll make sure Kail's memory is honored."

Her lips tremble, as though she's on the verge of speaking but can't find the words. Then, finally, she breaks. Her sobs erupt suddenly, harsh and uncontrollable, ripping through the quiet of the hut like a storm. Her entire body trembles as she cries, and I move toward her instinctively, wrapping my arms around her in a tight embrace. She collapses against me, her grief raw and consuming, a tangible force that I can almost feel pulsing through my own skin. I hold her, letting the waves of her sorrow crash over us both, as the weight of her pain seeps into my bones, deeper than the lie I've told her.

We stand together, bound by her anguish, her sobs muffled against my shoulder. Her pain feels so real, so tangible, that it cuts through me like a blade, and the lie presses down on my chest. Still, I hold her until her sobs slowly subside, until she pulls back, her tear-streaked face trembling with the effort to regain control. She wipes at her eyes with shaking

CHAPTER 16

hands, her breathing uneven.

"My brother," she chokes out, her voice barely more than a whisper, still thick with grief. She pauses, gathering strength. Anger flickers in her eyes, replacing the sorrow, and her voice hardens with conviction. "I need to know who did this to my brother."

I know that finding out will make no difference for her—it will change nothing and offer no solace. Shiwo has no power to exact vengeance, and perhaps she expects me to do it for her, to act on behalf of one of our own. I nod, my heart heavy with the weight of what I've set in motion. "We will," I reply quietly, the promise settling over me like a stone, cold and unyielding. "We will find out," I say again, the lie bitter on my tongue. "I'll make sure of it."

She takes a shuddering breath, her body sagging as if the fight within her has been drained entirely. She collapses further into me, her tears flowing freely, and I hold her tightly, offering what little comfort I can. But even as I try to soothe her, the gnawing guilt in my chest tightens its grip. I've chosen to shield her from the harsh truth, but at what cost? Why am I protecting the enemy over loyalty to my own? My mind spins with the weight of my choices, and the bitter taste of betrayal lingers on my tongue. I've chosen Gamu, the woman lying broken on the bed, over my own family, over the truth of Kail's fate.

"Shiwo," I say softly, trying to steady my voice "Will you stay with her? I have to go."

She pulls back, wiping her tears with a newfound purpose, attempting to mirror the strength of her brother, the strength she's always admired. Though Kail kept her away from the fight and shielded her from the brutal realities of our world, she now seems more determined than ever to honor his memory, to carry on in his place. Her eyes, once filled with grief, now gleam with a sharp edge of determination. She nods firmly, setting her jaw.

"You are not alone," I say, though the words feel hollow, weighed down by the lie that hangs heavy between us. I'm offering her comfort, but it's tainted, a promise built on falsehoods. The truth looms like a shadow, lurking just beyond our reach.

She nods again, her resolve hardening. With her now seated beside Gamu, her fingers lightly brush over the hand of her brother's murderer in a gesture of comfort. I step back, letting the moment sink in. There's no going back now.

I quietly leave the hut, my heart heavy with guilt and conflict, the rain outside feeling colder against my skin as I walk away from the mess I've created.

Chapter 17

I slip through the village and make my way toward the heart of Ndambira's regime—the soldiers' base. The jungle presses in on all sides, a living, breathing thing that feels as though it's biding its time, waiting to reclaim what was taken from it. The sunlight barely breaks through the dense canopy above, filtering down in fractured beams that scatter across the ground in ghostly patterns.

The base is a cluster of wooden structures, weathered and rough, their crude exteriors blending into the overgrown foliage. Vines creep up the walls like nature's defiant hand, slowly erasing the soldiers' presence, while the incessant hum of insects fills the air, their buzz a constant reminder of life beyond the brutality.

The base hums with activity, its rhythms foreign and jarring to the soul of Nakuru. These men—outsiders—move with purpose, but they are strangers to this land, unaware of the life it once held. As I push deeper into the base, the past floods my mind, vivid and unrelenting, each memory sharp and painful. I remember how Ndambira first arrived, draped in the guise of diplomacy, his words sweet with false promises of prosperity in exchange for access to Nakuru's lands. But his promises were nothing more than lies, veiled threats cloaked in the guise of negotiation. Slowly, methodically, his men began to infiltrate, worming their way into the village until they became part of the very fabric of daily life. Resistance, once a proud possibility, was gradually snuffed out.

When the village elders finally pushed back, Ndambira bared his teeth. His response was swift, brutal, and absolute. Blood soaked the earth where proud men and women once stood, and those who defied him were cut down with merciless efficiency. What was once a thriving, peaceful community has been reduced to a ghost of itself—its spirit crushed beneath the weight of checkpoints and patrols. Fear now prowls the streets where laughter once echoed, a bitter reminder of the price Nakuru paid for its defiance.

His commanders, handpicked for their cruelty and cunning, oversee the systematic draining of Nakuru's resources, their greed insatiable. What little wealth remains is siphoned off, flowing like a river of stolen lifeblood into Ndambira's war machine. The land that once provided for its people is now being pillaged, its riches fed to mercenaries who gorge themselves on the spoils of a land they have no right to claim. Nakuru is no longer a home—it is a carcass, stripped bare by the greed of men who never belonged.

"Munogamuchirwa, Tenda naAbu," I whisper under my breath, a quiet prayer for those lost to this madness. *"May you be welcomed, Tenda and Abu,"*

CHAPTER 17

Inside the base, the atmosphere is stifling. Smoke from burning wood mingles with the heavy scent of sweat as bodies shift in the cramped space. Maps line the walls, covered in scrawled notes marking patrol routes and checkpoints, the village transformed into a battlefield meticulously charted. I weave through the room, offering curt nods of acknowledgment to the soldiers I pass. My thoughts swirl as I approach Jengo, his sharp features partially obscured by the dim flicker of lantern light. He hunches over a map, the lines of strategy etched deeply into his brow. His short beard gives him a rugged edge, but the exhaustion in his eyes reveals a man who has carried burdens for too long. The weight of duty hangs heavily over him, as it does on all of us.

Weapons line the walls—rifles, pistols, knives—each one a silent promise of violence, waiting for the command to unleash them. Across the room, Zara and Malik converse in low whispers, their faces bathed in the soft glow of a nearby lantern. Zara's eyes blaze with fierce determination, while Malik's furrowed brow betrays concern, his gestures deliberate but strained. They halt their conversation abruptly when they notice me, their eyes locking onto mine. I meet their gaze, offering a silent warning: discretion. They nod, stepping back a few paces, allowing me the space to approach Jengo.

As I step closer, Jengo looks up. His eyes meet mine, and I see the flicker of recognition turn into a frown. He straightens, suspicion darkening his expression. *"What* are you doing here?" he asks, his voice low and guarded.

I glance around, ensuring no one else is within earshot before I lean in slightly. "We never made it," I say quietly, the words thick with the weight of failure. "There was… a complication."

His face tightens, concern replacing the wariness in his eyes. "What kind of complication?"

I hesitate for a fraction of a second, my mind racing to find the right words. The truth gnaws at me, but I know it's not something I can reveal now. Not here, not yet. I steady myself, exhaling slowly. "I need you to assemble everyone," I say, my tone measured. "Have them meet me underground."

Jengo's gaze sharpens, but a flicker of unease crosses his features. He lowers his voice further. "But where's everyone else? What happened to the others?"

The knot of fear tightens in my gut. We orphans—rebels who lived in the hidden tunnel, far from Ndambira's reach— were supposed to be untouchable. But Jengo's question cuts deep because he's asking about the ones who didn't make it back. The ones who were with me. I swallow hard.

"Dead," I say, the single word landing like a stone between us.

Jengo's face drains of color, his eyes widening in shock. "What? Dead? How—?"

I feel a surge of panic rising. The truth is too dangerous, so

CHAPTER 17

I force it down and give him a lie instead. "There was an ambush," I reply, my voice defensive, trying to hold steady. "We were outnumbered."

His gaze narrows, disbelief and suspicion battling for dominance. "An ambush?" His voice is sharp, his words cutting through the air. "That doesn't add up—"

"There's no time!" I cut him off, my voice rising in urgency. "We can't sit here debating the details. We need to be ready for what's coming next. Just do as I say, Jengo. Gather the others."

His frown deepens, but before he can voice his concerns, the entire atmosphere shifts, thickening with tension. The usual murmur of activity in the command center dies instantly as Ndambira strides in.

His presence is powerful, slicing through the room like a sharp blade through cloth. The air becomes charged with anticipation, and soldiers straighten as his piercing eyes scan the room. Every part of him radiates authority, with his prominent cheekbones and strong jawline emphasized by a closely cropped beard that gives his face a relentless edge.

The fear in the air is palpable, a living, breathing entity that tightens around each of us. "Line up outside," he orders, his voice cutting through the stillness with the crack of a whip. The command brooks no hesitation, no questions. The soldiers scramble to obey, their movements frantic and disjointed as they rush toward the exit. The clang of chairs and the scrape of boots against the floor echo through the room as everyone rushes outside, the oppressive weight of fear driving their every step.

The cold, unforgiving light of day greets us as we file out, forming a rigid line beneath the open sky. My pulse quickens, the anticipation of what's to come thrumming in my veins like an electric current. I exchange a glance with Jengo—his face tight, his eyes wide with unease—but neither of us dares to speak.

Ndambira strides outside like a storm incarnate, his shadow looming over us as he steps forward. He surveys the line, his eyes flickering over each of us with a mixture of disgust and cold calculation. His presence is almost suffocating; the fear he inspires hangs like a heavy cloud over us.

"You wither away," he snarls, his voice booming like thunder rolling across a desolate battlefield. "Our enemies have grown bolder, their defiance like weeds pushing through the cracks of your weakness. In these past weeks, the corpses have piled up like kindling, ready to feed the flames of war." His words lash out, sharp as a whip's crack. "Petty rebellions," he sneers, his contempt dripping like poison from every syllable, "yet still, they dare to defy me. Something festers in the shadows—a sickness, spreading among them." His voice drops, colder now, dangerous. "Or perhaps the rot has begun from within—treachery, a cancer gnawing away at the heart of everything I've built. If the rebels know what we prepare for, it is because someone among you has already

planted the seed of betrayal."

A wave of cold horror sweeps through the line, rippling like a current of doom. Our hearts race in unison, beating against our ribs like trapped animals. No one dares to move, to even breathe. The gun in his hand gleams, a cruel promise of what will follow.

His voice drops to a lethal tone, each word sharpened with the cold precision of a blade. "Betrayal," he hisses, "will not be tolerated. It unravels everything I've built, everything I've bled for." He moves with deliberate menace, pacing like a predator before us. His eyes sweep across the group, lingering on each face just long enough to make your pulse race.

"You two," Ndambira snaps, his gaze locking onto a pair of soldiers at the edge of the group. The blood drains from their faces, their veins running cold as the gravity of his attention settles over them like a death sentence. "Step forward."

The silence is suffocating, broken only by the hesitant scrape of their boots against the dirt, each step an admission of the doom that awaits. The rest of us remain frozen in place, as though bound by invisible chains, caught between the terrifying reality unfolding before us and the dark inevitability that looms like a shadow over our heads.

Their feet drag across the ground, sluggish and heavy, as if the earth itself resists carrying them to their fate. Time stretches taut, every second hanging in the air like a final breath held before the plunge. The gun in his hand feels alive, its presence almost sentient, as though it yearns for the violence it was created to enact.

"I expect full cooperation," he says, his voice smooth as silk, yet sharp as the edge of a blade. "If anyone has information about the traitors among us, now is your last chance to speak. Do not test me."

My thoughts spiral, frantic and disconnected, panic gnawing at the edges of my composure. I struggle to breathe, my mind racing to find a way to steady itself, but the fear is relentless, a wild beast clawing at the last shreds of my control. One wrong move, one stray glance, and I could be the next to die.

Ndambira turns his gaze to the first soldier. The man's body quakes under the weight of that gaze, his eyes wide, wild with terror. "Speak," Ndambira commands, his voice barely above a whisper, yet charged with deadly intent. "Confess what you know."

The soldier's lips tremble, his words spilling out in a disjointed plea. "I... I know nothing, sir. Please... I swear, I don't know anything."

For a moment, Ndambira's expression is as still as stone, unyielding and devoid of emotion. Then, with terrifying ease, he lifts the gun. The motion is smooth, and fluid— death in the shape of a single gesture. The crack of the shot rips through the air, sharp and sudden, its echo cutting through the forest like a scream that refuses to fade. The soldier collapses, his body crumpling to the ground in a lifeless heap. The smell of gunpowder lingers, mingling with the scent of dirt and blood.

Ndambira does not flinch, his gaze cold and untouched by remorse as it shifts to the second soldier. His voice is flat, devoid of any trace of humanity as he demands, "And you?"

The second soldier stands paralyzed, his breath coming in short, panicked gasps. The weight of his mortality presses down on him like an iron shackle, and I can see in his eyes the same terror gnawing at my insides—the kind of fear that knows no escape, no salvation, no mercy. *"Please,"* he cries, his voice a frantic plea, teetering on the edge of madness. "I swear on my life, I don't know anything!"

Ndambira's expression remains unmoved, carved from stone. The gun fires again, a thunderclap that reverberates through the air with deafening finality. The soldier's body crumples to the ground beside the first, an unsettling reflection of the carnage that now threatens us all. My breath catches in my throat, coming in shallow, panicked bursts. My chest tightens with the effort to stay composed, but inside, I'm unraveling, teetering on the precipice of blind panic.

His gaze sweeps over the remaining soldiers, each one of us standing like statues awaiting a crack of thunder. The silence is unbearable, every second an agonizing stretch of dread, each heartbeat a relentless countdown to oblivion. He gestures toward another pair, his voice a razor slicing through the stillness. "You two," he growls, "step forward."

The two soldiers shuffle forward, their dread hanging thick in the air, suffocating us all. They are like condemned souls trudging toward the gallows, and it feels as though even the earth recoils beneath their feet, unwilling to carry them to their fate. Ndambira's gaze remains unfeeling, his silence more terrifying than words, his finger resting on the trigger like a god poised to strike—impersonal, detached, inevitable.

Jameel's body trembles uncontrollably, his words barely a whisper, choked with terror. "Please, sir, I—I know nothing! Please, I swear—"

The gunshot cuts him off mid-sentence, sudden and absolute. It doesn't just kill him—it tears through the moment like a blade through flesh, leaving the air itself quivering in shock. The sound reverberates through our bones, a blow that lands not just on Jameel but on all of us. His body falls with a sickening thud, a lifeless heap that joins the growing pile of the dead at our feet. The sight of him—once a living, breathing man, now reduced to a corpse—awakens something primal in me, something cold and bottomless.

We stand frozen, every movement stilled by the crushing weight of fear. Our breaths have become shallow, muted whispers, as though even the sound of life itself could beckon the same swift and brutal end. Another pair is called forward, and the deadly cycle continues, a rhythm of slaughter dictated by Ndambira's unwavering will.

CHAPTER 17

Each death feels heavier than the last, the terror mounting with every life extinguished. And then comes the moment I've been dreading—Rugare and Zeal are summoned. My heart stutters in my chest, my vision narrowing to a tunnel of panic. The blood roars in my ears, drowning out everything but the pulse of my own fear. My legs threaten to buckle beneath me, but I force myself to stay upright, locking my knees against the overwhelming urge to collapse.

Rugare, usually so composed and strong, has unraveled completely. Her hands tremble violently, her eyes darting around in a desperate search for escape where none exists. Zeal stands beside her, but the bravado that once defined him has been stripped away, leaving him pale and hollow, consumed by fear.

Ndambira steps closer, his voice as cold and sharp as steel. "You know the drill," he says, each word dripping with authority. "Speak now, or face the consequences."

Rugare's throat bobs as she swallows hard, the words coming slow and shaky as if dragged from the depths of her fear. "I swear," she manages, her voice cracking, "I'm not involved in anything, Administrator. I'm loyal to the cause."

The words hang in the air for a fragile moment, suspended between life and death—then, with brutal indifference, Ndambira's gun fires. The shot hits like a physical blow, jolting me back into harsh reality. I flinch hard, my fists clenched tight, my heart pounding wildly in my chest. Rugare collapses. The sound of her body hitting the ground echoes louder than the shot, a heavy, sickening thud that sends a fresh wave of dread coursing through my veins. Her blood spills out, dark and gleaming, seeping into the earth to mingle with the blood of those who fell before her.

Zeal's turn comes next. He stares at Rugare's lifeless form, the horror etched deep into his face, draining the color from his skin. His lips twitch, but no sound escapes. He knows it's useless to plead, and knows that Ndambira's bullets care nothing for innocence or guilt.

But the pressure breaks him. His voice trembles, heavy with desperation. "Tau and Kundambire," he blurts, his words tumbling out in a frantic rush. "I overheard them… talking… complaining about being left out of meetings. I don't know everything, I swear!"

My stomach churns, twisting itself into a knot of dread so tight it feels like I might tear apart from the inside. The world seems to shrink around me and panic claws at my chest with icy fingers. I want to beg — to plead with any god, any omen, any spirit to intervene, to spare them from what's coming — but deep down, I know the truth. There is no hope. Only the cold, brutal certainty of what comes next.

"Come forward," Ndambira commands, his voice slicing through the oppressive silence with the precision of a blade.

Tau and Kundambire step forward after what feels like an eternity. Their faces are ashen, bodies trembling with fear, and I can feel their terror seeping into the air, poisoning it. Ndambira's gaze is cold, devoid of even the slightest hint of mercy. He raises his gun with grim finality, firing at Tau first. The shot echoes through the clearing, sharp and unrelenting, and Tau collapses to the ground in a heap of lifeless limbs. Kundambire's scream is brief, cut short by another gunshot that sends her crumpling beside Tau, her body hitting the dirt with a dull thud that reverberates through the oppressive stillness.

A soldier stumbles forward, drenched in sweat and trembling like a leaf caught in a storm. His voice is barely more than a whisper, hoarse and trembling. "Zara and Malik," he says, the words tumbling out in a rush. "They're always whispering, sir. I swear it."

Ndambira's eyes sharpen, his gaze locking onto the soldier with predatory precision. "Whispering?" He allows the word to hang in the air like a snare tightening around the soldier's neck. His lips curl into a cruel smile. "And what exactly have they been whispering about?"

The soldier's eyes flick nervously between Ndambira and the ground. His voice trembles as he struggles to find the right words. "They... they've been talking in secret, sir. About meetings. I didn't hear much, but... it sounded like they were plotting something."

Ndambira's lips curl into a sinister smile, his eyes gleaming with the dark satisfaction of a predator closing in on its prey. "Plotting?" he repeats, his voice low and lethal, carrying the weight of imminent destruction. He steps closer to the trembling soldier, his presence like the shadow of an oncoming storm, ready to break over us with merciless fury.

"Zara and Malik?" Their names fall from his lips like the pronouncement of doom. "Step forward."

Time seems to warp, stretching out into a cruel, agonizing moment, the tension unbearable. Then, as if sensing the very edge of Ndambira's patience, Zara and Malik step forward, their movements halting and heavy with dread. Malik is the first to speak, his words rushing out as if he can outrun his fate. He tries to steady his voice, but fear coils around him, squeezing out his confidence. "My loyalty to the cause is absolute," he says, but the words stumble over one another, betraying him with every quiver in his voice. "Any suspicion against me is baseless."

Zara's voice, when it comes, is fragile, like a piece of glass teetering on the edge of a precipice. "I'm loyal too," she insists, but the cracks are already there, her eyes darting desperately around as if searching for a way out that doesn't exist. She hesitates, choking on the fear lodged in her throat. "But... I don't know anything."

The silence that follows is agonizing, stretching out like an endless chasm. Every second drags on, unbearable, as Ndambira's gaze locks onto Zara, his expression unreadable, a void of emotion. His eyes are fathomless pits, and as they bore into her, it's as though he's already decided her fate.

CHAPTER 17

Then, without warning, he raises his gun. The shot rings out like a clap of thunder, splitting the air. Zara crumples to the ground, her body folding in on itself as her final breath escapes in a soft, almost resigned sigh. Her blood spills onto the earth, dark and thick like spilled ink, her life extinguished in an instant.

"Secure him," Ndambira orders, his voice cold and detached.

Malik's breath catches in his throat as Ndambira turns his attention to him. His body trembles violently, his knees buckling as two soldiers step forward and seize him by the arms. They drag him forward, and he doesn't resist—there is no fight left in him. The weight of Zara's death and his own impending doom presses down on him, crushing whatever spark of defiance once lived within him.

Ndambira's gaze shifts to *Idris Kamau,* his chief strategist, standing rigid near the back of the group. Idris, once the epitome of confidence and control, now seems small, diminished under Ndambira's relentless scrutiny. Where he once loomed large, a powerful presence, he now feels like a shadow of his former self, his influence eclipsed by the sheer force of Ndambira's will. The tension between them is a thick, oppressive thing that presses down on all of us.

"You have allowed this to happen," Ndambira growls, his voice low, simmering with menace. He steps closer to Idris, each word a dagger aimed at the man's pride. "Betrayal festers within our ranks, and you—my chief strategist—have failed to root it out."

Idris's jaw tightens, his composure fraying at the edges. "We've taken every measure, sir," he says, his voice steady but strained. "The patrols have increased, and surveillance is tighter. We will find the traitors—it's only a matter of time."

"Time," Ndambira hisses, his tone venomous. He looms over Idris, his presence as heavy as a storm about to break. "Time is a luxury we can no longer afford. Your failures are piling up, Idris."

Idris swallows hard, desperation creeping into his voice. "Perhaps we should change our strategy—"

"Shut up!" Ndambira's voice cracks. "Your incompetence," he says coldly, his eyes boring into Idris with icy disdain, *"is a stain on my rule."*

The gunshot rings out before Idris can respond. The sound reverberates through the clearing like a clap of thunder, sudden and jarring. Idris collapses, his body crumpling to the ground, lifeless. His end is swift and merciless, another casualty in the wake of Ndambira's relentless pursuit of power.

His gaze sweeps over us, his expression as cold and unforgiving as ever. He stands as a man devoid of remorse, untouched by weakness, ruling through fear and the ever-present specter of death. We are nothing but pawns to him—expendable, replaceable, utterly powerless. "Let this be a lesson," he intones. *"I demand loyalty. I demand results. Fail me, and you *will* meet the same fate."

He gestures toward Zeal, who stands frozen in the mud, his wide eyes brimming with terror. "Take him," he orders. "He will answer for his part in this treachery."

Zeal is dragged away, his body limp, his fate as dark and uncertain as the others who have fallen before him. Malik follows, his figure swallowed by the shadows, a condemned man walking toward the gallows. His face is pale, twisted with despair, his feet dragging through the mud as he's pulled toward the inevitable horrors that await him—torture, death, an agonizing end in the suffocating darkness of Ndambira's prisons. The thought of it churns my stomach, a nauseating fear twisting inside me as I imagine their final moments.

Then Ndambira's gaze shifts, landing on the soldier who had eagerly pointed fingers, the snitch. "Come with me," he says, his tone brooking no argument.

The snitch's eyes widen in terror, his earlier eagerness vanishing, replaced by the cold realization of what he's just done. He follows Ndambira with hesitant steps, knowing—as we all do—that his fate is already sealed. Ndambira may have spared him for now, but those who betray too eagerly never last long under his rule. His loyalty is suspect, and in Ndambira's world, even loyalty is a fragile, temporary thing.

As Ndambira strides away, the soldiers part for him like water before a passing ship, his authority absolute. We stand in the wake of his departure, the violence that unfolded before our eyes still clinging to the air like a thick fog.

I catch Jengo's gaze across the clearing, his face pale and drawn, the weight of what we've just witnessed pressing down on us both. We exchange a somber look—an unspoken understanding passing between us. Whatever illusions we once held about heroism, about rebellion, have been shattered into dust. The grim reality of our situation settles over us like a shroud, suffocating, unrelenting.

Rugare is gone. Zara is gone. Zeal and Malik will be next, their screams lost in the shadows before their lives are snuffed out. And with them will go whatever fragile hope we once clung to. What remains is the cold, brutal truth: *there is no escape.*

Chapter 18

The echo of gunfire still reverberates in my skull, relentless and unforgiving, like the last gasps of those we've lost. I stagger away from the others and my legs carry me to a secluded corner of the base where the world feels distant. But the memories... the memories are unforgiving, vivid. I collapse against the rough wall, every inch of my body trembling as if it, too, is trying to shake free from the horror.

I don't just crumble—I break. I unravel. My breaths come in jagged, uneven spurts, my chest heaving as though it might shatter under the weight of it all. The images flash behind my eyes, each one more harrowing than the last: the gunfire, the blood that stained the earth, the bodies crumpling, lifeless—gone, just like that. My mind claws at the memories, trying to grasp onto something—anything—that will make sense of it all. But there's nothing. There's just blood and death, the finality of it, and the aching emptiness that follows.

I clutch at my top, my hands shaking, the fabric warm and familiar beneath my fingers. But even that comfort is fleeting. My heart aches so fiercely that I'm sure it's breaking for real this time. Tears fall, scalding hot, streaming down my cheeks, and I make no effort to stop them. What's the point? The silence around me, broken only by the sound of my sobs, feels so vast—so hopelessly, suffocatingly vast. It's like the world is collapsing in on itself, dragging me down with it, and there's no way to claw my way back to the surface.

Seven of us executed—no, *eight*. Malik is probably already gone, too.

One by one, we've been picked off, as if each of us were nothing more than a pawn in Ndambira's game. *What's left of us?* A few scattered souls clinging desperately to the edges of survival? Most of them have probably turned, feeding our secrets to the enemy out of fear, leaving us exposed and vulnerable—barely a handful of us left, like ashes scattered in the wind.

I take a deep breath, but it does nothing to ease the crushing weight in my chest. Instead, it only tightens, as though something is pressing down on me, threatening to squeeze the life out of my lungs. My mind races, searching desperately for a way forward, a path that might lead us out of this nightmare, but all I find is darkness. I slam into a wall of despair, *over and over* again, and it's too much. It's too much for me to bear.

The thought of moving forward, of leading those who are left—leading them to their deaths—makes me want to scream. The sacrifice of my comrades looms large in my mind, and I can't shake the feeling that all of this has been for nothing. What have we gained? What has any of this bloodshed cost us except more pain and *more loss?* I feel the faintest tug of surrender creeping in, and for a moment, I wonder if that might be easier—just giving in, letting go of the fight.

I hear footsteps, and suddenly, Jengo is there, his presence pulling me from the abyss. I spin around, my heart slamming against my ribs, my breath quickening with panic as my wide eyes lock onto his. He takes a step closer, but all I can do is clutch at my clothes as if they might somehow hold me together when everything inside me is unraveling.

He doesn't speak, just watches me with a look that holds too much understanding. And at this moment, I hate him for it. I hate that he can see the wreckage I've become, that he knows exactly how close I am to breaking completely. I turn away, tears blurring my vision, but the weight of it all presses down, crushing me from every side. I can't escape it. I can't escape any of it.

The truth lodged deep in my chest—under layers of false hope and blind resolve—suffocates me now, raw and undeniable. That fragile hope I once held onto like a lifeline—it's gone. Ground down to nothing by the weight of our losses. Every sacrifice, every life lost, feels like a stone chained to my heart, dragging me into the depths. I don't know if I have the strength to pull myself back up again.

I force myself to face him, my tear-streaked face a mask of

panic and helplessness. "Jengo… I can't do this anymore. It's over. The fight—it's over. We've lost too many, and there's nothing left. Nothing to fight with, nothing to hope for."

His eyes darken with a fiery disbelief, his expression hardening like stone. "You think giving up is going to make their deaths mean something?" His voice is a sharp accusation, each word stabbing through my chest. "The lives you've lost, the blood that's been spilled—was it for nothing?"

"It *hurts,* I can't do it anymore—" My breath comes in jagged gasps, every word pulled from me like shards of glass. I clutch at my clothes, trying desperately to ground myself, but his rage is like a force of nature, bearing down on me until my legs tremble beneath its weight.

His gaze is unyielding, burning into me, and all I can do is try to defend myself.

"I never wanted this. I never meant for it to get this far. I didn't want anyone to die—we were naive." The words tumble out, a desperate plea for forgiveness, but there's nothing in Jengo's eyes to suggest he's willing to offer any. Only disappointment. Only fury. "There's no victory left to win. I failed you all. I failed."

Tears blur my vision, hot and relentless. My breath grows even more shallow, the guilt crushing my chest. "And if I hadn't turned back… if I had just kept going to Mvure, maybe this would've meant something. Maybe I wouldn't have failed so completely. But I did. I failed. I betrayed everyone."

Jengo's expression darkens, his anger hardening into something far more dangerous. His voice sharpens like a blade. "You never meant for this to happen? All of this was your idea, *Six*. Every. Last. Bit."

His words slice through me, cold and merciless, because he's right. Every part of me wants to deny it, but I can't. I started this rebellion. I lit the match that set our lives ablaze.

"You wanted a revolution, didn't you?" His voice drips with bitter accusation. "You rallied us, gave us hope—made us believe in something. And now look at what's left of us."

His words slam into me like a punch to the gut, and for a moment, I can't even speak. A laugh escapes him—harsh, cold, and disbelieving. Then, with chilling calm, he pulls a sleek pistol from his belt. Its metallic sheen glints menacingly in the dim light, and dread floods my veins like ice water. I back away instinctively, my heart hammering so violently in my chest that I fear it might tear through my ribs.

"What are you doing?" I whisper, my voice quivering with terror.

His eyes are hard, devoid of anything familiar. I search his face for some shred of humanity, some glimmer of the Jengo I once knew—my comrade, my friend—but all I see is a man hardened by fear, a man who has chosen survival over loyalty.

When he speaks, his voice is low and venomous, each syllable deliberately sharp. "Look at yourself," he spits. "You were supposed to lead us, supposed to guide us to victory, but all you've done is lead us straight into ruin. You've fallen apart, Six. And I'm not going down with you."

The barrel of his gun seems impossibly large, its shadow swallowing up the world around us. I open my mouth to speak, to plead for some sliver of understanding, but the words are stuck, suffocated by terror. His finger hovers over the trigger. But I see it—the tremors, subtle but unmistakable, in the hand holding the gun. Jengo, despite his cruel words, isn't as composed as he wants me to believe. His hand shakes, betraying the fear he's trying so hard to bury. The weight of what he's about to do is there, lurking behind the mask of cold resolve.

I swallow hard and reach out, my hand trembling just as much as his. "You can't do this, Jengo," I whisper, my voice barely audible. "It's me. It's Six. We've bled together, lost everything together. You know I never wanted any of this. I believed we could make a difference. And… and I never forced anyone into anything. They followed because they believed too. I didn't mean for any of this to happen. We're siblings, Jengo. We're not just friends or allies. We're family."

"Siblings?" he repeats, his voice flat, mocking. The word sounds foreign like it no longer has any meaning between us. "That *charade* doesn't matter anymore, Six. Dead people don't need siblings or friends. They don't need causes or beliefs." His voice is sharp now, cutting deep. "There's

nothing left. Malik's been captured, and it's only a matter of time before they come for the rest of us. You're a liability now." He shakes his head, his lips curling into something between a sneer and a grimace. "I'm not going to die for a lost cause."

His words crush me but I force myself to keep standing, to keep speaking. "Jengo, please," I say, my voice cracking under the weight of desperation. "You don't have to do this." I reach for him again, my hand trembling uncontrollably, but he doesn't move, doesn't flinch. He's already made up his mind, and I can see now that there's no reaching him.

"We're done here," he says flatly. He gestures for me to start walking with the barrel of his gun, the motion casual and terrifying all at once. "Let's go."

"Where are we going?" I manage to ask, my voice barely more than a ragged breath.

His expression set in stone. "I'm turning you in, Six."

"Don't do this, please," I am even more desperate. "I was wrong—I know that. But turning me in won't fix any of this. It won't save you. Ndambira will kill us all—whether you turn me in or not. He won't let you live. Not after everything we've done."

"Maybe it won't save me. But it might buy me some time. Time is all that matters now, Six. Time to get away. Time to make sure I survive. That's a risk I'll take," he mutters with icy finality.

His gun is trained steadily on me, the cold barrel almost grazing my skin. "Let's go," he says and the words are like a nail sealing my fate.

My legs tremble beneath me, threatening to give out with every faltering step, but somehow, I force myself to move.

Chapter 19

The ocean's rhythm is relentless, each wave a powerful, swelling breath that crashes against the shore. I stand at the water's edge, bathed in the eerie glow of a moonlit sky, where the world is drenched in a pale, ghostly blue. The air is thick with the scent of salt and something else—something ancient and unknown. It's as if this place is caught between worlds, teetering on the brink of the real and the unreal, where the line between dreams and reality is as fluid as the tide itself.

And then, she appears.

Her figure emerges from the mist, half-formed yet strikingly familiar, like a memory warped by time. There's a strange beauty to her, a familiarity that tugs at the edges of my mind, but something about her is unsettling—her features are distorted, as though I'm viewing her through a shroud of fog. Her eyes, though shadowed, seem to pierce through the darkness, locking onto mine with an intensity that sends a shiver down my spine.

She raises a hand, beckoning me, and I feel an almost

magnetic pull toward her. It's as if the very fabric of the night is urging me forward. My feet sink into the damp sand, each step heavy, as though the earth itself resists my advance. The wind picks up, carrying her voice to me—a haunting melody that threads through the roar of the ocean, weaving itself into the very air I breathe. It calls to me, luring me deeper into the night's embrace.

I follow her, my body moving of its own accord, drawn by a force I cannot name. With every step, she drifts further away, her form slipping into the shifting shadows of the ocean. The water climbs higher, cold and biting, first at my ankles, then my knees, but the chill doesn't stop me. Her voice grows more insistent, each note a siren's call that echoes through the night. The ocean's roar crescendos, and within it, I hear other voices—a chorus whispering my name, urging me onward.

The sky darkens above me, the moon's light swallowed by the encroaching blackness. The water is up to my waist now, the current pushing back with a force that makes every step a struggle. My heart pounds in my chest, fear mingling with the strange, unshakable compulsion to reach her. As I wade deeper into the ocean's depths, I see her eyes—they glow with an unnatural light, serpentine and mesmerizing. Her smile twists into something sinister, and the truth crashes over me like a wave: she is not human.

The water churns violently around me, and I feel something slick and cold slither against my legs. Panic surges, but her gaze holds me captive, a silent command that compels me to keep moving forward, even as every instinct screams at me to turn back. The ocean's depths yawn open before me, revealing an abyss so dark and infinite that it seems to swallow all light, all hope.

She dissolves into the darkness, her form unraveling like smoke in the wind, leaving me alone in the surging sea. The whispers grow louder, hissing and mocking, the unseen serpents beneath the surface brushing against me with evil intent. I try to retreat, to claw my way back to the safety of the shore, but the water grips me with an unyielding force, dragging me down, deeper into the abyss. The beach, the world I know, fades into a distant memory, a forgotten dream as the nightmarish sea pulls me under.

In the final moments before the darkness claims me completely, I hear a small, fragile voice—innocent and out of place in this hellish descent.

"Mama."

My eyelids flutter open, and the world is an unfocused blur of confusion and pain. I try to move, but my limbs feel impossibly heavy as if they're encased in lead, pinned down by an invisible weight. Sound reaches me in fragments—voices murmuring outside the hut, the metallic clatter of pots and pans, all muffled and distorted as though carried on a distant wind. Herbs; a sharp, earthy aroma filling my senses as I struggle to reorient myself.

My eyes slowly begin to adjust, and I notice the soft rustle of fabric, the dry whisper of leaves underfoot, and the texture of a woven reed mat beneath me, pressing uncomfortably into my bruised and battered skin.

Then, amid the haze, I see her.

Shiwo's face swims into view, a familiar anchor during the disorienting fog. Her features are tight with concern, her brow furrowed in concentration, but the moment she realizes I'm awake, her expression softens—relief flickers across her face like a brief respite from the storm. She kneels beside me, her hands moving with gentleness as she adjusts the blanket draped over me. The warmth of the fabric is welcome against the cool air, but even her touch, light as it is, sends ripples of pain through my fragile body.

"You're awake," she whispers, her voice quiet yet carrying a palpable urgency. Her words pull me, slowly, back to the present moment.

I try to speak, but my throat is dry and raw, the sound that escapes little more than a hoarse whisper. "Shiwo... where... where am I?" My mind clings to her presence like a lifeline, hoping that perhaps this is all just a lingering nightmare, that I'm still in Nakuru, and none of the horrors I remember were real.

Her eyes, full of empathy, darken with a sadness she cannot hide. There's a gravity in her gaze, a weight that tells me everything isn't as it should be. "You were hurt—badly," she begins, her voice carefully measured. "I don't know all the details, but Six brought you here. We're in Mama Tiso's hut now. Six asked me to stay with you."

The mention of Six drags me back into a harsh reality. The battle, the fear, the excruciating pain—it all slams into me at once, a flood of memories I can't hold back. I try to sit up, instinctively bracing myself against the rush of panic, but my body rebels. Pain lances through me, sharp and unrelenting, forcing me to collapse back onto the reed mat. I can feel every bruise, every wound, throbbing like a pulse beneath my skin.

The fear claws at my chest, my breath comes in short, shallow gasps, and a desperate question rises to my lips. "The baby…" My voice trembles, barely holding together. "Is my baby… is the baby okay?"

Shiwo's face pales. Her expression shifts from concern to something deeper—confusion mingled with a growing dread. Her eyes widen as if she's only just now realizing the weight of my words. "Gamu," she whispers, her voice strained, "I didn't know you're with child?"

I nod, tears blurring my vision as I struggle to hold them back. It feels like speaking the words aloud makes the fear that much more real, and I am terrified of what might come next.

Shiwo's face changes, her expression shifting in a slow, deliberate wave—surprise mingling with concern. Her lips part as if she's hesitant to give voice to what she's about to ask. "Gamu," she begins softly, her voice carefully laced with a tender curiosity. "Do you know who the father is?"

The question strikes me like lightning. Memories flash before my eyes—half-formed images of stolen moments, whispered promises in the dark, secrets shared in the quiet of the night. But then, like a shadow creeping into the edges of light, a darker memory surfaces—one I've tried to bury deep inside me. I see it again: the moment I killed Kail.

This terrible realization pulls me under in a drowning wave of guilt and sorrow. My heart clenches tight, a suffocating pressure building in my chest. How can I look at her now? How can I possibly meet her eyes, knowing what I've done? I feel trapped, confined by my own guilt. Across from me, Shiwo waits, her gaze fixed on mine, searching for something—some hidden truth I haven't yet given her. She doesn't know what I carry, and the weight of that unspoken truth presses down harder, threatening to crush me.

I push myself up into a sitting position, every movement slow and agonizing. My body is heavy, weighed down by more than just the physical pain. Shiwo's eyes follow my every move, her brow furrowed in deep concern. She can sense something is wrong, but she doesn't know the extent of it—doesn't know the extent of the monster I've become.

"Yes, I know," I choke out, the words barely steady, shaking as they leave my lips. My gaze drops to the floor, avoiding hers. Shame rises up inside me like a fire, burning hotter with every second. How could I ever explain this to her? How can I ever reconcile the bond we share with the unforgivable truth of what I've done?

She watches me closely, not moving, her eyes soft but intense. "Gamu," she whispers again, more gently this time. She reaches for me, her hand brushing mine in a tender attempt to comfort me.

But I flinch away, jerking my hand back as though her touch had seared my skin. Her warmth is unbearable—a kindness I don't deserve.

The gesture takes her by surprise. She hesitates, but only for a moment. She doesn't push further, doesn't ask why I recoiled, and instead, she presses on, her voice calm and steady, though I can feel the weight behind her words. "You can trust me, Gamu," she says, her tone filled with quiet compassion. "You meant so much to my brother, and now... now you're one of the last pieces of him I have left."

Her words cut through me like a blade, sharp and precise, slicing straight to the core of my guilt. She knows. I see it now, the grief etched into her face, hidden behind her attempts at strength. Her eyes are red and swollen, her skin puffy from weeping.

"I didn't mean to tell you like this," she continues, her voice cracking slightly under the weight of her own emotions. She wipes at a tear as it slips down her cheek, quickly glancing away before she meets my gaze again. "I don't know what Kail meant to you, but... he's gone."

Another tear falls, and she brushes it away just as quickly as if embarrassed by her own vulnerability. She's always been like this, always trying to appear not just strong, but unyielding, like nothing could break her. But now I see it for what it really is—a fragile facade, one that's beginning to crumble.

The truth festers in my throat, heavy and immovable, and for a fleeting moment, I wonder if Six told her already—if she knows more than she's letting on. But as I look into her eyes, I realize she's still in the dark. Six hasn't told her. *Why?* The question lingers in my mind, gnawing at me. Why would Six leave this burden on me, why leave Shiwo in the dark? What purpose could it serve? The uncertainty festers, a slow-burning ache in the back of my mind.

But even as these questions swirl around me, I know that none of it changes what's already been done. I see the depth of Shiwo's anguish and I can't bring myself to add to it. I can't tear her apart with the truth—not when she's barely holding herself together as it is.

The silence between us stretches taut, thick with shared grief and words we can't bear to speak aloud. We simply sit there, my heart aching for Kail, for the bond I severed with his death, and for the connection I now fear losing with Shiwo. She was never someone I truly knew but now I dread the thought of losing her too.

Without thinking, I guide her hand gently to my stomach. "There is another piece of him left," I whisper, my voice barely audible, almost afraid to give voice to the truth.

Shiwo's eyes widen, snapping from my face to where her hand now rests. Her expression shifts, flickers of confusion giving way to comprehension. Her lips part, but no sound escapes. For a moment, she simply stares, her chest still, as if she's forgotten how to breathe. Her touch is reverent, and gentle, as if she's holding something too delicate to risk breaking. Tears well up in her eyes again, but this time, they carry a new weight—something lighter than grief. I can see a spark in her gaze, a flicker of joy breaking through the clouds of despair.

"Could this be?" she whispers, her voice shaking with emotion. "You're... you're carrying his child?"

I nod, just slightly.

The tears fall freely, she makes no move to wipe them away. Instead, she lets them fall, streaking her cheeks, mingling with the dampness of our shared pain. And in that moment, something shifts between us. The suffocating weight of sorrow begins to ease, just slightly, making room for something else. It's delicate and tentative, but there's no mistaking it—hope. Fragile and uncertain, but hope nonetheless.

She pulls me into her arms, holding me so tightly that a moan of pain escapes my lips—but she doesn't even notice. "Thank you," she whispers, her voice thick with gratitude and love. "Thank you for telling me, for sharing this with me." Her embrace is strong, unyielding, yet tender in its care, and I find myself sinking into it.

But the truth gnaws at me from the inside out. The secret of Kail's death weighs heavily, a dark and festering wound I cannot reveal—not now, not yet. The guilt twists and coils within me, poisoning the moment of comfort I've found. It's a bitter burden, but one I have to carry in silence for just a little longer. For now, I can only hold on to her and hope that she doesn't sense the shadow I hide behind my words.

Eventually, she pulls back, her eyes searching mine with a gentle insistence that makes my heart ache. "I'm sorry," she says softly, her voice heavy with unspoken pain.

"I needed that too," I manage, my voice raw with emotion.

She gives me a small, tender smile, the kind that makes me want to hold on to her just a little longer, to keep the darkness at bay for a while more. "You need to rest, mama," she says, her voice filled with affection. "If not for yourself, then for my niece or nephew. You need to get your strength back."

The word *"mama"* pierces through me and a faint, fragile smile forms on my lips. I nod, grateful for the reprieve, the lightness she's trying to offer amid the darkness.

I lie back down, feeling the exhaustion settling into my bones, heavy and inescapable. She gently tucks the blanket around me and begins to hum. The lullaby is soft and soothing, its notes delicate and warm as they fill the small hut. I realize it's not a melody meant for me but for the child growing inside me—a lullaby for the future, for hope. And so, I let the sound wash over me, my eyelids growing heavier with each note.

As sleep begins to pull me under, the guilt remains, an ever-present shadow lurking in the corners of my mind. But despite it all, I cling to the *fragile* hope that one day, I might find the courage to face the truth and the strength to seek her forgiveness.

Chapter 20

Each step I take sends a crackle through the underbrush, the rustle of leaves, and the sharp snap of twigs echoing around us. Jengo is right behind me, the cold steel of his gun trained on my back. "Keep moving," he orders.

My mind is racing, desperate for a way out. Every instinct screams that I'm running out of time. The moment to act is slipping away, but I can't rush it. I can't afford to misstep—everything hinges on this. My body feels like a coiled spring, tension thrumming through every muscle, waiting for the right moment to snap.

I let my foot drag slightly, feigning exhaustion, my steps becoming deliberately erratic. I hear his irritation in the snap of his breath, the way his footsteps quicken as he closes the distance between us. His grip on the gun tightens—he's losing patience.

"What are you playing at?" he snaps. "Keep moving!"

His frustration is encouraging. I stagger more deliberately, letting my body sway as if I'm losing control. It's enough to make him step closer, his attention drawn entirely to my faltering steps. I feel the heat of his presence just behind me, his impatience erratic. He reaches out, his hand grazing my shoulder in an attempt to steady me. And that's when I strike.

In one swift motion, I pivot, my hand striking out like a viper. The gun is knocked from his grasp, and it hits the ground with a solid thud. In the same breath, I throw a punch. My fist slams into his jaw with all the force I can muster, sending him stumbling backward. His eyes flare with shock—he wasn't expecting this.

But the surprise doesn't last long. He's on me in an instant, lunging for the gun. We collide, a tangle of limbs and desperation, both of us scrabbling for control. The world around us blurs into a chaos of green leaves and brown earth as we wrestle in the dirt. My fists fly, instinct driving me, adrenaline pushing me forward. But Jengo is relentless, his strength a brutal reminder of the danger I'm in.

He lands a punch to my ribs, and the pain is immediate and blinding. My breath rushes out in a gasp, my vision blurring as the forest spins around me. I struggle to hold on, but his weight presses down on me, his larger frame overpowering me inch by inch. With one last surge of strength, he pins me to the ground, his face inches from mine, twisted with fury and triumph.

"You're done, Six," he snarls, his voice low and venomous as he snaps the cuffs around my wrists, locking them with a brutal finality. "Enough."

The fight drains out of me as the cold metal bites into my skin. My muscles throb with exhaustion, my ribs screaming with every breath I take. The forest looms around me like a silent witness to my failure. The indifferent trees sway in the breeze, their leaves whispering of defeat.

He yanks me to my feet, and a searing pain shoots through my side, tearing a groan from my lips. Jengo doesn't care—his grip is iron, unrelenting. He shoves me forward and the barrel of his gun digs hard into my spine. The trek resumes and the world is reduced to the monotony of the trees—tall shadows looming over us, their branches shifting. The ground beneath me feels like a blur of roots and rocks, the pain in my ribs a steady drumbeat keeping time with Jengo's sharp commands.

"Move," he barks.

Finally, the forest thins, the thick wall of foliage parting to reveal the outpost. It's not the fortress one would imagine—it's far humbler, a cluster of huts huddled together like animals seeking shelter from the storm. But there's nothing welcoming about it. The walls of woven reeds and timber are too clean, too well-kept, like bones picked clean by vultures. Soldiers linger everywhere, their eyes sharp and watchful, their rifles slung loosely but ready. The air here is different—tighter. The watchtowers loom above the courtyard, crude but effective, standing over the compound. They may not offer much in the way of protection, but they serve their purpose, reminding anyone who dares approach that they are always being watched.

Jengo leads me toward the central outpost. His grip tightens as we approach, and the guards at the perimeter shift their stances, recognizing me, but with narrowed eyes full of something else now—distrust, disdain. I can feel it in their stares. I'm no longer one of them. The heavy wooden door groans as it opens, a low, ominous creak. Inside, the room is cool and dim, shadows flickering along the walls, the bare light from oil lamps casting everything in a pale, sickly glow. There is a smell of dust and old paper, and the quiet here is different from the forest's. It's a silence that waits.

Commander *Otieno* stands at the center of it all. His uniform is crisp, every inch of it precise, not a thread out of place. He doesn't look up immediately, his eyes fixed on the documents scattered across the rough-hewn table in front of him. But when he finally lifts his gaze to meet mine, there's a coldness there—an emptiness that makes my blood run cold.

Jengo pushes me forward, his voice dripping with an unsettling mix of triumph and satisfaction. "Commander, I've brought a prisoner."

Otieno's eyes flick over to Jengo, then return to me. For a long, agonizing moment, there is nothing—just the cold calculation of a predator sizing up its prey, measuring the life it's about to consume. His gaze is a blade slicing through every layer of my defenses. Then, slowly, his lips curl into a smile—one that might have passed for amusement if it weren't so devoid of warmth, so empty of anything human.

"Six," he says, his voice low and chilling, the single word hanging in the air like a snare tightening around my throat. There's something almost intimate in the way he says my name, as though he's known me all along, and has been waiting for this moment.

Jengo stands beside me, tense, his desperation creeping into his voice. "She's the cause of the unrest," he says, a sharp edge of fear in his words. "She's the leader of the rebellion."

He almost sounds like he's pleading—like he needs Otieno to believe him, to validate the betrayal that's etched across his face. But Otieno doesn't rush to respond. He lets Jengo's words hang in the air, letting them fill the room with their weight, testing their truth against the silence.

Then Otieno shifts, his smile fading, replaced by something colder. He takes a step toward me, his eyes never leaving mine. "The leader of the rebellion," he echoes softly, as though he's tasting the words for the first time. His gaze narrows, darkening with suspicion, and something else—something more dangerous, more lethal.

My breath catches, and my heart pounds in my chest like a warning drum, but I force myself to meet his eyes, refusing to show the fear crawling through my veins.

Otieno simply nods, already resigned to whatever decision he's made. In this place, accusations are enough. Proof is secondary. If there's a whiff of disloyalty, the sentence is already written. His eyes darken again but with a kind of cold amusement, like he's already picturing how this will end. "Very well. Take her to the holding cell. We'll deal with her shortly."

The words send a shudder through me. Jengo's grip tightens, and I'm dragged forward, his hand digging into my arm as two soldiers step in to escort me away. Otieno doesn't bother looking at me again. I'm already dismissed in his eyes, already marked for whatever comes next.

The soldiers shove me into a small, dank cell, the door slamming shut behind me with a deafening clang. The air inside is thick and stifling, the stench of decay and mildew clinging to the walls like a living thing. The floor is nothing but hard-packed dirt and the barest layer of straw—no comfort, no reprieve.

I collapse against the wall, my mind racing. Every second brings me closer to whatever fate awaits me. The darkness feels like it's closing in, but I know that giving in now means the end. I force myself to breathe, to steady the panic rising in my chest. But with every breath, the reality presses down harder. I'm trapped. Alone. And the next time that door opens, it could be the last time I see daylight.

Chapter 21

Born albino, I became the living embodiment of difference—a glaring contradiction against the earth tones of Nakuru's village. My skin, pale as bone, and hair, white as the moonlight, set me apart, not only as an oddity but as a specter of things misunderstood. My eyes, red like embers in the dark, glowed with a flame that the villagers believed could see into their souls. To them, I was a symbol of something they feared—an unnatural force, an omen that disrupted their delicate balance.

Nakuru's people clung to their hospitality like a badge of honor, proudly proclaiming their village a place of kindness and inclusion. Yet beneath that veneer lay a darker truth—*xenophobia,* veiled as tradition, and fear dressed as righteousness. They condemned Mvure for their exclusion, for shutting their gates to outsiders, but in Nakuru, prejudice was no less potent. It was simply cloaked in polite silence, whispered behind hands and closed doors. My albinism became a living testament to their hypocrisy, my existence a daily reminder that they, too, were capable of cruelty.

They saw me as an ill omen. To them, I was cursed—a

harbinger of disaster sent by the spirits, a blot upon their pristine world. My mother died giving birth to me, her life slipping away the moment mine began. Her death sealed my fate in the village's eyes. They looked upon me with suspicion and fear, as though her passing had been a sacrificial offering to some darker force.

As I grew older, the villagers' fear of me transformed into something more insidious—hatred. They feared my condition made me tainted, a stain on their otherwise pure community. Their whispers turned to open hostility when one of their own—a village boy—came to me in secret. His advances were furtive, wrapped in lust but laced with shame. He courted me under the cover of darkness, his desires a secret he wished to bury. But when we were discovered together, he lied, saying I had pursued him, and forced him into my presence.

It didn't matter that it was his touch that had first sought mine, his whispered words that had coaxed me closer. It didn't matter that my own feelings had been genuine, my heart willing to explore the fragile connection we had begun to build. The villagers saw what they wanted to see—a girl who was different, tainted by a condition they couldn't understand, caught in the act of seducing one of their sons. To them, I was the embodiment of everything they feared—dark magic, forbidden lust, and a corruption of the natural order. My mother's death, my albinism, the boy's accusations—they all combined into a storm of superstition and hatred, a perfect excuse to cast me out.

And so, I fled. The dense forest that bordered Nakuru became my sanctuary. Its towering trees and thick undergrowth swallowed me whole, offering protection from the villagers' wrath. In that wilderness, I learned to survive alone, hiding from the world that had rejected me. That solitude was my companion until the day I met Six.

The small clearing we've found deep in the forest is hidden from prying eyes, a place of quiet refuge where the world's harshness cannot touch us. It's here, in this pocket of the wilderness, that we've made our home—a bed of leaves and moss, a shelter from the storms that rage beyond the trees.

As we peel away from each other, falling back onto the softness of our makeshift bed, the night seems to hold its breath. My skin, pale and luminous even in the darkness, contrasts sharply against Amani's deep, rich hue. Together, we are a striking tableau of light and shadow, of differences that somehow harmonize.

I turn my gaze to Amani, his brown eyes reflecting the soft glow of the moonlight filtering through the canopy. There's a warmth there, a quiet understanding that words could never fully capture. His hand reaches out, brushing a strand of hair from my face with the gentleness that has become so familiar.

"Is it always going to be this hard to leave?" he asks, his voice low and resonant, blending with the rustling leaves and distant calls of the forest.

CHAPTER 21

I smile, a soft chuckle escaping my lips. "I don't know," I reply, the sound like the wind stirring the treetops. "But it does seem like the forest is trying to hold on to us a little tighter every time."

Amani grins, his eyes twinkling with that mixture of humor and affection I've come to cherish. "Or maybe it's you," he teases, his fingers grazing my skin, "making it harder for me to go back to the real world."

I raise an eyebrow, amusement tugging at my lips. "A spell?" I ask, feigning innocence.

He shifts beside me, pulling his clothes back on, his uniform suddenly feeling foreign against the serenity of the forest. "If it is," he says with a playful grin, "then I'm not sure I want to break it."

Amani is not from Nakuru; he is one of Ndambira's soldiers. Our paths crossed during a chance encounter in the forest, where we discovered an unexpected connection. Despite the differences in our backgrounds and the danger surrounding us, we fell in love.

It was in this tranquil solitude that I first encountered Amani. I moved silently through the trees, my senses attuned to the calls of distant animals. It happened on a crisp morning, the sun barely filtering through the thick canopy above. I was tracking a bird when I caught sight of him. A tall figure, clad in the green, unmistakable uniform of Ndambira's soldiers, stood by the edge of a clearing, his attention fixed on something beyond my view. His presence sent a jolt of fear and anger through me—soldiers meant danger, and I had learned to avoid them at all costs.

Instinctively, I drew back, my heart racing. But as I watched him, a sense of curiosity mixed with my fear. There was something in the way he moved—a gracefulness and precision—that caught my eye. I remained hidden, observing him as he surveyed the area, his demeanor calm yet vigilant. My heart was pounding, my mind a mess of conflicting emotions. I should have fled and retreated deeper into the safety of the forest. But something held me there, compelled me to stay and watch.

Amani, unaware of my presence, turned slightly, revealing more of his face. His features were striking—strong and defined, with eyes that seemed to pierce through the shadows. At that moment, our eyes met, and a spark of recognition passed between us. It was as if time froze, and the world narrowed down to just the two of us.

Surprise flickered across his face, quickly replaced by suspicion. "Who's there?" he demanded, his voice firm but not unkind. He took a step forward, scanning the trees where I hid.

I hesitated, my instincts screaming at me to run, yet something urged me to step out of my hiding place. Slowly I emerged from the shadows, my heart pounding louder. His eyes widened slightly as he took in my appearance—my pale skin and white hair. For a moment, we stood in silence, assessing each other. There was tension, an unspoken challenge hanging in the air, but also an undeniable connection. Despite the fear, I felt drawn to him, as if our meeting was destined.

"I won't hurt you," he said, lowering his weapon slightly. His voice had softened, tinged with something I couldn't quite place—curiosity, perhaps, or understanding.

Maybe he felt sorry for me. My petite frame and pale skin made me look like a wounded, naked bird, exposed and vulnerable in the harsh light of day. Despite my fear, there was something about his presence that was unexpectedly comforting.

I nodded, feeling a strange sense of trust begin to blossom between us, even though we stood on opposite sides of a deep divide. Our conversation was cautious, each word a tentative step across a fragile bridge. He introduced himself as Amani, explaining that he was on patrol for his commanding officer. I shared a bit of my own story, revealing that I lived in the forest to escape those who wished me harm. As we talked, the world around us seemed to shrink, the forest fading away, leaving only the two of us in a moment that felt both timeless and surreal.

Over time, our encounters became more frequent. I would find myself waiting for his patrol, while he, too, would look for me, hoping to catch a glimpse of my pale silhouette among the trees. We were cautious, acutely aware of the danger our relationship posed, yet unable to deny the feelings that had taken root. Each meeting deepened our connection, and what began as a chance encounter grew into something neither of us had anticipated.

His broad shoulders and sculpted form move with a deliberate, almost effortless grace as he dresses. The fabric of his shirt clings to his frame, outlining every muscle, and he fastens the buttons. Each motion is infused with a natural ease that captivates me. His movements are fluid, and purposeful, but never rushed, and there's a quiet elegance to how he carries himself. He glances at me with that familiar playful glint in his eyes as he reaches for his trousers, a soft chuckle rumbling in his chest.

"I could stay here forever," he teases, the warmth in his voice soothing against the inevitable parting. "But duty calls."

As he slips into his uniform coat, the act feels like a ritual—one that pulls him away from me and back into a world where duty and consequence weigh far heavier than the fragile love we share. The sharp snap of him brushing off leaves and dirt seems louder in the quiet forest, like an unwelcome signal that our time is slipping away. When he kneels to tie his shoelaces, I sense the dread settling over him. The same reluctance gnaws at me, an aching desire to stay hidden in this secret haven we've carved for ourselves—a place where, for a few brief hours, we can be wholly and completely who we are.

Our relationship, a delicate thread spun from whispered promises and fleeting touches, is something we guard fiercely, knowing how easily it could unravel. Every glance, every brush of fingers, carries the weight of what we stand to lose. The thought that we could be torn apart—stripped of each other—hangs over us like a dark cloud, its presence inescapable. I can feel it now, pressing down on me, heavy and inevitable, a shadow lurking even in our most intimate moments.

"Don't linger here too long, Sparrow," he says softly, his playful tone replaced by a gentle concern. His eyes narrow slightly, his brow furrowed with worry. "Be careful out there," he adds, his voice barely above a whisper.

I nod, managing a smile that I hope conveys more reassurance than I truly feel. "I'll be right behind you," I say, though the sadness creeps into my words. There is always a goodbye between us, always the bittersweet knowledge that our time is limited.

Reluctantly, I begin to dress, feeling the cold weight of reality settle back in as I fasten my own clothes. There's a quiet ache in my chest as I watch him finish his preparations.

For a moment, he pauses, his eyes tracing the contours of my face as if trying to etch every detail into his memory. His gaze softens with a tenderness that threatens to undo me. He leans down, pressing a soft kiss to my forehead, the warmth of his lips lingering long after he pulls away. "Until next time," he whispers, the words filled with both hope and heartache.

And then, with one last look, he disappears into the shadows, the trees swallowing him whole. The forest, so alive just moments ago, feels emptier now, the weight of his absence settling over me like a shroud.

Chapter 22

After Amani leaves, the forest wraps around me like a living thing—its sounds, scents, and shadows pressing close, almost as if it knows I'm alone again. I pause, breathing in the damp, earthy air. Each step I take is deliberate and careful, my senses alert to every rustle, every subtle shift in the underbrush. I move with efficiency, the familiar path winding beneath my feet as I head toward the hidden entrance of our underground hideout.

I forge ahead, pushing through the hanging branches that obscure the entrance, and step into the tight, dark space. The tunnel wraps around me, shutting out the outside world. I smell burning candles and hear hushed voices filtering through the narrow passage. As I enter the chamber, I am immediately struck by the emptiness. The room feels cavernous, and yet thick with the kind of tension that grips you by the throat and refuses to let go.

Osi stands at the far end, leaning against the wall with his arms crossed, his eyes scanning the room with a contemplative intensity that speaks volumes. The others are huddled together, their bodies leaning toward one another as if the physical closeness could shield them from some danger. Their whispered exchanges stop when they sense me, replaced by wary glances. The weight of their mistrust is nothing I am not used to. Though they may try to hide it, I feel the tension in their gazes, their uncertainty about me—about my differences.

I move past them, aiming for Osi. If not for Six and him, I would have been cast out long ago. They see me for more than my appearance, beyond the pale skin and stark white hair that sets me apart. Six's trust, her unwavering belief in my value, and Osi's cool pragmatism are the only things that anchor me here. Without them, I would be adrift—an outcast, just like before.

"Was starting to wonder if you'd gotten lost," Osi says, his voice rough but not unkind. There's a warmth beneath the tension, the way he always tries to ease the weight of the moment.

"I didn't," I reply, though the words feel clipped, tight in my throat. My mind is with Amani. "Do you think he would run with me?" I ask, the question tumbling out before I can stop it, my voice barely more than a whisper.

Osi doesn't need to ask who I mean. He sighs deeply, the sound heavy with understanding. "He'd be a fool not to," he says softly. His eyes meet mine, a flicker of something close to sympathy in their depths. But then the moment passes, and his gaze hardens once more as he continues, "There was a mass execution today."

CHAPTER 22

Cold terror washes over me in waves. "Six?" I whisper, my voice trembling, desperate.

Osi shakes his head slowly, the lines on his face deepening with sorrow. "I don't know," he murmurs.

The uncertainty twists deep inside me, gnawing at my insides. The room seems to grow darker and colder as the enormity of the situation presses down on me. This is why the chamber is so empty, and now, with Six's fate hanging in the balance, the hope I've clung to feels more fragile than ever.

As Jengo enters the room, everything becomes still. His presence commands attention, and the seriousness of his expression immediately fills us with a shared sense of dread. His eyes sweep the room, and for a moment, it feels as if the air itself is holding its breath - just like we are. He begins with a sigh - the kind that seems to carry the weight of everything we've been running from, everything we've lost.

"This is the last of us."

The words land like a punch, reverberating through my body. My gaze flicks to Osi, whose expression mirrors my own—a deep, gnawing fear. "Six." The thought claws at my insides, and for a second, I can't breathe. The room closes in around me, a suffocating silence hanging on Jengo's next words.

"Six has been captured."

There is no sound but the dull thud of dread sinking into each of us, heavy as lead. It is hard for us to think, hard to feel anything beyond the shock of it. Six. Captured. The woman who held us together, who drove us forward, now at the mercy of the same forces we've been fighting to escape.

As for me, the shock is paralyzing, seeping into my bones, making it impossible to think, impossible to feel anything beyond the raw, gnawing dread that clings to me like a second skin. For me—Six is everything.

Lena, who is usually the sharpest among us, trembles. Her wiry frame seems to shrink in on itself, and she stammers in disbelief, her voice trembling with fear. "How... how could they get to her?"

Jengo's face hardens as he gives voice to one name. "Malik," he says quietly, his jaw clenched. The betrayal is bitter on his tongue, the word a cold blade. "They tortured him... and he gave her up."

A shudder runs through the group. Malik, broken. A name, a life given up in pain. It's a brutal truth, sinking into us like poison.

"They'll be coming here," Dele mutters, his wide eyes betraying the panic rising in him. He's tall, but right now, he looks so small, huddled in on himself as if trying to hide from the inevitable. "We have to leave—we have to go now."

The fear spreads like wildfire, a spark igniting the panic

CHAPTER 22

that had been simmering beneath the surface. The room erupts into chaos—voices overlapping, rising to a fever pitch. Everyone is talking, but no one is listening. The walls seem to close in, the air thick with desperation.

"Look at us!" Tariq roars. His voice booms with barely contained anger, his dark eyes flashing with raw emotion. Every inch of his body is tense, tight, coiled like a spring on the verge of snapping. "We never should have come started this rebellion." He sweeps his gaze over the others, his words biting, sharp as steel. "We're walking corpses now. All of us."

His words hang in the air, heavy, suffocating—a death sentence.

Amara's small frame trembles as she clutches herself tightly, her face pale and drawn with terror. Her braids, usually immaculate, are fraying, unraveling like her nerves. "This was suicide," she cries, her voice breaking. "We've sealed our own fate. What were we thinking?" Her words echo in the room, feeding the growing panic.

The room churns, the fear tangible, swirling like a storm ready to burst. The air hums with the urge to flee, to disappear into the shadows and never return. I feel it too—an instinct to run, to get as far away as possible from this doomed place.

"Maybe it's time to leave Nakuru," Ibrahim says, his voice quiet but resolute. It slices through the chaos like a lifeline, commanding the room's attention for a brief, fragile moment. He's always been steady, the calm amidst the storm, and now his words anchor us. "They've got our names. They'll come for us eventually." His gaze sweeps across the room, his expression clear-eyed and resigned. "We can't go back. It's over."

"He's right!" Tariq's voice booms, his frustration reigniting like a flame. "We should have left in the beginning—if we had, we'd never have been discovered!"

"And leave our people?" Amara snaps. "Would you be able to live with that? Abandoning them to this fate?" Her small frame trembles, but her words are fierce, her eyes burning with an intensity that defies her frailty.

"At least we'd be alive!" Caleb barks, his voice laced with bitterness. His hands curl into fists, trembling. "What good is staying if it only means we'll die with them?"

The room teeters on the edge of chaos once more, the tension crackling like the air before a storm. Ibrahim's calm gaze lingers over the group as they hurl accusations and deflections. The weight of every choice, every consequence, hangs heavy over them all, the fear of the unknown pressing in from all sides.

Jengo's firm voice douses the panic like water on flames. "We can't afford to lose our heads now," he says, his tone sharp and unyielding. "This is our last shot. We either fight now, or it's over. If anyone isn't ready for that, leave. Save yourselves. No one will blame you. But I'm staying, because we've lost too many siblings to let their deaths be in vain. If you remain here, you better be willing to die for the cause. Otherwise, you'll only hold us back—or worse, see enough to betray us."

His words hang in the air like a final ultimatum. The room is suspended in silence, the weight of his challenge pressing down on all of us.

Then the first person stands—Tariq, his hands trembling as he gathers his few belongings. He pauses, casting a desperate look at the door, then back at us, as if searching for some reassurance that he isn't alone in his fear. But when none comes, he slips quietly into the shadows of the corridor, his departure etched with uncertainty. He's not the last.

One by one, others follow. Their footsteps echo in the silence, heavy with the weight of their decision. Each step feels like a blow, each departure a tightening knot in my chest. It's like watching the last threads of a once-strong rope unravel before my eyes. What was once a movement, a cause, has been reduced to a scattering of frightened souls seeking safety over purpose.

When the final echoes of their footsteps fade, the silence that remains is deafening. It's as though the air itself has thickened, pressing down on the few of us who remain. We are fewer than I ever thought possible.

The last of us stand together, seven bodies still holding onto a fragile thread of hope: Ibrahim, Dele, Lena, Amara, Osi, Jengo, and me.

Ibrahim and Dele have been the backbone of our efforts many times with their physical strength and combat prowess. Lena may not exude the same fire as some of the others, but her agility and sharp mind have always made her an invaluable strategist. She is a problem solver, able to see paths where others see dead ends. Amara, who seemed ready to break under the pressure earlier, has chosen to stay as well. Her nerves may be frayed, but her skill as a sniper is unmatched, and she knows how to keep her hands steady when it matters most.

Osi, who barely spoke during the tense moments, stands with arms folded, his face unreadable but his commitment clear. This hideout has been more than a base. It's been our sanctuary, our home. I can't help but remember the first time I came here—how nervous I was, trailing behind Six like a lost child. Six had always been the confident one, the one who made us believe we could change the world. And in some ways, we did. But there was always an underlying naivety in our rebellion. We were orphans, broken by the world, but we'd found a family here. Six made it all possible. She made us believe that no one could touch us, not even Ndambira. But now, with Six captured, everything feels like it's crumbling.

"What exactly are our next steps?" Ibrahim questions.

Jengo's jaw is tight and his eyes are narrowed. "Let's assess our options. If Six's capture has compromised our location, we need to be prepared for any eventuality."

Amara shifts in her seat, her fingers twitching around the strap of her rifle. "They could be closing in on us already," she murmurs, her voice betraying her fear.

"Then we move now," Jengo replies, his voice low but commanding. "We don't wait."

But before Jengo can finish, Osi pushes forward, determination etched into every line of his face. "Sparrow and I are going to get Six."

His words send a jolt of fear and resolve through me. I can't lose her. I won't. Six won't betray us—they'll torture her immeasurably. If we don't act fast, they'll take everything from her, and the thought of what she's enduring right now burns a hole in my chest. I step toward Osi, ready to follow him into whatever hell awaits us.

Jengo, his face set in a grim mask, grabs my arm with a grip that's almost too tight, his dark skin contrasting sharply with my pale hue. His gaze flickers from our clasped hands to my face, something unreadable crossing his features before he releases me with sudden urgency. "That's not what Six would have wanted," he says, his voice rough with frustration and exhaustion.

Osi's eyes flash with defiance. "Well, it's what I want," he snarls, stepping closer to Jengo. "Who's gonna stop me?"

The room holds its breath. Jengo pinches the bridge of his nose, exhaling slowly. "You can't just rush out there, Osi. You'll be walking right into a trap. If we're going to save her, we need to be smart about it. Not reckless."

Osi's jaw clenches, his body taut with barely-contained anger. "If we don't act now, we risk losing her for good," he bites back. "I'm not waiting around while they tear her apart."

Jengo meets Osi's gaze, the tension between them is like lightning. Then, with a slow, deliberate breath, Jengo steps back, his face hardening with resolve. "Amara," he says, his voice cutting through the tension, "you're our best shooter. Get outside and find a vantage point. If anyone gets close, you take them out. No hesitation."

Amara's eyes meet Jengo's, and though fear lingers in her expression, she nods sharply, rising from her seat with renewed purpose. "How will I warn you?" she asks, her voice steady despite her anxiety.

Jengo turns to me. "Sparrow, we need a sparrow."

I nod, stepping forward with a sense of urgency. Closing my eyes, I call out to my namesake, reaching out with my mind to the little bird that often accompanies me. Moments later, a sparrow flutters in through the opening. landing gracefully on my outstretched hand.

Gently, I stroke the bird's head, whispering to it. "Go with

Amara," I instruct softly. "Watch over her and return to me if there's trouble."

The sparrow chirps, as if in understanding, and hops onto Amara's shoulder. She offers a small yet warry smile at the bird's presence, before slipping out of the chamber

But even as I watch her leave, I can feel the weight of their eyes on me, a strange mixture of awe and suspicion. They don't understand the connection I share with these creatures. To some, I am still an enigma, maybe even something darker. Yet they need me, and in that need, I've found a fragile acceptance—one that's always teetering on the edge of something far more dangerous.

Jengo's voice snaps my attention back to the present. "We don't have much time," he says, his eyes narrowing as he turns to Osi. "I need answers. Why did you and Six return from Mvure? What went wrong?"

Osi's expression hardens, and frustration bristles beneath the surface. "The prisoner was more powerful than we expected. She killed everyone on board before revealing she was pregnant. Then we had no choice but to turn back. She was losing too much blood."

Jengo's face darkens with suspicion. "So, Six made the call?"

Osi's jaw tightens. "The decision was mutual. It wasn't just her."

"What does this have to do with finding Six?" I interject softly, the tension in the room becoming almost unbearable. My patience is wearing thin, and my mind keeps drifting back to Six—whether she's alive, suffering, or already gone.

Ibrahim, standing off to the side, his fists clenched in frustration, demands answers. "Why is this so important? Why didn't we know about this mission?"

Jengo's gaze turns steely, his voice taking on an edge. "The mission was to remain classified for one reason: Gamu is no ordinary villager. She's the runaway heir of Mvure, and we intended to use her as leverage—force the queen to aid our cause with Mvure's military might."

He pauses, letting the gravity of his words sink in before continuing, his voice lowering to a near-growl. "But Six's failure has cost us more than lives—it's jeopardized everything we've fought for. If Ndambira gets wind of Gamu's identity, he'll use it to strengthen his hold, and every sacrifice we've made will be for nothing."

The room falls silent, the weight of Jengo's accusations heavy in the air. The flicker of doubt and distrust among us is undeniable, spreading like wildfire.

Osi steps forward, his anger building. "You can't put all of this on Six. The enemy ambushed us. The deaths on that boat weren't her fault. And even if they didn't happen then, the executions would have happened regardless."

CHAPTER 22

I speak up, frustration tightening in my chest. "Osi and Six were vulnerable going alone. It's a good thing they turned back, otherwise they'd have been captured and killed in Mvure. We'd be in a far worser situation. This woman—Gamu—she's a blood magic user. If she could take out four of our best fighters without lifting a finger, what chance did they really have?"

"She did it in an instant," Osi adds grimly. "We were foolish."

Dele finally breaks his silence, his voice a low rumble of grief. *"Akinyi, Kato, Zuberi, Kail,"* he recites, each name a punch to the gut.

We absorb the losses, the void left by their deaths tangible in the empty spaces around us. Jengo exhales sharply, his voice a mix of resignation and determination. "But we still don't have a choice. We still need Gamu. We still need to take her to Mvure while we still can. It's still our last chance."

Lena shakes her head, skepticism etched into her features. "Sparrow just said we wouldn't stand a chance. Not without her on our side."

Jengo's gaze turns to me, his eyes hard. "We make it work," he says coldly. "Sparrow will use a poison—a snake bite. It won't kill her immediately, but it'll keep her weak until we reach Mvure. The antidote will be our leverage."

A sick feeling coils in my gut. "That won't work," I argue. "She's a blood magic user. She can slow the poison, maybe

235

even stop it."

"We don't have time for doubts," Jengo snaps. "This is war, so we find a way to do what needs to be done. Otherwise, what use are you to us then?"

A cold knot tightens in my stomach at the way his sharp tone hints at a challenge; something laced with impatience and a hint of disdain.

Dele interrupts with a shout. "Shiri!" *"Bird!"*

The sparrow flutters back into the room, its wings frantic, eyes wide with urgency. "They're here!" My voice is barely above a whisper, yet it cuts through the room like a knife. "Ndambira's soldiers—they've come for us."

The sound of distant *gunfire* is cracking through the air and for a heartbeat, we stand paralyzed, the gravity of the situation sinking in.

Jengo, ever the steady hand in a storm, is the first to recover. His calm is unnerving. "Survive," he orders, his voice carrying an edge of urgency. "Do you hear me? Survive!"

The words spur us into motion, a chaotic scramble as we gather our gear. Hands tremble as we fumble with weapons, our movements frantic but driven by a singular focus— escape. We rush toward the tunnel that leads into the forest, the only sanctuary we have left.

CHAPTER 22

The canopy above shuts out the moonlight, plunging us into a blanket of darkness. The night becomes our shield, masking our movements as we slip through the underbrush. From somewhere above, Amara's sniper rifle fires with sharp, echoing cracks, each shot precise and deadly, cutting through the dense underbrush as she targets the advancing soldiers with cold efficiency.

"Stay low," Jengo whispers, his voice taut with intensity. His eyes dart through the darkness, scanning for threats as he signals for us to spread out. We obey, melting into the forest floor, our bodies moving with stealth. The dense undergrowth and tangled branches offer some cover, but their numbers feel overwhelming as if they've come to some absurd conclusion that the rebellion is more than just a ragtag group of teenagers.

Their presence tightens like a constrictor around us. Shadows flickering between the trees. The forest becomes our battleground, its darkness our ally. We move like phantoms—here one moment, gone the next—using hit-and-run tactics to disorient the enemy, to slip through the chaos.

Dele emerges from the shadows like a jungle predator, his tall, muscular frame moving with a grace that belies his size. He slips silently through the trees, his machete flashing in the moonlight. With a burst of speed, he lunges at a soldier. His blade finds its mark, slicing cleanly through a rifle strap, disarming the man before he can react. A swift spinning kick follows, sending another soldier crashing into a tree, dazed and stunned. Dele wastes no time, retreating back into the safety of the shadows, his breathing steady, eyes sharp as he searches for his next target.

Lena moves like liquid fire, dodging incoming shots with an agility that seems almost supernatural. Her every movement is precise, her gun an extension of herself as she takes down soldiers with deadly accuracy. The forest around her pulses with the rhythm of her gunfire, each shot a precise strike in the dark, each impact a victory.

Ibrahim moves with unshakable calm, directing us through the thick of it. Every shot is deliberate, and controlled, as if he's carving a path through the chaos with cold, tactical certainty.

Dele strikes again from a new angle, his bloodied machete gleaming like a predator's fang in the night. His blade swings through the air in deadly arcs, cutting down enemies with brutal, calculated force. The forest around him becomes a song of violence—the clash of metal, the guttural cries of the wounded, the heavy thud of bodies falling to the ground. It drowns out all else, the chaotic music of war.

And then, in an instant, everything changes.

A shot rings out—sharp and unseen—and the world narrows for Lena. The bullet finds her with brutal precision, striking her side with a sickening thud. Her body jerks violently, her breath stolen by the force of the impact. Her eyes widen in shock, confusion flashing across her face as she stumbles, desperately searching for the source of the attack.

"Lena!" The scream tears from my throat, raw and panicked, the sound splitting the night.

Jengo's grip tightens on my arm. His fingers dig into my skin, burning with urgency. "Move!" he snaps, his voice cutting through the madness like one of Dele's machetes. There's no room for hesitation in his tone, no warmth, just the cold, hard command of survival. He calls for Osi, his shout sharp with authority.

Before I can protest, he yanks me forward, the force of it nearly sending me sprawling. My legs scramble to keep up, the ground beneath me a blur of uneven roots and underbrush. The world spins in a chaotic whirl, disorienting and oppressive, but Jengo's pull drags me through it, his pace relentless.

He moves with a predator's precision, his sidearm, and knife glinting briefly in the dim light as we weave through the trees. He doesn't hesitate—he disarms, disables, and moves on with ruthless efficiency. The confusion of the soldiers behind us becomes our shield, their disarray giving us precious moments to gain ground. Jengo turns any hesitation into an advantage, slipping through the shadows like a ghost. Osi is right behind us, his presence a fierce shadow at our backs. His knife glistens with the blood of those who dared cross our path, his strikes unflinching and brutal. He's a force of raw aggression.

My heart slams against my ribs as I struggle to make sense of Jengo's sudden urgency, questioning why we're abandoning the others—why we're leaving them behind to fight while we flee into the shadows. But there's no room for it, no space for second-guessing. I am being forced to push my legs to move faster and my lungs to gulp down air in sharp, burning breaths. The ground is treacherous, riddled with roots and debris that threaten to trip me with every step. But Jengo's relentless grip and urgent pace drive me forward, making me dodge and weave through the underbrush with grim efficiency. My mind races, but my body moves on instinct, following Jengo's lead. Because at this moment, there's nothing else I can do.

Chapter 23

I can't shake the haunting images of the others—their faces burned into my mind, etched with a mix of fear and resolve as they faced the grim fate that awaited them. Each heartbeat hammers with the terrifying possibility that they could be killed at any moment, or worse, forced to surrender to the very forces we've been fighting against. The thought of capture sends a chill down my spine, colder than the fear of death itself. And as we race through the darkened forest, my thoughts keep circling back to Six—already in their hands. The dread tightens my chest, squeezing the breath from my lungs.

"Stay close and be ready," Jengo commands, his voice low and gruff, carrying the weight of urgency and authority. "We're getting close."

But something feels off. My instincts, the ones that have kept me alive this long, are screaming that something isn't right. I've spent years listening to the subtle shifts in nature, to the small signals that betray danger lurking nearby, and right now, every sense is heightened. A deep unease gnaws at me, a prickling awareness that there's a threat I can't quite see, but I force myself to keep moving, to follow Jengo. He's the one with the knowledge—he knows where they've taken Six, where they might be holding her. That's the only thing that keeps me running beside him, my legs aching with the effort.

I want to trust him. He's explained it all—how survival is key, how the cause demands sacrifices. That, getting Six back will turn the tide in our favor. But the pit in my stomach tells me something else. I don't have it in me anymore to be cruel, to justify this level of cold calculation, even for the cause. I swallow hard, the taste of bile rising in my throat, and push forward.

We press on, the darkness of the forest deepening with each step. But I can't shake the feeling that the trees are whispering to me of a danger yet unseen. Then, abruptly, the trees begin to thin. The thick canopy overhead breaks apart, and we step out into an unusually large clearing. The shift is so sudden it feels like a blow to the chest, the forest giving way to a barren, empty stretch of land. The ground beneath our feet is hard and unforgiving, scattered with jagged rocks and patches of dead, brittle grass. It's as if the forest has been forcibly pushed back, leaving behind a vast, unsettling emptiness that makes my skin crawl.

Jengo's pace falters as we reach the edge of the clearing. He stops short, his usual confidence giving way to confusion. His eyes scan the area with increasing desperation, his brow knitting in frustration. "It should have been here," he mutters, more to himself than to us. His voice wavers

CHAPTER 23

with a note of disbelief as if the ground itself has betrayed him. "There were structures here. They were supposed to be here."

A cold dread curls its way up my spine as I take in the desolate scene. My heart thunders in my chest, the eerie stillness pressing in from all sides. The absence of anything—of life, of shelter, of soldiers—is wrong. My stomach churns as the realization claws at the edges of my mind. This clearing isn't a sanctuary; it's a stage. And we've walked right into it.

Osi steps forward, his face carved in suspicion. "This doesn't make sense," he says, his voice low and sharp. "Why would the structures be gone? And where are the soldiers?"

Jengo's face tightens, panic beginning to fray the edges of his calm. "I don't understand. This was the location. We've been betrayed." His voice breaks on the word, and for the first time since we've started this desperate mission, I hear real fear in his voice.

The truth hits me like a blow to the gut. The silence is broken by a rustling sound in the trees. I whip around just in time to see soldiers emerging from the shadows. Ndambira's men. They close in from all sides, cutting off any hope of escape.

"Jengo—" I whisper, my throat tight with betrayal. "You lured us into a trap."

But before the words can even fully register in my mind, *I see him.* Standing among the soldiers, his gun pointed directly at me. *Amani.* His face, so familiar, so achingly dear, is now a mask of cold duty. The shock of seeing him here—of seeing him on the other side—sends a wave of disbelief crashing through me, threatening to knock the air from my lungs. His eyes lock onto mine, and for a moment, the world seems to freeze, becoming colder. Though he tries his emotions, his features hardened into an unreadable mask of duty, I can see the storm brewing behind his eyes—the conflict between his love for me and the role he has been forced into. The sight of him, so close yet so unreachable, intensifies the agony of our situation.

Osi's eyes blaze with fury as he lunges toward Jengo, but the soldiers are faster. In one synchronized motion, they raise their weapons, the metallic clicks of safeties being released echoing in the tense night air like a countdown to death. Osi freezes, his muscles coiled with barely restrained rage, the wildfire in his gaze refusing to die down.

Jengo stands tall, his normally composed expression now tinged with something colder—calculation, cruelty. His eyes sweep over us with a detached sort of precision. He takes a deep breath, and when he speaks, his voice is as smooth and icy as the steel barrels trained on us. "Isn't it obvious?" he says, his tone almost bored.

Osi's face twists with disgust, Jengo's words hitting him just as hard. "You sold us out," he spits, his voice trembling with rage.

He doesn't even flinch. "I secured my place. I survived."

CHAPTER 23

I force myself to maintain a neutral expression, fighting against the rush of emotions threatening to overwhelm me—for *him*, for Osi. There's too much at stake. I push down the hurt and force my voice to stay steady. "But why bring Osi and me out here, instead of just killing us with the others?"

It doesn't make sense.

Jengo's eyes narrow as he looks at me, calculating, weighing his words. "My only concern," he begins, his tone as cold as ever, "is proving my worth to Ndambira. You and Osi are valuable—crucial players. You can't be thrown away so easily. The others?" He shrugs as if they were nothing more than pawns in a game. "They were expendable. Exposing their location was just another way to demonstrate my value to Ndambira."

"What do you mean?" I ask, giving my voice strength.

Jengo's lips curl into a faint, bitter smile. "It's all about consolidating power and positioning myself advantageously with Ndambira. If I can demonstrate that I've neutralized significant threats, I'll be rewarded—promoted, perhaps even given more control over operations. Gamu, is it? Anyway, represents the ultimate prize—both a formidable threat and a key advantage. I brought you here for a reason. She trusts you both, and that trust is my leverage. I need to lure her into a trap, and for that, I need you. I can't simply ambush her—her power is beyond my full comprehension. But with you two, I can exploit her trust and get her to lower her guard."

Osi's face contorts with a mix of anger and betrayal. "So, this was all about you climbing the ladder? You used us as pawns for your gain?"

Jengo's eyes flash with cold resolve. "It wasn't clear at first," he begins. "I didn't grasp the full extent of the situation until the numbers began to dwindle and the executions started. The reality hit me hard—I was facing death unless I acted. Seeing Six's weakness only fueled my panic."

Six's weakness? Six is anything but weak—a fleeting moment of vulnerability, as he suggests, is all that it is. I despise him, and I realize now that I've always harbored that hatred. His treatment of me, so distinctly different from everyone else's, stands out in my memory. He regarded me as though I were contagious, and that condescension has festered into a deep, burning loathing.

He pauses, his voice dropping to a hushed, conflicted tone. "I handed her over," he confesses, the words trembling on his lips, "and that decision nearly broke me. I stood there, gun in hand, guilt crashing over me like a wave, desperate to confess and abandon the path I had chosen. The weight of my betrayal nearly drove me to pull the trigger on myself—an act befitting a true Judas. Yes, Judas." His gaze hardens a flicker of unyielding conviction piercing through the regret in his eyes. "But by then, it was too late. I was ensnared by my own choices, forced to continue down this dark road. My focus now is on survival and advancement. I made my choices, and there's no turning back. In this ruthless world, it's about who can endure, adapt, and rise above the rest."

CHAPTER 23

Osi's eyes blaze with defiance. "Well, your plan has one major flaw. We'd rather die right here and right now than betray Six," he says, his voice tight with pride and anger.

Jengo's lips curl into a bitter smile, a glint of menace darkening his gaze. "I know," he sneers, "but she's in my possession—so drop it, will you? If you refuse to cooperate, if you don't do exactly as I say, I won't just kill her. I'll make sure she endures unimaginable torture, and you'll have the privilege of witnessing her suffering from the other side of life."

I don't hesitate; my voice edged with resolve and desperation. "What do you need from us?"

Jengo's expression hardens further. "Help me lure the blood witch into a trap, and I will present her as a gift to Ndambira."

A note of skepticism creeps into my voice. "How do you expect us to do that? She's a blood witch, and we're powerless against her magic. We don't have any means to counteract her abilities. What's your plan to deal with her?"

Jengo's gaze sharpens. "You know her better; use that trust to your advantage. Find a way to draw her in, and I'll provide whatever you need to set the trap. If you succeed, it'll ensure Six's escape."

Amani's eyes meet mine, and I can see the tension coiled in his jaw. It's a raw, aching exchange, a silent conversation fraught with regret and unresolved emotion. I'm overwhelmed by longing to reach out, but the reality of our situation presses down on me, paralyzing me in place.

As they move away, Amani's figure fades into the darkness, leaving me rooted to the spot. A cold emptiness spreads through me, settling in the hollow spaces he once filled.

Chapter 24

I am standing in a vast, misty landscape where the air shimmers with a soft, golden glow. The ground beneath my feet feels both solid and ephemeral, like walking on a surface of swirling mist that responds to my every step. The sky above is an endless expanse of rich purples and deep blues, streaked with delicate, shimmering lights that resemble distant stars. In the lower distance, a singular, majestic tree stands alone amid this vast emptiness. Its trunk, ancient and imposing, is wrapped in rugged, masculine bark, while its roots weave intricately across the realm, anchoring it deeply.

As I approach the tree, I see an elderly woman seated beneath its expansive branches. She exudes strength and dignity, her face etched with the lines of age. Her tired white dreadlocks are loosely gathered atop her head, and she is dressed in simple traditional attire made of animal skin, adorned with an array of white beads around her hands and neck. She sits barefoot, her legs folded gracefully to the side. Her presence radiates warmth and serenity, an anchor in this surreal landscape.

As she tends to the soil around the tree, her weathered, knobby hands move with a rhythmic grace that complements her song. The tune, soothing and haunting, fades as I draw closer, and her eyes meet mine with a deep, penetrating gaze, both gentle and profound. "What are you doing here?" She asks, sounding alarmed, but her voice is warm and welcoming.

I sink slowly to my knees, overwhelmed by the beauty of the scene and the comfort of her presence. "I think I am lost," I admit, my voice low.

She gazes at me with understanding, a gentle smile touching her lips. "Well, that must be frightening," she says, her tone imbued with the wisdom of someone who has long learned to find peace in the unknown. She gestures to the space beside her, patting it with a welcoming motion. "Come, sit with me for a while. I have found much clarity in the presence of this tree."

I move closer and settle beside her, feeling the strange but comforting solidity of the ground beneath me, despite its misty appearance. The tree's branches stretch protectively overhead, creating a soothing canopy of light and shadow.

As I sit there, she resumes her gentle humming. After a moment of shared silence, she looks at me with keen interest. "It's lovely here, isn't it?" she says. "Sometimes, the world outside can be so chaotic, but here, it's like time stands still, and we can just be."

CHAPTER 24

I nod, absorbing the tranquil ambiance. "Yes, it is beautiful. Have you tended to this tree alone?"

"Only since I was born, it has been my life's work," she replies, her fingers continuing their gentle work as her humming fills the air.

"You've been here your whole life?" My voice is raised with concern and sadness.

"Yes," she answers simply.

"That sounds very lonely," I say, with empathy in my tone.

"Oh, but I am not alone," she replies with a gentle smile. "Look at this tree; isn't it majestic? Its roots run deep, anchoring it firmly in the earth, while its branches stretch skyward, ever-reaching for the light. This tree is more than just a living entity—it embodies the collective spirit and effort of those who have cared for it before me and those who will continue its legacy after I am gone. It stands as a living testament to the strength and continuity of our lineage."

Her gaze turns tender and knowing. "In this continuity and with resilience, they have nurtured it with their wisdom and care. Before me, there was another who tended it, and now it has become my source of hope and endurance." She pauses, and her gaze softens. "And now it is your turn."

Her words stir something deep within me—a mix of awe

and fear. "I don't think I can—" I begin, my voice trembling, "I don't think I can bear such a weight of duty and responsibility. When I look at this tree, I'm overwhelmed by the fear of watching it wither and die if I fail. What if I tend to this soil and ruin everything? I know myself too well; I am fragmented and lost. When I look at my past, all I see are shadows of failure and broken dreams."

She listens quietly, her eyes filled with compassion. "It is natural to feel afraid when faced with such a profound responsibility. But remember, the tree's strength comes not from any single branch or root but from the entire network of support it has beneath and around it. You are not alone in this. Just as this tree has thrived because of the collective care of those who came before, you too have the support and legacy of your ancestors guiding you."

Her words offer a semblance of comfort, though the fear still clings to me. "But how can I trust myself to nurture something so significant?"

"Trust in the roots of your own lineage," she says softly. "The wisdom and strength of those who came before you are woven into your very being. Their guidance flows through you, even if it's not always visible. By embracing their legacy, learning from both their triumphs and their mistakes, and daring to carve your own way forward, you will discover your own path. The tree grows not only through its own efforts but through the enduring support of the earth and the care it receives."

CHAPTER 24

I nod, feeling a fleeting sense of comfort—until her expression changes. Her face darkens, a solemn shadow creeping across the dreamscape. The world shifts, the tranquility morphing into something unsettling. Her voice changes too, no longer singular but an eerie symphony of many, layered and haunting, reverberating with an unnatural echo. The dream, once peaceful, warps into something darker. "But a tree, in its magnificence, is not an end in itself but a source of sustenance and beauty for all who come near—is it not?"

The words crawl under my skin, and in a heartbeat, I'm wrenched from the dream, jolting upright with a sharp gasp. My heart races as if it's trying to escape my chest, my breaths come in frantic, shallow bursts. The remnants of the dream cling to me like a cold sweat, and I struggle to shake off the lingering dread.

"Gamu!" Shiwo's voice slices through the haze, pulling me back to reality. She appears at my side, her face tight with concern. Her eyes search mine as if trying to anchor me back to the present.

I press my hand to my chest, trying to calm the rapid rise and fall of my breath, but the weight of the dream still clings to me like a shroud. It was more than a nightmare—it felt like a warning, a message veiled in shadow.

"It's just a dream," Shiwo says softly, her voice warm and steady, a counterpoint to the terror still clawing at me. "It was only a bad dream, Gamu."

My hand reaches for hers, gripping it tightly as if she's my only tether to the world. "I have to go to the river, Shiwo," I manage to say, my voice trembling under the weight of the inexplicable urgency that has taken hold of me.

Her eyes widen slightly, but she nods, her compassion overcoming her confusion. She helps me to my feet with a steady hand, her touch warm and reassuring even though she doesn't understand.

"Let's go," she whispers, guiding me with gentle care.

We step outside, and the dawn greets us with its sharp, clear light. The air is cool, biting against my skin, but it helps clear the last remnants of the dream from my mind. This has been waiting for me all along.

Chapter 25

As I step out from beneath the thick canopy, the village unfolds before me, bathed in the soft light filtering through the trees. The sounds of daily life reach my ears—the rhythmic thud of hoes hitting the earth, the murmur of voices sharing stories, and the distant, joyful laughter of children at play.

At the village's edge, soldiers stand watch, their eyes flicking toward me with brief suspicion before shifting away, like shadows disappearing beneath the trees. I stick to the story we've built—a simple miner, returning sporadically to the village, a face blending in with the others. It's a fragile cover, but it keeps them from looking too closely and keeps their scrutiny from piercing too deep. I know the importance of maintaining this illusion. One crack in the facade could unravel everything.

The air carries with it the rich scent of freshly turned soil and the faint aroma of cooking fires. It's a comforting reminder of home, grounding me in memories of simpler times. My heart swells with a deep sense of belonging as I take in the familiar sight of the towering baobab tree.

And then I see Chinai. Her face lights up the moment she spots me, and she comes bounding toward me, her small form dusted with dirt from playing in the sunbaked fields. Her laughter spills through the air like a melody, bright and unburdened by the weight of the world. "Mhoro, Osi!" she shouts, her voice a joyous call. She launches herself into my arms with reckless abandon, and I catch her, lifting her up with ease.

"There's my little warrior!" I say, lifting her easily and spinning her around. "Uri kudyei kuti ukure zvakadai!"—*"What are you eating to get so big!"* I tease and kiss to her forehead.

She giggles, her eyes bright with mischief, her hair wild from play. She clutches a half-chewed sugarcane in one hand, and her friends hover nearby, curious but shy. They watch us from a distance, their faces a mix of wonder and excitement.

The women gathered around their cooking pots pause to look up, their faces breaking into warm smiles. I raise my hand in greeting, and they respond with eyes that sparkle with recognition and quiet joy that my return seems to bring them.

"Bamboo," I say, tousling the hair of a little boy with a mischievous grin. "Panashe, Andon, Princess." I greet each child by name as Chinai squirms out of my arms to rejoin her friends.

Neighbors call out to me, their voices warm and familiar, rising above the crackling fires. I press my hands together and bow my head in a gesture of respect. "Mhoro, ma! Mhoro, mama Genzi, mama Ruparanda, mama Mhoroma. Mhoro mama Rwedzi."

Their smiles widen as they see me, and a chorus of compliments follows, their words playful and affectionate. The women exchange knowing glances, their laughter mingling with the comforting sounds of the village.

I knock gently on the wooden frame of my sister's hut and step inside, ducking under the low doorway. The interior is dim and cool, fragrant with herbs hanging from the rafters to dry. My sister stands by the hearth, the morning light filtering through small windows to cast soft patterns across her face. Her expression shifts from relief to radiant joy as she sees me.

"Osi!" she exclaims, rushing forward to embrace me. Her grip is tight as if she's afraid I might vanish. *"Nguva dzese paunodzoka uchiri mupenyu, ndinotenda zvikuru."*—*"Every time you come back alive, I'm grateful."*

I hold her close, offering silent reassurance. The crackling of the fire and the gentle hum of village life drift in through the open door, blending with our shared breaths.

"I will always come back to you," I murmur, resting my chin on her head, speaking the words as much to reassure myself as her.

"How are you and Gogo?" I ask.

She laughs with a soft, melodic sound. "Gogo—you won't believe what you'll see."

My brow furrows in confusion, but before I can ask, she grabs my arm and pulls me toward the garden at the side of the house. "Come, you have to see this."

I follow her, curiosity drawing me in. As we round the corner, I freeze, astonished by what I see. Gogo, once so frail and bedridden, is crouched among her garden plants, her hands working the soil with a steady, familiar rhythm. Though her movements are slow, there's a new vitality in her that I haven't seen in years.

"Gogo?" I whisper, my voice thick with disbelief.

She looks up, her eyes crinkling into a warm smile that seems to light her entire face. "Osi, mwana wangu,"—"Osi, my child," she says with a clarity and strength I hadn't thought possible. "Come, come," she beckons, excitement dancing in her voice.

"Gogo," I approach cautiously, still processing the sight before me. "You're... you're up and about," I say, wonder lacing my words. "Nguva yekupedzisira yandakaenda, wanga usingakwanise kunyange kugara zvakanaka."—*"Last time I was here, you could barely sit up."*

Gogo chuckles softly, her laughter earthy and rich, like the soil she tends. With deliberate care, she presses her hand against her knee, pushing herself upright. The sun catches the sweat on her skin, making it glisten like dew on leaves. As she stands, her back curves slightly with age, but her strength is undeniable. "Sango rine nzira dzaro, Osi," anodaro, izwi rake richirema nehuchenjeri. "Midzimu inotichengeta."—*"The forest has its ways,* Osi. *Spirits watch over us."*

Nia stands beside me, her face alight with pride. "It was Chinai who led them here."

"Chinai?" I ask, startled, my voice edged with surprise and concern. "How?"

Nia's expression shifts, the brightness fading into something heavier. Regret flickers in her eyes before she speaks. "Osi... the soldiers ambushed Chinai," she says quietly, her tone grave. "They were going to harm her," she gestures to emphasize the danger Chinai faced. "But a young woman saved her. Manawe knows what could've happened if she hadn't intervened. They were grown men, and Chinai—she's just a child."

Her words hit me like a blow, and anger surges through my veins, hot and unrelenting. My fists clench until my knuckles ache, the image of Chinai threatened by those men searing itself into my mind. "How could they?" I growl, my voice low and dangerous. "How could they do that to a child?"

Nia's eyes widen at the intensity of my reaction, but she nods slowly, understanding the depth of my fury. "These are dark times, Osi. The soldiers don't see innocence anymore—just targets."

My anger simmers beneath the surface, barely restrained. "They will pay for this," I vow, my voice shaking with the weight of my rage. The thought of Chinai—my sweet, innocent niece—facing such terror fuels the fire inside me. It takes every ounce of control not to let it consume me completely.

Nia places a hand on my arm, her touch gentle but firm. "You must be wise," she says softly, her voice soothing, though it does little to extinguish the storm still raging in my chest.

I clench my jaw, fists curling tight as my eyes scan the soldiers scattered around us. Any one of them could be the one who threatened Chinai, their indifference a sickening reminder of the rot that festers within this broken system. Rage coils deep in my chest, a burning desire to strike—to tear into them and make them feel the fear and pain they've caused. But I hold myself back, knowing that if I act on this fury now, I risk shattering the fragile safety my family clings to. We can't survive if I lose control. To win this war, it's not enough to fight these men; I have to dismantle the entire foundation that allows their cruelty to thrive. The grief inside me is a well of sorrow, but it fuels my rage, pushing me forward. We've lost too much already, and I won't lose any more.

Nia's voice draws me out of the storm in my head. "The young woman who saved Chinai," she says, her words soft but insistent, "she's the one who healed Gogo. I prayed for help, and the spirits led her here. She didn't refuse us."

Her words settle over me like a revelation, and a wave of gratitude swells in my chest for this unknown savior.

"Ndinopira minamato kwaari mazuva ese."—*"I'll offer prayers for her every day,"* Nia vows, her tone resolute, filled with the weight of belief."If not me, then Chinai—who's become absolutely obsessed with the idea of being powerful," she says, dropping her voice to a dramatic, wary whisper, her eyes widening for effect. "You know... a *witch* like her."She laughs, shaking her head in mock disbelief. "A good witch, though, she insists. She says she has kind brown eyes that remind her of yours."

The air grows heavy with meaning and a cold realization trickles through me. *"Wicth?"* I ask with my voice tight with urgency. "Who was this woman?"

Nia's expression shifts into something almost reverent, her voice tinged with awe as she replies, "Chinai hasn't stopped talking about her. She says the woman wielded magic, that she commanded spirits to fight by her side. Her name was *Gamuchirai,* and it's burned into my memory."

The name strikes me like a blow, knocking the breath from my lungs. Gamuchirai. The recognition hits like a landslide, overwhelming and terrifying in its clarity. She was here—already woven into the fabric of our lives, and we didn't even know it. My heart pounds as the urgency tightens around me like a clenching hand. Every second we waste now is a second lost. A mistake has been made, and we are on the verge of something disastrous.

The spirits have spoken, guiding me to this moment. I was torn before, uncertain of the path, but now there is no question. I know what needs to be done. The time for doubt has passed.

"I have to go," I say, my voice hard with resolve. There is no hesitation left in me—only purpose. Every moment matters now; every step is crucial. I will protect what's left of my family, and I will seek justice for what's been taken.

I share one last look with Nia, a promise unspoken between us. Then I turn and sprint into the fading light, my heart hammering with the force of my decision.

Chapter 26

The river stretches before me like a shimmering ribbon of silver, slicing through the landscape with quiet grace. Sunlight dances across its surface, casting dazzling reflections that glint like scattered diamonds. It flows with a steady, gentle strength, winding through rocks and reeds with an ease that seems almost effortless. I inhale deeply, catching the familiar sweet fragrance of wildflowers that line the banks—bright bursts of color against a backdrop of lush green and deep blue.

I kneel by the water's edge, letting my fingers trail through the cool, clear liquid. The sensation is both refreshing and grounding, as though the river itself whispers secrets only I can hear. I've always felt a pull toward the water. The rhythmic lapping of the waves and the constant, soothing rush of the current seems to tap into something deep within me, a place that longs for stillness and renewal. Here, by the river, it feels like my soul finds its home again, connected to something far older, far deeper than words could ever express.

I cradle my belly, the soft curve of it where new life stirs. It is a presence I can't help but marvel at, both delicate and powerful, and I am overcome by a deep, fierce love for this child I have yet to meet. It is here, by the river, that I feel most connected to them—a connection that stretches beyond flesh and blood, one that roots me deeper into the world around me. The tree from my dream rises in my thoughts again, its mighty roots anchoring it to the earth. I realize then that I, too, am planting seeds. The choices I make now, the dreams I nurture, the fears I face—all of it will shape the legacy I leave behind. The soil I tend will nourish the future.

The river murmurs softly, a song of renewal and persistence, and I find myself thinking of the tree not just as a symbol of life but as a reminder of the generations that came before me. We are all part of something greater, each of us woven into the story of our ancestors' struggles and triumphs. The wisdom of the woman in my dream comes back to me—her gentle voice echoing with truth: we are all connected, bound by the roots of those who walked before us.

I take a deep breath, the crisp morning air filling my lungs, and as I exhale, a whisper of resolve passes my lips. "My name is Gamuchirai Danai Darare," I say softly, but the words feel strong and certain. "I am the first daughter of Chief Anesu Hondo Darare and Chiedza Danai Darare." My hand rests protectively on my belly, feeling the flutter of life within. "Ndakugamuchira,"—*"I receive you."*

A single tear slips down my cheek, not from sadness but from the release of everything I've held so tightly within. It falls into the river, disappearing in an instant, yet leaving behind a sense of peace, a moment of acceptance.

I rise to my feet, the weight of my decision settling into my bones like steel. I turn to Shiwo, meeting her gaze with unwavering certainty. "I'm going back to Mvure."

"Back? A shadow of shock falls across Shiwo's face, her eyes clouded with a mix of emotions—fear, and disbelief. "Why?" she asks, her voice tinged with concern.

"I am the princess of Mvure, Shiwo," I confess, letting the truth hang between us. "I ran away because I didn't understand the destiny that was laid upon me. For so long, I've crucified myself for the decision I made when I was unaware and naive, but now I see that leaving was necessary. It was a journey I had to take to learn certain truths, understand myself, and grow stronger."

Shiwo's eyes widen, her shock giving way to astonishment. She opens her mouth as if to speak, but the enormity of my revelation roots her in place.

"Mvure cannot continue as it has," I continue, my voice gaining strength. "It cannot remain isolated, serving only its own interests while ignoring those who suffer. I have to reclaim my place—to take the throne from my mother and make things right for our people."

Shiwo takes a step closer, her face lined with worry. "But what about me? What about the child?"

I place my trembling hand over my belly, feeling the faint but unmistakable flutter of life stirring within. "This child will be born into a world where people stand together." I look into Shiwo's eyes, her expression shadowed by doubt, by the same fear I feel gnawing at the edges of my resolve. "We've allowed fear to rule us for too long," I continue, "It's that fear—insidious, creeping into our hearts—that has kept us divided, that's made us easy prey for our enemies." I reach for Shiwo's hand, and when our fingers entwine, I grip it firmly, but with a tenderness that I hope conveys my conviction. "I must confront it head-on, Shiwo."

Her expression shifts from concern to fierce determination. "Then I'm coming with you," she declares, her voice steady and filled with deep loyalty.

I smile, warmth spreading through me despite the gravity of the moment. "I wouldn't dream of refusing you."

Our quiet moment is abruptly interrupted by the flutter of wings. A bird swoops down from the sky, its movements graceful as it lands on a nearby branch. Its gaze locks onto mine, unblinking and intense, piercing through the air between us as if it knows something I don't.

"I know that bird," I whisper, more to myself than to Shiwo.

Shiwo glances at the bird with mild curiosity. "It's just a sparrow. There are so many around here."

"No," I say softly, my eyes fixed on the bird, sensing something familiar. "This one is different."

The bird tilts its head as if beckoning me closer. Its presence draws me in, like a whisper from something beyond the physical world. My heart stirs with a connection I can't quite explain. "It's you, isn't it?" I murmur, half-believing the words as they leave my lips.

"Gamu?" Shiwo's voice is laced with concern, her eyes flicking between me and the bird.

"This bird," I say, my voice distant, "it's been in my garden. I see it often." My words trail off as the bird's dark eyes remain locked on mine, filled with an intensity that feels almost human.

The bird takes flight, a streak of feathers darting above our heads, circling with purpose before diving low and gliding into the thick embrace of the forest. An invisible tether pulls at me as if the very air around us is urging me forward. Without a word, I follow, my gaze locked on the bird's graceful movements through the branches. Every instinct in me screams that this creature is more than it seems—a guide, perhaps, or a messenger sent to illuminate the path ahead.

Shiwo hesitates behind me, her voice rising with concern. "Gamu, where are you going?" Her footsteps quicken as she follows, though her uncertainty is clear.

"I don't know," I admit, glancing over my shoulder at her,

the forest swallowing my words. "But I feel like we're meant to follow."

The forest deepens around us, the undergrowth thickening and the towering trees weaving a canopy so dense that the light barely filters through. Shafts of sunlight pierce the gloom here and there, but shadows rule this place, casting everything in shades of green and grey. The bird flits ahead, always just out of reach, its path deliberate, leading us ever deeper into the unknown.

The air turns cooler and sharper, and the bird settles on a low branch, its dark eyes watching us with a strange, unnerving awareness. My heart quickens—this place feels significant, like a moment on the cusp of revelation. But as I take a step forward, a foul odor slips into my senses—a sharp, chemical tang that cuts through the natural fragrances of the forest.

Alarm flares within me, my instincts sharpening as I try to place the smell. Too late. A pale mist drifts lazily from the surrounding trees, curling like a serpent around us. Within moments, my lungs begin to burn, each breath a laborious, choking effort. Shiwo's eyes widen in panic, her breath quickening to shallow, desperate gasps. The weight of the gas presses down on us, pulling at our limbs, and dragging us toward the ground. My head spins, the world twisting in on itself, colors bleeding together in a chaotic blur.

I stagger, the strength in my legs abandoning me as if my muscles are turning to water. My vision swims, darkening at the edges, and I know I'm breathing in more of the poison

CHAPTER 26

with every rasping inhale. Desperately, I try to call on my blood magic, to summon the power that thrums beneath my skin, but it's as if I've been severed from it, my limbs leaden, my thoughts clouded in thick fog.

Shiwo collapses beside me with a lifeless thud, her body hitting the earth in a tangle of limbs. Panic claws at me, but my own strength is slipping away, my knees buckling as I sink to the ground.

Through the swirling haze, another figure steps out of the trees. Tall, his face obscured by shadow, his movements slow and purposeful, like a predator closing in on wounded prey. The man's steps are methodical, his presence growing larger with each heartbeat as if the very space around us bends to his will.

And then I see Sparrow. He moves through the mist, his face partially concealed by a cloth tied across his mouth and nose. Only his eyes are visible above the mask, and what I see there sends a chill through my bones. There's a pain in those eyes, a deep well of anguish, but there's also something far darker: resolution. His hands bring a syringe into view, its needle promising no mercy. My body struggles weakly against the gas, but I know it's futile. I am paralyzed, trapped in the grip of whatever nightmare has taken hold of this place.

As Sparrow kneels beside me, the syringe poised and ready, my mind screams at the betrayal, but I am powerless to act. My breaths are shallow, barely enough to sustain me, and the world around me begins to fade into the cold embrace of oblivion.

But then, through the creeping darkness, a voice rings out—deep and commanding, cutting through the fog like a blade.

"Mira," Sparrow, *"stop!"*

The shout slices through my fading consciousness, and for a fleeting moment, hope flares in my chest. But the darkness presses in from all sides, and I slip beneath its suffocating weight, spiraling into a place where even the light cannot reach.

Chapter 27

Sparrow freezes, his hand shaking as he stares at Jengo, fear flickering in his eyes. I melt into the shadows, my breath shallow, my heart pounding in my chest like a war drum. From my concealed position, I line up the shot, feeling the alien weight of the gun in my hand. I squeeze the trigger, and the explosion of sound is jarring, but the bullet flies true. One of Jengo's men crumples to the ground, the sound of his fall lost in the chaos of battle.

I hate guns. The disconnect between the pull of a trigger and the damage it inflicts unnerves me. With a knife, there's a closeness, a brutal honesty to the kill. This is only the second time I've ever fired a gun, and the cold metal still feels unnatural in my grip. It's nothing like the sure, familiar heft of a blade.

Across the clearing, I catch a glimpse of Jengo's face twisting with fury, his eyes alight with rage. In a swift, violent motion, he grabs Sparrow, pressing a gun to his temple. Sparrow's eyes widen in shock, his breath catching in his throat as the barrel digs into his skin.

"Step out, Osi," Jengo snarls, his voice a razor slicing through the air. "Or I blow his brains out."

The world narrows to this moment. Every sound—the rustling leaves, the distant gunfire, even my own heartbeat—fades into a low hum. My thoughts are racing, each one more desperate than the last, but they all collide against one unyielding truth: I cannot lose Sparrow. Not him, not now.

I step from the cover of the trees, my gun trained on Jengo, muscles coiled tight like a drawn bowstring. "Let him go, Jengo," I say, forcing my voice to remain steady, though my insides are twisting with panic.

Jengo's lips curl into a cruel, humorless smile. "You really think you're in any position to make demands?" His eyes gleam with malice as he tightens his hold on Sparrow, pushing the gun harder against his skull. "I've already won. You're outnumbered, outmatched, and out of options."

Sparrow's gaze locks with mine, pleading silently, his terror palpable. Every instinct screams at me to act, to end this standoff before it's too late, but the tension coils tighter with every passing heartbeat. We're balanced on a knife's edge, one wrong move and everything shatters.

"You've got what you wanted," I say, my voice hardening, fighting to regain control. "We've held up our end. Now let him go—at the very least, let Sparrow go. We both know this doesn't have to end in more blood."

There is a heavy, tense silence before Jengo's face twists, his expression shifting from cold contemplation to something far uglier. His eyes narrow with venomous hatred as he fixes his gaze on Sparrow. "I've always despised him," he hisses, his voice seething with malice. "Look at him—pale, sickly, like a damned ghost. And there are whispers, Osi. Whispers that he *prefers* men. Do you know what kind of man does that? Only a twisted, sick abomination. He uses dark magic to prey on others—who knows how many of us he's defiled, maybe without us even knowing. A man's got to satisfy his filthy urges somehow, right?" He spits on Sparrow, the act dripping with contempt.

His gaze flicks to me, and his lips curl into a sneer of disgust. "You knew, didn't you? Of course, you and Six knew all along." He spits again, this time with even more disdain. "Disgusting. How could we have ever followed someone like her?" His voice drips with loathing. "You're all freaks—every single one of you," he snarls, his fury only deepening. He turns his attention back to Sparrow, his eyes burning with revulsion. "I've had to endure him—endure the thought of accidentally touching him, fearing I'd catch whatever *sickness* he carries."

Sparrow's attempts to hold himself together are pitiful. He shakes like a leaf in a storm, his resolve crumbling under Jengo's cruelty. Watching him crumble under Jengo's cruelty makes my chest ache helplessly.

But I can't stay silent.

My voice forces its way through the tight knot in my throat, urgent and desperate. "You've gotten what you wanted—now let him go!" The plea erupts from me, gaining strength as fear, frustration, and helplessness flood my veins. "You don't have to like him, Jengo—just let him go! We don't have the right to snuff out what we don't like, what we don't understand, or what makes us uncomfortable. A human life doesn't need to make sense to us to be worthy of it—please, let him go."

Jengo's face contorts with a seething rage, his fury blazing out of control like a wildfire. "Is *it* even human, Osi? Look at it," he sneers, his gaze filled with venom as it shifts back to Sparrow. "You're an abomination—a disgusting freak of nature!" His words drip with contempt as he presses the gun harder against Sparrow's temple, the cold metal biting cruelly into his skin. "Say it," Jengo growls, his voice a low, menacing snarl. "Tell him that you're an abomination. You know it's true—so say it out loud, damn it! Admit it!"

Tears fill Sparrow's eyes, his body shaking uncontrollably as the last vestiges of his strength slip away. He tries to choke back the sobs, but the pressure, the pain, is too much. His dignity, his spirit, is crumbling under Jengo's relentless cruelty. My heart shatters as I watch him break, his suffering like a knife twisting in my chest.

Jengo's patience snaps, his grip tightening on the gun. "Say it!" he roars, yanking Sparrow's head back so violently that it forces a gasp of pain from him. The brutality of the motion leaves no room for defiance; it's an order meant to break, not just to humiliate. Each second stretches agonizingly, his cruelty mounting with every passing moment. His rage seems to feed off Sparrow's suffering, each flinch and wince from Sparrow spurring him on, his face twisted into a mask of sadistic glee.

I can't stand it any longer. Every fiber of my being screams for action, but I know that one wrong move could end Sparrow's life.

"I'll show you what happens to freaks who don't know their place." He twists the gun against Sparrow's temple, his finger twitching dangerously on the trigger.

But I can't stay silent.

"Is he human?" I finally shout, my voice cracking with emotion. "Of course, he's human, Jengo! Can't you see? His fear, his pain, his tears—they're all human! Look at him—really look at him. He's no different from you or me. He bleeds like we do, he suffers like we do. The only abomination here is the hatred consuming you."

My father taught me this: You can't claim righteousness while you live in ignorance. Compassion isn't about who looks like you, thinks like you, or believes what you do. It's about recognizing humanity, even when it challenges your comfort. Until you learn that, you're just hiding behind the illusion of virtue.

There's a brief flicker of hesitation, but it vanishes almost instantly. Jengo's hand trembles, his finger poised on the trigger, his face still twisted with disgust as his breath comes in harsh, ragged bursts. My heart thunders in my chest, drowning out all other sounds as his finger starts to press down, each beat echoing with a terrifying finality. My instincts falter, paralyzed by the looming specter of loss, grief already gripping me in its merciless hold.

The gunshot rips through the air—a deafening crack that shatters the silence, freezing everything in its wake. I flinch, my eyes clenching shut as a harsh, burning lump lodges in my throat, striking with the force of a blade. I brace myself, every muscle in my body tensed with dread. My mind races ahead, conjuring a vivid, harrowing image of Sparrow crumpling to the ground, his life ebbing away as crimson blood spills from the bullet wound on his head, staining his pale skin. I wonder if his eyes will remain open—his life brutally cut short, a last defiant stand of his soul against the grasp of death.

But what I see stops me cold, shock rooting me to the spot. Instead, it's Jengo who staggers backward, his face twisted in shock and disbelief. His hand instinctively flies to his side, where dark, wet blood blossoms through his shirt, spreading like a sinister flower. He gasps, his body swaying, teetering on the edge of collapse. For a moment, everything narrows, the world reduced to the sight of Jengo crumpling, his expression one of stunned agony.

Confusion sweeps through the clearing like a wave, gripping us all in its cold, paralyzing grasp. My mind races, struggling to process what just happened. Then, in the corner of my vision, I see him—one of Jengo's own men. His gun is still smoking, his face impassive, as if the chaos around him is nothing more than an everyday occurrence. He's the traitor, the source of the shot that felled Jengo, and for a moment, the air itself seems to hold its breath.

But I don't waste the opportunity. With reflexes honed by survival, I spring into action. My hand darts to the dagger at my side, and before I even register the motion, the blade is spinning through the air. It finds its mark with deadly precision, burying itself in the neck of one of Jengo's soldiers. He crumples to the ground, his life bleeding out in choked gasps, his eyes wide with shock as crimson spills down his chest.

And then, in the same instant, another crack cuts through the clearing. The traitor fires again. The bullet finds its target—a soldier who had been advancing, his weapon raised for a killing blow. He drops in an instant, his skull shattered, his body collapsing like a puppet with its strings cut. The report of the gunshot echoes, reverberating through the trees, a brutal punctuation to the chaos that surrounds us.

The adrenaline surges, sharp and unforgiving. I move without thinking, drawing my own gun in one fluid motion. The forest erupts in a cacophony of violence, my shots ringing out in quick succession. Two more of Jengo's men fall, their bodies hitting the dirt with sickening thuds, their deaths swift and merciless.

The gunfire fades, replaced by the ringing in my ears and the heavy thrum of my own heartbeat pulsing like a drumbeat. My gaze locks with the traitorous soldier. His eyes burn with an intensity that matches the storm of emotions swirling inside me: fear, defiance, and something more—resolve, perhaps, or resignation. His chest rises and falls with sharp, controlled breaths, but it's clear—he's no longer poised to strike. With slow, deliberate care, he lowers his gun, the barrel dipping toward the ground. His hands rise in the universal gesture of surrender, his fingers spread wide in the air between us, like fractured branches reaching out for something to hold on to.

Every movement he makes is slow, deliberate—each step measured with the care of someone approaching something fragile, something sacred. His face softens, the hard edges of his demeanor melting away. The soldier lifts and wraps his arms around Sparrow with the kind of tenderness that makes the air around them seem to be still, his touch light yet protective, his fingers trembling as they press into Sparrow's back.

Sparrow crumples into him, his body shaking violently as sobs wrack his frame—sobs born from fear, exhaustion, and a flood of emotions too long held back. His tears wet the soldier's chest as he clings to him, his grip desperate, as if he's terrified that this moment, this person, might slip through his fingers like a fading dream.

He murmurs soothing words to Sparrow. Watching them, I feel the weight of the scene crash over me like a wave, knocking the breath from my lungs. This isn't just a moment of rescue—it's a reunion, intimate and raw, brimming with a love so fierce it cuts through the brutality of the night. The realization strikes me with sharp clarity, like a blade slicing through fog: this man, this soldier who just betrayed his comrades, is Sparrow's secret lover. The one he's fought to keep hidden, the one who's now risked everything—his life, his honor—to save him. In this moment, they are each other's refuge—the world around them can burn, but for now, they are safe in each other's arms.

Chapter 28

"Sparrow," I say softly, though urgency sharpens my tone. "We have to go. Now."

He lifts his head from his lover's shoulder, his face streaked with tears but carrying quiet bravery beneath the vulnerability. He meets my gaze, and in his eyes, I see the delicate balance between fear and resolve. The soldier gently releases him, whispering something tender, something meant to hold Sparrow together for just a little longer.

"What's your name?" I ask, my voice steady, though the air around us still hums with danger.

"Amani," he says, a flicker of uncertainty in his tone, as though bracing for judgment. His eyes search mine, seeking not just gratitude but an acceptance of the bond between him and Sparrow—an unspoken plea for understanding in a world that often refuses such love.

"Thank you, Amani," I reply, and I let the warmth in my words show him there is no judgment here, only gratitude.

CHAPTER 28

He manages a faint smile, hesitant but filled with hope, a fragile thing that hints at relief.

"We need to move quickly. You carry Shiwo, I'll take Gamu," I say, the urgency in my voice undeniable.

Amani nods, the gravity of our situation pulling him into action. Sparrow stands, his tears wiped away, leaving behind a resolve that gleams in his eyes. Amani gently lifts Shiwo, his arms steady and strong, while I scoop Gamu into my arms with care, cradling her against me like something precious and irreplaceable.

We move through the thick forest with purpose, the shadows deepening as we plunge further into its depths. The canopy above grows dense, the twisted branches forming a protective veil over us as we weave through the undergrowth. The path is narrow, winding, and relentless, but we press on, our determination outpacing our exhaustion. Finally, we emerge into a secluded glade, a hidden sanctuary wrapped in soft moss and dotted with ferns. Sparrow's belongings are scattered here—items that speak of the life he has lived in secret.

We gently lower Gamu and Shiwo to the ground, their bodies settling into the earth's welcoming arms. Sparrow kneels beside them and rummages through his pouch. He selects herbs with precision, his touch steady as he begins crushing the leaves into a fragrant mixture. The sharp, revitalizing aroma fills the air around us, carrying the promise of healing.

"These will help," Sparrow whispers, his voice soft but filled with conviction. He presses the crushed leaves beneath Gamu and Shiwo's noses, the scent sharp and pungent.

Gamu is the first to stir. Her eyes flutter open, the confusion in her gaze giving way to a flicker of recognition and determination. Shiwo follows soon after, her breaths deepening as she blinks away the remnants of the gas-induced haze. Relief washes over us, brief but sweet—until Sparrow stiffens.

He gasps, his hand flying to his throat. Panic floods his eyes as he begins clawing at his neck, choking on invisible hands that seem to grip him. The air around him thickens, and I feel my heart lurch. We all freeze, horror gripping us as we watch him struggle, desperate to understand what's happening—what new horror has claimed him.

Gamu's power tightens around Sparrow's throat like an invisible snare, a subconscious defense mechanism born of fear and confusion. I can feel the energy crackling in the air, wild and untamed, as her magic constricts him without intent, her disoriented mind reflexively lashing out.

"Gamu!" I shout, urgency sharpening my voice. "Let him go! You're safe now—it's a mistake!"

Amani, still reeling from his own brush with death, raises his gun with a fierce resolve. I see it in his eyes—if it's a choice between Sparrow's life and Gamu's, he won't hesitate. His gun quivers in his hand and his finger hovers over the trigger.

But this only pushes Gamu further. The force of her magic lashes out again, and Amani gasps, his hand flying to his throat as the invisible grip squeezes tighter. He drops his weapon, his fingers clawing at his neck in desperation. Gamu's face twists, her expression darkening with anger and confusion, lines of exhaustion etched beneath her eyes as raw power radiates from her, electric and terrifying. She doesn't seem like herself—she's become something more primal, more dangerous, like a force of nature unleashed.

"Gamu, please," I plead, stepping closer, my voice steady despite the chaos. "Six—she's in danger. They've taken her. We don't know if she's still alive, but this... this is all a misunderstanding!"

Her eyes flicker, the fog of confusion briefly lifting. Her grip loosens. "Six?" she whispers, her voice soft and broken with concern.

Both Sparrow and Amani collapse to the ground, gasping for air as they are released from Gamu's power. The tension in the clearing begins to ebb, leaving behind only the sharp relief of survival. Shiwo kneels beside them, her touch gentle as she checks them for injuries, her eyes wide with concern.

"Yes, Six," I say, my voice steadier now. "She's in trouble. We need to find her—Jengo betrayed us. He lured us into a trap."

Gamu's expression shifts. The brief moment of confusion

is replaced by something fiercer, her remorse transforming into cold, burning rage.

"Where is she?" she demands, her voice hardening like steel.

"We don't know exactly," I reply, sensing her frustration mounting. "Jengo was feeding us lies, claiming to know where she was, but—"

"I know where she is," Amani interrupts, his voice hoarse from the recent struggle. He looks up, his eyes filled with grim determination. "She's at the intelligence outpost, where Commander Otieno is stationed. They're holding her there."

Gamu's face darkens further. Her hands ball into fists, her fury barely contained. "Then we have no time to lose," she says, her voice fierce. "We need a plan."

Amani quickly takes charge, his mind already working through the details. "The outpost is heavily guarded, but I know its layout. We'll approach through the forest—it's dense, and they won't expect an attack from that direction."

He turns to Sparrow. "Your birds will be crucial here. Send them to scout the perimeter, especially the watchtowers and entry points. We need to know where the guards are stationed and if there are any weak spots in their defenses."

Sparrow, still shaken but resolute, nods, and his lover continues, his voice sharp with focus. "Gamu, you'll use your blood magic to take out the guards in the watchtowers. Once that's done, Osi and I will take care of the soldiers on the ground. When the immediate threats are neutralized, you'll join us in securing the area. Once we have her, we retreat into the forest. If things get too hot, Sparrow, create a distraction—something to throw them off our trail."

A flicker of pride crosses Sparrow's face as he glances at him. The bond between them is so tangible and deeply felt. Amani, continues, "The outpost won't be at full strength. Ndambira has pulled most of his troops for the campaign against Mvure. We have an opportunity here."

Gamu's fear is intense, her breath catching in her throat. "What? They're mobilizing against Mvure?" Her voice trembles at the edges, disbelief woven through the words.

Amani's expression is grim, eyes shadowed with the weight of the news he carries. "Yes—they plan to strike before dawn."

Gamu's shock only lasts a moment before it hardens into something sharper, more resolute. The flame of fierce determination lights in her eyes as she straightens her posture. "Then we have to stop them."

"We can't," Amani replies firmly, as if delivering a truth neither of them wants to accept. "There are too many. We'll be slaughtered."

She shakes her head, eyes blazing with a fire that refuses to be extinguished. "Then we warn them. Shiwo, you have to go. You must reach Mvure before it's too late."

Shiwo's face drains of color, her breath catching in her throat as the weight of the responsibility crashes down on her. Her wide eyes reflect both disbelief and fear. "But... what if I don't make it?" she stammers. "What if... I fail?"

Gamu steps closer, gripping Shiwo's shoulders with a steady firmness. She locks eyes with her with an intensity that leaves no room for doubt. "Do you think I'd ask this of you if I doubted you?" Her voice is low but fierce, carrying a strength that seems to flow directly into Shiwo, like a lifeline anchoring her to something solid amidst the storm of fear. "You are stronger than you realize, Shiwo. I trust you with this. And right now, you need to trust yourself. We all do."

For a moment, the air is suspended, crackling like a live wire between them. Shiwo's gaze flickers from Gamu to the rest of us, doubt shadowing her expression—the enormity of the task before her is overwhelming, a mountain too steep to climb. She hesitates, fear and indecision holding her in place. But then, something within her shifts—a small but undeniable change, as if she's tapped into a hidden reservoir of inner strength. Her spine straightens, her shoulders pull back, and though the fear still lingers in her eyes, it's now accompanied by something deeper, more powerful. *Resolve.*

"I'll do it," she says quietly. The trembling uncertainty in her voice is still there. "Your people are now my people. I won't let you down."

Her words are unexpected but powerful. There's something about the way she says it that makes us all pause. The bond between her and Gamu is clear—something has shifted, something beyond duty. Perhaps it's the gravity of the situation, or perhaps it's something more profound, a connection forged in fire. Whatever it is, it transcends mere loyalty, and though I don't fully understand it, I don't question it either. Not now.

Gamu's expression softens as the tension ebbs, her fierce exterior melting into something tender. She lifts her hands to cup Shiwo's face, her touch gentle yet firm, an unspoken promise passing between them. "Thank you, Shiwo" she whispers.

Amani, who has been checking his gear with tactical efficiency, looks up, his expression hardening with purpose. "We don't have time to waste," he says, his voice sharp. "We're cutting our resources thin, and this could jeopardize everything."

I catch his drift. "I'll lead her there and return. We leave immediately."

Gamu takes Shiwo's hands in hers, her voice soft but urgent. "We'll meet before sunrise. Stay safe, my sister."

With a final, heartfelt embrace, Shiwo steels herself and prepares to depart. Her fear is palpable, but her resolve is fierce.

"Let's move," I say, and together, we step into the night.

Chapter 29

I am dreaming again.

Nakuru, my village—my home before Ndambira's rule darkened our world—unfurls before me, alive with the memory of freedom. The air hums with a forgotten lightness, a sense of peace that now feels distant. The bustling marketplace is a riot of color and sound: vendors calling out, selling fresh fruits, vegetables, and handmade crafts. Friends and neighbors chatter and laugh, their faces warm and familiar. Children dart through the streets, their laughter ringing out like music, unburdened by fear. But as I move through this vibrant world, my steps feel heavy, as if the earth beneath me is trying to pull me back, reminding me that this is no longer real.

I push open the door to our old hut, and there he is—my father—lying on his mat. The sight hits me like a blow. He is a shadow of the man I remember, his body gaunt, his skin pale and drawn tight over his bones. He looks so much smaller than he once was, his strength eaten away by illness. Every rib stands out beneath his tattered clothing, his once-powerful frame reduced to something fragile and fading.

My chest tightens, the pain sharp and raw as if the years since I last saw him have dissolved, leaving only the fresh ache of loss.

I force myself forward, each step feeling as though I'm wading through thick mud. My feet shuffle across the dirt floor, hesitant. His eyes flicker open as I kneel beside him. They are dull with exhaustion, but behind the weariness, there is still a glimmer of love—a depth of feeling that reaches across the distance of time and suffering. His breath comes in shallow gasps, each one a fight, and I take his hand in mine. His fingers are limp, his grip barely there, but I cling to him, needing to hold on to what little remains.

"Tariro," he whispers, his voice rasping like wind through dry leaves.

"I'm here, Baba," I reply, my voice trembling as I fight to keep it steady.

He watches me with an intensity that cuts deep, piercing through the fragile walls I've built around my heart. "You must stop coming here," he says softly, the words barely audible yet filled with a quiet strength. "It is not good for you."

I swallow back the tears burning at the corners of my eyes. "I know," I say, my voice thin and brittle.

His chest heaves with the effort of speaking, but he persists despite the exhaustion dragging him down. "I am with her, where we all belong." He pauses, his eyes searching mine. "But *you,* Tariro... you're running. You keep looking for me here. She needs to be acknowledged. And you... you need to find peace."

The dam breaks. Tears spill over, blurring everything. "I don't know if I can," I choke out, the words raw in my throat.

His hand, weak and trembling, gives the faintest squeeze. "You must," he whispers, "She is part of you. You must find a way... to make peace with her—she forgives you."

I nod, though his words crush me. The tears fall unchecked, sliding down my cheeks. I sit by his side, his hand still in mine, as time seems to stretch and warp around us. The hut, the village, the world outside—everything fades. It is just the two of us, suspended in this moment of shared grief and love. His breath grows more labored, each exhale a struggle, but I hold on, unwilling to let go.

"Don't come here again," he gasps, his voice barely more than a whisper. "Do you understand?"

I nod again, my throat tight, my hands shaking as I wipe away the tears with the back of my hand. I try to find the words, but they stick in my throat, tangled with the weight of everything unsaid.

His grip on my arm weakens, and I feel the last remnants of his strength slip away as if the very essence of life is draining from him. His eyes close slowly, surrendering to a profound stillness that envelops him completely. I know in that instant—he is gone.

"I hope this grief has not misled me, Baba," I whisper, my voice cracking under the burden of uncertainty and sorrow. "I hope I've made the right decisions."

In my dream, the hut around me begins to dissolve, the vibrant colors of Nakuru's past fading into a haunting silence. The once lively sounds of the village are replaced by a suffocating quiet, leaving me enveloped in shadows. I wonder if this is all she has ever known—just shadows, lingering in a world stripped of light and life.

"I am sorry," I whisper.

Chapter 30

There's a fire in me that refuses to be snuffed out. It burns hotter than the fear creeping at the edges of my mind, pushing me forward with unwavering resolve. We are standing on the precipice of danger, but there's no turning back now. We will find Six, and we will bring her home.

Osi arrives, his presence solidifying the air of urgency around us. "What about the others?" he asks, his voice low but firm as he turns toward Sparrow. His expression is grim, the unspoken loss already felt in the tightness of his jaw.

Sparrow's face hardens, his eyes dark with the knowledge he carries. "I've sent the birds," he replies, his voice barely more than a murmur, yet steady with the finality of it. "All three bodies have been accounted for."

For a moment, a flicker of grief crosses Osi's face, a quick flash of sorrow that lingers in the air between us like a shadow. But there's no time to give it space. No time to let the sadness root itself. The flicker fades as quickly as it comes, replaced by the hard edge of focus. There will be time for mourning later—if we survive.

Sparrow's birds return, their wings slicing through the dark like whispers, slipping back to him as if drawn by some invisible thread. He kneels and draws out the map before us on the dirt. His voice is calm and precise. "Each watchtower has two guards. They're not particularly vigilant, but their placements cover the crucial entry points."

He turns toward one of the birds and the creature flits toward me. The same bird had frequently visited me in the garden, a silent companion during my moments of solitude. I wonder if it was Six who'd asked Sparrow to keep an eye on me. Or perhaps it was simply a shared connection, a mutual enjoyment of each other's presence.

His finger traces a path on the map. "The bird will lead you," he says, gesturing to a hidden route. "Neutralize the guards here." He taps the dirt map precisely. "If you can handle them quietly, no alarms will be raised." The finger shifts to a point within the dense woods. "From here, you'll have cover. The trees and the ropes from the east shelter will shield you. It's a blind spot—perfect for concealment." He continues. "Once the tower is clear, I'll take over and monitor the communications. If anything comes through, I'll keep up the illusion."

Amani steps forward, every inch of him radiating purpose and precision. His eyes are sharp, and unflinching, as he looks over us with quiet authority. "Alright. We move fast," he says, his voice calm but laden with intensity, "quiet, and with no mistakes."

The finality of his words sinks into the group like a shared breath. We know the stakes. We know what failure would mean. There's no room for error, no room for hesitation. Without another word, we begin.

The plan is simple, but the weight and fear are still crippling. The wind stirs the trees as I exhale slowly, trying to release the tension, but it persists. Above us, a bird flits through the treetops, a ghostly shadow leading the way. Its wings beat in near silence, blending with the soft rustle of the forest as we follow, every muscle primed for what's to come.

The outpost is near now, with its rough-hewn structures huddled together like animals seeking warmth. As we approach, the soldiers' murmurs become clearer—a casual mix of laughter and idle talk that feels out of place against the tension thrumming through my veins. The bird leads us to the edge of the clearing. Osi signals for us to halt, his sharp gaze sweeping the compound. His hand raises, two fingers indicating the guards' positions and the way they patrol in slow, predictable loops.

We advance quietly, moving low through the dense underbrush. Every step is precise, each breath measured. Ahead, the nearest shelter comes into view—a decrepit structure, its wooden supports overgrown with vines, reclaimed by nature. We slip silently along its edge, our bodies pressed low against the ground, hidden within the dense foliage. The guards' voices grow louder, their careless chatter drifting lazily through the air. They're completely unaware of us, and their ignorance is our greatest advantage.

The first watchtower comes into view. We slow our pace, measuring our steps as we close in. My heart pounds in my chest as I see them—two soldiers slouched beneath a flickering lantern. The weak glow casts long shadows across their faces, their posture relaxed, and they are more interested in their idle conversation than the responsibilities of their post. The lantern swings gently in the breeze, casting fleeting glimmers of light on the surrounding darkness, the soldiers' shadows swaying as if they're already being swallowed by the night.

"We need to take them out simultaneously," Osi whispers, his voice tight and urgent. "No alarms."

Amani nods, his expression set with determination. "I'll circle around," he whispers back, his voice barely audible. He slips away like a shadow, his form disappearing into the blackness. Every movement is deliberate, and fluid, as if he's one with the darkness itself.

I exhale slowly, steadying myself, feeling the familiar thrum of my blood magic awaken beneath my skin. It hums quietly, a dark promise stirring in the pit of my stomach, eager to be unleashed. I focus on the soldiers, their unsuspecting forms illuminated in the faint light of the lantern. Slowly, I attune my senses to their heartbeat, the rhythmic pulse of life flowing through their veins. The magic inside me coils, waiting. I reach out with it, invisible tendrils slipping effortlessly into their bodies, connecting me to their very essence.

I can feel their confusion first—a slight unease, like a chill brushing against their skin, but it's too subtle for them to react. Then, as the magic wraps tighter around them, their breath hitches. Panic flickers in their minds, but it's already too late. Their muscles seize, their throats constrict, and their eyes widen as they struggle to comprehend what's happening. I tighten my grip, and their bodies go limp, slumping in their chairs without a sound. The lantern flickers once more, casting fleeting shadows over their still forms. Silence follows—deep, unbroken silence.

I release the breath I've been holding, my pulse steadying as the magic recedes. It's done. No sound, no struggle—just darkness.

Across the clearing, Amani strikes with lethal grace. His dagger glints like silver under the faint lantern light, a flash of metal followed by the swift fall of two more soldiers. The blade slides through flesh as if slicing through air, precise and deadly. Blood pools at his feet, seeping into the earth, but no one notices. No one sees.

We move toward the nearest watchtower, our footsteps silent against the damp ground. My magic surges again, wrapping around the guards perched above. I can feel their hearts hammering in their chests, their pulses like drums in the quiet night. With a simple, silent command, I tighten my hold. Their bodies seize, a final spasm of fear before their minds slip into oblivion. They collapse against the railings, their limbs lifeless, and the soft thud of their fall is swallowed by the night.

With the watchtower secured, I glance toward Amani and Osi. They move toward me, their faces set in grim determination. Amani gestures to the largest structure at the heart of the compound, his voice low and steady. "That's where they'll be holding her," he says, his eyes gleaming with resolve. "It's the most fortified."

We advance through the outpost's central courtyard, slipping between the structures and approaching the central building, where we suspect Six might be held. The shadows cloak us, and the soldiers, lulled by a false sense of security, are our only obstacles. Osi and Amani dispatch soldiers with swift, brutal efficiency, extinguishing their lives without sound.

Ahead, another pair of guards stand at the entrance, relaxed and unaware of the danger creeping closer. Amani makes the first move, his dagger plunging into the nearest guard's side, the man's eyes widening in shock before he slumps to the ground. Osi follows seamlessly, dispatching the second guard with a brutal twist of his neck. The soldiers crumple to the ground, their lives snuffed out before they can raise the alarm.

I extend my senses, letting my magic flow out like tendrils, brushing against the flickering energies of life in the building.

CHAPTER 30

The guards inside are faint, barely noticeable, their presence dimming like dying embers. I sense the final flicker of life snuffed out before Amani peers through a small window, his brow furrowed in concentration. With a quick, reassuring nod, he signals that the way is clear.

We slip through the door carefully, the click of the latch as quiet as a whisper. The room we enter is dimly lit, its sparse furnishings giving it an almost desolate feel. A few scattered tables and chairs bear the marks of use, and the scent of stale air lingers. It feels more like a place where plans were hatched than a holding cell. Amani motions toward a back door, and without a word, we follow, our movements sharp and silent. Every second counts.

The narrow corridor ahead is dim, the walls lined with vines that twist and weave around the crude wooden structure. Four small wooden cells stretch along the passage, each one fortified with strong rope and reinforced with sturdy locks. Faint light seeps through their cracks and inside one of the cells, we hear the stir of movement—a figure shifting in the shadows, startled by the sound of our approach. Instinctively, they stand, their posture tense, preparing for the worst.

Osi and Amani move swiftly to the locks. They twist and pry, unscrewing and beating the stubborn metal loose with a focused urgency. Finally, the last lock gives a sharp snap, and the door creaks open. Inside, Six stands bathed in the dim light. Her eyes are wide, a mix of surprise and disbelief etched into her features, and then, the weight of recognition washes over her. Relief floods her gaze, softening the sharp lines of tension that have marred her expression.

Osi moves forward in a heartbeat, enveloping her in his arms. The embrace is fierce, and desperate, as though he's afraid she might disappear if he lets go. Six gasps, a wince of pain escaping her lips as her bruised body protests, but she clings to him just as tightly, her fingers curling into the fabric of his shirt as if grounding herself to this moment. Tears spill down her cheeks, carving paths through the dirt and grime, but she makes no effort to wipe them away. She buries her face in Osi's shoulder, her body trembling as the tension she's held onto for so long begins to unravel.

"I thought I'd lost you," Osi whispers, his voice thick with emotion. He pulls back just enough to meet her gaze, his eyes searching her face with quiet desperation. The bruises, the cuts—they tell the story of what she's endured, and the sight of it tightens something deep in his chest. "What did they do to you?"

Six shakes her head, her voice a rasp, fragile from disuse. "I'm okay now," she insists, though the strain in her voice betrays the truth.

Our eyes meet in the thick silence that stretches between us. So much unspoken. The last time we had been face-to-face, we were adversaries, caught in the undertow of opposing forces, pulling in different directions. Now, fate and survival have spun us together like threads of some unfinished tapestry much bigger than us, binding us in ways neither of us could have foreseen. At this moment, despite everything, we had each chosen the other. Six was right—our destinies were tangled, interwoven by something far more ancient than our own decisions. The spirits had led us here.

She breaks the silence first, her voice soft but piercing in its simplicity. "How's the little girl?" Her gaze drifts downward, lingering on my stomach, where new life grows, fragile yet determined.

I can't help but touch my belly, the motion is instinctive and protective. "Girl?" I ask, the word almost slipping away, quiet and uncertain.

Six nods, her expression softening with something close to peace, as if she's seen a future I can only dream of. "I can only hope," she murmurs.

A gentle smile breaks across my face, tentative yet hopeful. "I can only hope too."

The tenderness of the moment settles around us, thick as the night, but Amani's voice cuts through the haze of emotion, pulling us back to the urgency of our situation. "We need to get out of here," he says, his tone sharp but not unkind.

Six straightens, the pain in her body flickering briefly across her face before being swallowed by sheer will. I watch her push the agony aside, her determination a force that seems to reshape her entirely. And in that moment, a realization strikes me with such clarity, it feels like the ground beneath my feet has shifted.

We are no longer just fighting for survival. We are fighting for each other now.

Chapter 31

The small fire crackles softly, its warm light casting our faces in shifting shades of amber and gold. The low murmur of conversation hums around us, a comforting backdrop against the vast stillness of the forest. I am kneeling beside her, my focus on the rise and fall of her chest as she lies prone in the firelight, her body marked by the brutality of battle. Her muscles twitch involuntarily beneath the strain, delicate tremors betraying the immense effort she's putting into keeping herself still, holding on to her last threads of control.

I reach out, hovering my hands just above her battered form. My magic stirs beneath my skin, eager and alive. Slowly, I guide it forward, feeling the familiar warmth bloom in my fingertips before it flows into her. The initial contact is sharp, biting—her body tenses, and I hear the sharp intake of breath, the involuntary flinch as the magic threads its way through her, touching on the raw edges of pain. But then, as it settles deeper, it begins to soothe, to unwind the tension in her muscles, releasing her from the tightness that has gripped her body for hours.

My gaze moves across her form, tracing the contours of her lean, powerful frame, built not just for battle but for survival. Her strength is undeniable, even now as she lies beneath the weight of her injuries. But there's something else there too, something fragile beneath the layers of resilience and grit. Her skin bears the story of countless battles, not just from today but from long ago—faded scars crisscross her arms and shoulders, each one a mark of endurance, of survival. One particularly brutal scar runs diagonally from her left shoulder to her right hip, a deep groove that must have been inflicted by a strike meant to kill. The skin there is rougher, and slightly raised, a reminder of a wound that once came too close to taking her life.

The urge to reach out and trace the scar rises within me, to ask her what happened, but I resist. This moment feels too delicate, too charged with a vulnerability that neither of us is prepared to confront. Instead, I let the silence stretch between us, my magic continuing its quiet work, weaving through her body, knitting together what was broken.

"Six," I finally say, breaking the silence with a voice that feels fragile against the weight of the night. My heart quickens, the question that has been gnawing at me since the boat finally pushing its way to the surface. "There's something I need to ask you." I hesitate, gathering the courage to continue. "Why did you risk everything to save me on the boat?"

She doesn't respond immediately. Her eyes remain closed, her face resting over her folded arm. For a moment, I wonder if she's even going to answer, but then she takes a deep breath, her chest rising and falling with a slow, deliberate calm. "Honestly," she begins, her voice steady but carrying a weight of sincerity that tugs at something deep inside me, "it felt like a chance for a new life. For redemption."

"Redemption?" I repeat, my voice soft, almost as if the word itself might break under the weight of her confession.

She opens her eyes, meeting my gaze with a raw openness I hadn't expected. "I've done things," she says, her voice low and steady, but there's a tremor beneath the calm, a shadow of regret that flickers in her eyes. "Things I'm not proud of. Saving you... was selfish," she adds with a slight, self-deprecating laugh, "but it also felt like the right thing to do. Like maybe, if I could save you, I could save something in myself too."

Her words linger in the air between us. "Did it work?" I ask, my voice faltering slightly, unsure of the right thing to say.

She smiles faintly, a weary smile that doesn't quite reach her eyes. "A little bit," she says softly, her eyes fluttering closed once more.

I let the silence take over, giving her space, unsure whether to push further or let her rest. But before I can decide, she speaks again, her voice quieter, and more vulnerable than before. "I was pregnant... but I ended it." The words seem to weigh heavy on her, each one dragging itself out from a place of deep, unhealed pain. "The mistake wasn't the pregnancy itself—it was what I did… ending it."

Her confession drops between us like a stone into still water, sending ripples of quiet shock and sorrow through the space. I feel the weight of her words, the vulnerability she's laid bare, and the unspoken grief that lingers behind them. My heart clenches as I try to absorb it all, fumbling for the right words to offer her. "I'm so sorry," I whisper, my voice thick with empathy. It feels inadequate in the face of her pain, but it's all I can offer.

Suddenly, she rises, startling me, breaking the spell of the ritual. The effort is visible in every movement, her body stiff and slow, as if every shift costs her more than she has to give. She reaches for her shirt, and I instinctively avert my gaze, a flush of heat rising to my cheeks at the intimacy of the moment. Though she's still wearing a bra, there's something deeply personal about it, something that feels intrusive to witness. She slips the fabric over her head, her movements deliberate, almost ritualistic, as she adjusts the shirt. Her muscles ripple beneath the worn fabric.

"I couldn't bear the thought of letting another innocent child die," she confesses. "When we start to view death as just another cost of survival or advance, we're no better than the ones perpetuating the violence. We become part of the cycle that's been tearing us apart."

I want to reach out, to offer some kind of comfort that goes beyond words, but the distance between us feels insurmountable—built on shared grief and regret, but also the walls we've each constructed to protect ourselves. I force myself to find the right words, feeling the burden of gratitude I never thought I'd have to express.

"I'm grateful," I begin, stumbling over the words, "not for your loss—no, of course not—but for how it reshaped you. Because of what you endured, my child is alive today."

For a moment, something shifts between us, a shared understanding that hovers in the space. Then she laughs softly, but it's the same hollow sound—self-deprecating, tinged with a bitterness that's all too familiar. "It was my mistake," she says, the laugh fading quickly, her voice dropping to a quieter, more resigned tone. She averts her gaze, as though feigning some sudden need to busy herself, her hands absently adjusting her shirt. "No one caused the suffering but me," she adds, as if she's trying to shrug off the weight of her own choices but failing.

I shake my head, stepping closer now, emboldened by something that feels like conviction. "It was a mistake that caused you pain, yes, but you took that pain, and you turned it into something else. You saved my child's life, Six. That's not something small—that's powerful."

The moment is long before her gaze meets mine, and the sadness in her eyes softens. Her hand rests gently on her knee, her fingers tracing invisible patterns as if she's trying to find her way through the past. "I'm sorry for everything, Gamu," she says quietly.

I shake my head again, standing as I do. The firelight casts long, wavering shadows behind me, flickering with a new sense of resolve. "Don't be," I reply, my voice carrying a newfound strength, one that feels like it's been forged in the crucible of everything we've endured. "Everything we've been through has led us to this moment. Now, it's time to set things right."

She searches my face, her brows furrowing with concern. There's something almost protective in the way she watches me. "Alone?"

I take a deep breath and say, "I'm not alone. I have the strength of my lineage, a heritage that has survived every trial thrown its way. Those who came before me are with me." Her amused smile sends a ripple of warmth through me, and I feel my cheeks flush despite the gravity of our conversation. The amusement in her eyes only deepens as she watches me stumble through my words. "I mean, Shiwo has already gone ahead to warn them. Ndambira is leading his campaign as we speak. This is the moment that could define us both—Mvure and Nakuru." My voice softens, filled with reflection as I speak the words that have been stirring within me. "A tree, in its magnificence, is not an end in itself but a source of sustenance and beauty for all who come near."

She laughs, and it surprises me—a sound I'm hearing for the first time. It's genuine, almost child-like, light, and airy in a way that feels completely out of place given that she's, well, *Six*. "Shiwo is not exactly a fighter," she says, her tone

CHAPTER 31

carrying that gentle, teasing note.

The corners of her eyes crinkle with amusement, and I feel my cheeks heat up even more, a warmth rising inside me that I can't seem to control. I'm terrified—terrified of doing anything to ruin this moment, to break this fragile connection we've somehow found ourselves in. I ruin everything, I think, the familiar doubt gnawing at me, but please, not this.

"I know," I admit softly. My voice is quieter, too afraid to shatter the moment with too much intensity. "But I'm going to set things right." I glance away for a second, gathering the courage to say the rest, feeling the weight of everything I've been carrying. "People are suffering, and I can't just stand by. Not anymore."

She rises then, and when our eyes meet, the warmth and amusement vanish, replaced by a fierce intensity that holds me in place. "My real name is Tariro Munashe."

I blink, not quite sure how to respond. "Tariro is a boy's name," I blurt out, caught off guard.

She smiles as she shrugs her shoulders. "It is," but her gaze sharpens once more, and the weight of her words pulls the atmosphere back into focus. "My father came to Nakuru driven by his love for my mother, an outsider, and Mvure wronged her deeply." Her voice deepens, growing strong and unshaken. "And I will go with you, Gamu."

Her words settle over me like an anchor, grounding me in a way I hadn't expected, and for a moment, I feel overwhelmed. My hands, which had been limp and uncertain at my sides, slowly curl into fists. But this time, it's not out of fear or tension. It's out of purpose. I meet her gaze with equal determination, a new fire burning in my chest. The bond between us feels stronger now, like our fates have become inextricably intertwined.

"I am honored," I say, my voice carrying the sincerity of my heart.

Chapter 32

Osi, Sparrow, and Amani have stayed behind, seizing the slim window of opportunity to fortify our position while Ndambira's forces are drawn thin. The days ahead loom heavy with uncertainty, every move is fraught with danger. Securing safe passage for the people of Mvure now feels like our most urgent task. Amani, slipping once more into his role as one of Ndambira's commanders, is planning to free some of the boys from the mine, rallying them to our side. It's a risky maneuver, but one we desperately need.

Meanwhile, Six and I cut across the moonlit waters, the boat gliding smoothly through the night. The silver glow of the moon casts a path before us, turning the river into a gleaming ribbon that stretches endlessly ahead. I clutch the edge of the boat, my fingers curling around the rough wood, the weight of the journey pressing against my chest. My thoughts drift to Shiwo—my promise to her.

There is no room for hesitation or fear. The path has been set, and we have no choice but to follow it. This voyage represents my return to Mvure for the first time since I fled—

a return fraught with a whirlwind of emotions. Each wave that gently slaps against the hull seems to echo the memories of my departure and the fragile hope of reconciliation. Yet a more somber realization settles in: the truth behind Mvure's seemingly blissful facade and the shadowy secrets that lie beneath it, hinting at the trials and revelations that await.

Chapter 33

Part Two.

As dawn approaches, our boat silently maneuvers through the winding river. The narrow waterway, veiled in mist, snakes through dense foliage. This hidden route, untouched by Ndambira's larger forces, has become our lifeline - a secret passage known only to those who understand the land's deeper veins.

I turn to Six, my concern threaded with curiosity. "What do you know of the powerful magic that Ndambira seeks in Mvure? The serpent spirit."

Her eyes shift to the thick jungle closing in on either side of us, her expression clouding with a mixture of apprehension and reverence. "Mvure's strength lies in its pact with Nyoka, the serpent spirit," she begins, her voice low, almost as if she fears the spirit might be listening. "They say the island's protection, its veil of seclusion, is tied to Nyoka's power. It's an ancient agreement, one rooted in necessity."

The words send a chill through me, the name *Nyoka* pulling

something dark and primal from the recesses of my memory. "Nyoka?" I whisper, the word feeling heavy on my tongue, like a forgotten curse.

"My father told me stories of Nyoka long before I ever heard the name Ndambira," Six continues, her gaze distant, lost in the past. "He spoke of a serpent-like spirit born from the depths of the sea, summoned when Mvure was at its most desperate. Back then, the village was under constant threat—pirates, rival clans, and nature itself seemed bent on tearing it apart. So the elders, in their fear, called upon Nyoka. They made a deal: protection in exchange for something precious, something irreplaceable."

I pause, my mind racing to piece together the fragments of her tale. "What did they offer in return?" My voice is barely audible over the soft splashing of water.

Her brow furrows, "I don't know the full truth," she admits. "All I know is that what they offered wasn't just a material treasure. It was something of immense value—something that went beyond gold or land."

I feel a tight unease in my chest, heavier than the mist clinging to the boat. What could be more valuable than land, wealth, or power? Could it be that Mvure—this place I thought I knew—had hidden such dark secrets right under my nose? The realization washes over me like a cold wave, bringing with it a deep, sinking dread. How could I have been so blind?

CHAPTER 33

The river winds once more, twisting and coiling through the fog. Six's hands grip the wooden oars tightly as she guides us through the dense mist. The oars dip into the water with rhythmic splashes, propelling us forward with a steady, almost meditative cadence. I, however, sit in silence, the weight of our thoughts pulling us deeper into the unknown. As we approach the mouth of the river, the mist begins to part, slowly lifting like a veil to reveal the rugged coastline of Mvure. The island, once a distant shadow, now emerges in sharp relief against the soft hues of the rising sun. Dense palm trees tower above us, their silhouettes standing tall and unmoving, while the fringes of the forest appear lush and impenetrable, holding secrets within their depths.

Our boat edges closer to the dock, a modest wooden structure bathed in the golden morning light. The scene is almost surreal—peaceful, tranquil, untouched by the chaos we expected. The air feels unnaturally calm, a stillness that hangs heavily in the atmosphere, making me question the reality of the moment. It's as if the island exists in its own world, separate from the conflict that looms on the horizon. Villagers move about with an almost unsettling serenity. Fishermen tend to their boats, children chase one another in playful abandon, and vendors begin setting up their stalls, all in a peaceful, almost idyllic manner that feels out of place.

As the boat gently nudges the dock, my heart pounds heavily in my chest. I take a deep breath to steady myself. I've brought Six here, and there's no room for hesitation or doubt now. The moment for second-guessing has passed; fear and dread are no longer options. This is it – the point of no return. The worn wood creaks beneath me as I step onto it.

I had hoped for anonymity, but it hasn't been very long since I left, and I was already becoming a woman then. It doesn't take much for the unease to ripple through the silence. Heads turn slowly, and the familiar hum of the village falters, replaced by a palpable tension. Whispering begins, growing in intensity as people recognize me. Their eyes widen with a mixture of disbelief and awe, their expressions shifting from casual indifference to stunned recognition. They hesitate, their steps faltering as they keep their distance, unsure if the figure before them is truly their long-lost princess. No one speaks, yet the silence brims with unspoken questions, a collective wariness that hangs between us like a wall. I can feel their eyes on me, their collective gaze a heavy weight pressing down on my shoulders, and suddenly the quiet stretches too long, too thin.

Six glances my way, her sharp gaze flitting between the villagers and the overgrown path ahead of us. Her voice is low and cautious. "Do you think Ndambira's forces have been delayed?"

I steady my nerves under the weight of their uncertain gazes. "Perhaps," I reply, injecting a note of calm into my voice. "I suppose we'll find out soon enough. Let's go and look for my mother and Shiwo."

Together, we walk along the narrow, winding trail away from the dock. The river has led us to a secluded inlet, and we must navigate through hidden trails to reach the heart of Mvure. The forest surrounds us, with its dense canopy casting shifting shadows on the narrow path. The trail is overgrown and tangled; each step crunches softly on the forest floor, a sound that seems louder in the stillness of the morning. The path twists and turns, leading us deeper into the island's heart, where the air grows thicker and the shadows longer. Six walks beside me, her presence steady, though I can sense the sharpness in her gaze as she scans the surroundings with habitual vigilance. I'm unsettled too, despite the forest being alive with the rustle of leaves and the occasional bird call. Under these familiar sounds, there's an underlying silence that creeps in, heavy and unnerving. The forest feels alive with something unspoken, and I can sense something stirring within the magic inside me, like a distant alarm. Branches seem to me to be twisting into dark, claw-like fingers that scrape the sky. Every step we take feels as though we're trespassing, the peacefulness we just witnessed clashing with the uneasy energy that clings to the forest like a shroud. I can't shake the feeling that something is terribly amiss.

After what feels like an eternity of pushing through tangled vines and thick undergrowth, we finally emerge into a clearing. The village of Mvure sprawls before us, bathed in the soft, golden light of dawn. Towering palm trees sway gently overhead, their leaves rustling in the breeze as the thatched roofs of huts glisten with fresh dew. The wooden structures, weathered by time and sea air, stand nestled among the dense foliage, their edges blurred by creeping vines and scattered wildflowers.

The village is slowly coming to life, the quiet hum of morning routines filling the air. Vendors are setting up their stalls, arranging fresh fruits, woven baskets, and handmade trinkets with the ease of long-practiced movements. Women sweep the well-trodden dirt paths, their brooms moving in unison as they exchange soft laughter and idle conversation. The scent of cooking fires mingles with the salty tang of the nearby sea and the earthy aroma of the damp ground beneath our feet. It's a scene of serene normality, untouched by the troubles beyond, as though time itself has slowed to a languid crawl here in the heart of Mvure.

But our relief is fleeting, a brief glimmer of peace shattered as we spot the distant shoreline. The docks, barely visible through the trees, are lined with soldiers—Ndambira's forces. They've secured the perimeter, their presence a dark blot on the otherwise tranquil landscape. But what strikes me most is this disconcerting normalcy of the village. Despite the looming threat, despite the soldiers lurking at the shore, there's no sign of alarm, no indication that the villagers are aware of the danger that creeps ever closer. The village seems frozen in a bubble, suspended in time, untouched. The laughter, the idle chatter, the calm preparation for another day—it all feels like a dream, a fragile illusion that could shatter at any moment.

Six steps closer to me, her brow furrowed in concern. "Do they not know?"

"This can't be right," I murmur, my eyes darting around in confusion. "How can everything seem so peaceful when the docks are under enemy control?"

"This must be some kind of spell," Six said, her eyes narrowing with suspicion. "Maybe it's an illusion or enchantment—the *veil*. They say the magic of Mvure hides the true state of the village from its inhabitants and outsiders. I've been here before, but there was never any danger to compare, and the villagers were never alarmed by outsiders. I assumed it was because they were innocent."

The truth continues to deepen, there is something profoundly dark and deceptive about Mvure. But another question lingers. "What were you doing in Mvure?" I recall her cruel words about my father's death and the underlying malice they carried.

Her response is almost wistful. "My father's home—his family. I was curious, but I never found any trace of him. Still, I enjoyed watching the children play and witnessing the life here, seeing how he grew up."

A shadow of unease settles in my heart. I hope she doesn't believe that anything malevolent was done to his family because of his actions. My family has led Mvure since its inception; to think they could be capable of such evil is a grim prospect I can hardly bear.

I gather my resolve, pushing forward with a renewed sense of urgency. "We need to get to the royal shelters," I say decisively. "That's where my mother—and," *hopefully* "Shiwo—will be."

As we move carefully through the narrow streets, every step feels increasingly surreal, as if we're walking through the remains of a dream. The villagers glance at us with a mixture of disbelief and awe, their eyes wide in recognition. However, instead of panicking or showing alarm, their expressions quickly shift from cautious curiosity to reverent acknowledgment, as if they're witnessing a figure from a legend coming to life. Despite our presence, their demeanor remains oddly placid, as if they've been conditioned to accept the extraordinary without question. They continue their tasks with an unsettling calmness, their hands working on tasks so familiar that they don't seem to fully grasp the gravity of our presence. The scene around us feels disjointed, like an illusion where reality and dream overlap.

The royal family's shelters loom before us, imposing and fortified, their wooden frames overgrown with thick, twisted vines that wrap around them like sinewy armor. The air crackles with tension here, the kind that precedes a storm. It's as though this place and the village we passed through are caught in two different worlds—one oblivious to the danger at its doorstep, the other bracing for a battle yet to begin. Reflecting on it now, it seems this has always been the case; as if my family *understands* danger.

As we approach the entrance, the guards' eyes snap at us, their stances stiffening with vigilance. I brace myself, preparing to explain our presence, my mind racing with how to demand entry without revealing too much. But before I can speak, my gaze locks on a figure just inside the gatehouse.

CHAPTER 33

My aunt.

Her posture is rigid, her hands gripping a scroll as if it anchors her in place. At first, she doesn't move, her eyes widening with shock as they take me in. The disbelief etched on her face is so profound; it's as if she's seen a ghost. Time stretches impossibly thin, and for a heartbeat, we are locked in this moment of stunned silence, the world around us holding its breath. Then, suddenly, the scroll slips from her fingers and hits the ground with a soft thud. It unfurls at her feet, the parchment flapping uselessly in the breeze. She doesn't even notice. Her composure shatters, and the elegant, restrained woman I've always known is nowhere to be seen. Instead, there is only raw, desperate urgency in her movements.

With a cry that catches in her throat, she rushes toward me, her steps quick and unsteady. Her usually graceful movements are replaced by something far more primal, driven by the need to reach me. There is no hesitation, no decorum—just the force of love and shock propelling her forward. She reaches me, and the embrace that follows is fierce, almost crushing; her arms wrap around me with a strength I didn't know she possessed. I sink into her embrace, feeling a rush of emotions swirl within me: relief, warmth, and a sense of home that I hadn't realized I'd been longing for until this very moment. I feel her tears against my skin as she pulls me closer, murmuring words I can barely make out through her sobs, but I don't need to understand them. Her presence, her love, is enough.

The guards exchange glances but say nothing, their alertness softening as they witness the reunion. She pulls back slightly, her face flushed, and tears streaked. She looks at me with a mixture of awe and relief, her eyes searching mine for the truth of my presence. "We thought we'd lost you forever," she says, her voice trembling. "But you've come back."

"I had to, *tete.* There is trouble. I sent a friend with a warning. Please, did you receive her message?" I ask, my voice urgent, the weight of what's coming pressing against my chest.

She nods, but her expression shifts slightly, a flicker of confusion crossing her features. "Gamuchirai, you're with child?" Her brows knit together as she studies me more closely, concern deepening the lines on her face.

Startled by her observation, I blurt out, "Did Shiwo tell you this?"

"No," she replies softly, shaking her head. "Have you forgotten me?" She seems offended. But then something more creeps behind her eyes—something she's not saying. She hesitates, a shadow of unease passing over her face, as if on the verge of revealing something critical but deciding against it.

Before she can say more, a voice from behind pulls me back, echoing through the space between us. "Gamuchirai?"

I make a sharp turn, my heart stuttering as I see my mother emerging from the inner part of the compound.

CHAPTER 33

Her eyes lock onto mine, and in that moment, the world around us seems to freeze. Her face is a mixture of disbelief and overwhelming relief, emotions playing across her features like the morning light breaking through a storm. "Gamuchirai," she repeats, her voice trembling with the force of emotions she's held at bay for far too long. Her wide eyes, filled with unshed tears, cling to me as if trying to piece together the reality of my presence.

My heart aches at the sight of her. A single, hesitant step carries me closer, but the sheer weight of this moment holds me still. She closes the distance between us, and the moment her arms wrap around me, I feel the dam break. We cling to each other in a desperate embrace, our tears mingling as years of separation and sorrow collapse into this single, bittersweet reunion.

"My daughter," she whispers against my ear, her voice ragged with emotion. "You've come back to us. I feared I'd never see you again." She pulls back just enough to cup my face in her hands, her touch both fragile and fierce. Tears pour down her cheeks, and though she tries to smile, the grief cuts through. Her lips tremble as she chokes on her words, her joy muted by sorrow. She glances upward, her gaze softening as she speaks to the one who is no longer here. "Anesu," she breathes my father's name like a prayer, "she has come back—she is here," her voice thick with the aching knowledge that he will never answer.

She looks back at me, and the pain in her eyes sharpens, her smile crumbling into a mask of regret. Her hands tremble against my skin as she whispers, "I am so sorry."

The grief I had been holding back crashes over me, uncontrollable, relentless. My sobs are violent, spilling out from a place so deep it feels bottomless. "I know, I know," I whisper through the tears, my voice breaking. "I'm sorry... I'm so sorry I wasn't there—I'm sorry I failed, I'm sorry it's—"

"Stop it, Gamuchirai!" Her hands remain gently on my face, her thumbs moving softly, futilely brushing away my tears. Her eyes brim with her own sorrow, but her voice is steady, trying to anchor me in the storm of my own emotions. "He was proud of you. He spoke of you all the time, right up to the end. He never held anger, only love and hope—for this moment, when you would return to us. It wasn't your fault. It was just his time."

I clutch her arms desperately as if holding her will keep me from drowning in all that I've lost. "I wish I could have been here," I whisper, my voice cracking with the weight of my regret. "I wish I could've said goodbye."

She shakes her head slowly, her eyes filled with sorrowful understanding. Then she pulls me in again, tighter this time as if trying to compress all the lost years into this single embrace. We hold each other for a long moment, the only sound between us is the shared quiet of grief and love. Finally, she releases me gently, her hands trailing down my arms before dropping to her sides.

Her attention shifts, her gaze falling on Six. Her expression softens, her grief giving way to something else—gratitude. "We owe you so much," she says quietly, her voice thick with sincerity.

Six meets her gaze with a calm, unreadable expression. "There's no debt," she replies, her tone edged with something like disdain but softened by exhaustion.

She nods, wiping away the last remnants of her tears, and turns to me once more. Her grip on my hand is firm, her resolve returning. "Come," she says, her voice regaining strength. "There's much to be done. We must prepare for what is to come."

As we follow her through the compound, the atmosphere around us shifts from the raw emotion of our reunion to something more urgent, more focused. Garden workers, once engrossed in their tasks, pause to watch us pass, their eyes full of curiosity. The entrance gives way to a grand space—vast, yet intimate. The high ceiling is crisscrossed with carved beams, and the soft light of oil lamps flickers across the wooden walls, illuminating symbols and artwork that pulse with the spirit of Mvure's deep history. The floor is a patchwork of woven mats, their rough, natural textures grounding the space with a warmth that feels both welcoming and distant, a connection to simpler times in the gathering storm.

The maids freeze in their tracks at the sight of us. They stand in hushed silence, eyes lowered but glancing sideways at us, their expressions a mix of reverence and unease. The air smells of incense and herbal remedies, familiar scents that wrap around me like an old blanket, pulling me back to my childhood days when such smells meant healing and safety. But now they hold a different weight—one steeped in uncertainty.

She leads us with purposeful steps into a secluded room at the far end of the hall. The atmosphere shifts as we enter. What little noise there was vanishes, replaced by a thick silence that fills the room. The people gathered here are not speaking, yet their bodies tell the story: a subtle slump of shoulders, downcast eyes, and hands fidgeting with unease. A palpable sense of resignation hangs in the air, heavy and oppressive.

My mother's presence demands attention, her urgency unmistakable, but it's my arrival that truly electrifies the room. Conversations that had been teetering on the edge of despair now fall away completely, replaced by wide-eyed stares and hushed disbelief. In the center of the room stands a large, oval wooden table, worn smooth by age and use. High-backed chairs encircle it like sentinels. The shift in the air is palpable—recognition spreads like wildfire through the room.

The gathered people, my family, react as if jolted awake. Faces mirror shock, joy, and disbelief, their movements hesitant, tentative, as though afraid that this moment might shatter like a delicate illusion. My nephew Taiwo is the first to move. He strides forward, his tall frame cutting through the stillness, his deep-set eyes locking onto mine, searching as if to confirm that what he sees is truly real. "Gamu," he says, his voice thick with emotion, the word carrying more weight than a simple greeting. It is a declaration of relief. His presence, so strong and grounded, wraps around me in a way that feels both steadying and overwhelming.

Sekuru Tiritese steps forward next, his eyes shining with unshed tears. "Mvure's daughter," he murmurs, his voice heavy with the weight of our shared loss. The air around him seems to hum with the unspoken—the absence of my father hangs between us, thick and oppressive. His hand reaches out, trembling slightly as it brushes my arm, and in that touch is everything: the grief we have carried, the acknowledgment of what has been taken from us.

Mwendo, another Sekuru, approaches as well, his demeanor calm and stoic as always, but his eyes reveal more. "You have grown, Mzukuru," he says, his voice deeper, his tone filled with a mixture of pride and sorrow. His hand settles gently on my shoulder, its warmth a grounding force. "We feared the worst," he adds, and though his words are simple, they linger in the air, thick with the weight of unspoken fears that have haunted us all. His eyes convey both relief and lingering sadness, as though my return has answered some questions but raised others.

Tete Mirembe and Tete Chipo are next, moving forward with open arms. Their embraces are warm and tight, filled with a mixture of greeting and comfort, their familiar scents and soft murmurs grounding me further. The years apart seem to vanish in their touch, though beneath the warmth lies an undercurrent of worry.

Nyasha stands back, watching from the edges of the room. Her arms are folded tightly across her chest, her sharp eyes scanning me with an intensity that feels almost clinical. Her face remains impassive, her lips pressed into a thin, skeptical line, but I know her well enough to recognize the flicker of disbelief in her gaze. There's no mistaking the fierce protectiveness in her posture—Nyasha has always been the one to guard the family with an intensity that borders on ferocity. Her mistrust now isn't personal—it's protective, a shield she has drawn around all of us, even against me.

Though I long to see my cousins, I know they would not be allowed in this room—not for discussions of this gravity. The absence of their familiar, joyful faces stings, but I understand the necessity. This meeting holds the weight of our future, and the decisions made today will shape the fate of Mvure.

In the far corner of the room, my Gogo, frail and bent with the years, struggles to rise from her chair with the help of her cane. Her eyes, milky with age, still manage to gleam with tears of joy at the sight of me. The deep lines etched into her face seem to soften, and a slow, tender smile unfolds across her lips. My mother, ever attentive, nudges me forward gently—a gesture of both support and reverence, ensuring that Gogo doesn't have to strain further.

I step closer, feeling the fragile, trembling hand of my grandmother reach up to touch my face. Her skin is warm against mine, a comforting reminder of the roots that still hold me. She smiles wider, revealing the sparse teeth that remain, and whispers my name, her voice barely more than a breath, trembling softly. I fight to hold back my tears as a single tear slips down her cheek, tracing a path along the age spots and moles that mark her weathered skin. I nod, the unspoken words between us carrying the depth of years and love.

"Come now—we are not prepared," my mother says, her voice soft but firm. She draws me gently toward the head of the table and gestures for me to sit beside her. It is the seat of the chiefess or the most senior family member, and her invitation carries with it an unspoken acknowledgment of the responsibility now placed on my shoulders.

As I move to sit, I glance toward Six, silently inviting her to join me at the table. She shakes her head firmly, choosing instead to position herself near the door. Her stance is that of a soldier, vigilant and protective, ever watchful. I nod at her, understanding her choice, and take my seat beside my mother, feeling the weight of the moment settle over me like a heavy cloak.

I lean in close to my mother, my voice barely more than a whisper. "Where is the friend I sent?"

Her eyes meet mine, a flicker of understanding and urgency crossing her features. She subtly gestures to my tete, who steps forward swiftly. My mother's whispered words are brief but clear, instructions flowing quietly between them.

My tete nods, her face tightening with purpose, and she moves toward Six. After exchanging a few hurried words, Six glances at me—a final, searching look—before following my aunt down the corridor, her figure disappearing into the dim light. The absence of Six fills me with unease, but there is no time to linger in that feeling.

She turns back to Taiwo, her tone taut with impatience. "Have the villagers been warned to stay away from the docks?"

Taiwo nods solemnly, his expression a reflection of the gravity that has seeped into every corner of the room. "Yes, ma," he replies, pausing to clear his throat, though the weight of his words already seems to choke the air. "They see the ships, the camps, but they don't recognize the danger. It's as if... they see nothing at all."

A ripple of unease spreads through the room like a chill wind, sending goosebumps along my skin. The reaction is swift and unmistakable—faces shifting in sudden fear and disbelief. A chorus of soft grumbles fills the space, low mutters of *"Haiwa kani!"* and *"Zvakaoma!"* spilling from their lips as heads shake in disbelief. Tongues click in disapproval—sharp, loud, and full of meaning. Anger smolders just beneath the surface, the reaction of those who feel they are unjustly victimized.

"We've told them the docks are off-limits," Taiwo continues, his voice straining to remain steady amid the growing dread. "We've claimed it's for festival preparations. They trust us, but…" He hesitates, "Something isn't right."

My Gogo's fragile voice, trembling and weathered with age, slices through the air with the force of a machete. A voice seldom heard yet carrying more power than any spoken command. "Is it not clear?" Her sudden zeal reminds me of the old woman from the village who I spoke rudely to, though the absence of teeth softens her words. "The veil is upon us! The legend we feared now stands before us, *just* as it always has."

Her words are a stone cast into a still pond, ripples spreading outward as they sink into the collective consciousness of the room. Gogo, always the silent observer, a figure who has lingered on the edges of action for years, suddenly steps into the spotlight.

The room is plunged into stunned silence. Eyes dart nervously from one person to the next, searching for meaning in the void left by her declaration. The truth she speaks appears to be unavoidable and inescapable. My mother, her usually stoic expression shaken, tightens her grip on the arms of her chair. Lines of tension harden her face, but behind them, I see the glint of something urgent—a resolve born from desperation.

"Gamu, my daughter," she says, her voice sharp but edged with worry. "Do you know anything more? Does this Ndambira have another plan, something we haven't uncovered?"

My mind races, pulling together the scattered pieces of knowledge, and threading them into a coherent answer. "Ndambira's hunger for power runs deeper than we've imagined," I say slowly, the realization forming with every word. "His interest in Mvure isn't just about conquest. He believes the magic here can amplify his strength, and give him an advantage that could extend his reach far beyond Nakuru. He's aware of the magic protecting Mvure and is actively seeking a way to dismantle it. His forces are testing our defenses, probing for weaknesses. He wants to neutralize our magic completely."

Her gaze sharpens, her lips pressed into a thin line. "He's playing a dangerous game," she mutters as if speaking to herself, "one that could unravel everything we've worked to preserve. If he gains control of Nyoka's power..." She doesn't finish the thought, but the implications are out in the open.

The name Nyoka lingers like a specter, its shadow dark and looming. The very sound of it seems to tighten the walls of the room, the space around me feeling smaller, more oppressive. My frustration surges, boiling over into anger that bubbles in my chest like a rising tide. I stand abruptly, my chair scraping harshly against the floor.

My voice rises, sharp and demanding. "What's really happening here?" Each word is taut with frustration. "I sent my warning to give us the upper hand, but all I hear is fear! Rumors said Mvure held magic as its strength, but I never believed it—refused to believe it." I laugh, the sound

CHAPTER 33

harsh, mocking, incredulous. "And now, you are speaking of it so casually in *my* presence, to say the least." Again, the harsh, mocking laugh, as though my mind is unraveled. "But instead of power, all I see is fear and dread. Why does it feel like we're the ones being hunted?"

The air shifts in the room—small movements, the tension crackling like dry leaves about to catch fire. Faces that once exuded quiet confidence now falter, unease rippling across them. My heart races, but not from fear. It's a fierce, simmering determination—an urgency for truth. I didn't come back for whispers and half-answers. I came back for clarity, for the raw, unfiltered reality of whatever they've been hiding from me.

"Will you remain silent, even now?" I press, the edge of frustration sharpening my words. "You speak of Nyoka as though it's a mere afterthought—yet, why was I kept in the dark about such crucial magic? Why wasn't I told? What *more* haven't you told me?"

Eyes flicker away from mine and a new sense of disdain takes root in my chest. The familial affection I once held has all but evaporated, leaving only a bitter realization that the people I once revered are now tainted in my eyes, reduced to something unclean and insidious.

My mother's gaze softens, but there is no warmth there, only the weariness of someone who has carried a burden too long. Her voice, when it comes, is quiet but heavy. "We didn't want to burden you, Gamu. You weren't ready for the responsibility that comes with the knowledge of Nyoka's power. The magic that protects Mvure is not just a secret—it's a pact, a delicate balance between the village and the forces that guard it. To maintain that balance... sacrifices must be made."

I cannot let assumptions fill the void. "What kind of sacrifices?" I demand, my voice firm and resolute. The darkness will not be vanquished by half-truths. If we are to confront this evil, every truth must be spoken aloud.

"Blood, Gamu," she whispers, her voice faltering and gaze faltering. "A firstborn son from our family."

I struggle to keep my composure, but the betrayal and horror writ large on my face are unavoidable. "And you *kept* this secret from everyone?" I ask, my voice trembling with a mixture of outrage and disbelief. "While pretending everything was fine? How could you do this? Do you understand how *despicable,* how *evil* this is?"

Her eyes brim with deep, haunted regret, and her voice hardens, defensive yet filled with sorrow. "This was never our choice! This curse—this burden—was inherited, passed down through blood, bound to us by a pact our ancestors made in their darkest hour. They forged a desperate bond with the serpent, and ever since our family has carried this terrible obligation. The curse binds the leaders of Mvure, a chain of servitude stretching back long before any of us were born. We tried to break free of it, to defy its demands, hoping that the legend of its power would be enough to shield us from harm. But now... now it seems the serpent stirs once more." She gestures towards my Gogo, her voice trembling. "Ambuya vako—*your Gogo,* has never sacrificed a child in her long life, and many believed that the serpent had faded into mere myth. But this new threat... perhaps it has woken it from its slumber. Or perhaps it was never truly dormant, only waiting, biding its time."

I can feel the gravity of what she's saying pulling me under. Anger and betrayal war with the deep sense of responsibility now gnawing at my soul. This curse—this dark pact—has defined not just our family, but our entire village, and it has shaped every decision made in Mvure for generations. I had always believed we were free, that we were powerful in our own right. But now I see the truth, or at least a glimpse of it—the power we thought we wielded was never truly ours. It came at a cost, and we've been paying it with our lives, our secrets, and our silence.

Suddenly, a strange sensation grips me, and the edges of the room blur, the voices of my family fading into the background. My vision darkens as whispers unfurl in the recesses of my mind, pulling me into a world beyond the physical. The shadows around me deepen, and then, from within the darkness, something stirs. The murky haze shifts and thickens, like fog rolling in over still water, and from its depths, the serpent emerges. Its scales glisten like wet stone, shimmering with an eerie, otherworldly light. Its eyes glow with a malevolent intelligence, sharp and unblinking, and I can feel its gaze piercing through me. The serpent coils sinuously, its massive body winding in and out of the shadows, encircling our village. Its presence is oppressive, ancient, and powerful, and as it moves, the darkness grows thicker, spreading like an ominous veil over everything I hold dear. The serpent seems to devour the light itself, casting long shadows over our homes, our people—our future.

My heart pounds in my chest as I watch the serpent's movements, entranced and horrified. Its power is undeniable, but so is its hunger. It moves with an eerie grace, coiling around the shadows of my mind like a predator biding its time. This is no protector—it's a force that thrives on sacrifice, a darkness that feeds on fear. The whispers that once swirled murkily now grow louder and more urgent. Suddenly, Ndambira appears before me. His eyes are glazed, vacant, as though his soul has been swallowed whole by some unseen force. He stands frozen, a puppet on strings, his will twisted and bent to the serpent's dark desires. The massive creature wraps itself around him, its energy twisting through him like a parasite, siphoning his very essence. The scene is horrifying, yet in that moment, the truth becomes all too clear—Ndambira is not the mastermind of this nightmare. He is merely a pawn, a vessel manipulated by the serpent's influence. It seized on his ambition, his hunger for power, whispering dark promises into his dreams, shaping his every move to serve its own ends.

And all the while, the serpent has been *watching me too.* I can feel its eyes on me, slithering through my thoughts, through the very fabric of my being. Its attention is unnervingly sharp as if it has been biding its time, waiting for my return.

CHAPTER 33

And now, I understand the most chilling part of its scheme: it has been waiting for me, waiting for the one thing I will never give.

My child. The revelation steals every breath from my lungs. My body tenses, every muscle fighting the urge to cradle my belly protectively.

Is my child what the serpent truly seeks? A male, born into the line of Mvure, destined to fulfill its ancient demand? The very thought sends a cold shudder through me. But as that revelation sinks in, so too does another, far more terrifying thought. Could my family—my own blood—truly allow this to happen? I think of their story of defiance, their claims of holding strong against the serpent's demands. But those were times of relative peace when the threat of war did not hang over our heads like a sword. Now, with Ndambira pressing on our borders, with the serpent awakening and its hunger gnawing at the edges of everything we hold dear, I fear their resolve may crumble. What if their commitment to resisting the serpent's demands is weaker than they've led me to believe? What if faced with the threat of annihilation, they would offer up my child—my innocent child—in a desperate bid to save themselves? *I must keep my knowledge to myself. Trust is a luxury I cannot afford.*

The vision fades, and with it, the voices retreat. I can still feel them echoing in the back of my mind, like a whispering wind that refuses to die. My heart pounds against my ribcage but I force myself to stay calm, to gather my thoughts before the panic overwhelms me. I acknowledge the whispers, pushing them to the recesses of my mind, trying to lock them away for now. I cannot allow myself to lose control, not here.

When I finally come back to myself, I realize that my mother is holding me, her hands firm around mine. I don't know how or when she reached me, but her touch is grounding, even if only for a fleeting moment. Her eyes, filled with concern, search my face. She's waiting for an answer.

"Are you alright?" she asked softly, her voice fragile with worry.

I nod, swallowing down the fear, trying to make my voice steady. "Is it only firstborn sons who are targeted?" I push the words past the tightness in my throat.

The room falls deathly silent. My mother looks taken aback by the directness of my question, her lips parting slightly in surprise. She hesitates, her gaze flickering to the elders, seeking some form of silent consensus. Sekuru Tiritese, with his weathered face and deep-set eyes, clears his throat.

"Yes," he begins slowly, his words measured, "the serpent's hunger is for firstborn sons. It is the nature of the pact—blood for protection, and the serpent demands the purest blood of the line to satisfy its appetite."

Taiwo adds his voice, steady but somber. "Its logic is steeped in ancient beliefs about lineage and power. The firstborn represents the continuation of the family line and the strength of our bloodline. To the serpent, this makes the firstborn the most valuable offering."

The knot in my stomach tightens, a cold, unrelenting twist of dread, but I keep my face impassive, my expression unreadable. I can't afford to betray the terror seizing me from within, can't allow them to see the cracks forming beneath my calm exterior. Inside, I'm trembling, my mind spinning with the gravity of what's at stake.

"Then we're all agreed," I say, my voice sharp with conviction, forcing strength into the words. "None of us want our children condemned to such a cruel fate, no matter what the future demands of us."

The room shifts like dry leaves rustling in the wind, eyes flicking toward Tete Mirembe and Nyasha. Their faces are etched with a mixture of dread and reluctant acceptance, the kind that settles deep into your bones when the inevitable is staring you in the face. Tete Mirembe's mask of composure finally cracks, and I can see the weight of her decision pressing down on her like a boulder she can barely carry.

Her voice trembles, quivering on the edge of her shame and regret. "I... I'm so sorry," she chokes, her words barely a whisper at first. "I've already sent Tafa away... from Mvure." The admission sinks, "he left for the north docks before dawn." Her voice cracks, unraveling as she presses on. "I knew this moment might come... I couldn't bear the thought of him being chosen for sacrifice. I had to protect him... even if it meant sending him away."

The room stills, a collective intake of breath and Tete's hands tremble at her sides. As I study the loyal and defiant Nyasha beside her more closely, my gaze falls on the subtle curve of her abdomen, unmistakably revealing her pregnancy. A chill runs through me as I contemplate the grim possibility that her child might be a boy. But even if it isn't, the nature of evil spirits means that no compromise is ever truly out of reach.

I glance at Sekuru Mwendo, whose jaw tightens, his eyes narrowing into slits of barely controlled fury. He steps forward, his hand lashing out to grip Tete Mirembe's arm with brutal force. "You sent him away without telling us?" His voice cuts through the air like a whip, harsh and biting.

Tete Mirembe flinches visibly, her body recoiling from the pain of his grip. Her body shrinks away, instinctively curling into herself as though to make herself smaller, to lessen the blow. Nyasha flinches as well, her reaction immediate and familiar—like a child used to violence, her shoulders hunch as if bracing for a blow that might come at any moment. The sound of it—a collective gasp—ripples through the room, echoing in the stunned silence. Chairs scrape against the floor as others rise to their feet, torn between shock and action, unsure whether to intervene or avert their eyes as they've done countless times before. It's no secret that my Sekuru Mwendo has been beating my tete for as long as they've been together. The rumors have always been there, hushed whispers behind closed doors, stories shared in quiet corners. And Nyasha—Nyasha has borne her own share of that cruelty. She has tried to intervene, to protect her mother, but it always ends the same way: Nyasha caught in the crossfire, enduring the same blows meant for her mother. It is a truth everyone knows but no one speaks of. No one has ever done anything to stop it.

My heart hammers in my chest, a fierce pulse of anger rising inside me. "Sekuru, enough!" My voice breaks through the charged air, louder than I've ever let it be before. It cuts across the tension, sharp and clear, demanding to be heard. Everyone in the room freezes, their eyes snapping toward me.

I surge forward, every muscle tense with the need to intervene. "This is not the way, Sekuru! Do you think this is strength? Do you think this earns you respect? There's no honor in hurting the very people you're supposed to protect! Your anger," I continue, my voice rising with conviction, "means *nothing* here. There will be no more sacrifices, Sekuru! Even if Tafa were still present on this island, even if the serpent itself demanded it!"

He whirls on me, his eyes blazing with a fire I've never seen before, something fierce and dangerous. "Gamuchirai—who do you think you are?" he demands, "To dictate the terms of this matter? To interfere in my marriage? Who gave you the right to speak here?"

I lock eyes with him, my own gaze steely and unyielding. "With all due respect, sekuru, you are correct to address me by my full name. Yet it seems you have forgotten who I am. I am Gamuchirai Danai Darare, my father's—your brother's—

heir! My mother was his wife, and in her presence, her authority is secondary. Every choice made here falls under my final command. Or has our tradition changed in my absence?"

His face twists. "You will be silent!" His words drip with disdain, a sharp accusation meant to wound. "You abandon your land and your people, and now you come *to impose?*"

"I do not impose upon you; I uphold tradition!" I declare, my words ringing with a fierce authority, reverberating through the room like the toll of a great bell.

His breath is now heavy and uneven. But the fire in his gaze doesn't die; it simmers beneath the surface, tempered but not extinguished. "You dare to speak of tradition?" he sneers, but his voice wavers, a crack forming in his ironclad authority. "Tradition binds us all to this island, to the serpent's curse. You cannot defy that. No one can."

The truth ripples out of me. "Tradition *does not* bind us—it shapes us. But we are not slaves to it. We are its keepers, its protectors. I will not let the past dictate the fate of our children. The time for sacrifices is over. We must find another way. And I will ensure that we do."

Sekuru Tiritese steps in, his voice a blend of firmness and desperation. "Mwendo, we must listen to Gamuchirai. She speaks with the authority of tradition, which is not to be disregarded."

CHAPTER 33

Despite his intervention, Sekuru Mwendo's anger remains unabated, his defiance evident in every tense muscle of his body.

The very atmosphere around us seems to root itself in the force of my conviction, the ghosts of our ancestors standing with me. "Do you not understand why my father had no sons? Why our family is burdened with daughters alone?" My gaze pierces him, daring him to deny the truth. "The ancestors seek to end this cursed lineage. They refuse to bring more sons into this world—refuse to feed the serpent any longer!"

His eyes blaze with uncontrolled fury. "And who are you to presume to know the will of the ancestors?"

"I will no longer tolerate repeating myself," I snap, "My name is Gamuchirai Danai Darare. I am a voice, a conduit. I carry the will and the vision of all those before us. I have come to end this curse, and you would be wise to acknowledge my rightful place in our lineage and on the throne." I turn to my mother, my gaze piercing. "Will you challenge my claim? Will you stand against me? Let's settle this once and for all."

The room tightens like a constrictor, stretched to its limit with anticipation. My mother's eyes meet mine, sadness flickering in their depths—a quiet sorrow and *disappointment*. Her lips part, "No, your claim is true," she concedes, her tone like a whisper carried by the wind, reluctant but resolute.

I turn, my gaze hard and unforgiving, locking onto Sekuru

Mwendo. Every word I speak now feels as though it reverberates in the bones of this old house. "Release tete." The command leaves no room for hesitation, my voice is cold and unyielding, stripping away any pretense of negotiation.

For a brief moment, he hesitates. His jaw clenches, his grip still firm as if his stubborn pride might keep him rooted in this moment of defiance. But just as the tension threatens to snap, a voice—unexpected and potent—slices through the silence. My Gogo speaks, her voice strong, cutting through the air with the authority of a matriarch whose power has not diminished with age.

"Yield to your chiefess, Mwendo!" A mother's reprimand, disciplining her son as if he were still a child. The authority in her words is a reminder of the order he has forgotten, a call to obedience that even his pride cannot ignore.

The effect is instant. The room shifts around her, the energy recalibrating as though the center of gravity has moved. Reverence ripples outward, washing over us like a wave. At this moment, my Gogo is no longer frail and bent by the weight of time; she is a pillar, a monument of authority that still commands respect. Sekuru Mwendo's eyes flicker, his grip loosening as though it is no longer his decision to make. Slowly, with great reluctance, he lets Tete Mirembe go. She stumbles back, and Nyasha catches her, pulling her into a protective embrace.

She sobs, and everyone quietly settles back into their seats, their expressions heavy. The atmosphere grows almost reverent as it resumes its formality with a renewed sense of gravity.

"Tete Mirembe," I continue, "you did what was right. It is a blessing that there are no more sons to sacrifice."

"The darkness will not be vanquished by half-truths," my own words belittle me.

"It is time we cast aside this cursed legacy and forge a new path forward. I pause, letting my words settle. "We are depleted," I continue, "weakened by our own selfishness over centuries, and now we stand alone, with no allies to turn to. Yet I am here—not by choice, but because duty has called me. My duty now is to consult with our ancestors; they must guide us toward a better path."

My mother's voice wavers, her frustration blending with desperation. "Ancestors? You will consult them? Gamuchirai, this is not a game. Your imagination will not save us! Perhaps we should plead with the serpent, perform a ceremony—"

I cut her off. "The morning my father passed away," I begin, my voice steady despite the storm within. "Your final words to him were sharp and unforgiving. You cursed him for his inability to give you another child, lamenting the one son you had lost and the promise unfulfilled. On that cold dawn, you spat your venom and walked away, leaving him with your chilling words: if he were ever to find you dead, it would be his fault for failing you so miserably. Is this my imagination, mama?"

Her eyes widen with shock and defensiveness. "How could you know this?" She demands.

A wave of guilt washes over me, realizing these words are out of place. Yet, something beyond me has taken hold—an urgency that now speaks through me. "I am not here out of ambition or a hunger for power—" I reply firmly. "I am here because I have been called—to forge a new path forward. I am here because I am simply what *needs* to be done." This *calling* is not just a gift—it's a command to change everything, and my gaze sweeps across the room, daring anyone to challenge my conviction. "The past will no longer dictate our future. You speak of pleading with the darkness that has enslaved us, but I refuse—no more! How long will we live in fear, bowing to this curse? Our children will be free; this is the path I am forging. I will not raise a generation of beggars!"

The room continues in its heavy, subdued, silence—disbelief and shock etched on every face. Their stunned expressions only fuel the fire inside me. I meet their stares, the anger simmering just beneath my skin. "And what will you do in the meantime? You will carry on, won't you? As if nothing has changed, as if you're the cursed puppets beyond these walls—fishing, cooking, sweeping the pavements. All of them, so obedient, so small. Trapped in a life that isn't theirs."

Chapter 34

The meeting of the family council has ended, but the tension still lingers in the air like an unshakable fog. As I wait, I pace the room, my thoughts a whirlwind of plans and emotions, grappling with the weight of what has transpired. The door creaks open, and Six steps in, her presence a blend of strength and reassurance that nearly pulls me into her arms. Behind her, Shiwo follows, her eyes wide with a mix of anxiety and relief.

Without a word, we close the distance between us, and our arms envelop each other in a tight, heartfelt embrace.

"Sisi," *"Sister,"* Shiwo whispers, her voice trembling with emotion, "you made it."

I smile, the expression is bittersweet as I hold her close. "How have they treated you here?"

"They've treated me well," Shiwo replies, her voice soft but tinged with a hint of sadness. "Though I've been left alone since I arrived."

I gently cup her face, my voice lowering to a tender murmur. "It's alright. You're safe now. Have you been fed?"

She glances downward, her slight shake of the head betraying her discomfort. Anger flares within me at the thought of her being neglected. "How dare they!" I exclaim, taking her hand with renewed determination. "Come with me!"

But Shiwo stops me gently, her other hand resting on mine. "Please, I'm not hungry yet. I don't eat so early in the morning."

I study her for a moment, my frustration giving way to understanding. "But they should have offered you something."

She offers a small, reassuring smile, her eyes warm and calming. "It's alright. I'll be happy to eat with you and Six."

I squeeze her hands gently. "Alright then."

Six, who has been standing quietly by the door, steps forward. Her presence commands attention, her voice low but firm. "Gamu," she begins, "we need to discuss our next move. Ndambira won't wait long before he makes another attack."

I nod, reluctantly releasing Shiwo but keeping her close by my side. "Ndambira isn't acting on his own. He's a pawn, controlled by the serpent. His attacks on Mvure are driven by its command."

CHAPTER 34

Her brow furrows, her expression a blend of curiosity and concern. "That, uh—sounds crazy, but I believe you."

Taking a deep breath, I gather my thoughts, trying to calm the storm of fear and uncertainty brewing inside me. "Ndambira... he's just a pawn. The serpent is using him, pressuring us into fulfilling an ancient pact."

Six's eyes flicker with understanding. "Finally," she exhales, "They admitted it to you. There's no room for doubt now, Gamu."

I glance between her and Shiwo, my heart heavy. "Yes. Long ago, my family made a pact with Nyoka, a powerful serpent spirit—one steeped in darkness and greed. But those who came after refused to honor that pact," I pause, swallowing hard. "It required blood sacrifices—human sacrifices."

Shiwo gasps, her eyes widening in horror, her hand flying to her mouth as if trying to contain the shock. *"Human?"* she breathes, disbelief flooding her features.

I nod, and a cloud of doom and shame is already hanging over me, suffocating but I continue. *Truth, truth is what matters.* "Everything Ndambira is doing—it's the serpent's bidding. Forcing us to give it the blood we've withheld for generations." I lower my gaze, instinctively placing a protective hand over my belly. The unspoken fear grips me—what if my child is next?

Shiwo's breath catches in her throat, and suddenly she's

on her knees, her voice breaking as she pleads. "No!" Her trembling hands reach out toward me, desperation lining every word. "Gamu, this is my brother's child—it's all I have left of him. Please, don't let the serpent take my baby. You can't be so cruel. There must be another way. Please..." Her voice wavers, unraveling into sobs, her strength crumbling beneath the weight of this terrible truth.

"I would never, Shiwo" I reply firmly, my voice steady with determination. "I will not sacrifice my child—or anyone else."

Six's frown deepens, her anger simmering beneath her furrowed brow. I can see the way she swallows it down, how she attempts to stifle it, but it's too late. I've already seen it. Her eyes burn with something fierce and betrayed, and I know exactly what's triggered it—I hadn't told her about the baby. The fact that it belongs to Kail hangs between us, unspoken but heavy. *Have I finally ruined it?* The fragile relationship that had bloomed now feels shattered. I feared it all along—*I destroy everything I touch.* Now, she's reminded of what I truly am: a monster. How could she not be, knowing I killed the father of my own child? It's a secret that now follows us like a shadow, growing darker, and larger, demanding to be acknowledged.

But she doesn't even look at me. She just presses forward, her voice clipped and urgent. "Ndambira is here with most of his forces," she says, her tone hard. "We don't need to kill them all. If we eliminate him, we cut off the head of the snake that has enslaved Nakuru. We can defeat both."

CHAPTER 34

My heart pounds in my chest from the heartache, and the devastation of watching her slip away emotionally. It aches, this unspoken rift between us, but I force myself to focus on what's ahead.

"Merely killing Ndambira won't end the serpent's threat," I say, trying to temper her with caution. "The serpent doesn't rely on just one person. Killing him won't be enough. We need a deeper solution. And even if we could kill him," I pause, searching her eyes, "how do you suggest we do it? He's been invincible up to now, made even more powerful with the serpent's favor."

Six's face hardens even more, her face a mask of determination and frustration.

"We need to find a way to address both threats," I continue. "To understand why we have been brought here? Together." I say it attempting to reconcile the situation, futilely. "I am to consult with the ancestors. Hopefully, they will show us the way forward soon."

The door creaks open, and my mother steps into the room, her presence heavy with unspoken tension. Worry lines her face, but there's an edge of anger behind it, deep and cutting. The room seems to shrink as she stands there, waiting, her gaze sharp as steel. Shiwo and Six slip out silently, leaving the air thick with unresolved conflict.

"Gamuchirai," she starts, her voice taut and strained, like a string pulled to its breaking point. "You disappeared—

vanished without a word. And now you return, *pregnant—*" Her voice rises, filled with raw emotion, "—and you think you can just step back into this house, take command as if you never left? As if you are not a symbol of shame and dishonor! How can we—how can I—accept this so easily?"

Her words cut deep, like thorns pressing into old wounds. My mind reels. Tete Chipo told her. The truth about my pregnancy is out. My heart slams in my chest as panic flares. Who else will she tell? And then, a darker thought creeps in—how far will I go to keep this secret? Will I silence her? Is that who I've become? My skin crawls with the weight of the question, but I force it down. I must not let her see my fear, the storm brewing behind my eyes.

"This isn't about me," I say, trying to keep my voice steady, trying to suppress the rising dread. "It's about Mvure, about stopping the serpent's curse. The ancestors want us free—pregnancy doesn't strip me of that purpose."

Her gaze wavers for a moment, a flicker of hesitation crossing her face. But anger quickly replaces it, flashing hot in her eyes as her voice sharpens. "It was the ancestors who cursed us in the first place!" she hisses. "And now you expect us to trust them to save us? After all they've done?"

"They were once human, *Mama,*" I counter, my voice growing stronger despite the ache inside me. "They made sacrifices, just as we do now. But they didn't mean for us to be bound by their choices forever. We have the power to end this. We can change what they could not."

CHAPTER 34

"You think it's that simple?" she snaps, her tone cutting deep. "You think the ancestors care now, after all this time? Perhaps you never should have returned at all—maybe you should have stayed gone, you and that seed. They'll come for it, you know."

"Are you the one who will tell them?" I ask, my voice colder than I intended, the challenge clear in my words.

Her eyes flicker, a mix of disappointment and hurt flashing in them. She exhales sharply. "Of course not," she cuts back. "You are my daughter, Gamuchirai—how could you think I would betray you? Do you think so little of me?"

Her words sting, but there's something else beneath them—a tenderness I hadn't realized I longed for. I didn't know how much I needed her affection until I heard it, even wrapped in anger. My throat tightens.

"As for your tete," she continues, "she will remain silent. I have made sure of it. Regardless of what you may think, I've protected you. Even if you sought to hurt me and put me to shame in front of the entire family with your words." Her voice trembles slightly, pain evident in her eyes. "I loved your father—and weakness, it favors us all."

"I'm sorry, Mama," I whisper, my hands trembling as I speak. "And thank you." I swallow hard, forcing myself to confront the weight of my own choices—my words, and actions. "This child... it was a mistake," I say softly, shame creeping into my voice. "The father—he's dead."

Her face pales, and she steps closer, enveloping me in a tight hug. The warmth of her arms, the pressure of her embrace—it feels foreign. I stiffen, ashamed of what I've become, ashamed of the distance between us. "I'm so sorry, Gamuchirai," she murmurs, her voice filled with sorrow. Her scent is both comfort and a blade, wrapping around me with a warmth that threatens to draw out the tears I've fought to hold back. It's suffocating, like a knife pressed against my throat, demanding that I surrender to the grief.

But I recoil. I step back, my body retreating as though fleeing from the truth that her presence forces me to confront. She sees it—the way I shut down, how quickly I cast aside the unbearable weight of the loss I still can't face.

I pull myself together, straightening my spine, forcing the words to my lips. "I didn't come back for a throne," I say, the tremble in my voice barely contained. "The ancestors have guided me here—pushed me, even. Demanding that I come and face this." My voice hardens with conviction, though inside, I feel anything but steady. "I cannot deny it, Mama. I have to believe. We all have to believe. Fear can't dictate our future anymore."

The disbelief flickers in her eyes, clear as day. I've moved on from the subject of my child's dead father with a speed that shocks her, but not me, shutting out the reality of it as though it were a door I can lock behind me.

She stands there, watching me, her face carved in disbelief. Her hands move sharply, clapping together in a gesture that

CHAPTER 34

cuts through the room with a snap, like the breaking of brittle wood. Her eyes narrow, her mouth set in a line that barely contains her frustration. But she is my mother, and mothers know when to push and when to hold back—to bury things deep within, locking them away for another time, another conversation. She recognizes the barriers I've put up—the ones she, too, knows how to build.

So, she says nothing, but I can feel the weight of her judgment lingering between us, heavy and unspoken. "Fine," she concedes, lowering herself to my pitiful reality. "You say the ancestors speak to you? You speak of faith?" She scoffs, her expression hardening into something fierce and brittle. "Do you not see what we face? The threat is tangible—not hanging somewhere in the air with the whispers—it sits at our docks!" Her voice rises, each word punctuated by growing frustration—mocking me. "Our situation is dire! We cannot rely on vague promises or ancient voices. We need action now, not faith!"

"Action?" I laugh bitterly, my voice gaining strength as I meet her gaze. "The serpent's influence has left the villagers numb, complacent, and blind to the true danger. They lack the will to fight. Convince them of the threat, and then what? Will you face down their weapons with nothing but spears?"

Her lips press into a thin line, the pain behind her eyes visible, if only for a moment, her expression shifting to one of profound disappointment. "Are you mocking our ways, Gamuchirai? Kutambura kwedu hakubvi mukushaiwa kwemhirizhonga, asi kubva mukukudza kwatinoita rufu pacharo. Hupenyu hunofanirwa kuwanikwa zvakaoma, kwete kutorwa nyore—kutora kwahwo kunofanira kuve kwakarongwa uye kunzwisiswa. Panga—hatitsvaki kuenda kure nemutoro werufu, nokuti mutoro wekutakura, kwete kukunda kwekuzorora."—*"Our suffering does not stem from a lack of violence, but from the reverence we hold for death itself. A life must be hard-won not dealt with ease—its taking deliberate and felt. A spear—we do not seek to distance ourselves from the weight of death, for it is a burden to carry, not a victory to celebrate."*

Her words cut deep, sinking into my core.

"We don't have all the answers, Gamuchirai," my mother says, her voice quiet but firm. "We're doing our best with the limited resources and knowledge we possess. But you cannot just return and expect everything to fall into place seamlessly. It's not just about the serpent; it's about the people who have persisted in your absence. All I ask is that you share the burden. Prove to them that you're not here to demand blind obedience but to earn their trust and support. Lead them with genuine intent."

I want to be angry—want to rail against her for daring to question me—but guilt gnaws at the edges of my frustration, cutting deeper with every second. She's right, and it stings because I've been trying so hard to outrun the truth, yet here it is, staring me down like an unforgiving specter. *My intentions are not all that genuine.* I can't shake the growing sense of hypocrisy in me, festering like an old wound.

CHAPTER 34

I've come here, placing myself on a pedestal of righteousness so high they don't stand a chance to reach up and pull me down—to confront me as an equal. It was never about leading them, not truly. It was about protecting myself, insulating myself from the judgment I feared most— their disappointment, their anger, their questioning. So, I built walls of superiority, cloaking myself in the guise of authority and purpose, convincing myself I was untouchable. That way, they couldn't challenge me, couldn't hold me accountable for the things I've done.

Who am I to demand anything? I disappeared, left them to fend for themselves, and now I return, expecting loyalty and submission as if nothing has changed. Expecting them to embrace me, and forget how I failed them—while I cling to bitterness as if it's armor that protects me from the weight of my own shame. I preach about the need for change, yet I carry resentment like a shield, clinging to my anger as if it's the only thing keeping me upright. I've buried my own sins, hidden behind the mask of urgency and righteousness. *How can I expect them to follow me when I haven't even confronted the truth of my own failures?* I demand transparency from them while I remain cloaked in lies, preaching strength while drowning in my own unresolved bitterness. The truth is, I'm terrified. Terrified of facing what I've done, terrified of facing the disappointment I earned and their rightful anger. I thought if I could just stay angry, stay distant, I wouldn't have to deal with the pain of their judgment—or worse, their forgiveness. Because forgiveness would mean I'd have to forgive myself, and I'm not ready for that.

I'm not strong because I've locked away my pain; I'm a coward because I'm too afraid to face it. I told myself that pushing it all down was power, that pretending none of it mattered anymore was some kind of strength. But the truth is, it takes so much more courage to let it rise to the surface, to admit that I've failed, that I've run away from my own demons instead of conquering them.

My mother's eyes are searching, waiting for a response, for some sign that I understand, that I'm willing to meet them halfway. But I don't know if I can. The bitterness feels safe and familiar. It keeps me at arm's length from the hurt I know is waiting to consume me if I let my guard down. But maybe that's the problem. Maybe I've built my walls so high, even I can't see over them anymore. *This power,* this *self-importance* that has taken root—I have become exactly what I claimed I came to overcome.

My mother's expression softens, her eyes giving way to something deeper—*understanding. A mother knows.*

"It's never too late, Gamuchirai," she says quietly, her words sinking into me like a gentle but insistent tide. "But you have to let them see you. Not the mask, not the anger. You. Because they're scared, too. And they need to know they're not alone in their fear. They need to see that you respect our traditions and value their wisdom—that you're not putting them under your feet like dust. If not, you will face resistance at every turn. Enforcing change can easily become tyranny, even on a smaller scale—slavery is slavery. True leadership lies in inspiring, not coercing."

CHAPTER 34

Tears slip from my eyes before I can stop them. I turn away instinctively, trying to hide my shame from her, but she takes me gently by the arm and pulls me into her embrace. The hug is long and silent, a place where I feel *safe,* where I am not chosen or the leader, but just her daughter. For a moment, I let myself rest in that space, allowing the burden to ease, if only briefly.

When I finally pull away, I feel a renewed resolve. My tears are gone, but their trace lingers on my cheeks as I sniff and wipe them away. "We need to ensure a safe passage for the women, children, and elderly," My voice is stronger now, regaining the mantle of leadership. "Can we arrange boats at the north dock for a possible escape route to Nakuru? I have allies there and have asked them to secure the river path if we need to evacuate."

She nods, though concern shadows her eyes. "It's not a bad idea," she says, her voice calm and wary. "But how will you convince the people to board the boats?

"Indifference to danger doesn't mean we can't appeal to them as their leaders or command them," I reply. "You and Nyasha are the most trusted—perhaps you can persuade them. But regardless of the outcome, we must prepare the boats."

After a moment's hesitation, she nods again. "I will do as you've requested." She pauses, her gaze thoughtful. "But why don't you accompany Nyasha, dear? Your return, seeing you after so long, will underscore the urgency of our situation."

"Won't my presence just add to the confusion?" My voice is tinged with uncertainty.

"I don't think so, dear," she says softly, sensing my fear. "Your return will reinforce the gravity of our situation."

To be honest, I'm terrified. I'm not ready to face the people, so I try to dismiss her with a sense of urgency. "We can't afford the risk, Mama," I reply, trying to sound firm.

It's a flimsy excuse, and I know it. I hope she'll accept it, seeing through my fear.

"Alright then, dear" She gazes at me for a moment longer, her expression softening into something almost bittersweet. "I can hardly believe you're here, right before my eyes. You left, you returned—conquered the sea, did you? Remember what I used to call you? My star of the sea?"

I nod, but the sadness is too heavy to hold back. My father's absence looms like a shadow over this moment. I miss him. I miss the man who once held me high on his shoulders. And I failed him. I failed him in every way that mattered.

"Consult your ancestors," she continues, her voice pulling me from the fog of my guilt, "but let us not dismiss the other voices—their concerns, their fears, their opinions. Take them into account, Gamu. Truly listen." She reaches out and lifts my chin, forcing my gaze to meet hers. Her eyes are searching, like she's reading parts of me. "It's your cheeks—your eyes," she murmurs, her gaze distant, teasing but knowing. "That's how your tete sees these things. It is a boy indeed—he sits there, in your eyes—a skilled eye can note the subtle sharpness that comes with a little boy."

My heart clenches as I feel the truth of them settle like a stone in my chest. My child. *My son.* I swallow hard, forcing myself to stay calm, though I feel like I'm standing on the edge of a precipice, the ground beneath me ready to give way.

Chapter 35

As twilight descends, we enter the village of Mvure, the fading light casting a warm glow over the landscape. The air is alive with the laughter of children and the soft rustling of leaves in the gentle breeze. The tantalizing aroma of fresh fish being grilled drifts through the village—we don't have fish in Nakuru, only chicken. Villagers, initially absorbed in their evening routines, pause and look up, a wave of recognition spreading through the crowd. Murmurs of surprise evolve into a chorus of welcoming voices as more faces turn toward us, their expressions shifting from astonishment to delight.

Children, their faces alight with excitement, rush towards Gamu's mother and Nyasha. *"Princess Nyasha!"* one little girl exclaims, tugging eagerly at Nyasha's dress. *"Mama!"* they call to Gamu's mother, presenting her with a collection of colorful shells, trinkets, and wildflowers, their small hands overflowing with their treasures. The adoration is *worship,* their smiles warm as they gather around us. Their eyes brim with wonder and gratitude, and they reach out to touch Nyasha and Gamu's mother, some even offering heartfelt blessings and praises. "We missed you!" they cry out, their voices filled with genuine affection.

Women and girls approach Nyasha, their hands resting gently on her pregnant belly. "Is it a boy or a girl?" one woman inquires, her voice alight with excitement. Others lean in, eager to hear the baby's heartbeat, their faces glowing with curiosity and affection. Gamu's mother, her bright skin glowing in the twilight like a canvas, engages with women who sell textiles. Her voice is soft yet animated as she discusses fabrics and patterns, her hands moving gracefully as she examines their wares. The women nod eagerly, their faces reflecting the pride they feel in their craft.

As we make our way through the village square, the vibrant life of Mvure envelops us—the chatter of families, the playful banter of children, and the soothing murmur of the evening breeze create a sense of peace and community. Yet beneath this serene surface, a current of urgency pulses through our group, a reminder of the critical task that lies ahead. Taiwo and I walk apart, our presence less marked by reverence. I prefer it this way. Taiwo, with his solid build and quiet strength, reminds me of Osi—a silent force of resilience and determination.

"Nyasha," a young mother calls out, her baby cradled on her hip. "Will you stay long this time?"

Nyasha's smile falters briefly but she swiftly regains her composure. "I wish we could, sisi, but we have pressing matters to address. Please gather everyone in the square."

As we step into the square, Taiwo rings the bell. The clear, resonant tone slices through the evening air, reverberating off the clay walls and stirring a ripple of urgency in the sleepy village. The familiar signal spreads like wildfire, and the villagers begin to stir, calling out to their neighbors, and huddling their families together. There's a restless hum, but it carries with it the quiet reassurance of routine—until Gamu's mother raises her hand.

A wave of silence follows her gesture, the crowd falling still as if nature itself bows to her command. Even the children, squirming at their mothers' sides, are gently hushed and told to pay attention. The air feels fragile, as though it's holding its breath.

"My friends," she begins, her voice strong yet imbued with a gentle warmth, "it brings me great comfort to stand here with you, but I carry grave news." Her eyes sweep over the crowd, her words hanging heavy in the air. "I urge you—to find your courage. A perilous threat is approaching, and we must evacuate immediately."

The words land and send ripples of confusion and unease through the gathered villagers. The joy that had once filled their faces vanishes, replaced by a shadow of concern that creeps slowly across them. I can almost see it—*fear*, not of the danger itself, but of change. It's the unknown that makes their hands tremble, the idea of leaving this place they've called home for generations. Change, I realize, is as crippling as a gun pressed to their heads.

CHAPTER 35

"Why?" A man's voice pierces the tension, sharp with an edge of panic. "What is happening?" More voices echo, asking the same question, refined by their varying tones and genders. This is the most discord or dissonance I've ever seen in this place

Nyasha steps forward then, her hand instinctively cradling her belly, a shield against the unseen storm brewing on the horizon. Her voice is calm, but beneath her collected facade, there is the tremor of uncertainty. "We have to leave," she says, her words carefully chosen, as though testing their weight in the air. "But only for a little while. There is a great storm coming, one too fierce to survive."

The villagers, who have known only the steady rhythm of peaceful days and the occasional trials of life, stand frozen, their expressions a mix of disbelief and fear. An old man shuffles forward, his voice trembling. "A storm?" he echoes, confusion and doubt battling in his eyes. "We have storms all the time. Why must we abandon our homes because of the weather?"

Gamu's mother meets his gaze and speaks gently. "This is no ordinary storm," she says, keeping her urgent tone. "The shelters will not hold. The cobblestones will flood. Imagine the children playing, swallowed up by torrents of water. The elders swept away."

Her words hang in the air like a curse, striking deep into the hearts of those gathered. The crowd shifts uneasily, murmurs rising again as uncertainty gnaws at their resolve.

Nyasha speaks once more, her voice rising above the mounting anxiety. "We are family. We protect one another." Her words spread like a gentle embrace, soothing the sharp edges of their fear, though the unease lingers, stubborn and persistent. "It will only be for a little while," she adds, her eyes pleading, "but what matters is that we will face this together. We will survive—together."

They hesitate, their feet rooted in place, torn between the familiar safety of their homes and the terrifying unknown that beckons them to leave. The thought of abandoning everything they've ever known for the first time in their lives hangs like a stone around their necks.

"Come on now, friends," Nyasha urges, stretching her tone just a little too sweet, a little too innocent, as though trying to coax a stubborn child. "You know how much we care for you. Please, gather your things, and let us move swiftly."

For a moment, no one moves, the tension crackling in the air like the distant roll of thunder. They glance at one another, uncertainty in their eyes starting to give way to understanding. Slowly, reluctantly, they begin to move. Then, reluctantly, they begin to stir, shuffling toward their homes with heavy steps, their minds still grappling with the fear of what lies ahead.

But then something in the air shifts—something invisible yet tangible, prickling the skin like icy breath on the back of the neck. What should be urgency and unity curdles. Faces once softened by familiarity and trust seem carved from stone now. Their smiles vanish, replaced by an emptiness that swallows warmth whole that quickly twists into something far more sinister.

A chill snakes up my spine as I scan the faces around me. The change is subtle, a slow poison seeping into the air, but undeniable. "Do you sense it too?" I whisper, my voice barely more than a breath, directed at Taiwo. His brow furrows deeply, a shadow of worry crossing his features as he nods. "I feel it," he murmurs, his voice thick with dread.

A sudden shout tears through the uneasy quiet. "What threat? Zvinoramba!" A villager, his voice edged with disbelief and anger, steps forward. His eyes are wild, a darkness settling in them like a storm cloud. "It's inconceivable!" he spits, his body vibrating with growing aggression. Shadows grow behind his eyes, and a malevolent sneer twists his lips.

Another voice rises from the crowd, a young woman's sharp and furious: "Varikuda kutinyepa!" she cries, her words biting through the air. *"They're trying to deceive us!"*

Gamu's mother, her face now pale, confusion etched deep in her features, raises her hands in a pleading gesture. "Hapana anokunyeperai," she insists, her tone straining to stay calm. *"We would never deceive you."* But her words falter as the villagers close in, their hostility palpable.

My heart pounds, and suddenly, thoughts darker than the night itself coil within my mind. *Liar,* a whisper claws its way through my consciousness. *They are all liars.* This family, steeped in betrayal and cruelty, now hides behind a mask of false concern. They've sacrificed innocent lives, and their supposed care is nothing but a facade.

The crowd stirs, their whispers turning venomous, escalating with a feverish energy. "Vatengesi!" a voice shouts from the back, the word like a knife flung into the thickening tension. *"Traitors!"*

"Why should we trust you?" another villager demands, his voice taut and unforgiving. Their eyes narrow with suspicion, as if every word from Gamu's mother is an assault on their very existence. Even the children—innocent only moments ago—begin to mirror the same twisted anger, their small voices adding to the swelling chorus of malice. "Traitors!" They echo their elders.

Gamu's mother tries again, her hands trembling despite her effort to appear strong. "We are not deceiving you!" she insists, her gaze darting frantically from face to face, desperate for even a flicker of recognition, of trust. "Tiri pano kuti tikudzivirire," she adds, voice faltering. *"We are here to protect you."*

But the crowd doesn't listen. Their expressions harden, the warmth once shared between neighbors now replaced by something cold and menacing. I watch as the faces of the children—those small, once-gentle souls— possessed as though they were grown women and children. It's as if the village has been consumed by a sinister force, twisting every mind in its grip.

CHAPTER 35

"Ndapota!" Nyasha cries, stepping forward, her voice laced with fear, her hands protectively resting over her belly. *"Please!"* Her voice wavers, cracking under the weight of their growing fury. "Fungai nezvevana! Ticharwirana tese—ndapota!"—*"We must leave immediately, think of your families!"*

But her words seem to be swallowed by the rising tide of anger. A man steps forward, his face contorted in rage. "Tichakuuraya!" he roars, his voice a violent boom. *"We will kill you!"* The threat ripples through the crowd like a shockwave, stunning everyone—me most of all. Here, in the sanctuary of Mvure, such words are unthinkable.

The atmosphere turns cold, thick with an almost tangible hostility. "Uurai vatengesi!" someone shouts, and others quickly echo the call, their voices raw with fury. *"Kill the traitors!"* The crowd surges forward, a terrifying wall of bodies and rage. Fists clench. Objects—sticks, stones, whatever they can find—are raised into the air, ready to strike. "Uurai vatengesi!"

The mob's chant grows louder, more insistent: "Uurai vatengesi! Uurai vatengesi!" The words pound in my head, their dark energy twisting through my thoughts like a venomous serpent. And before I can stop it, I feel it—a shadowy urge pressing down on me, trying to pull me into the frenzy. *Kill them,* it whispers. Join the others. *Kill them.*

"Kill the traitors, uurai vatengesi, kill the traitors, uurai vatengesi!"

My heart races as I fight the pull, gritting my teeth against the dark command echoing through my mind. I glance at Taiwo, whose eyes are locked on the villagers, his jaw clenched tight. He steps forward, his body tense with determination, and stands beside me. I find my feet moving, too, stepping into the path of the mob, positioning myself between them and Nyasha, who stands trembling behind me.

"Zvikangwai!" Gamu's mother cries, her voice cutting through the chaos. *"Stop!"* Her eyes meet mine, wide with terror, pleading for something, anything, to halt this madness. "We are not your enemies,"

I force myself to push back the dark whispers gnawing at my thoughts. *Kill them, kill them, kill them.*

Taiwo nods, his gaze never leaving the crowd as he speaks too, voice firm. "Hatikunyepi," he says with unwavering resolve. *"We're not lying."*

But the mob's chant only grows louder, their fury boiling over.

A man with a pitchfork lunges at Nyasha, his movements are erratic and driven by an unseen, malevolent force. Without hesitation, I spring forward, wrenching the pitchfork from his grip and shoving him back, fighting to keep my own mind clear. Another woman, her eyes glazed with feral rage, swings a heavy wooden club. Taiwo and I work in swift, coordinated motions, disarming and pushing back the aggressors while striving to avoid unnecessary harm.

CHAPTER 35

"We need to get out of here!" I command, my voice sharp with urgency. "Now!"

Taiwo nods in agreement, and together we brace ourselves against the swelling tide of the crowd, positioning ourselves as shields for Nyasha and Gamu's mother. Our retreat devolves into a desperate scramble, the once-familiar path to the royal shelter now a chaotic battleground. Insults, threats, and thrown objects bombard us from every side. The mob's anger is a relentless assault that challenges our every step. Each advance is met with a surge of opposition.

Kill the traitors. My mind echoes the chant, a dark mantra that blurs my thoughts. *No. Stop.*

The mob's roars, its rage undeniable—growing louder with each chant. The screams, the shouts of "Uurai vatengesi!" are like blows, each one pounding against us. The words are not just shouts—they are a terrifying command, an all-consuming force that takes root in every body and mind until the anger in their eyes becomes a violent storm, churning and crackling, manifesting in every stone hurled, every fist raised. Pressing in on us, their shoves becoming more violent, their faces twisted with unbridled fury. Objects fly through the air—rocks, sticks, anything they can grasp, each one landing with a brutal thud or crack, sparking cries of pain and shock.

Nyasha's breath comes in ragged gasps beside me, her hand pressed protectively over her belly, her eyes wide with terror. Her fingers are interlocked with Gamu's mother's, the two women bracing each other as if drawing strength from that connection, anchoring themselves against the torrent of rage surrounding us. Though the mob swells like a living thing, a storm of fury pressing in from all sides, they have not yet crumbled under its weight. Urgency claws at my throat, tearing the words from me. I turn to them, urgency clawing at my voice. "Go! Run!" I shout, my words cutting through the deafening noise of the mob. "We'll hold them off—just run as fast as you can—forget the royal elegance, abandon it all!"

Their eyes meet mine for a brief, fleeting second, filled with fear and understanding. There's no time for hesitation. Nyasha gives a quick nod, her hand clutching her belly tighter as if drawing strength from the life she carries within her. Gamu's mother, her chin raised with defiance only she could muster in such terror, nods too. Then they turn and bolt up the cobble path with desperate agility. Nyasha stumbles once but catches herself, pushing forward with a force that defies her fear. Gamu's mother, despite her age, moves with surprising speed, her royal grace shed like a cloak left behind in the fray.

I watch them go, a brief flicker of relief threading through the chaos that surrounds us. But there's no time to dwell. I struggle to breathe, the sheer force of the crowd pressing against me like an unforgiving wave. Taiwo stands firm beside me, his body braced against the crush, his hand gripping my arm tightly as we try to carve a path through this sea of hostility. Every step forward is a battle, every inch gained a victory against the relentless tide. Another

CHAPTER 35

shove sends me stumbling, my knees buckling, but I manage to stay upright, my heart pounding in my ears. Every shout, every shove, every object thrown feels like the world itself is collapsing around us.

Chapter 36

"Before Mvure cloaked itself in secrecy, a small, formidable tribe thrived under the watchful guidance of the Darare ancestors—people famed for their resilience and autonomy. Their verdant, bountiful lands lay exposed to the relentless advance of merciless pirates, whose cruelty and ambition knew no bounds.

As the shadow of invasion drew closer, Mvure's leaders found themselves in a desperate plight. Their defenses were crumbling, and their very existence teetered on the edge of oblivion. In their desperation, they turned to ancient legends that spoke of a formidable spirit residing deep beneath the sea: Nyoka, a colossal serpent with dominion over the tides and the power to wield darkness itself. With their fate hanging by a thread, the leaders made a fateful decision—to summon Nyoka through an ancient and perilous ritual.

The chosen site for this ritual was a rocky promontory jutting defiantly into the sea, surrounded by roiling waves and the distant roar of the ocean. Here, nature's raw power seemed to converge with the supernatural forces they sought

CHAPTER 36

to invoke. A young woman of the tribe, steeped in the ancient magic passed down through the ages, prepared the ritual. She carved serpentine symbols and storm clouds into the stone altar—emblems of consuming darkness and ravenous rage. Flickering torches cast eerie shadows across the sacrificial slab, etched with ancient runes.

As night descended and the sky darkened, the leaders assembled in solemn silence. The woman began her chant, invoking Nyoka's presence as the air thickened with tension. Waves crashed violently against the rocks, a chaotic symphony to accompany the ritual's crescendo. The firstborn son of Chief Darare, his life a sacrificial offering, was laid upon the altar. His life was the price for sealing the pact with Nyoka, ensuring the serpent's protection and favor.

The sea churned and bubbled as the ritual neared its climax. From the depths emerged a great shadow—Nyoka, a towering black serpent with eyes like burning embers. The serpent's presence was both awe-inspiring and terrifying. With trembling hands, the woman offered the child to Nyoka, her voice a mournful whisper as she completed the final incantations. Nyoka enveloped the child's spirit in a dark, swirling mist, drawing the boy's essence into itself.

Nyoka's power bound itself to the tribe, and the serpent's protection manifested in a frenzy of violence. The invaders began to slaughter each other, their own hands becoming instruments of destruction. Men were thrown overboard, cast into the turbulent sea with violent brutality, their screams lost amid the storm's roar. The once-formidable fleet disintegrated under the weight of internal strife and Nyoka's dark power, leaving behind a scene of utter carnage.

Yet, as the storm raged, the woman was seized by an overwhelming force. An otherworldly darkness awakened a primordial hunger within her. Her desperate incantations, drawn from a source both profound and incomprehensible, fused with the sacrificial power in a vortex that transformed her essence. The serpent's full strength was siphoned away, leaving behind only a diminished echo of its former majesty, while the woman became its new, terrifying vessel.

Nyoka, you see, was a *blood bender*—a being of unimaginable power who commanded the very life force that courses through our veins. Blood bending is no ordinary art; it is an ancient and forbidden practice that grants the ability to manipulate the blood within living beings, bending it to one's will. This dark craft transcends mere physical manipulation. It plunges into the deepest, most primordial realms of existence—life and death themselves. Nyoka wielded this power with chilling precision, turning it into a tool of both domination and terror. By controlling the blood of its victims, Nyoka did more than exert influence; it invaded their very essence, bending their bodies and minds to its will. The serpent instilled fear, sowed discord, and perpetuated cycles of dependence and manipulation.

The storm reached its zenith, and the woman's transformation was both profound and tragic. Despite her newfound powers, she died instantly, her body collapsing as the last echoes of the storm's energy dissipated. Her lifeless form lay untouched by the very power she had claimed, her transformation marked only by the violent end she met.

The tribe was saved, but the pact with Nyoka came with a heavy price. Over the centuries, the promise of protection became a yoke of obligation, demanding regular sacrifices and binding the tribe to Nyoka's will. Each generation saw the offering of a firstborn child, a tradition that bred fear and resentment. Bound by the ancient pact, Nyoka's power was restricted, exerting influence only within the confines of the agreement. Even when the sacrifices ceased, Nyoka's influence remained, subtly manipulating events to maintain its tethered duty.

Then, a prophecy emerged—a foretelling of a momentous rebirth. It spoke of a girl, a direct descendant of the Darare clan, carrying an unborn child who would serve as the vessel for Nyoka's full strength. This prophecy promised the return of Nyoka's terrifying power through the girl and the sacrifice of the unborn child, signaling a pivotal shift in the balance of power.

And so, on the foretold day, a storm erupted with unparalleled fury—a manifestation of Nyoka's restrained yet potent will. Nyoka, in its resurrection, vowed to unleash its rage and vengeance upon all who dwelt by the salt and the water.

Yet, gifted one, when something profoundly wrong occurs, a solution is set into motion simultaneously. You will come to see the truth in my words and understand the weight of your burden. Within each of us, within all our trials, lies the answer to the wrongs we face. We are not wronged merely for the sake of suffering, but to illuminate the necessity of correction and to guide us toward the resolution we seek—for the greater good of all people. This is our collective duty."

Chapter 37

The back of the royal shelter is more than just a cooking spot; it is a sanctuary of memory, an altar to the unspoken rituals of daily life. For generations, the women of my family stood here, hands working with the grace of familiarity, tending to the fire that has never truly gone out. In this place, my ancestors sustained their families by preparing meals. It may not have been consecrated by ritual, but it is sacred all the same. This is where life was nurtured.

The cooking spot itself is simple, a circle of stones arranged neatly around a shallow pit, blackened by years of use. The fire within crackles steadily, its warmth a constant presence, casting flickering light that dances on the stone walls of the house and across the nearby trees. Above the flames, a bent and slightly rusted metal stand holds the heavy pot where tonight's sadza bubbles away, thickening slowly. Nearby, logs are stacked haphazardly but efficiently, and a bundle of dry kindling rests against the wall, ready to stoke the flames when needed.

Here, my mother once knelt, her hands stirring the same

bubbling porridge, her face lit by the same flickering flames. Her mother before her did the same. And the women before her. Tonight, I kneel in the same spot, the thick wooden spoon resting heavily in my hand, its surface worn smooth from years of use yet fitting perfectly in my palm as if it had always been meant for this moment now that I am a woman.

I lean over the fire, the heat licking at my face, the scent of the bubbling maize porridge mingling with the smoke. I move with the same deliberate grace as the women before me, stirring, shaping, and feeding. The *sadza* thickens beneath my touch, the bubbling water transforming into something solid and rich. My hand dips into the mealie meal bag, the fine grains slipping through my fingers like sand. As I lift a handful and let it fall into the pot, the familiar soft hiss of grain meeting water fills the twilight air. I stir, my movements rhythmic, the spoon carving circles through the thickening mass. My forearms tighten as I work, coaxing the sadza into its familiar shape.

The air around me thickens with the rich scent of cooking maize, wood smoke, and the earthy heat of the fire, sweat gathering at my temples in response. I add another handful of mealie meal, watching it swirl into the pot, the texture shifting beneath my spoon, becoming heavier, more substantial. The effort builds in my muscles, but it's a familiar resistance, one I welcome as the sadza takes form beneath my touch, its weight now tangible. I tune out the hushed whispers of the maids and vatete vangu, *my aunties*, the curious eyes that pry, and the distant echoes of my cousins' playful footsteps in the shelter's halls. Instead, I let the crackle of the fire and the rhythmic scrape of the spoon against the pot anchor me, drawing me into their simplicity.

Beside me, the pot of beef stew simmers, its scent—a savory blend of tender meat and rich, dark gravy—rises into the air, so enticing it makes my mouth water. Garlic, onions, and tomatoes have melded together into a fragrant blend, punctuated by the earthy notes of cumin and bay leaves. I stir it gently, watching the meat fall apart in the thick broth, the steam rising to meet the violet sky, carrying with it the promise of something hearty and nourishing. In another pot, the rap greens sizzle, their leaves glistening with oil, softened by heat, and flavored with onions, tomatoes, and a subtle hint of peanut butter that adds richness to the dish. The smell of fresh vegetables mingles with the savory stew and the comforting weight of the sadza, each aroma weaving into the next like strands of well-worn drapery.

The fire beneath the three pots crackles steadily, each one contributing its own music to the evening—the bubbling of the stew, the hiss of the sadza, the gentle sizzle of the greens. I stir the sadza one last time, feeling it resist the spoon, its familiar density now just right.

I move the pot off the fire, shaping the sadza into neat balls, and placing them carefully on the plate beside me. Next comes the stew, ladled thick and rich into a clay plate, the beef falling apart under the touch of the spoon, the deep red gravy spilling over the sides. The rap greens follow their bright green vibrancy a beautiful contrast against the dark stew.

I step back, wiping the sweat from my brow, and for a moment, I simply stand and breathe. The plates before me aren't just sustenance; they are an offering, a link between the living and the dead, a bridge between past and present. I carry the plates to the small shrine at the back of the shelter, a humble collection of stones and relics that I've prepared, and place them there gently, reverently.

I kneel before the offering, hands resting on my thighs, and bow my head. The words of my prayer come naturally, flowing from me like water, carried by the smoke up to the stars.

"Vadzimu vangu, Ambuya, Sekuru, ndauya pamberi penyu nechinangwa chizere nekutya nemibvunzo. Makandiunzazve kuMvure, kunyika yedu, nekuti hamuchadi kuti tsinga yangu itore vamwe vakomana kunzi rubatsiro rwemweya wezvinyoka. Asi zvino handichazivi kana nzira yekumberi. Ndorwisa sei mweya wezvinyoka, ndisina humbowo kana zvombo? Ndiregerereiwo kana ndiri kure neicho chaizvo."

"My ancestors, Grandmother, Grandfather, I come before you filled with fear and questions. You have brought me back to Mvure, to our land, because you no longer want my lineage to sacrifice our sons to the serpent spirit. But now I do not know what lies ahead. How do I fight the serpent spirit, without proof or weapons? Forgive me if I am far from the truth."

"Ndinoziva kuti ndimi makandisarudza kuti ndisiye nzira yevakuru vedu yekubayira mukomana. Zvino, vadzimu, mundiratidzei nzira, musangundipe ndangariro, musangundipe matambudziko. Ndiratidzei nhanho yekuzopedzisa zvakagadzirwa nemweya wezvinyoka, ndisingatyi."

"I know it was you who chose me to abandon the path of our elders,to stop offering our sons. Now, ancestors, show me the way, do not leave me with memories alone, do not leave me with burdens. Show me the steps to finally end what the serpent spirit has wrought, without fear."

As I kneel here, I hope that my ancestors will answer from the beyond, offering clarity where there is none—and soon.

I rise slowly, leaving the food as it is, a humble offering nestled within the shrine. Gathering my pots and spoon, I hold them with care—they are more than tools today; they are vessels of tradition, worn but precious. Cleaning them is as much a tribute to my ancestors as preparing the meal itself. As I walk past the maids, I catch their soft whispers, their curious eyes tracing my every step. Though I feel their attention, I choose to focus on my task. My feet carry me to the corner where a large clay jug awaits, water sloshing gently inside as I tilt it into a shallow basin. The coolness soothes my hands, offering a brief respite. Vatete—are watching too, their presence a quiet weight on my back.

I move to the side of the house, where the earth is packed hard and dry, a perfect spot for scrubbing. Kneeling once more, I set the pots before me, their blackened surfaces streaked with soot from the fire. My hands instinctively reach for the dish and a handful of sand—the grains are coarse, and rough between my fingers. Sprinkling the sand over the pots, I begin scrubbing in tight circles, the friction biting into the stubborn black residue, each stroke deliberate.

Tete Chipo approaches, her feet shuffling softly against the ground. I feel her gaze on me, lingering as she bends beside me. "Hazvisiri kudaro, mwanangu,"—*"That's not how it's done, my child."* She says it gently, taking the dish from my hand. She demonstrates the right angle, showing me how to press the sand into the pot just so, ensuring it scours away the soot without damaging the metal beneath. Her hands, strong and sure, make quick work of the task, and I nod, accepting her correction.

I glance at her as she finishes, noticing the softening in her eyes. I see the unspoken question forming there—the one about my pregnancy that she doesn't dare voice. Her gaze flickers to my belly, then back again. Whatever my mother told her earlier has stopped her from asking about the pregnancy. The space between us fills with unsaid words, but I find great peace in her silence.

She pats my shoulder softly, her instruction complete, and rises to leave. I return to scrubbing, the sand biting once again into the pots, slowly revealing their gleaming surface beneath the layers of black. Bit by bit, they shine under my hands.

Chapter 38

I walk slowly, my fingers absently picking at the stubborn black coal embedded in my skin, the gritty residue clinging no matter how hard I scrape. Lost in the motions and my own thoughts, I don't even notice the door until I've passed it. My steps falter, a sudden awareness pulling me back, and I stop abruptly, retracing two careful steps as the moment sharpens into focus.

Sekuru Mwendo sits hunched in his low chair, his broad shoulders drawn back like a man bracing for a battle he knows too well. His face is a fortress, all hard lines and unyielding pride, weathered by years of resentment and stubbornness. The firelight dances across his features, but it does nothing to soften them. He is a man who has built walls, not just around his heart, but around every part of his being. Reaching him will be like chiseling through stone.

I linger in the doorway, the weight of the moment pressing down on me, heavy and suffocating. *Should I take advantage of this moment while he's alone, or should I simply keep to myself?* My mother's words echo in my mind. *But how do you reveal yourself to a man who refuses to see beyond his anger? How do you reach someone who has spent years wrapped in bitterness like a second skin?*

Steeling myself, I inhale deeply before stepping into the room. "Sekuru," I say softly, testing the waters, my voice foreign to my own ears.

He doesn't move, doesn't even acknowledge me. His jaw clenches, and I notice the veins bulging in his hands as they grip the arms of his chair. His eyes remain fixed on the fire, as though its glow offers him a solace I am not capable of giving.

"I need to talk to you," I try again, forcing strength into my voice though it trembles with uncertainty. Standing before him, I feel small—like a child before a giant, seeking some form of mercy.

His response is a low, guttural growl, thick with contempt. "Talk? What more is there to say? Another speech about how you've come back to *'fix'* things? Another empty claim to some newfound wisdom?"

I swallow hard, willing myself not to retreat. "No, Sekuru, I want to apologize," I manage, the words heavy in my throat. "For what I said earlier. It wasn't right."

"An apology?" His head snaps toward me, eyes cold and hollow, but his lips twist into a mocking sneer. "You? *Apologizing?* Since when do you care about anything other than yourself?" His gaze sharpens, daring me to falter under the weight of his scorn.

"I'm not the same girl I was." The words feel brittle, as though they could shatter at any moment under the pressure of his gaze.

His laugh is a harsh bark of derision. "Oh? And who was that earlier then? A ghost? The same girl who looked down on us like we were beneath her?"

"You're right," I whisper, feeling the fragile facade crack. "I was selfish. I left when you needed me most." I pause, my throat tightening, wondering if he will understand—if he even cares. "I built walls around myself, thinking I could come back and force things to be right, that I could control it all with intimidation. But I was wrong, Sekuru."

His scoff is sharp and dismissive, and he turns back to the fire, his face a mask of indifference. "And now? What do you want? Forgiveness? Redemption? You want me to pretend nothing ever happened?"

I steady myself against the surge of emotions threatening to overwhelm me. "I don't expect forgiveness," I admit, my voice faltering but honest. "Not now, maybe not ever. But I need you to know that I'm not here to erase the past. I'm here to make things right—to earn back your trust, your faith… your respect." My hands tremble as I kneel before him, lowering myself to the cold, hard ground. "We don't have to keep hurting each other, Sekuru. We don't have to let this anger destroy what's left of us."

The silence that stretches between us is suffocating, a chasm so wide it feels impossible to cross. The fire crackles, its restless energy filling the unbearable quiet. I watch him, my heart heavy with hope and fear, uncertain if there is any way to bridge the gap between us.

Finally, his voice breaks the stillness, raw and cracked. "Do you even know what it feels like?" His eyes never leave the fire, distant and haunted. "To lose a brother?"

His words cut through me like shards of glass, each one slicing deeper than the last. I flinch but hold my ground.

"What you did… the mess you left behind… it's nothing compared to what your absence did to my brother, your father. It destroyed him. Do you think your apology can bring him back?"

His accusation hits me squarely, and the weight of my guilt is almost too much to bear. My throat tightens, my breath shallow as I fight to stay composed beneath the crushing force of his grief. I remain kneeling, feeling the cold earth press into my skin, sharp like the edges of his disappointment.

"Sekuru…" My voice cracks, barely audible under the crushing weight of my regret. "I didn't know. I didn't mean for any of this to happen."

His voice rises in a fierce roar, resentment boiling to the surface. "You *didn't know?*" He finally looks at me, his eyes blazing with fury. "Of course you didn't know! You didn't care!"

Every word lands like a physical blow, and I feel myself shrinking beneath his rage. But I can't deny his truth. I did leave. I ran when I should have stayed, and abandoned my father when they needed me most. And in doing so, I broke him. The guilt tightens its grip around my heart until I can hardly breathe.

"I'm sorry," I whisper through tears that blur my vision. "I know it doesn't fix anything. I know I can't bring him back. But I'm here now, Sekuru. I'm trying—"

"*Sorry?*" he spits. His fists clench, his knuckles white as he struggles to contain the storm within him. "Sorry won't bring back the dead. Anesu is gone, Gamuchirai. Gone. And you think you can sweep it all away with a few words and a bow of your head?"

The power of his rage, the depth of his grief—it's overwhelming, a storm that rages through both of us. But I hold my ground. There is no easy path forward, no words that can undo what's been done. But I won't run this time. I will face him, face the pain, and somehow, somehow, I will rebuild what I destroyed.

I stay rooted to the spot, my heart pounding in my chest. The fire crackles between us, its heat licking at the silence that falls heavy and unforgiving. I brace for another wave of anger, but slowly, something shifts. His rage cools, like a dying ember, and I watch as his shoulders slump, his entire frame seeming to shrink. He looks smaller now, diminished by the weight of a burden too heavy for one man to carry alone.

For the first time, I truly see him—not just as a towering figure of resentment, but as a man hollowed out by years of unspoken pain. Could this really be about my departure alone? No—this anger, it's too much, too tightly wound, always searching for a crack, an excuse to erupt and break through the surface. He is a man carrying something far greater than one loss, something gnawing at his insides. For the first time, I realize his anger is misplaced—not because he lacks reason, but because he has nowhere else to empty it.

He chooses me. *Tete Mirembe, Nyasha*—we are all victims of a man trapped in his own torment, a man who never learned how to release his anger in a way that didn't break everything around him.

"You remind me of him," he says at last, his voice quieter now, his gaze distant once again. "Your father. He was always so stubborn. Always so determined to fix things, even when it was too late."

I blink back my tears, my throat tight. "I just want to honor him," I whisper. "And you. I want to make things right, Sekuru. Not just for me, but for him. For all of us."

He doesn't respond, but he doesn't turn away either. Instead,

CHAPTER 38

he stares into the fire, its flickering light dancing across his face. The silence is too full, heavy with all the things we can't yet say to each other. Reconciliation feels like an impossibility at this moment. Slowly, I rise, deciding not to push any further.

I won't force his forgiveness or rush his healing for my own sake. This has to happen on his terms when he's ready. Stepping back, I leave him with the fire and his thoughts, giving him the space he needs. As I walk away, my mind races, the weight of the conversation lingering in my chest. But I know I have to move forward, even if it's only one step at a time.

Just as I turn the corner, I spot Shiwo, but before I can reach her, a sudden noise freezes me in place. My ears strain as chilling chants fill the air: "Uurai vatengesi!" The roar of violence follows, frantic and growing louder with every heartbeat.

Kill the traitors? I jolt into action, rushing to the balcony where Shiwo stands, both of us peering over the edge.

"What's happening?" she breathes, her voice barely a whisper, her eyes wide with disbelief.

The sight below sends an icy shiver down my spine. The villagers, once peaceful and indifferent, have transformed into a seething mob—twisted with rage and hatred, as if a dark spell has descended upon them, shattering their calm in an instant.

Why this sudden, brutal violence?

I can feel it, deep in my blood—the magic. It seethes within me, responding to the fury spreading like wildfire through the crowd. It pulses through me as if the very essence of their fury is alive within my veins. The sensation is unbearable and unsettling.

The mob surges forward, their movements wild and chaotic, like a storm gathering force. Their makeshift weapons are barely visible in the new night and the shouts of hatred slice through the night like jagged shards of glass. They're coming for us. Panic surges within me, yet I remain rooted to the spot, paralyzed as a cold, serpentine realization coils through my mind.

"No, please," I murmur, the weight of the warning finally settling in—pressing against me like a cold knife of terror.

Jolted into action, I spin on my heel and sprint toward the gates of the royal shelters, desperate to reach them before it's too late. I race past the room where just moments ago I had stood toe-to-toe with Sekuru. Now, there's no time to linger. Shiwo follows closely behind, her breath quick and sharp, her confusion evident, but she matches my pace without question.

I tear through the winding corridors of the shelter, my feet pounding against the stone floors, the sound echoing off the walls. Worrying murmurs rise from the rooms I pass, anxious eyes peeking from behind curtains and doorways.

CHAPTER 38

They call my name, their voices heavy with fear, but I cannot stop. There is no time to explain. Bursting out into the evening air, I am met with a scene that feels like a chilling manifestation of a nightmare.

A woman, her face streaked with dirt and tears, stands at the gates, clutching her child tightly in her arms. Her eyes are wide with terror, and her breath comes in ragged sobs. The moonlight glints off a gleaming knife she clutches in her trembling hand. "Ndapota, ndibatsirei!" She cries, her voice echoing with desperation. *"Please, help me!"*

"Zvakafaya—zvakafaya—ndichakubatsira,"—*"It's okay—it's okay—I'll help you."* I say it stepping forward, my hand reaching out to her.

But the words falter as a chilling aura envelops her, something dark and *hungry.* I hesitate, and in that split second, regret sinks its claws into me. "No!" I shout, but the sound is swallowed by the night, lost in the void.

The child, too young to sense the danger, clings to her with innocent trust, oblivious to the horror looming just moments away. And then, with a single, heart-stopping motion, she plunges the knife into his chest. His scream rips through the air, a piercing, gut-wrenching cry that fractures the night. Blood spurts from the wound, splattering onto the ground, onto her tear-streaked face. Her sobs twist into something agonizing, an echo of the child's final desperate breaths.

Behind me, Shiwo and the others stand paralyzed—all of us locked in the grip of the grotesque scene unfolding before us.

She pulls the knife from her son's limp body with a sickening jerk, her expression shifting from tortured grief to a quiet, resigned serenity. *No.* Then, with the same agonizing calm, she turns the blade on herself. With deliberate, excruciating slowness, she drives the knife into her abdomen. Her body crumples to the ground beside her child, their lifeless forms intertwined. Her final breaths come in ragged gasps, each one a struggle as her body convulses, the life draining from her. And then, silence.

The maids and workers who have gathered out of morbid curiosity, display a chilling indifference. Their faces are strangely detached, failing to grasp the gravity of the scene. A sinister whisper coils into my thoughts, its voice dripping with malice: "Chibayiro,"—"*Sacrifice.*" The word wraps around my consciousness like a cold *serpent.*

My sekurus rush past me, their voices sharp and urgent. Sekuru Mwendo's commands slice through the chaos as he berates the guards for their sluggishness, ordering them to seal the gates. The once passive guards snap into action with startling precision, rushing to barricade the entry.

Out of the confusion, *my mother* and *Nyasha* appear, sprinting with desperate urgency. Six and Taiwo arrive just after them, and behind them, the furious mob surges forward with makeshift weapons and accusatory shouts of treachery—

CHAPTER 38

their anger fueling their pursuit.

I feel as though I am watching it all from outside myself, detached and distant, yet my body moves instinctively. My feet carry me forward, trembling until I stand over the bodies. Slowly, I fall to my knees, my heart heavy with a sorrow that feels impossible to bear. With shaking hands, I lift the boy's lifeless form from the pool of blood, cradling him gently in my arms.

As the gates begin to shut, a desperate surge of villagers reaches them, their shouts growing more frantic. Hands claw at the narrowing gap, but with a resounding clang, the gates slam shut, sealing out the frenzy. The mob presses against them like a ravenous beast, their fury and hateful shouts defining the borders of our world. The guards stand resolute, yet their eyes, though fixed on the chaos, betray a detached, analytical gaze, as if they are struggling to grasp the enormity of the madness that has consumed them.

Six, breathless and flushed from her frantic sprint, turns to me. Her eyes, wide with a mix of relief and deep-seated fear, fall upon the bloodied child cradled in my arms and the lifeless mother lying beside me. Her expression darkens with sympathy and horror. Nyasha, tears streaming down her face, runs to her mother and the other elders, their cries filling the air. Though I don't look directly at them, I can picture them huddling together, clinging to one another in their shared fear and despair.

The scene is heart-wrenching. My own mother collapses

to her knees, clutching her chest in a gesture of profound despair. "Tatarika," she murmurs while struggling to catch her breath. *"We are lost."*

I glance behind me, noting the younger ones—all girls—how thin and fragile my family has become. They stand in stunned silence, their faces etched with terror, eyes wide but devoid of tears. They are frozen, their fear manifesting in their vacant stares rather than in tears or embraces. Sekuru steps forward, his face etched with concern and sorrow.

He places a comforting hand on my mother's shoulder, his own voice filled with grave urgency. "What can we do? How do we fight something like this?"

How?

It becomes glaringly apparent that any remaining shred of order or reason that once characterized Mvure has been entirely eclipsed by all-consuming darkness. The village's former facade has been swept away, leaving only the raw, unbridled force of the dark powers that should never have been meddled with.

Chapter 39

The mob outside the gates grows increasingly violent, their rage manifesting in frenzied assaults against the barriers. Every crash and thud reverberates through the royal compound, amplifying the sense of impending doom within its walls. Their fear and confusion are so thick I am breathing it.

"We can't stay here," one of Gamu's aunts—Chipo, I think, though I can barely keep track—urgently insists. She clutches two terrified children to her chest, their wide eyes reflecting her own terror and confusion. The little girls, each with two side ponytails and long lashes that echo Gamu's features, tremble in her arms.

This entire family is a mirror of girls, each one a reflection of the next.

"Vachaputsa magonhi chero nguva."—*"They'll break through the gates any moment."*

The older children, more aware of the danger, are visibly anxious. They shift nervously, exchanging worried glances and whispering hurriedly to each other. Their clothes are rumpled, and they cling to any semblance of normalcy they can muster, though it's clear that the looming threat has shattered their sense of safety.

Another voice, her uncle, cuts in, his tone laced with panic. "We're trapped! What can we do but wait? We don't have enough men to fend them off—and those demons outside aren't like anyone we've ever known. There's something supernatural driving them."

Taiwo chimes in, "Their strength—it's beyond human. I felt it."

The main hall, though packed with the family—perhaps ten or fifteen people—feels claustrophobic. All the children have been gathered here for safety; their parents, too fearful to leave them alone, have followed suit. The maids continue their tasks with a veneer of calm, but their every movement is scrutinized with suspicion. It's almost satisfying to see Mvure brought to such fear.

Gamu paces the room with a restless energy. Every step is a manifestation of her anxiety, her movements sharp and erratic as she searches for a solution. *Damn it.*

Her mother raises her hands as if to calm the fears and hysteria hanging in the air. "We must at least remain calm. Panicking will only make things worse."

"*Calm?* How can we be calm? The gates won't hold forever!"

CHAPTER 39

Mwendo shouts, his words sharp with desperation. I remember his name for his violence.

The other uncle, more calm and composed, interjects "He is right, we need a plan. We can't just stand here and wait for them to break in."

A teenage girl, her face flushed with urgency and frustration, blurts out, "Sei tisingagoni kungovasiya?"—*"Why can't we just leave them?"* Her face, flushed with emotion, stands out against the chaos, her disheveled hair falling loosely around her shoulders. She says it so softly, so innocently, as if it were the most logical thing in the world.

Her mother reacts quickly, silencing her with a stern, anxious look. Fear and dread washes over the woman's face, her eyes darting nervously between her daughter and the uneasy crowd. It's as if her daughter has voiced a forbidden truth.

The other children around her, with their wide, innocent eyes, glance up eagerly, waiting for an answer. The idea of escape is simple, so clear to them—why are the adults making it so complicated?

The adults, who had clearly been entertaining the same thought in secret, now exchange glances. Their faces betray a mix of quiet agreement and rising hope, silently acknowledging that the girl had voiced what they had been too afraid to say out loud.

It's almost *laughable*.

"Hamunyari here? Hatigone kusiya vanhu vedu!"—*"Are you not ashamed? We cannot abandon our people!"* Gamu's mother rebukes. "We must find a way to protect them here!"

Her declaration stirs a mixture of hesitation and unresolved tension among the crowd.

But Mwendo, unrelenting Mwendo, cuts through the silence. "What can we do against them? They don't need our protection!" His voice is sharp, his eyes darting wildly in search of someone to blame. His gaze locks onto Gamu, and with purposeful strides, he storms toward her, cutting off her restless pacing. "You came here, full of bravado, barking orders like you had all the answers. And now? Now you're as quiet as a mouse?" His voice drips with accusation.

Gamu's face hardens, a storm brewing behind her eyes. "I am trying my best!" she shouts, her voice cracking under the weight of frustration and desperation.

"Your best?" Mwendo's face twists, a mask of rage and bitterness. "You're a fraud!" He steps closer, his accusations sharp and cutting. "You pretend to care, but you've kept us all in the dark—about the male life you carry. The one thing that could save us, and yet you hoard it while we suffer. How dare you call yourself a leader?"

Fuck, fuck, fuck—how does he know that?

CHAPTER 39

I think I can hear Gamu's heart slam, and her mind racing.

Her mother's face drains of color, eyes wide with shock as she scrambles to rise, panic etched into her features. But before she can act, I step in, pushing past the invisible line that's been crossed. I lock eyes with Mwendo, my voice low and ice-cold. "I'll count to six," I say, each word deliberate, deadly. "And if you haven't released her by then, I'll break your wrist."

Mwendo's eyes flicker with uncertainty for a split second, but a sneer quickly twists his lips. "Do you see this?" he spits at the crowd. "They are against us! A serpent slithering quietly in our home, waiting to strike!"

"One," I start, my voice icy and resolute.

His face contorts with fury, his anger erupting like a storm. "What right do you have to threaten me?"

"Two," I continue, undeterred.

He grabs my arm, yanking me closer, his grip tightening painfully. Now he's holding both me and Gamu, but I don't flinch. Instead, I keep my eyes locked on his, a cold smile curling my lips. "Three."

"Silence!" he bellows, his voice cracking under the weight of his fury. "You've no respect for your elders! Foolish girl—you deserve to be taught a lesson. Beaten!"

"Oh, really? *Beaten?*" I mock, feigning shock, my voice dripping with sarcasm as I push him further.

"Six, enough!" Gamu's voice breaks through, demanding attention.

"No," I say firmly, barely pausing. "Five."

"If you truly wanted to save your people," Mwendo snarls, turning to Gamu with a feverish intensity in his eyes, "you'd do what's right. The ancestors brought you here for the child! Prove your repentance, and earn your place as a leader—not by barking orders, but by sacrifice!" His face twists in zealotry, his voice rising like a preacher inciting the crowd.

Gamu's eyes widen, disbelief etched across her face. "You would have me do such a thing, Sekuru? Inspire it?"

"Six," I finish, my voice unyielding. Without hesitation, I twist Mwendo's arm sharply, the sickening crack of bone breaking the silence. His scream cuts through the air, raw and piercing, a sound that reverberates with pain and shock.

I grip his shattered wrist tightly, a dark satisfaction simmering beneath the surface. "Men like you disgust me," I say, my voice dripping with contempt. "You prey on the weak to inflate your ego, but you wouldn't last a second against someone stronger."

"Six!" Gamu's voice rises again.

CHAPTER 39

"Chiefess," I acknowledge, my grip still firm on Mwendo's broken wrist, the tension between us taut like a drawn bowstring.

"Please," she pleads, her voice softer now, urging me to let go.

Reluctantly, I release him, the weight of my anger still burning beneath my skin. "Fine," I say, stepping back, though the fire in my eyes remains unextinguished.

Stumbling, Mwendo tries to regain his composure.

I let my contempt show, my voice cold and sharp. "You're all pathetic. You act as if you don't understand what's happening—your serpent has turned against you. Ndambira, the serpent itself has allowed a breach in your defenses to force you to fulfill our bargain! Mvure brought this upon itself. It's not Gamu's fault, and it might not be yours, but what's happening here is a consequence of your own mistakes. Your ancestors' selfishness has left you isolated. You thought you could remain on top forever, never needing anyone else. Now, you've pushed away your fellow Africans, built borders, and allowed yourself to be ruled by your own arrogance. You're alone in your false superiority, and now you suffer alone. In your desperation, you're willing to embrace darkness, even when it's right before your eyes."

Their eyes droop, the weight of shame settling over them.

"I am from Nakuru—you denied us aid for years! You

mistreated us when we sought refuge, and you flaunted your supposed superiority. I despise what you've become. I'm not here to help you because you deserve it; I'm here because it's the right thing to do. I stand with Gamu because she dares to challenge the mistakes of the past. That is true leadership—not merely doing what's popular or celebrated, but doing what is right." I pause, a severity falling upon my features. "And I'll protect that child with everything I have, even if it means I have to kill every last one of you. That is not a threat; it's a promise."

The weight of my words settles among them like immovable boulders, heavy and unshakable.

Taiwo, his face set in grim determination and big arms folded, clears his throat and speaks up in the weighed-down silence. "She's right." He pauses and clears his throat. "We need to stand together—alright, let's start barricading the doors and windows. Gather anything that can be used as a weapon. We are not going to surrender without a fight."

Reluctantly, the gathered people spring into action. They move furniture to create makeshift barricades and arm themselves with whatever they can find. The clamor of their efforts fills the air—a desperate, chaotic symphony of survival.

Gamu's mother is speaking to her in hushed, soothing tones, the air around them heavy with tenderness. I wait patiently for a moment before approaching and requesting a private conversation with Gamu. We move to a quieter corner, away from the anxious crowd. "Something happened while we were outside—something I believe is important."

Shiwo watches us from across the room, seated beside two girls who are huddled together in a fitful sleep.

"What happened?" Gamu asks, her voice low and urgent.

"When the darkness fell upon the villagers," I begin, "I felt it too. Something strange was unfolding. Every time your mother and Nyasha insisted they were not liars or traitors, it only seemed to provoke the spirit further, intensifying the villagers' agitation."

Gamu's eyes narrow as she processes this, her expression turning serious and thoughtful.

"I think," I continue, "that the spirit's power is being fueled by deception. It's drawing strength from the lies and confusion that surround us."

A look of realization dawns on Gamu's face. "You might be onto something. The serpent's power seems to stem from the very deceit embedded in Mvure—the curse is rooted in secrecy and manipulation that has plagued this village for years. To truly dispel this darkness, we need to expose every lie. Perhaps revealing the whole truth is the key to breaking the curse." She pauses, her gaze intense and resolute. "By shining a light on the truth, we can lead Mvure out of the shadows and into the light.

I frown, a note of skepticism in my voice. "But how will you persuade your family to confess and relinquish their power and respect? This will ruin them, and I suspect they won't comply. If you command it, they will likely turn against you. These people are more concerned with saving themselves than with doing what's right—I see it clearly."

Gamu contemplates my words, her expression thoughtful. "What I've learned about leadership is that to inspire change, you must lead by example, not by command. That's what I intend to do. We'll bring three villagers and demonstrate the truth to them. If it works, it might give others the courage to follow suit."

"Or it could backfire spectacularly. The villagers might react with even more hostility upon hearing the truth, revealing a more deep-seated hatred. Your family could become even more fearful and resolute in their refusal to expose the truth."

"I'm not sure, Six. But if the truth is what will break this curse, then we have no choice but to prove it. Showing them that the truth is the real solution might bolster their courage, however uncertain it may be. Perhaps, deep down, they do care about doing what's right."

"Alright," I sigh, resigning myself to the task. "I'll go find two volunteers, at least."

Her brow furrows with concern, but her tone remains soft and sincere. "Be careful, Six" she says gently. "I need you."

CHAPTER 39

My gaze softens, and for a brief moment, I'm captivated by the sincerity in Gamu's expression. The way the light highlights her features sparks a warmth inside me that tugs at my heart. I quickly look away, feeling my cheeks flush, unsure if Gamu noticed or if I'm just misinterpreting my own feelings. This sudden, intense reaction leaves me disoriented, questioning the depth of my emotions. What the fuck was that?

As I'm heading out, Shiwo rushes up to me, her voice tinged with urgency. "Six, where are you going?"

"Kunze."—*"Outside."*

Shiwo's frown deepens, her eyes brimming with hurt. "You and Gamu have been whispering together, and it feels like you're shutting me out. Do you have any idea how that feels? You, more than anyone, should understand the weight of how these people look at us. They might act kind, but there's always that flicker of disdain beneath the surface." Her voice trembles as she continues, "I'm one of your own, Six. I want to be involved, to help—especially for my brother. I need to be part of this fight to feel like I'm contributing something meaningful. But when you isolate me like this, it feels like you're abandoning me, like you've somehow switched sides. It's tearing me apart inside. I don't want to grow bitter and resentful, believing you've left me behind. I'm here too, and I'm your sister. I need to know that you still see me as part of this, that I still matter in this fight we're in."

"You're valuable, Shiwo—both to me and to Gamu. We want

to keep you safe and out of harm's way. Your well-being matters to us, and we don't want to see you caught in the crossfire. Your support is important, but we also need to protect you. That's why it might seem like we're keeping you at a distance, but it's only because we care about you."

Her eyes flash with determination as she presses on. "I understand that you want to keep me safe, but I need to be there with you. I want to fight alongside you, not just stand on the sidelines. If I stay here, it feels like I'm invisible, like I don't matter in this fight." She takes a step closer, her voice earnest. "Let me go with you. If people see that I'm not alone, if they see that I'm with you, maybe they'll stop judging me for being excluded. I don't want to be left behind, feeling like I'm just a bystander. I want to prove that I'm not just here to watch—I'm here to help, to be part of this struggle. If you truly see me as valuable, then let me stand by your side. Let me at least show them that I'm not alone and that I belong somewhere."

I consider her words, realizing there's no reason to keep secrets from Shiwo. My private conversation with Gamu was driven by urgency, not sentiment. I can handle this mission with one hand tied behind my back. Why not make it a bit more challenging—and a little more enjoyable? Not that Shiwo's presence will make a difference.

"Alright," I say, a hint of a smile tugging at my lips. "Let's go, *tete*."

Chapter 40

Shiwo and I slip out of the palace under the cover of night. The mob's frenzied cries pierce the silence, their shouts of "Vatengesi" and "Vanyepi" echoing off the royal shelters, closing in around us like a tightening net. *"Traitors—liars."* The crowd presses in relentlessly, their angry faces illuminated by the flickering torchlight as they surge against the royal barriers, creating a chaotic wall of bodies and noise.

My fingers find purchase on the rough stone, and with a final push, I haul myself over the edge. Finding an opening is nearly impossible; the mob's relentless press and shifting shadows make it hard to spot a clear path. I scan the chaos from above, searching for a way through. Shiwo follows closely from below, her anxious breaths barely audible. At last, I spot a narrow gap, a fleeting opportunity. Shiwo struggles but I reach down with a steady grip and pull her over the edge. We drop silently into the courtyard, our landing cushioned by the damp earth beneath us.

We weave swiftly through the narrow alleys and backstreets, sidestepping the surging swarms of enraged villagers. There is burning wood in the air and the village is a dark maze of flickering torchlight and shadowed huts. I cast a quick, reassuring glance at Shiwo. Her face, illuminated briefly, reveals a mix of determination and anxiety. Her eyes dart toward the roiling mass of the mob. "Relax," I murmur urgently. "We approach from the back and move fast."

She nods, her breath quick and controlled, though she makes a valiant effort to mask her fear. Our mission is straightforward: infiltrate the outskirts of the mob, extract two villagers without drawing attention, and make our escape.

We slip into the shadows, slipping behind the structures and edging closer to the commotion. We position ourselves discreetly behind the clustered groups of villagers, our presence nearly imperceptible amid the chaos. The roar of the mob swells, growing louder as we approach the fringes. Finally, we reach a narrow alleyway that offers a vantage point, allowing us to observe the outer edge of the chaotic throng. I scan the crowd, quickly identifying our targets. A man with a noticeable limp and a young woman adorned with a distinctive necklace that glints faintly in the torchlight.

I signal to Shiwo, and we slip into action. I approach the first target—the man with a limp who is struggling to keep up with the chaotic crowd. As he stumbles along, I creep up behind him, and with a quick motion, I deliver a sharp blow to the base of his neck. He crumples to the ground without a sound, his unconscious body barely making a whisper against the earth. Shiwo is already on the move, helping to drag the man into the safety of the shadows.

The young woman with the glinting necklace is more alert, but I approach her from the side, my hand steady as I strike with surgical precision. She falls quietly, and I pull her into the shadows where Shiwo is already waiting. Shiwo and I work quickly to bind their hands and ensure they remain unconscious.

"You carry the old man, he's lighter," I instruct.

Shiwo nods, her determination evident as she hoists the man's limp body by his shirt and begins dragging him with considerable effort. Each of us grips our respective burdens, moving steadily backward toward our escape route.

How we're going to get these two over the walls, I have no idea—but we'll take it one step at a time. "You got it?" I ask, glancing over to Shiwo. My breathing is tight.

"Yes," she replies firmly. Her breath comes in strained bursts, but she refuses to show any sign of weakness. Determination sharpens her every move.

Suddenly, two interconnected huts burst into flames, their fire spreading aggressively due to their close proximity. The blaze quickly intensifies, casting an ominous, hellish glow across the village. No one reacts but us.

"We need to put out these fires," I urge, frustration edging my voice. "They'll spread further if we don't act now."

Shiwo's eyes are wide with determination, though her anxiety and exhaustion are evident. She nods, taking a deep breath to steady herself. We spring into action. I dart toward the closest hut, flames already roaring through the roof. My heart races as I grab a makeshift bucket from a nearby well, desperate to combat the blaze. Each splash of water seems almost futile, evaporating before it can make a dent in the inferno, but I press on, every second critical to prevent the fire from consuming the entire village.

Shiwo is equally resolute. She locates a hidden well and starts hauling water with urgent, strained motions. Despite her trembling hands and the sweat and soot streaking her face, she pours the water onto the encroaching flames with relentless focus. The heat is suffocating, and thick smoke billows around us, obscuring our vision and choking our breaths.

We work in synchronized desperation, despite the surrounding chaos. I concentrate on the flames devouring the roof of one hut, while Shiwo battles the fire spreading to the adjacent structure. The inferno is merciless, the heat oppressive, but gradually, we begin to see signs of progress. The flames subside, their intensity fading as we manage to control the worst of the blaze. The two huts, though blackened and smoldering, are no longer in immediate danger of spreading further destruction.

Exhausted and covered in grime, Shiwo collapses against a

wall, her chest heaving with every ragged breath. "We did what we could," she says, her voice hoarse but tinged with relief. "Now let's get these villagers back and get out of here."

"Agreed."

I take a swift inventory of our surroundings, ensuring that our captives remain secure. Each of them is tightly bound, their unconscious forms leaning against one another, vulnerable but safe. Shiwo and I exchange a terse nod of mutual understanding before we set off, moving cautiously through the village. The chaotic roars of the possessed mob continue to echo ominously in the distance. I lead the way and my eyes constantly scan for any signs of trouble—though, more out of habit than necessity. The villagers are heavy but manageable, and we drag them along with grim determination.

Her voice shakes with exhaustion, labored with short, ragged breaths. "Six, did you ever find out who killed my brother?"

The question hangs in the air, a heavyweight that sends my heart racing. I clear my throat, trying to steady my voice. "No, I didn't—but I haven't forgotten *or* stopped searching."

"Have you discovered any leads? Anything—just to keep my mind occupied. Otherwise, I'll go mad with not knowing." She sounds so desperate and wounded.

I force myself not to look at her, instead focusing on the task at hand. "I'm sorry, Shiwo. I don't."

A wave of self-recrimination washes over me. The hypocrisy stings—lying to Shiwo to serve whatever purpose I think is righteous, the same deceit I despise in Gamu's family. It's a bitter pill to swallow, and I'm left feeling both humbled and conflicted.

We press on, our skin slick with sweat and grime, our throats parched. Beneath the exhaustion, a knife of guilt twists in my gut. Shiwo stumbles, a sharp cry escaping her as she bruises her knee. I drop the burden and rush to her side. "Hey, are you alright?"

I kneel beside Shiwo, examining her knee. "It's not too bad, at least," I reassure her. But her sudden shift in demeanor catches me off guard. She moves with startling swiftness, and before I can react, I feel a sharp sting at my neck. "Ouch!" I instinctively press my hand to the spot, rising quickly.

My vision sways and the world tilts. "Shiwo, what have you done?" I manage to croak, my breathing growing heavy and erratic, struggling to stay upright.

My sight blurs, but I catch a glimpse of her cold, detached expression—the last thing I see before the world starts spinning uncontrollably. "Sh..." I begin to speak, but the word is swallowed by a wave of numbness. Darkness closes in rapidly, my legs buckling beneath me as I collapse, the fading muffled chaos of the village the last thing I hear before everything goes black.

Chapter 41

I wake up groggily to the sound of creaking wood and the relentless sway of the sea. My head throbs with a dull ache, and my limbs feel heavy and bound. Blinking slowly, I take in my surroundings: the dimly lit interior of a wooden ship, its walls lined with rough planks and sparsely decorated with nautical knick-knacks. The ship's gentle rocking and the distant sound of waves are oddly soothing, but a creeping sense of dread fills the air.

The remnants of my last memory come back in fragmented flashes—Shiwo's sudden, unsettling change, the sting of a needle, the disorienting plunge into darkness. I shift slightly, testing the restraints around my wrists and ankles, realizing I am tied to a rough wooden bench in a small, confined space—captured again. *Fuck.* The ropes binding me are tight, though not excessively intricate, allowing for some limited movement. I turn my head, and my eyes fall upon a sight that drains all vitality from my body.

In the dim, oppressive room, Ndambira's lifeless form hangs from a rope, suspended grotesquely from the ceiling of the ship. His face is contorted in a mask of excruciating pain.

His suit is barely recognizable, reduced to tatters, and his skin is marked by unmistakable signs of severe torture—deep cuts, bruises, and burns. From the holes in his white socks, it's evident that several toes are missing.

My breath catches in my throat, an overwhelming wave of shock and confusion flooding my senses. *How is this possible?* The formidable, untouchable Ndambira, now reduced to a pitiful, tortured spectacle, hangs lifelessly on his own ship. This man, who came here with his company to seize Mvure, was supposedly an instrument of the serpent. He was the enemy, yet here he is, dead. My heart pounds erratically as I struggle to make sense of this horrifying scene. *If Ndambira is dead, then who is orchestrating this chaos?*

A low murmur of conversation draws my attention, pulling my gaze toward a small, barred window. Through the narrow slits, the pale light of early morning filters in, casting an eerie glow over the choppy sea outside. The muffled voices become clearer as I strain to listen, catching fragments of their urgent conversation.

I hear footsteps.

"She's coming to," a much closer voice says, hushed yet filled with a sense of urgency. "Good," replies another voice, colder and more authoritative. *Shiwo's voice.*

The door to the small hold creaks open, and she steps into view. Her face is a mask of grim determination, her eyes holding a hint of something dark and unsettling. She meets

CHAPTER 41

my gaze. "You're awake." Her voice is cold, her eyes hard. "Comfortable?"

I glare at her, my voice hoarse but defiant. "Very."

A tense silence stretches between us. I continue glaring at her, waiting for an explanation, my eyes demanding answers even as the weight of betrayal settles in.

"We only needed you to lure her," she says. "But then you lied to protect her, proving your loyalty."

"Lied? Loyalty, Shiwo? What are you talking about?" I struggle to make sense of her accusation.

"Your loyalty to Gamu!" she snaps. "You lied about her killing my brother. You knew the truth, but you chose to cover it up!"

Her accusation lands like a punch to the gut, leaving me stunned and disoriented. "No, Shiwo. I was protecting you," I try to explain, my voice faltering as I struggle to make sense of this unraveling reality. "I was—I *promise.*"

"No!" Her voice rises, cracking with anguish and anger. "You were protecting her. You cloaked it in compassion, but your loyalty shifted to her, Six. Whether you realized it or not, you chose her over us."

"No, that's not true," I protest, but my voice lacks conviction. And then, suddenly, the weight of the truth hits me—I realize it is. Something had shifted within me, something quiet yet undeniably powerful, something tied to Gamu. "Shiwo, I never meant to deceive you—to *hurt* you. I struggled to find the right words, and we needed Gamu on our side, alive. I didn't want to add to your pain, especially when I learned about the baby—when you told me it was Kail's. I was torn between revealing the truth and protecting something precious from you. Please, you have to believe me." My voice trembles, cracking under the weight of my guilt.

"Oh please. That lying whore deceived us!"Her voice shakes, wavering between fury and heartache. "That fetus isn't my brother's!"

I'm stunned, my mind reeling. "No, she couldn't have done that; she wouldn't do such a thing to you—or anyone."

"Well, she did," she retorts curtly.

"How can you be so sure? Did the serpent tell you? It thrives on deception, Shiwo. You can't trust it."

She scoffs, her expression darkening. Without warning, she makes a subtle, almost imperceptible gesture with her hand. A cold, invisible grip tightens around my throat, constricting my airways with a crushing force. It feels as if my blood has turned to lead, clogging my veins and suffocating me from within. My lungs are squeezed shut, and a searing pain constricts my windpipe. Panic surges as my vision darkens, edges of reality blurring into a suffocating void. Just as the darkness begins to close in and I teeter on the brink of unconsciousness, she releases me with a cold, detached ease.

Gasping for breath, I struggle to steady myself, my body trembling. Her voice, calm and chilling, cuts through my disoriented state. "I can sense that the blood in that fetus is not mine." Her tone is unsettlingly serene as if the terror she's inflicted is merely a casual observation.

My heart pounds against my chest as I fight for each desperate, ragged breath. My throat burns, the phantom of her invisible grip still lingering, as if icy fingers are wrapped around my windpipe. The reality of what just happened crashes over me—Shiwo has magic. *Has she always had it?* No, it's impossible. *But how has she done this?* The disbelief is overwhelming, my mind spinning as I try to grasp the full scope of this revelation. *How could it come to this?*

"Shiwo," I manage to croak out, my voice weak and trembling, "if you see nothing to envy about this place, then why would you align yourself with the very darkness that has corrupted it?"

"I don't care!" Her voice lashes out with a venom I've never heard before, raw and seething with anger. "Everything else—Mvure, the serpent, even you—means nothing to me anymore. Ndambira's ambitions were all-consuming, driven by a relentless desire to conquer Mvure and every other village within his reach. Tragically, this grand vision reduced him and his men to mere spectators, confined to the docks where they could only spread fear without ever taking decisive or meaningful action. The serpent, bound by its pact, had to protect Mvure—it couldn't extend Ndambira's power beyond that. If anything, it was an act of desperation from its side. It was an act of desperation on its part.

It came to me on that boat ride here, whispered promises of power and vengeance. I was a better tool, more willing to do whatever it takes. Someone who could achieve its goals without jeopardizing its own interests. I arrived with ample potential, thanks to you. I am unburdened by any attachment to Mvure's insipid history of selfishness and arrogance. All I seek is vengeance for my brother. The serpent saw in me the opportunity to fulfill its dark desires, to harness a power that Mvure's insipid, self-satisfied denizens could never hope to wield. My quest for revenge aligns perfectly with its goals, and it has chosen me as the instrument of its reckoning."

"In exchange for what?" I manage to breathe out, my voice shaking with disbelief. "The fetus? Shiwo, this isn't you—you'd never harm an innocent child. Please, you have to fight this."

"I don't have to fight anything, Six," she replies coldly as if the words alone justify everything. "I've secured Ndambira's company, and I will withdraw his forces from Nakuru. You can thank me for accomplishing what you failed to."

"I can't let you do this, Shiwo," I say, my heart breaking.

"You see exactly what I mean?" she snaps, her voice rising. "Your loyalty is with her!" Her face contorts, twisted by rage and anguish, her eyes burning with a feverish intensity that's terrifying to witness. A dark influence seems to warp her features, turning her into someone I can hardly recognize.

"It's you!" she screams, her voice a mix of fury and despair. "You did this to me! Turned me into a victim. Your lies—your deceit—unleashed a torrent of whispers that plagued me. The serpent whispered betrayal, grief, vengeance—seeds you planted, seeds that have festered into madness!" Her voice cracks, climbing into a high-pitched, frenzied wail. "I fought them—the relentless whispers, the tempting promises. I reasoned with myself until I couldn't any longer. The darkness—oh, the darkness—it consumed me!"

She's trembling violently now, her eyes wild and unfocused, as if she's lost in a nightmare she can't escape. "And when I arrived, the way that family looked at me, the way you and she schemed in the shadows, the way you followed her around like a slavering lapdog!" Her voice erupts into a piercing shriek, her fury spilling over like a dam breaking. "I hate you both! I hate you! I hate you!" Tears stream down her face, mingling with her furious cries. "This way, I can finally claim my justice and grasp at a shred of freedom from this endless torment!"

This isn't the Shiwo I once knew; the person standing before me is a twisted reflection, a stranger born from the darkness she has embraced. I am paralyzed, unable to fully grasp the horrifying transformation unfolding before me. It's like watching a nightmare come to life—her once kind and innocent demeanor has been replaced by something far more sinister, something more horrifying than the unsettling changes I've witnessed in the villagers. The intensity in her voice, the depth of her emotions, feels like a force that has been consuming her for decades, though she arrived in Mvure just yesterday. The serpent's influence has twisted her grief and anger into a nightmarish distortion of reality. Her suffering has been magnified beyond the bounds of sanity, creating a reality that is both horrifying and incomprehensible.

"Shiwo," I plead, my voice breaking. There's nothing more I can say. She's beyond help.

Her voice drops to a chilling whisper, her face contorting into a twisted sneer that seems to revel in the horror she's become. "Since I began to embrace this rage and thirst for vengeance, I've felt a sickening exhilaration, a lightness that makes me feel more alive, more powerful than ever." She rises with a jerky, unsettling grace, her movements eerily fluid and unnatural.

Her eyes, once warm and familiar, have transformed into cold slits, narrowing like those of a serpent. The shift in her gaze is both mesmerizing and horrifying, as though her humanity has been eclipsed by something far more sinister. Out of the shadows, a black snake materializes; it moves with a deliberate, sinuous grace, coiling itself around her neck with an unsettling intimacy. Shiwo's voice takes on a serpentine hiss, an echo of the creature draped around her. "She'll come soon," she intones, the words slipping from her lips with a slithering, almost hypnotic rhythm.

Chapter 42

Outside, the fog clings to the ground like a living entity, swirling around my ankles as I walk. The grass is slick with dew, and the biting chill of the night air seeps through my skin, numbing me. My feet sink into the soft earth with each step, but I press on. I make my way to the backyard, where the darkness deepens and the fog thickens, wrapping around me like a suffocating shroud. The only sound around me is the occasional rustle of leaves and faint whispers of the night breeze.

I reach a small clearing in the grass. I pause, my breath coming in shallow, ragged gasps. Though my eyes are open, they see nothing of the world around me, locked instead on the knife now clutched in my hand—a slender, gleaming cold instrument with an edge that seems to hunger for blood. With the knife raised, I hold it poised in the air, my heartbeat pounding in my ears. The thought of the impending pain sends a thrill through me, a mix of fear and anticipation that almost feels intoxicating. My grip tightens, my hand trembling slightly as I prepare to plunge the knife into my flesh. But then, a sharp, authoritative voice—*"Iwe!"*—cuts through the silence like a bolt of lightning. The elderly woman's rebuke pierces through my haze, jolting my body and halting my movement as though struck by lightning.

My eyes snap wide open, filled with raw terror and confusion and the angry murmur of the mob floods my senses immediately with sudden clarity. Their voices have grown weary and strained as if they're being forced to continue despite their exhaustion.

The encroaching light of dawn illuminates the scene, and I am washed by the realization of how much time has passed without my awareness. The weight of the moment settles heavily on me. Breath coming in ragged gasps, I look down at the knife in my hand. The horror of what I almost did crashes over me like a mighty tidal wave, leaving me shaken and disoriented. The fog begins to lift, and with panicked breaths, I stagger backward, my heart racing in my chest. The knife slips from my fingers, meeting the ground with a muted thud.

My body trembles violently as my mind reels from the chilling realization of what could have happened if I had not awakened in time. I steady my breathing, trying to steel my nerves. The world is suddenly deathly quiet—the mob worn out. Suddenly, a gentle sound breaks the silence. From the shadows in the corner, a small yellow snake, a child snake, slithers quickly past me. I gasp and step aside, my heart pounding.

As I gaze into the darkness where the snake disappeared, my curiosity and fear mingling, I take a tentative step forward.

CHAPTER 42

The shadows seem to shift, almost as if they are alive, watching my every move.

"Gamu, "a voice jolts me, breaking the eerie silence. "Uri right here?"—*"Are you alright?"*

I turn sharply, my heart still racing, to find Taiwo standing at the edge of the clearing, his face etched with concern. The moonlight casts a pale glow on his features, highlighting the worry in his eyes.

"I'm fine," I stammer, my voice barely above a whisper. "I was just getting some fresh air."

Taiwo steps closer, his gaze shifting to the spot where the snake had disappeared. "Fresh air?"

"Yes," I reply, trying to sound more confident than I feel.

He takes another step forward, and a shiver of unease runs down my spine. There's something unsettling about his presence, a feeling that the snake's appearance has only heightened. My instincts scream at me to be cautious.

I instinctively take a step back, widening the distance between us.

"You're not thinking of running, are you?" He asks, suspicion heavy in his voice.

"No," I say, though my past actions keep me from elaborating.

"I'm not."

"Your friends have been gone too long—Six, right? Where did they go?"

"Six, well, is restless—she wanted to go and survey the docks." I trust Shiwo and Six too much to think they'd desert me. Now I'm concerned something's happened to them.

"But Shiwo is *soft*."

"And Six is stubborn," I hope to dismiss the topic.

The suspicion does not budge. "Well, let's hope they return soon," he says, his tone unsettling. "Meanwhile, we should use this quiet, chiefess."

"Yes, of course," I reply.

His words seem like a veiled threat, and the way he watches me… But I try to brush it off—it's natural to be suspicious in times like these, but I need to stay grounded in reality. He gestures for us to walk back in, opening a space beside him. I step forward, and together we move back inside.

"Taiwo," I start as we walk, "is it true that my father grew ill when I left… because of me?"

Taiwo—there's something about him that reminds me of Sparrow—something familiar, something safe. It's the kind of feeling the mind instinctively grasps, running with it, desperate for an escape from the echoing chambers of its own skull. It's as if, in that rare moment of peace, it has found something that will not only listen but embrace it fully, a calm that longs to be filled.

He frowns, his expression a blend of sympathy and discomfort. "I disagree," he begins softly. "Let me share something with you—an observation. The men in our family have long struggled, not just with their circumstances but with their minds. Their inability to produce sons, the thinning of the lineage—it weighs heavily on them, leaving them feeling like failures. Soon, there will be no male to carry on our surname. They carry a deep anger born from a sense of injustice. And I think your father bore the brunt of it the most. To be a chief and yet... nothing. What does a chief do with that kind of emptiness? There's a root to the turmoil in their minds, but they refuse to acknowledge it, burying their pain in anger and blaming everything else."

I pause, his words sinking in like cold water washing over me. Suddenly, everything begins to make sense—Sekuru Mwendo, his relentless anger, his willingness to demand that I offer myself and my son as a sacrifice. It wasn't just cruelty—it was desperation, a frantic attempt to end the curse that had shadowed his life, to claw his way toward some elusive redemption. Though understanding it doesn't excuse it, not by any measure.

The puzzle pieces fall into place, and I can finally see the burden that's been passed down through generations like a silent curse, festering in the darkness. "Do you... feel this way too?" I ask, hesitating. Then quickly, I add, "But you don't have to answer that. I realize I might be prying."

"No, it's alright," he says after a moment, his voice softer. "I'm happy to talk about it." He pauses, his gaze distant. "It's good to talk about it."

"Please," I urge gently. "I would love to understand."

He takes a deep breath before speaking again. "The struggle of the mind—it's like a creeping darkness. It seeps in slowly, eroding your will, until you start to believe you're failing, that you're not enough. It weighs heavier than anyone lets on. It's a constant battle within, trying to live up to impossible expectations, trying to find a place in a world that no longer makes sense. It's like being trapped in a fog, unable to find a way out. But we don't talk about it. We don't seek help. We just… endure it, suffering in silence."

His words strike deep, and I find myself thinking of my father—the distant, haunted look in his eyes, the way he withdrew from everyone, the nights I heard him pacing endlessly, restless and tormented. He was crushed by the weight of unspoken expectations, unable to bear the burden of disappointment.

"It's wrong to suffer in silence," I say, surprised by the intensity of my own voice. "Why does it have to be this way?"

We pause just outside the entrance. Inside, a few people have succumbed to exhaustion, lying awkwardly on the floor in positions that speak of discomfort but also a deep fatigue. Others sit rigidly, fighting to stay awake, their eyes wide and alert, clinging to some sense of maturity or dignity. Despite the silent struggle to remain present, the hall is eerily still, punctuated only by the rustling of clothes or the occasional sigh of resignation.

Taiwo looks down, a shadow of grief passing over his face. "There is no help available—no ear for it. It's what we were taught," he says quietly. "For us men, strength means never showing weakness. It's been drilled into us—that speaking of our struggles makes us less... capable. Less of a man. But it's a lie. A dangerous one."

I nod, feeling a surge of anger and sadness. "From what I've learned, suffering in silence only deepens the shadows that enshroud us. True strength, contrary to what I once thought, isn't merely about enduring pain. It's about resilience—standing firm in the face of overwhelming darkness. Darkness thrives behind closed doors and shut windows, convincing us that opening them will make no difference. It whispers that darkness is all there is and that light is just a false promise. But how can we know unless we try to let in the light? How can we be sure that the light it fears isn't really out there, waiting to shine through?"

He meets my gaze with a serious intensity. "I'm glad you see it that way—because I do as well. This perspective might be crucial for what's unfolding around us. The darkness has loomed over us for too long, and perhaps it's time we confront the secrets we've kept hidden. Maybe now is the moment to let the light in and challenge the shadows that have shaped our world."

His words catch me off guard and I speak, encouraged by them. "It seems too simplistic, doesn't it? Too simplistic to be a solution... But confronting ourselves and the truth is far from simple. It's easier to pick up weapons and fight, to distract ourselves from our inner battles. That's Nyoka's strength—he knows we'd rather shed blood than face the truth. That blood will indeed be shed here before anyone here is willing to begin to expose the truth and set everybody else here free."

His face is etched with gravity as he nods in solemn agreement, the gravity of our conversation settling heavily between us. His eyes lock onto mine, carrying a profound intensity. "Gamuchirai, I need to tell you something important," he says with earnest conviction. "You may have wandered and lost your path before, but that was necessary. You had to find a new way to confront your own challenges so you could bring about true change. Your father, wherever he may be, understands this and takes pride in your journey. Getting lost is almost inevitable, but finding a better way through that loss—that's the real challenge. I believe in your calling." He rests a comforting hand on my shoulder, his gaze steady and reassuring. "Forgive them," he advises gently, "and be patient. They lack the experience to make better choices."

I nod in understanding.

Taiwo's expression shifts to one of concern as he continues, "But now, we face another challenge. I'm not sure how we can move the unconscious children all the way to the north dock without assistance."

"Perhaps we don't need to move them after all," I suggest. "If we bind them securely and prevent them from causing any more harm—even if the serpent tries to invade their minds—they'll only exhaust themselves without causing damage. This way, we can focus on confronting the evil at hand. We'll need to act swiftly with that because we can't afford to let them suffer any longer than necessary."

"But how can we act without a solution? You mentioned consulting the ancestors."

"I have consulted them," I reply. "I've made offerings to the spirits, hoping to hasten their response, but so far, there's been no sign. Timing is crucial. The ancestors can guide us and offer wisdom, but they do not have the power to alter destiny itself—that is governed by a higher force beyond them. Perhaps the moment for their guidance has not yet come."

He nods, his expression shifting with unease. "In the meantime, we must do what we can and focus on what's within our control. But can we trust the guards?"

"I don't know," I admit, trying to make sense of the situation. "It's unusual that the serpent hasn't targeted the workers or the guards. It seems there was never a true intention to harm us directly. For some reason, the serpent is relying solely on fear tactics now. Patience is no longer a valid excuse—it's as if the serpent is operating from desperation."

At that moment, my mother, wrapped tightly against the cold, approaches us. She looks tired, her movements slow. "They've lost consciousness at last," she murmurs, a yawn escaping her lips.

A sense of urgency drives me to step outside the gates now, my determination fueled by the realization that I have waited far too long. The mission was never meant to be a test for Six; I had only allowed this time to pass to avoid causing chaos and backlash if all of us were to vanish—there would be an uproar that I have run away again. But I've been anxious and praying for their return for far too long now—opinions don't matter anymore.

But Shiwo emerges unexpectedly from the shadowed edge of the shelter. She stumbles into view, looking as if she's just survived a harrowing ordeal. Her clothes are disheveled, her face bruised and swollen, as though she's stepped out of a fiery chaos. Her eyes, red and swollen from crying, reflect a depth of anguish that grips my heart. I rush to her, my breath catching in my throat.

"Gamu," her voice is a strained whisper, fraught with pain and urgency. "He took her."

The words hit me like a physical blow, tightening around my chest. "Who took her?" I manage to choke out, my voice trembling.

Her voice is barely more than ragged whispers. "Ndambira—he took her. They're inside the village."

My blood runs cold at her words, but an intense, boiling urgency ignites within me—a singular, all-consuming drive to go after Six immediately and to deal with Ndambira once and for all. I turn to leave, but my mother's voice stops me.

"Gamuchirai Danai Darare!" She snaps, her tone sharp with frustration. "Where do you think you're going? Have you forgotten your duty? You came here to assume your role, yet now you act impulsively, driven by personal vengeance and neglecting your responsibilities to your people. If these men are inside the village, what will happen to your people? Will you not lead them?"

"The people aren't the immediate threat!" I retort, my frustration boiling over. "The soldiers aren't going to fight against men, women, and children who are barely conscious. Every second I waste here could mean Six's death."

Taiwo steps in, his voice firm and steady. "This isn't just about your people. This whole situation has been a trap designed to lure you out. Taking Six is the final move to draw you into the open."

"Ndambira isn't interested in harming civilians directly," Shiwo adds urgently. "His plan is to infiltrate the village, plant his forces, and then seize control from the royal family—just like he did with Nakuru. This is the perfect moment to strike while he's busy spreading his forces. That's if you're prepared to confront him head-on."

"Nonsense!" my mother exclaims, her face etched with worry. "How can Gamuchirai take on an administrative commander?"

I meet her gaze squarely, feeling the weight of her doubt and fear. "I have magic, Mama."

Her eyes widen in shock and disbelief. "Magic? What kind of magic, Gamuchirai? Do you too have a pact with darkness?"

"No, Mama," I say firmly, trying to calm her fears. "It's not what you think. My magic comes from our ancestors. It's blood magic, a sacred legacy passed down through our family. Yes, it's powerful, but it's not dark. It's meant to protect and serve our people."

Her face is a mix of confusion and fear. "Blood magic? But that's not—there's no such thing in our family, and you certainly have never shown any sign of such strength."

"Mama, please!" I plead, desperation cracking my voice. "I need you to understand." I channel my magic. The energy courses through me with a fierce intensity, and Taiwo's body tenses before he collapses to his knees, gasping for air. His eyes roll back, and for a moment, he is completely incapacitated.

CHAPTER 42

I release the spell immediately, my heart pounding as I watch him struggle. Taiwo's breaths come in ragged, desperate gasps, his chest rising and falling with violent intensity as he tries to regain his composure. The silence is deafening, punctuated only by his strained breaths. My mother's face has drained of color, her eyes widening in horror. She stumbles back, unable to process what she's just witnessed.

"How can you wield such power without succumbing to darkness?"

"Discipline and respect," I reply softly, rushing to Taiwo and helping him as he clutches his throat, his breaths coming in ragged gasps. "I am so sorry, Taiwo."

Taiwo continues to massage his throat, tears streaming down his face from the strain. The gravity of my magic hangs over us, its impact settling in with overwhelming intensity. I straighten up, my resolve hardening. "You need to leave without me. Escape while you can—I'm going to confront him." I begin to walk away, the urgency to escape the judgment and rejection pushing me forward. "Come on, Shiwo."

"Gamuchirai!" My mother's sharp and pleading voice halts me in my tracks.

My heart rushes with unexpected relief at her reaching out to me. Tears brim in her eyes as she reaches out, her hands trembling as they touch my face. "You're only one person. You're just a girl; you're my daughter."

"I will go with the guards, but I must go," I insist, my voice breaking under the burden of urgency and emotion.

"Guards?" She scoffs, her despair evident. "They're no match for what's coming. They're mere decorations."

"What do you suggest we do, Mama?" I plead, my voice trembling with desperation. "This magic was given to me for a reason. Power isn't a gift of privilege but a responsibility, given because there was a duty I was meant to fulfill. It wasn't meant to make me exceptional but was given because I was destined to be in the right place at the right time to face this challenge. If I don't confront him, he will come to us, seize control, and we might be left defenseless—or worse, all of us could be in grave danger. We have no way to protect ourselves if he attacks us first!"

The silence is defeating, the gravity of our predicament paralyzing. Taiwo steps forward, his voice steady and determined. "I will go with her."

I look at him, overwhelmed by his offer, "Thank you, Taiwo."

My mother's tears flow freely now, her eyes fixed on mine with a mixture of deep sorrow and reluctant acceptance. "Gamuchirai," she says, her voice quivering as she looks up. "What have we done? What have I done? She is my daughter—will you really take her away from me?" Her gaze meets mine, filled with anguish. "You've grown into a woman beyond anything your father and I could have ever hoped for," she sobs. "And yet, you're still my daughter."

CHAPTER 42

"I am your daughter," I say softly, taking her hands in mine, trying to offer comfort. "But I also have a destiny. You and the others are in more danger than you realize. These unconscious people were never the true target; they were a distraction. What Ndambira truly desires is the serpent's power, and he won't stop until he gets it. I need you to take the boats and use the river to escape. Please."

She sobs intensify, her grip on my hands desperate. "I cannot abandon you. I cannot abandon our people. If you die." Her voice breaks, choked by her anguish. "We will have failed them."

"No, Mama," I insist, my voice steady despite my own fear. "You wouldn't be abandoning anyone. It's far better to escape now, gather our strength, and fight another day. If you stay here and die a prideful death, we lose not just the battle, but the war."

The desperation in my voice seems to cut through her anguish. She looks at me with a blend of defeat and reluctant acceptance, her tears flowing freely. "But how can I live with the knowledge that you're risking your life? That we might never see you again?"

"I know it's hard," I squeeze her hand. "But you have to trust me. Trust that the force guiding my path wouldn't have set this in motion just to see me fail. There's a purpose behind this, and I need you to believe in it as much as I do."

"I will go with you," declares Sekuru Mwendo, stepping

forward from the shadows, his jaw set with newfound determination. "Even after I opposed you, even when I raised my hand against you, you never once used your power against me—you knelt before me, humbled yourself. That kind of humility and restraint, mzukuru, speaks volumes about the woman you've become. My eyes have finally been opened to the truth. We cannot allow this darkness to define our lineage—I have certainly let it define me for far too long. But no more." He pauses, his voice softening with the weight of his confession. "I am grateful for your courage, for how you've held onto your belief in a better path, even when it seemed impossible and terrifying. If I, your Sekuru—older, supposedly wiser—dismiss this knowledge, then I deserve to be a beggar."

I turn to my Sekuru, my heart swelling with gratitude and relief. "Thank you, Sekuru. But the family needs you and Sekuru Tiritese here—to guide them through the forest and ensure their escape. We don't know what might be lurking there, if anything at all, but it's not a risk we should take lightly. Every moment counts. You must all get to safety while there's still time."

My Sekuru Tiritese, standing behind him with arms folded and a smirk on his face, says, "I could handle this myself, but I suppose I'll take Mwendo along. He's so clumsy he might trip over his own feet. Better to keep him out of your way, daughter," he jests.

I can't help but appreciate his attempt to lighten the mood. Sekuru Mwendo shakes his head, giving a resigned sigh as

CHAPTER 42

he places a hand on Sekuru Tiritese's shoulder. My mother looks at me, her face streaked with tears and exhaustion. "Do you really think this will be enough to face Ndambira and his forces?"

"I have to try. Six's life is on the line too, and she has been a great ally; a friend. And if I don't act now, we risk losing everything. We can't let Ndambira seize control. I need to confront him while he's vulnerable."

"Very well, Gamuchirai." She nods, her voice a blend of sorrow and reluctant pride. *"You are chiefess."*

I nod, feeling the weight of the title settle over me with a fierce determination. "I will see you again, Mama. I promise."

Sekuru Mwendo steps closer, placing a reassuring hand on my shoulder. "You are brave—your father would be proud."

I manage a smile through the knots tightening in my stomach. With renewed urgency, he steps into the hall and begins clapping his hands, the sound echoing through the space. "Wake up! We need to move!" he shouts, rousing everyone from their sleep.

Sekuru Tiritese lifts his fist in a playful gesture, and I meet it with a solid fist bump. With a final, reassuring glance at my mother, I turn to Shiwo and say, "Let's go, Shiwo."

"Ndokuda, Gamuchirai!" My mother shouts to me, her voice

trembling with urgency and fear, the words echoing through the air like a plea. *"I love you, Gamuchirai."*

I love you too, mama.

Chapter 43

Lightning splits the sky, jagged veins of raw energy flashing through the canopy. The thunderclap follows, shaking the very ground beneath my feet. It's dark in the forest, and I sprint through the underbrush, my heart pounding like a drum. Branches and leaves whip at my face, leaving stinging welts, and the ground is a blur beneath my feet. Low foliage snags at my legs, and sharp sticks scratch and bruise my skin, but I can't slow down. Every fiber of my being pushes me forward, the urgency of the moment driving me faster and faster.

I know a story *from a dream.*

In this dream, there's a woman who resembles my mother, though it isn't her, but a great ancestor. She is white like me, an albino, with skin as pale as moonlight, untouched by the sun's harsh rays. Her hair is a striking shade of ginger, with fiery strands that seem to catch and reflect even the faintest glimmers of light. Each strand is as delicate as spun gold, framing her face in a halo of warmth and intensity. Her eyelashes, too, are a vivid orange, curling gently like the fronds of a fern. She says she was the first in her family, born after her mother, a woman from an unnamed tribe, was struck by lightning.

This woman visits me in my dreams, her presence shrouded in an eerie glow. She speaks of the lightning that struck her mother, revealing it was no ordinary bolt. It wasn't a natural occurrence, but the chaotic aftermath of a ritual gone horribly wrong. The energy from the ritual, like a wild storm, surged uncontrollably, striking everything in its path, including her mother while she was pregnant. That fateful strike was the catalyst for her becoming a magic wielder—a witch, they would call her. It wasn't just her skin that set her apart, but her ability to commune with and command snakes, a power born from the very essence of that errant lightning.

In the dream, she reassures me with a calming presence, her eyes reflecting a deep, knowing light. "You are not alone," she says softly. "It is because of me that the snakes do not strike you. They recognize you by your blood, a connection we share." She gazes at me with a mixture of awe and pride, marveling at my rare and wondrous gift.

Her words wrap around me like a protective cloak, filling me with a sense of belonging and strength I had not known before—before Six and Osi, and before Amani. At first, I thought I had conjured her from the depths of my own mind, a creation born from my desperate need to soothe the aching void of loneliness. She seemed like a figment of my imagination, a balm for my solitude. After all, I had heard about the serpent from Six long before the dreams started

CHAPTER 43

to take hold. It only made sense that my subconscious was drawing upon those tales to fuel my visions.

Yet, recent events have solidified her presence, making her more tangible and immediate than anything I can touch or feel with my own hands. Her reality now overshadows even the steady, reassuring beat of my own heart. Her words, once dismissed as mere whispers of a dream, have acquired a gravity and urgency that I can no longer ignore. This is precisely why I have been so careful to follow her guidance and keep what I know to myself.

She shares a prophecy, warning me to never reveal it, not even to those closest to me. One of them, she says, will be taken by the will of the snake, but she doesn't know who, and neither will I until the moment comes to act. My silence has been a deliberate act of preservation. It's happening, *it's here*—the *prophecy* is here.

I am sorry, *Amani* and *Osi*. I had no time to explain.

I push through the dense forest, my breath coming in ragged gasps. The path ahead is obscured by shadows and undergrowth, but I can't afford to hesitate. The dream's warning echoes in my mind, urging me onward.

Another bolt of lightning illuminates the world in a blinding flash, and I stumble over a root, my ankle twisting painfully, but I catch myself and keep running. The pain is nothing compared to the fear driving me. Branches snap underfoot, and I dodge around trees, my eyes darting for any sign of the path I need to take. The forest is alive with the sounds of the storm, the wind howling through the leaves, and the distant rumble of thunder. Each step is a battle against the terrain, but I can't stop, *won't* stop.

In the distance, I see a glimmer of light—a break in the trees, a way forward. I push harder, my muscles screaming in protest, but I force myself to ignore the pain. Every second counts.

She told me, "Kana chimwe chinhu chakanyanya kukanganisika chikaitika, mhinduro inotanga kufamba panguva imwechete. Uchazozviona chokwadi chemashoko angu uye unzwisise uremu hwemutoro wako."

"When something profoundly wrong occurs, a solution is set into motion simultaneously. You will come to see the truth in my words and understand the weight of your burden."

I've come to understand that my albinism is not the burden—despite how others have tried to make me believe it was. The true burden was the weight of their judgment, their stares, their whispers. But even that, I realize now, was necessary. I had to feel that pain, had to carry it, so it could ignite the fire within me—the fire that would drive me to bring about change.

On *that day,* during the sacrifice, something profoundly wrong was unfolding. A solution, set in motion generations ago, had been designed long before anyone could have imagined my arrival. This gift was bestowed upon me because I was destined to be in the right place at the right time to set things right and mend what had gone wrong. Indeed, there exists a power greater than memory itself, transcending both mortals and spirits alike.

Finally, I burst through the last line of trees, emerging into a small clearing. The rain begins to fall, heavy drops soaking me instantly.

Chapter 44

The morning sky darkens further, the clouds churning like a cauldron as distant thunder hints at an approaching storm. The village lies in a haunting silence, the villagers are unconscious so navigating and reaching this point—this close to the docks—was relatively easy. Taiwo, Shiwo, and I crouch behind a stack of crates near the docks, peeking around the edge. My gaze locks onto the enemy boats anchored just offshore, their dark silhouettes ominous against the brooding sky. The sea churns violently, the waves crashing against the hulls of the boats with a menacing force, sending sprays of saltwater into the air. The scent of brine is potent with the fresh, metallic tang of the approaching rain.

The soldiers disembark from their boats, relaxed and absent-minded, given the village poses no threat. Their only task is to secure the unconscious villagers and take over the unguarded royal family, forcing them to submit. Hopefully, my family has made significant progress to the north docks, where they might escape.

Ndamira's forces are clearly advancing, but the absence of

CHAPTER 44

any soldiers so far makes me question the situation. Why was Six taken if their mission was only to round up a few villagers from the protest near the royal shelters? If the soldiers are positioned this far out, what could Shiwo and Six have been doing here?

Taiwo's eyes widen as he surveys the scene. "This is worse than we thought. They're everywhere."

"Yes, but only out here," I say, my voice tight with concern. "Shiwo, how did Six get abducted? What were you two doing out here?"

Shiwo doesn't hesitate. "There were a few soldiers by the crowd. Maybe they were sent to gather intelligence on the protest and the royal family."

I nod, still troubled. "But why the sudden move? If Ndamira's agenda hasn't changed, Nyoka should still be keeping them at bay, even with a peaceful infiltration. A takeover is a takeover."

"I don't know," Shiwo admits, frustration evident in her voice.

"It's not our main concern right now," Taiwo says, his face grim. "We should stay hidden and wait for them to spread out. We can handle the few guarding the boats. We can't take on all of them, and I'm not sure of your fighting skills."

"Taiwo, don't overestimate your strength," I warn. "Each

soldier is armed with a firearm. No matter how formidable you are, you can't use sheer strength against a gun. We need to be strategic and avoid direct conflict."

Taiwo looks bewildered. "What exactly are these firearms?"

It's clear he has no idea what a firearm is. His experience comes from village life, not from modern warfare. In Mvure, the idea of such weapons is foreign. I take a breath, knowing I need to explain quickly. "Pfuti izvombo zvinouraya kubva kure nekutsikirira kabhatani. Zvinorira, zvinokurumidza, uye zvinouraya. Hatigone kuzvidzivisa nesimba chete."—*"Firearms are weapons that can kill from a distance with a pull of a trigger. They're loud, fast, and deadly. We can't match them with just brute strength."*

Taiwo's face pales as the gravity of the situation sinks in. He swallows hard, his hands trembling slightly. "So they can kill us without even getting close? How are we supposed to fight against that? What about your magic?"

"In close combat, I can control an opponent's movements by manipulating their blood. But against firearms, I wouldn't stand a chance to get close enough to use it effectively. My magic is useful for precise control and defensive maneuvers, but it doesn't negate the need for strategy and stealth."

Taiwo's apprehension deepens. "If your magic can't protect us from guns, what's the plan?"

I notice his fear and place a reassuring hand on his shoulder.

"We need to be strategic. Direct confrontation isn't an option. We'll use the darkness to our advantage, avoid their patrols, and find a way to outsmart them."

Despite my words, the fear in his eyes and posture remains. "Taiwo, I don't expect you to go through with this if you're not ready. Your bravery has already been shown by standing with me and coming this far. You can turn back if you need to."

He takes a deep breath, his expression hardening with resolve. "I'm not going anywhere."

I offer a grateful smile. "Thank you."

The wind picks up, howling as it whips through the village, and the waves grow even more turbulent. The soldiers move into the village, their relaxed demeanor and confident chatter cutting through the silence. We stay hidden, waiting for the right moment to make our move. "I'll need to get closer to sense Six's blood and locate which boat she's on." My voice is now trembling from the cold that seeps in. The first heavy drops of rain begin to fall, their impact sharp and sudden.

"Shiwo, you will stay close to me." I lock eyes with her, my voice barely audible.

She nods.

Slowly, cautiously, we inch forward, emerging from our

hiding places with a quiet, shared resolve. But then, without warning, the sky splits open. A torrential downpour crashes down on us with an unforgiving intensity we hadn't braced for. The rain falls in thick, unrelenting sheets, pummeling our faces and bodies, drenching us within moments. We glance at one another, silently acknowledging the same truth—there's no turning back now. Despite the deluge, despite the cold biting through our skin and the wind howling like a restless spirit, we push forward, struggling to catch our breath as the storm rages around us.

The soldiers react to the sudden downpour with a mix of annoyance and frustration. Their relaxed demeanor quickly shifts as the rain drenches their uniforms. Some scramble to adjust their gear, trying to shield themselves with improvised rain covers or huddling under whatever shelter they can find. Their chatter becomes more strained, and voices are raised in irritation as they try to keep their equipment dry.

We step onto the beach, the coarse sand crunching underfoot. Suddenly, a sharp, urgent cry cuts through the thick curtain of rain.

"Gamu!" The sound is unmistakable—a desperate voice I know too well.

My heart skips a beat as I turn toward the village, straining to see through the torrential downpour. Barely visible through the rain, Sparrow's form emerges. Behind him, a flock of birds rushes in, their wings beating furiously against the storm. They dive at the soldiers with fierce determination, their beaks and talons plucking out eyes and rending flesh. Chaos erupts as the soldiers, caught in the downpour, scramble and scream. They fire wildly into the storm while others drop their weapons, futilely shielding their faces. Cries of agony pierce the storm's relentless roar. Flashlights cut through the dark, rain-soaked air, and frantic gunfire disrupts the sheets of rain, creating a dissonance of panic and violence. The birds, relentless in their assault, drive the soldiers into disarray and confusion.

A gunshot rings out, shattering my stance and the sky seems to rip open in response, a blinding flash of lightning splitting the heavens. In the distance, a voice shouts, *"We've got movement!"* The words are nearly drowned by the storm's roar.

I glance to my side and I freeze, my blood running cold. Taiwo collapses beside me, his body hitting the wet sand with a heavy thud, shock, and agony etched on his face, his eyes wide with the brutal realization of his fate. The source of the gunshot is glaringly clear—*Shiwo* stands a few feet away, her gaze as cold and unfeeling as the storm itself.

"Aiwa!"—*"No!"* I scream, the word tearing from my throat as I lunge toward Taiwo.

The rain washes my tears away as I frantically assess the damage, my hands trembling over his bloodied form. His blood seeps into the sand, spreading rapidly and darkening the pale grains. My heart pounds as I struggle to grasp the severity of his injuries.

Shiwo steps closer, her gun still trained on me, but something more sinister begins to occur. I feel a draining sensation as if my very life force is being siphoned away. I glance up in horror as her face seems to twist and elongate, morphing into something serpentine and malevolent.

"Fuck!" She screams, her voice twisted with deranged fury. She whirls around, her eyes burning with frenzied intensity as she takes in the nightmarish scene. "Find him!" she roars, her command slicing through the storm with ruthless authority. Her soldiers, witnessing their comrades being torn apart by birds and collapsing under the relentless assault, scramble in terror. Some try to shield themselves, while others flee in chaotic desperation. Spurred by Shiwo's icy command, their search escalates into a frantic scramble, a horrifying display of panic and desperation.

"Shiwo, what have you done?" I cry out over the storm's roar.

"You did this, Gamu!" She hisses, her voice dripping with malice. "You did this!"

Chapter 45

The ship's gentle rocking turns violent as rain hammers against the wooden hull, driven by howling winds. The storm amplifies the vessel's creaking, making the tiny cabin I'm confined in shudder and fill with water. The downpour is deafening, each droplet assaulting the deck above. The wooden walls groan with every gust, and the flickering lantern casts erratic, menacing shadows. My restraints dig into my wrists as I tug desperately for freedom, my heartbeat racing with each agonizing second.

A sharp crack of gunfire pierces the storm's roar. My heart leaps, freezing me in place as I strain to pinpoint the source. The gunshot is close and clear, cutting through the ceaseless rhythm of the rain. Panic surges within me as I grapple with the implications.

Gamu's name echoes in my mind. Shiwo was supposed to lure her here under the guise of my capture by Ndambira. The thought tightens my chest, and tears of frustration threaten to spill. I clench my jaw, fighting back the tears, but with renewed determination, my efforts become more frantic.

"Damn it!" I scream, my voice raw and desperate. The tears break free. My strength wanes, but I pull and tug at the ropes with every ounce of energy I have. The thought of Gamu being shot, possibly dead, leaves me gasping for breath, each inhale coming in ragged, shallow bursts. It feels as though it might burst from my chest. The ropes cutting into my wrists are like razors, and the force with which I'm tugging at them feels like it could crack my bones. "Damn it!" The desperation is so intense that it feels like I could tear my arms off just to free myself, to run to her.

The possible message flutters away, struggling against the relentless rain, while the echo of the gunshot lingers in my mind. The thought of them battling through the storm to reach me fuels a fierce urgency, battling the terror that it might be one of them who has been shot. I redouble my efforts against the ropes, my resolve hardening even as my heart remains fragile. With a final, desperate yank, my hand slips free, and a sharp pain shoots through me—I've cracked one of my wrists. I let out a moan of agony but quickly tear my tank top and wrap it around the injured wrist as a makeshift bandage. With the back of my hand, I wipe away the tears and snot, the urgency of the moment sharpening my focus despite the pain.

I hear footsteps hurrying in the corridor outside in my direction. I position myself against the wall, my heart pounding. In my view, this is Ndambira's tortured and rotting body. Though the sight fills me with a sense of relief and victory, it also churns my stomach. I want to vomit, my insides twisting in revulsion at the grotesque display of his suffering. The stench of decay assaults my senses and makes me gag.

The door hinges groan and a soldier steps inside, his gaze sweeping the room. I spring into action, my hands instinctively finding his throat despite the sharp pain from my cracked wrist. I squeeze with just enough force to cut off his air supply but not enough to kill, my strength faltering under the agony. His eyes widen in shock as he struggles against me, but I twist his body with a grim determination and slam his head against the wall. He collapses, unconscious, and I quickly strip him of his firearm and knife.

Armed now, I move cautiously along the dimly lit hallway. The narrow, swaying corridor seems to stretch endlessly; the ship's chaotic rocking is making it difficult to maintain my balance. I can hear the muffled shouts and clanging of metal from above, and my heart races as I approach a stairway leading up to the deck.

I ascend the stairs. The noise outside is deafening, and I finally reach the top, peering through a narrow gap in the hatch. The deck is a chaotic scene, but fewer soldiers are present than I anticipated. They move frantically in their drenched green uniforms, their attention fragmented. It seems that something on the shore has captivated their full attention and curiosity. I push the hatch open and slip through, instantly enveloped by the storm's fury. The rain stings my face, and the wind tugs at my clothes. I keep low, moving with purpose, battling the slick, rain-soaked surface to avoid sliding off and falling.

The first soldier I approach doesn't see me coming. I drive the knife into his side, and he collapses with a grunt. His comrade turns, eyes widening in shock, but I'm already firing. The shot is deafening in the storm, and he falls to the deck, clutching his chest. Chaos erupts. The remaining soldiers scramble to respond, their shouts lost in nature's roar. I dive behind a stack of crates, narrowly avoiding a volley of gunfire. Peeking out, I fire again, taking down another soldier. My movements are instinctual; each shot is deliberate and deadly. I move along the edge of the ship, using the rain and darkness to my advantage. The soldiers struggle to see clearly, and I pick them off one by one. Each shot brings another soldier down.

A group of soldiers desperately pulls on thick ropes, trying to secure the sails and stabilize the mast. I approach them from behind, my footsteps silent on the rain-slicked deck. I fire rapidly, the gun's recoil jarring my arm, but I don't relent. The soldiers cry out; some collapse immediately, while others stumble, clutching their wounds. Alarmed shouts and frantic clattering boots converge on me. A bullet whistles past, and I spot a soldier aiming directly at me. Without hesitation, I fire first, the shot ringing out. The soldier crumples, his gun clattering to the deck.

With the immediate threat neutralized, I sprint for the railing, vault over it, and plunge into the churning sea below.

CHAPTER 45

The icy water shocks my system, dragging me down in its cold embrace. I fight against the current, struggling to keep my head above water as I swim away from the boat. The gunfire fades into the distance as I push through the turbulent water, every muscle straining against the water's relentless fury. My arms, cracked wrist, and legs burn with pain and exhaustion, but I press on, driven by sheer will.

Finally, I reach the shore. My teeth chatter uncontrollably as I claw my way up the beach, the sand rough against my raw hands. My body aches from the cold and exertion, each movement a battle against the fatigue threatening to overwhelm me.

The rain lashes at my face like icy needles, and the wind howls in my ears, distorting every sound and reducing visibility to mere feet. Despite the storm's fury, the urgent commotion onshore cuts through. Enemy soldiers scream in panic as sporadic gunshots ring out. Flashes of light intermittently cut through the rain, offering unsettling glimpses of soldiers stumbling in disarray and the chaos unfolding around them. Birds swoop through the storm with brutal intensity, their talons raking at the soldiers' eyes, sending them sprawling in terror.

It feels like a surreal nightmare, a scene so outlandish it's hard to fully grasp. Is this Sparrow's doing? Has he always possessed such immense power? A surge of awe mixes with a pang of betrayal and anger—how could he have hidden this strength from us? This ability, if revealed earlier, might have helped us overcome the enemy in Nakuru before we lost so many friends and family. We knew he could communicate with birds, but to command them in such a devastating, all-encompassing assault—this is beyond anything I could have ever anticipated.

I feel something dark and unfamiliar settling over me—an overwhelming, oppressive weight that slowly transforms into a consuming rage. It's a sensation so intense and alien that it seems to seep into every pore, wrapping itself around my heart and mind. This anger, deep and primal, feels as though it's been waiting in the shadows, ready to surge forth at the perfect moment—it's not just mine anymore. I recognize it for what it is—the serpent's power. I can almost feel its cold, slithering presence lurking beneath the surface of my anger, feeding off the negative emotions that surge within me. The serpent's influence is insidious and pervasive, subtly whispering to me from the shadows of my mind. Its voice is faint but unmistakable, coaxing me to embrace this rage, to let it consume me and drive my actions.

The whispers are not loud, but they are persistent, an insistent murmur that urges me to take this personally, to let the anger fester and grow. They push me to view every setback, every loss, as a personal affront, a betrayal that justifies and amplifies my fury. The serpent wants me to feed this anger, to let it dominate my thoughts and actions, because it knows that by doing so, it can draw power from my suffering and deepen its hold over me. If I let this darkness take root now, I risk becoming like Shiwo—utterly consumed and possibly beyond redemption. This is the moment I must choose to trust that Sparrow, who has fought by our side and sacrificed so much, wouldn't have allowed our suffering to continue if he had the means to end it. He has stood with us, borne the weight of our battles, and made countless sacrifices for our cause.

Yet, the darkness presses in, gnawing at my resolve, hungry and voracious. Its whispers are insidious, echoing through my mind. I take a shuddering breath, trying to anchor myself, but the images of betrayal and loss invade my thoughts, each one a piercing reminder of the pain, each one stoking the fire of the darkness within. I grit my teeth and clench my fists tightly until my nails dig into my palms. I force myself to remember Sparrow's unwavering loyalty and his sacrifices. I've trusted him with my life more times than I can count, and he has never failed me. He stands with us now, fighting on our behalf. He would not have let us suffer if he had the power to change things. There must be a reason, a broader perspective that I cannot yet see.

"Leave me alone!" I shout, my voice cracking with raw desperation. The storm's intensity seems to lighten, becoming pure once more, though it continues to rage around me. I collapse to my knees, gasping for breath. I must find Sparrow and understand the truth before this darkness consumes me entirely.

Chapter 46

The soldiers, frantic and disorganized, scramble in their futile attempts to counter the onslaught of my feathered allies. My breath comes in ragged gasps, the downpour making every movement a struggle. "Go!" I shout. The birds dive and swoop with fierce precision. A soldier stumbles, a raven pecking savagely at his eyes. Another collapses, his throat torn open by a hawk's talons.

I weave between the huts, my heart pounding. The village is a battlefield slick with mud and blood. A soldier raises his gun at me, but a raven descends, its talons sinking into his flesh. His scream is swallowed by the wind as he falls. I slip and slide, barely keeping my footing. The soldiers are everywhere, but my birds are relentless, attacking with deadly precision.

I need to get to Gamu. Her safety is my only concern. I push forward, determined to reach her. The soldiers falter, their ranks thinning. With each fallen soldier, my hope grows stronger. Through the rain, I glimpse her on the beach, forcibly pushed by Shiwo, who has a gun trained on her. They move toward a rocky promontory jutting into the sea,

CHAPTER 46

just as the prophecy foretold. She stumbles against Shiwo's relentless push.

I have to save her—*this is my destiny.*

I push through the remaining soldiers, my birds clearing a path of carnage and terror. The soldiers cry out, try to flee and fight desperately, but they can't withstand the fury of my flock. The beach is a storm-lashed war zone, bodies littering the sand, their green uniforms soaked and stained. I step onto the beach, the transition from muddy ground to gritty sand barely registering as I break into a run. The waves crash violently against the shore as if the ocean itself is angry.

A sharp gunshot cracks through the air, and a searing pain rips through my calf. I stagger, my leg buckling under the sudden agony. Shiwo and Gamu whirl around, and Gamu's face contorts in horror. "Sparrow!" she screams.

Despite the intense pain radiating from my calf, I grit my teeth and focus. Without looking back, I command my birds with unwavering resolve, directing them to converge on Shiwo. They dive toward her, their talons and beaks poised to strike with lethal intent.

"Look at me, Sparrow!" Six's voice cuts through the storm, sharp with fury and betrayal.

My heart sinks as I turn to face her, dreading what I'll see. She's standing there, eyes blazing, her face twisted with anguish. "You lied to me!" she screams, her voice raw and gutted. "You lied to all of us!" She advances on me, gun trained unerringly, and through the rage and pain warping her features, she's almost unrecognizable.

"Six!" I shout, desperate, pleading. "What are you doing?"

"You kept this strength hidden while our friends and family died!" Her voice trembles, each word laced with bitter accusation. "Why, Sparrow? When you could have helped us—*saved* us."

It's not truly her. I know that. "Six, you have to fight this!" My birds circle above, agitated, sensing the tension, ready to strike. "I didn't have a choice!" My words are clipped, the pain in my leg sharpening my tone. "If Gamu reaches the top of those rocks, it will unleash something far worse than we've faced. Mvure, Nakuru—everything will drown in darkness. We're standing on the brink of disaster!"

Her eyes flick to the distant rocks, then back to me. Confusion and pain wage war on her face, but the gun remains steady. "Why should I believe you now?" she cries, her voice cracking under the weight of betrayal.

"Because it's me!" I shout, desperation clawing at my throat. "You know me, Six! I've always been there, by your side—you mean everything to me. We have to stop Shiwo. I didn't know who the traitor was—that's why I couldn't say anything! The mission was too dangerous to risk!"

CHAPTER 46

Blood drips steadily from my leg, staining the sand beneath me. I catch a flicker in her eyes, a shadow of the person she once was. Her gaze drops to the blood, her expression softening, just for a moment.

"No, you haven't always been there for me—you stood by as I suffered through every loss, as our home fell apart—you watched us suffer, refusing to offer your strength."

"No, Six. I had to make a choice—I knew this day was coming, I've always known. But the spirits warned me—they told me to stay silent. The reckoning that was coming was too great to risk telling even one wrong person. This darkness, it could have spread far beyond here. Look, Shiwo has betrayed us, just as the prophecy foretold—but it could have been you, Osi, or anyone else—look at what happened with Jengo. I wanted to tell you so badly, but I had a duty, Six. You have to believe me—I knew the day would come when Nakuru would be free, and it tore me apart to wait silently and watch you suffer. To know that if I did anything, lending my strength, it would risk the chance for Nakuru to be truly free in the end."

Her hesitation is painfully evident, her body shaking as the darkness claws at her from within. "No," she chokes, her voice thick with pain and resistance. The gun wavers, her hands trembling violently.

"Please," I beg, my voice cracking under the weight of desperation. "You and Osi—you're the only family I have. I've given everything for you. Don't let this destroy us. I know you can fight it, Six. Please, fight it!"

"You lied to me," she gasps, each word a battle against the shadow that tightens its grip on her soul.

"Tari?" I call out, voice trembling, fear gnawing at me.

"No!" Her cries echo through the storm, each "no" a tortured whisper of her inner struggle. She tries to lower the gun, but her hands shake uncontrollably. Her body trembles with the effort, her breath coming in ragged sobs.

"Tari, please," I call out again. "See me again. The way you saw me when no one else did."

She breaks down, her body wracked with uncontrollable sobs. "Leave me alone," she begs, her voice splintering into a fractured whisper. "Please… just leave me alone." Her head jerks from side to side, her face contorted in sheer desperation as if trying to shake off the darkness suffocating her. Her pleas dissolve into broken, gasping murmurs, "Ple—no—plea—sss— Don't make me—plea…" She cries, her hands trembling as she fights against the cold, unyielding grip of the gun.

Her entire being wrestles against the encroaching darkness, its shadowy fingers coiling tighter around her, dragging her deeper into its suffocating grasp. Then, in a moment both sudden and agonizingly slow, like frost creeping over glass, she goes deathly still. Her body stiffens as if the cold has consumed her completely. With a terrifying calm, she

CHAPTER 46

adjusts her grip, the gun steady in her hands. The barrel lifts, its cold gaze locking onto me, her eyes empty and unyielding.

Her gaze is empty. The warmth, the recognition—gone.

My heart pounds with a sickening dread, but I can't fully comprehend the reality until it happens. The gunshot's roar rips through the storm's fury, a deafening crack that slices through the relentless rain. I cry out—a sound—*a word? Her name? I don't remember*—but it's a desperate plea swallowed by the storm's unrelenting beat.

Chapter 47

The birds descend upon Shiwo, their talons, and beaks poised for a fatal strike. But what follows is a horrifying spectacle—a nightmare unfolding in the blink of an eye. With a single, fluid motion, Shiwo's hand sweeps through the air, and suddenly, a dark power unfurls from her, a force that mirrors my own—a blood-bending ability. The birds' cries transform into a twisted symphony of agony. In an instant, their small forms crumple mid-flight, plummeting to the ground in a lifeless heap. Blood streams from their eyes, pouring from their tiny bodies as Shiwo's power constricts and crushes them all at once, their lives snuffed out in a violent surge of darkness.

Horror grips me as I watch the carnage, my strength draining away with every heartbeat. Nausea rises, the pounding rain slashing across my skin, but all I can do is stagger back, my voice barely a whisper in the howling wind. "How... how is this possible?"

She turns to me, her expression sharp, her eyes gleaming with cruel certainty. "You still don't understand, do you?" Her voice is cold and biting, as though to outdo Mother

CHAPTER 47

Nature herself. "Do you even know the true source of your blood-bending power?"

I shake my head, trembling with disbelief. "No," I whisper weakly. "That's impossible—it belongs to my ancestors."

She lets out a bitter laugh, sharp and cold as shards of ice. "You fool! And where do you think they got it?" Her laughter fades, leaving only the sting of her words. "You mean your ancestors who dabbled in dark magic they never truly understood?" she retorts, her voice dripping with scorn. "It was on that fateful night when they dared to summon Nyoka's presence. The woman—your ancestor, *a witch* who succeeded in forging the pact—unleashed a power far greater than she could ever understand. Though she may never have admitted it, she was a woman consumed by hunger—greedy for power, obsessed with ridding herself of any trace of weakness. "Sound familiar?" she taunts, her voice laced with accusation.

I struggle to comprehend the sight before me—she looks almost unrecognizable now, her face twisted, and contorted in ways I never imagined. Her very essence has shifted, her features warped into something grotesque. The transformation is haunting.

"It's not the darkness itself that holds power," she continues, her voice rising, "but the force of the spirit that seeks it out. When conviction is strong enough, when desire or desperation pushes beyond reason, the spirit becomes like a magnet, drawing the darkness closer, and bending it to its will. She absorbed Nyoka's blood-bending abilities, a power so immense that it has lingered within your bloodline, dormant and untouched by those who came before you. But you—you've awakened it from its slumber at last—and the owner is eager to *whole* once more."

She revels in a cold, chilling satisfaction as if the serpent itself had become her god. "Move," she commands, her hand remaining steadfastly aimed at me.

I claw my way up the jagged promontory, the sharp edges of the rocks tearing at my hands and feet with every desperate scramble. The merciless sheets, turn the stone beneath me into slick, treacherous surfaces that threaten to send me tumbling. Behind me, faint but insistent through the relentless downpour, I hear Six and Sparrow shouting, their voices nearly lost to the howling wind and the thunderous crash of the waves below.

A particularly powerful wave crashes against the rocks, sending a surge of water up the promontory. I cling to the rock, my fingers slipping on the wet surface, but I manage to hold on. Shiwo holds on too, and for a moment, I consider attacking her. But even I have to focus on remaining alive. The water recedes, and we push forward. As we near the top, the rocky promontory reveals a small plateau where wind and rain converge in a chaotic dance.

I stagger to the summit, my legs trembling beneath me, and the world opens up into a storm-wracked panorama. The sea churns angrily below, waves crashing against the cliffs with deafening force. The village lies far beneath, barely visible through the thick veil of rain and mist. The beach is a blur of darkness and water, almost lost in the chaos.

"Shiwo," I manage, my voice ragged, fighting to rise above the noise. "This isn't you. You're not a monster. We can end this—you have to fight it!"

Her voice trembles with barely contained anger. "You murdered my brother, Gamu! And then you had the audacity to lie to me, to everyone. You stand there, pretending to be righteous, but you have no right—none at all—to speak about character or to pass judgment on anyone else's choices. You're a sinner—twisted and corrupted—and you should be focusing on your own judgment, your own reckoning. Not that it matters, though," her voice lowers, cold and venomous, "because you won't live long enough to seek redemption or repentance. You've already sealed your fate."

The accusation jolts me cold and I am stunned with guilt and sorrow. The memory of that night flashes before my eyes—the horror of what I had done, and my desperate hope to make amends without her ever knowing the full truth. But now, with the storm raging around us, there is no escape from her anger, no hiding from the truth.

I try to speak, but my voice falters, barely rising. "Shiwo, please, I never meant to hurt him. I didn't know. It was a mistake—a terrible, terrible mistake. I'm so sorry. I cared for Kail, I swear—"

But my words hang hollow in the air, unable to bridge the vast chasm of anguish that flickers in Shiwo's eyes. Her expression hardens into something implacable, a fury so deep and cold it seems to freeze the space between us. "A mistake?" she hisses, her voice cutting like ice. "You whore! Was lying to me also a mistake? Lying to me again and again and again," she spits, her voice colder than the rain pouring down on us. "And all the while carrying that thing inside you—that fetus that doesn't even belong to Kail! You know it, and yet you used his name like filth! You twisted it to manipulate me!"

Her hand, gripping the gun with white-knuckled intensity, trembles—not with fear, but with the sheer force of her rage and heartbreak. "You used his name to get inside my head, to control me!"

I collapse to my knees, the jagged rocks biting into my flesh as waves of nausea churn inside me. Desperation claws at my throat. "I would never do that. Please, Shiwo, you have to believe me. It belongs to Kail—I swear it on my life!"

She pauses again, her head tilting slightly as if she's listening to some insidious whisper that only she can hear. Her eyes darken further, her expression hardening into something cold, something terrifyingly resolute. My stomach knots with fear. The Shiwo I once knew is gone—replaced by something far more dangerous, something unstoppable. Fear grips me, cold as death, sinking deep into my bones.

But I can't give up. Not yet. "Shiwo," I rasp, my voice

trembling but insistent. "Please, think about Kail. Would he want this? Would he want you to become a monster in his name?"

"Shut up!" Her voice cracks, a raw edge of pain cutting through her fury. "Shut up! You don't have the right! Just be quiet!"

Her anguish is laid bare before me, a dismal display of grief and rage. Her drowning tears tear through me like shards of glass. All I want is to reach out to her, to hold her, to somehow make her see the truth buried beneath all the pain.

"Shiwo," I say softly, trying to rise, my limbs shaking beneath me, weak with fear and exhaustion.

"No!" She thrusts the gun forward, her hand trembling, but her eyes flashing with deadly certainty. "You're right to swear it on your life! You deserve to die for what you've done. All you've brought is death and suffering, Gamuchirai! We were better off without you."

Her words strike like a physical blow, knocking the air from my lungs. She's right—I can't deny it. I've ruined everything, over and over again. Self-loathing washes over me, drowning me in its cold embrace. A harsh, unforgiving voice rings in my head. It's your fault. You deserve this. Every ounce of pain, every drop of blood—they're because of you.

"I never meant to hurt him," I plead, my voice breaking

under the weight of my own guilt. "I cared about him deeply, Shiwo—he knew that. This baby… it's his. It's ours, Shiwo. I would never use it to manipulate you. Please, believe me. I cared for him, and I care for you."

My voice cracks as the tears I've been holding back finally break free. "I love you," I choke out. "I wanted so badly for this to be real—us, this baby. I wanted something that felt like a new start, a chance to finally get it right." My body shakes with grief, the words pouring from me like a confession. "I was selfish," I admit, my voice hoarse. "I'm so sorry, Shiwo. I care about you more than you know, and I never wanted to hurt Kail. They kidnapped me, and when I found out, it was already too late. You're right—I deserve to die. But this baby… he doesn't. Please, Shiwo. If you let him live, I'll give my life for his. I'll give him to you because I know you'll love him. You'll see Kail in him, I promise."

I am begging now, not for myself but for the life growing inside me, a plea for mercy that I know I do not deserve. "Please, Shiwo," I whisper, my voice barely more than a breath. "Let him live. Let something good come out of all this suffering."

I watch her face flicker between rage and deep, haunting sorrow, a storm of emotions battling behind her eyes. For a moment, I think I see a crack in her resolve, a hint of the Shiwo I once knew, but it vanishes as quickly as it appears. Her expression hardens again, settling into a mask of unyielding determination. "It doesn't matter anymore, Gamu," she says with chilling finality. "You can cry all you want, but I know the truth. You finally get what you deserve. Right here, right now, you're standing on the altar where all of this began." Her gaze sharpens, eyes cold and unforgiving. "And where all of this will end."

She steps closer and, with a decisive movement, tosses the dark, tangled cords aside. The weight of the ropes hits the rocky surface with a dull thud, quickly swallowed by the storm. "Bind your hands," she commands. Her hand trembles slightly, but her resolve remains.

With the gun pointed directly at me, I have no choice but to comply. My fingers, numb and slick with rain, fumble as I tie the ropes around my wrists. Each knot is a struggle, my hands shaking with fear, cold, and desperation. The coarse ropes bite into my skin, but I manage to secure them.

Her eyes never leave me as she grabs the ends of the knots to ensure control, quickly putting down her gun before pulling the ropes tighter. She ties additional knots, the rough rope cutting into my wrists with every movement.

As she finishes tightening the ropes, desperation drives me to use my blood magic. I seize her throat in a vise of magical force, and her eyes widen in shock. Her hands fly to her neck, clawing at the invisible grip tightening around her windpipe. She gasps for breath, stumbling back, her struggles frantic. For a moment, she loses control.

But then, I feel an intense pressure around my own throat. Instinctively, I claw at my neck, my bound hands reaching the source of the pain. Her face contorts with rage and determination as she fights through the suffocating force. Her blood magic flares to life, tightening the pressure around my throat further, her will pressing down with brutal intensity.

My vision blurs as the pain in my neck becomes unbearable. I struggle to maintain control over my magic, focusing on her despite my ragged breathing. The clash of our powers creates unbearable tension. Her fury and determination drive her to push through the pain, her magic relentless. My strength wanes, and darkness closes in. Finally, overwhelmed, I collapse against the rocks. She releases me, and I gasp violently for air.

Shiwo, still gasping and clutching at her neck, rises with triumph on her face. She takes a shaky breath, her body trembling as she recovers from the magical struggle. As I lie on the rocks, my strength ebbing away, I watch helplessly as Shiwo stands over me, her resolve solidifying into something cold and final.

Chapter 48

My birds swoop in, their bodies intercepting the shot meant for me. They spiral through the air, wounded but still fighting to shield me. I watch in horror and gratitude as they struggle, their wings fluttering weakly but their sacrifice preventing a fatal blow.

I turn to Six. Her eyes are wide, glazed, her body trembling under the weight of the unseen force tearing at her soul. The battle within her is savage, relentless, ripping her apart. "Tari! I forgive you!" I shout, my voice raw and fraying, caught between hope and desperation. "I forgive you!"

She gasps, her head jerking in recognition, but her hands stay frozen, the gun trembling violently in her grip. The barrel wavers, but doesn't lower.

"It's okay," I shout, trying to keep my voice steady, even as fear twists inside me. "We've won, Six. Gamu will change everything—I believe in her! All the pain, everything we've sacrificed, it's led to this!"

Her nod is fragile, desperate, but the serpent's grip tightens, its unseen coils squeezing ever tighter, feeding on her fear. Her body convulses violently, the gun trembling in her shaking hands. Her voice cracks, barely more than a strained whisper. "I... I—I am trying—t-t-to figh…"

The gun wavers between us, her pain etched in every quiver. I can see the war raging in her eyes, the agony tearing her apart. "I know, Six. I trust you," I murmur, willing her to hold on.

Her face contorts with torment, her voice breaking like shattered glass. "I—I… sorry… I." Her hands refuse to release the gun. The serpent's dark aura pulses around her, tightening its hold with every passing second, feeding on her despair.

"It's okay, it's okay," I say, fighting to keep my voice steady despite the terror clawing at me and the bone-deep cold from the relentless rain. "You're stronger than this. You've fought so hard—don't let it win now."

I try to inch closer, but her voice lashes out, sharp and desperate. "Don't!" Her body convulses again, her sobs torn from her throat, raw and jagged.

"Okay, okay—it's okay," I say, trying to calm her, but I can feel her slipping away, the darkness consuming her, the serpent wrapping tighter. "I'm here, Tari," I whisper, my voice trembling with emotion. "You're not alone. We're so close. Just hold on a little longer—don't let it take you." I can't lose her. Not now. I inch closer. "I love you, Tari."

CHAPTER 48

For a moment, her eyes meet mine—a fleeting spark of the Six I know—the one who's been through so much and fought so hard. I see her mouth the words I love you too, but the darkness swallows them, snuffing out the light in her eyes. She's trapped, caged in her own pain, her guilt, and the serpent feeds on it, its coils squeezing her tighter as her hands shake violently around the gun.

My heart shatters, the weight of helplessness pressing down on me. "It's okay," I say, my voice soft, flooded with sincerity. "It's okay. I forgive you, Tari. I'll always forgive you."

But I can feel it—the darkness has claimed her. It seeps into my bones like the cold of the storm, the dread coiling around my heart, sinking into my soul.

Our eyes lock one last time, and I know it's over.

Her sobbing slices through me, each sound a dagger to my chest. Her finger tightens on the trigger, slow, inevitable, devastating.

"I forgive you," I whisper again, closing my eyes. "I forgive you."

And I brace myself, waiting for the sharp crack of the bullet that will finally end it all.

"Put down the damn gun, Six!" Osi's booming voice pierces the roaring and whistling chaos, cutting through just enough for her to waver. "What are you doing? Put it down!"

Her head jerks, a flicker of recognition in her eyes as she fights against whatever has overtaken her. "He lied to us, Osi! I tried—I fought—but it's too strong! I can't stop it!"

His voice remains steady and unyielding. "You have to push harder! Sparrow is your best friend—he needs you! Put the gun down, Six!"

Her body convulses, twisted with anguish as she struggles. "I know—I love him, I love you, Sparrow!" she cries, her voice breaking. "Oh God, please—help me!"

Osi's tone hardens, more urgent now. "Fight it, Six! It's always been you and Sparrow—he's your little brother! Focus on that! You've always protected him—don't let this win, not after everything you've been through!"

A raw, tortured scream rips from her throat. Rain slashes down, blurring the space between us, but her eyes find mine, wide with torment. "Sparrow…"

"Tari," I breathe, clinging to the last shred of hope.

"Fuck!" She spits the word, her voice shattering. "Osi!" It breaks again, sharp and frantic. "I can't hold on! You have to do it—please!"

Dread grips me. "Do what?"

"No!" Osi bellows, his voice raw with pain. "I won't do it, Six! You have to fight! Don't give up!"

CHAPTER 48

"I can't!" Her voice cracks, a desperate plea, trembling with anguish. "You know me, Osi! I can't—if you love me, just end it! Please!" The words tear out of her, barbed and jagged, desperation shredding her from the inside.

"No! Wait!" The scream tears from deep within me as the horrifying truth crashes down. The world collapses around me. "Shoot me instead!" I cry out, over and over, my voice raw with despair. "Shoot me, Osi!"

I lunge toward her, desperate, but her voice lashes out, sharp as a whip.

"Don't fucking move, Sparrow! I'll kill you—I swear!"

For a heartbeat, everything feels suspended in the air, teetering on the brink. Then, the gunshot cracks through the downpour, louder than anything, tearing like a jagged bolt of lightning.

I freeze, the world blurring around me, and slowly open my eyes. Six collapses to her knees, her body crumpling with a brutal finality. The scene feels like it's playing out in slow motion—her fall, the devastation rippling through me, the sinking reality of what's happened.

Pain explodes in my leg, but it barely registers. I push through it, stumbling forward, my heart in pieces, every step a struggle. "Tari!" I scream, my voice breaking, raw with desperation and grief.

Another gunshot pierces the air, jolting me into tense readiness. Osi staggers, clutching his arm in pain. Grimacing, he returns fire, his shot finding the soldier responsible for wounding Six and sending him sprawling across the beach.

She looks up at me with a wan, bittersweet smile, her eyes reflecting a deep sorrow and resignation. Blood drips from her lips, quickly washed away by the relentless rain. Her smile, hauntingly gentle, falters as her body goes limp. A sob tears from my throat. "No, no, no!" I cry, cradling her lifeless form in my trembling arms. "Please, Tari, stay with me. Don't leave me like this." But her breathing grows slow and labored, each breath shallower than the last. Her gaze turns distant, as though her soul is retreating from this world.

She's gone.

The ocean roars with increasing fury, its waves battering the rocky promontory with escalating violence. The sea transforms into a primal, malevolent force, shaking the very earth beneath us. The air thickens with oppressive energy, sharp with an eerie, dangerous, dark presence. In this moment of chilling clarity, the prophecy unfolds with grim inevitability. The boundary between the mortal realm and the supernatural has dissolved into a nightmarish haze.

Destiny's crushing weight bears down on me but a hollow numbness has settled within, a profound apathy overtaking every thought. All that remains is a relentless void where hope once resided. I no longer care about anything but this

CHAPTER 48

excruciating loss. I want Tariro back. If not, I want to be consumed by the darkness because nothing else seems to matter anymore.

Violent sobs wrack my body as I clutch Tari's lifeless form to my chest. Her weight is a crushing burden, and the pain is unbearable—a gaping chasm that threatens to swallow me whole. The thought of a world without her is a knife twisting in my heart. Yet, deep below this unrelenting despair, a faint whisper of Tari's spirit seems to linger. Even as the darkness threatens to engulf me, I sense her urging me not to surrender. "I can't, Tari," I sob desperately. But through my tears, her voice, faint but insistent, pushes me to believe in my own strength and to find the will to continue. "I can't." My voice is raw, breaking with each repetition of the words. I sob until a moment of silence falls between us and urgency takes hold.

"Osi," I choke out, forcing myself to my feet despite the agony that wracks my body. His arm is bloodied, the crimson staining his clothes. "Tari," I cry out, "Tari is gone." Osi, despite his injuries, extends a bloodied hand and grips my arm firmly. His gaze, though pained, is resolute. "Go," he says through gritted teeth, his voice strained but unwavering. "Go and help Gamu—Six was in love with her."

The shock of his words hits me like a cold slap. All this time, Tari was… Did she know this about herself? But there is no time to dwell on the sudden truth. I nod, my heart pounding with a mix of grief and newfound urgency. "I will never let you go, Tari," I vow silently, steeling myself for what lies ahead.

Chapter 49

Shiwo hauls me to the precipice of the rocky promontory, where the storm's wrath drowns out everything but its own thunderous roar. The waves crash violently against the cliffs below, each one threatening to drag me down into the abyss. Darkness claws at the edges of my vision, pulling me closer to unconsciousness, but I fight it with everything I have left. Blood trickles down my face, warm and bitter as it slides past my lips.

She stands firm beside me, her grip on the gun unyielding, eyes wild with fear and desperation. "She's here!" She shouts over the storm.

I squint through the blinding rain, my heart pounding, and then I see it—a shadowy figure emerging from the deluge. My heart plummets to my stomach as the figure comes into focus. *Sparrow.* No.

Panic surges through me, but my voice is caught in my throat, trapped in a scream that never escapes. I want to shout, to warn him, to stop him from stepping into the line of fire, but the words die before they reach my lips. My magic—

useless now—fails me when I need it most. I can only watch, helpless, as he advances.

Sparrow moves with purpose, undeterred by the storm. His eyes lock on Shiwo, and without hesitation, he releases a flock of birds from his grasp. They burst into the air, their wings cutting through the rain like blades, diving toward her with deadly precision.

Shiwo flinches, her finger twitching on the trigger.

No.

The gunshot splits the air, swallowed almost instantly by the storm's howl, but the damage is done. Time seems to freeze for a breathless moment, and then Sparrow staggers. His expression shifts from shock to pain as the bullet finds him, and he crumples to the ground, his body folding in on itself.

A scream tears through me—raw, desperate—but it's lost to the wind. I collapse to my knees, reaching out for him, but the distance between us feels impossibly vast. His eyes find mine, wide with disbelief, as the life begins to drain from them.

"No!" The scream tears from my throat, raw and broken, shattering the storm's relentless roar. "No, no, please—no." The sight of his lifeless body rips something deep inside me, an unspoken fracture that tears through my soul. My strength crumbles in an instant, and sobs wrack my body, raw and uncontrollable. Every breath feels like a wound. "I can't do this anymore," I cry out, my voice unraveling into a desperate plea. "Please... I don't want to do this anymore." I don't even know who I'm begging—*Mwari,* my ancestors, the indifferent hands of fate. My heart buckles under the unbearable weight of grief, too heavy to hold. All I want is for it to end, to escape this relentless torment that won't let go.

He lies there, his pale skin like porcelain against the dark, rain-soaked ground. His beautiful white hair, once so full of life, is now plastered to his forehead, lashes dusted with water like frozen petals. Blood pools beneath him, turning the earth beneath him into a river of crimson that flows into the storm's hungry embrace. His eyes, once bright with kindness, now stare blankly into the void—empty, distant, and gone.

"Sparrow," I whisper, my voice breaking as I fall apart. Anguished sobs rack my chest, tearing through me. The rain swallows my tears, but it feels as though pieces of my soul are being torn away, leaving behind nothing but raw, gaping wounds.

My cries become a torrent of grief, raw and visceral, ripping through me. The weight of loss suffocates, twisting my pain into something darker, more monstrous. It consumes me, drags me under, drowns me. I scream—a ragged howl against the storm—begging for release. "I can't do this anymore!" The words splinter as they fall from my lips, each one laced with desperation. "I don't want to fight anymore! Just end it—kill me!"

My mind spirals into a pit of darkness and regret, cruel whispers stabbing deeper than any blade. I should have been faster. Stronger. Smarter. I should have seen this coming. I should have known. *But I failed him. I failed all of them.*

My body trembles wracked with guilt that crushes me under its unbearable weight. I don't deserve to survive this. I don't deserve the air still filling my lungs. *How many have died because of me?* My arrogance, my naive belief that I could protect them all—it's killed Sparrow, Taiwo… and Osi will fall next, all because of me.

Sobs choke me, my breath is jagged and broken, shame tightening its grip around my chest. "I should be the one lying there," I whisper hoarsely, barely audible above the storm's roar. "It should have been me." The thought claws at me like a barbed hook, twisting, tearing at my insides. My mind becomes a relentless assault of self-loathing, each thought sharper, more venomous than the last.

I *deserve* this pain. I deserve every agonizing moment.

But as deep as I sink into this self-hate, anger stirs in the shadows, an ember smoldering in the darkness. At first, it's small, barely a flicker. But it grows, catching fire as the vultures circle in my mind. The grief twists, sharpens, and reshapes into something hotter, something violent. Fury. Rage. It simmers beneath my skin, and I welcome it. Let it flood every corner of me. The grief has hollowed me out, and now anger rushes in to fill the void.

CHAPTER 49

How could this have happened? How could the ancestors just stand by as everything I love is torn from me? I've done everything right—returned, fought, sacrificed, bled—*and for what?* Was I just a tool to be used, a sacrifice to feed their dark whims? To be left here, broken and hollow.

This is what they wanted all along. I see it now—I was blind, misled by false promises and illusions of destiny. They wanted me here, wanted me to suffer, to be the sacrifice. It all makes sense now—their whispers, their cryptic guidance—it was never about salvation. It was about offering. I was their pawn, and they waited until this child was conceived, pleased that the final piece of their plan had fallen into place. They were never here to help me; they came only for this—another sacrifice sowed in blood.

I'm such a fool. I've led everyone into death's jaws, following whispers in the dark. They wanted this all along. They wanted me broken. And now... I am.

The anger consumes me and wraps itself around my heart like armor. I'm done with righteousness and done fighting against the darkness. The darkness is easier. Safer. And I let it take me, let it burn through me.

The force of my rage explodes outward, transforming my magic into a wild storm of uncontrollable power. My sorrow, my fury—they fuse into something unstoppable. The air vibrates with it, and the storm around me pales in comparison. My magic lashes out, raw and primal, tearing through the space between us with terrifying intensity.

I seize Shiwo by the throat, my will manifesting as a crushing grip. Her eyes widen in terror, her hands clawing desperately at her neck. But there is no control left. The storm I've become is beyond restraint.

She fights back, her magic lashing out in frantic arcs, trying to choke me, to overwhelm me. But my fury eclipses hers, an all-consuming inferno. It crushes her magic and drowns her resistance in its wake.

I struggle to my feet, my body trembling uncontrollably, but I refuse to stop. A guttural cry tears from my throat as I push forward, every fiber of my being vibrating with raw, unchecked power. Pain rips through me as I break my thumb, but it only fuels me further. My hand thrusts out, my magic tightening its grip around Shiwo's throat. I pour everything into it—every ounce of my rage, my pain—until it becomes a relentless force of destruction.

I glare down at her, her eyes locked with mine, wide with terror. Her fear feeds my anger and fans the flames inside me. She deserves this. She deserves every single moment of it. My magic tightens around her throat, and I savor the sound of her struggling breath. "Isn't this what you wanted?" I growl, my voice low and menacing. "You wanted me to become this—to prove I'm the villain, to force darkness and failure into my very soul? Well, here I am."

The grip of my magic tightens even further, and Shiwo's eyes bulge with terror. Her fingers claw at her throat, but I don't relent. I push harder, every ounce of my fury and grief

CHAPTER 49

pouring into that single, crushing moment. She gasps, and struggles, but I drive the pressure deeper, savoring the raw power coursing through me.

In this moment, nothing else matters. Not righteousness. Not sacrifice. Just the storm within, and the reckoning it brings.

A shadow looms behind me, vast and alive, an abyss swallowing the rocky expanse. It churns the stormy waves into chaos as if even the waters recoil in disgust. Tendrils of darkness slither around me, siphoning my life force, leeching my strength. My gaze stays locked on Shiwo, even as the shadow coils tighter, suffocating me in its sinister embrace.

If Sparrow came alone, then Six and Osi are dead. The thought gnaws at my soul, relentless, unbearable. I've failed them all. I was supposed to break the curse, become something greater, a hero—yet all I've done is lead them to their deaths. *Why did they believe in me? Why did I let them?* I tricked them into putting their faith in a lie, and now they're gone because of it. The darkness presses in, whispering accusations with every breath.

This is your fault. You killed your father. Everyone around you dies.

Pain tears through my abdomen—sharp, searing, relentless. I clutch my stomach, gasping for breath as a cry breaks from my lips. The darkness coils tighter, pulling at the fragile life inside me, draining the last of my strength. I feel it—

the serpent's claws deep inside, twisting, ripping away what little hope I had left. My grip on Shiwo slackens, the power I once wielded now slipping through my fingers like sand. My magic is fading. And all that's left is terror.

Am I really going to lose him too? The thought shatters me. Panic claws at my throat as I try to fight the dark force suffocating me. But it presses harder, my own demons clawing at my mind, whispering that it's too late. That there's nothing I can do.

The pain deepens, cutting through me with brutal precision, and I feel him—my baby—slipping away. I try to hold on, but it's like trying to catch smoke. Lightning splits the sky, illuminating a haunting vision—a flicker of ancient memories not my own. Stone altars etched with serpentine symbols. Flickering torches casting long shadows over a sacrificial slab. And a woman—her face eerily like mine—chanting to Nyoka with a cruel smile. In a sickening instant, she transforms into a yellow snake, slithering through rivers of blood, her tongue flicking out as she drinks deeply, reveling in the carnage. Her satisfaction is unmistakable.

The vision sickens me. The ground beneath me feels as though it's crumbling away. I am losing him. Losing everything. My baby, the last piece of hope I had left. I can't save him. I couldn't save any of them. I'm failing, just as I always have.

My strength fades, consciousness slipping further with each labored breath. The life force that once sustained me drains

CHAPTER 49

into the abyss, leaving nothing but emptiness behind. *"When this soul reaches into the abyss, it is forever altered, for no one can touch the void without carrying a piece of it within."* The old woman's voice haunts me.

My heart breaks and shatters into pieces I can never reclaim. This darkness... it isn't just an external force. It's inside me. It's always been there, waiting for this moment. I was never meant to escape it. I was never meant to protect anyone. My fate was written long before I ever thought I could change it.

I feel my baby fading, slipping further from me with every passing moment. I am losing him, and all I can do is let go. Let the darkness take him. Let it take me. This was always my fate.

Something cuts through the storm—a presence, startlingly familiar, emerging through the torrential rain. My heart lurches. It's impossible. *My mother.* She's walking toward me, clear as day. She was supposed to leave on the boats with the others. *Is this real?* Or is it just my fractured mind, offering me one last illusion before the end?

"Gamuchirai," her voice breaks through the storm, soft but full, like the quiet before dawn, heavy with the weight of ages. It cuts through the howling wind as if it was meant for me alone. "Nyoka thrives on your doubt, your guilt. It latches onto every insecurity you've buried, every unspoken fear, every whisper of inadequacy that's haunted you. It feeds on the shame you carry, the regrets that cling to your soul like iron shackles. It grows stronger with every stone you cast upon yourself, every time you believed you were not enough."

Her eyes, fierce yet full of love, meet mine. "You've been fighting the wrong enemy," she says, her voice heavy with sorrow. "You've been battling yourself, piece by piece, trying to carry burdens no heart should bear. And in doing so, you've let Nyoka grow in the cracks of your soul."

Tears stream down my face, my chest tight with grief and disbelief. "You're not real," I stammer, my voice breaking, but her steady gaze holds me in place.

"I am as real as your pain," she says softly. She steps closer, kneeling before me, her hand reaching out, glowing with an inner light. The rain seems to slow, as if even the storm bows to her presence.

I cry out, clutching my belly, pain rippling through me like the waves breaking against stone. "Mama, please… I'm losing him. I'm losing everything."

Her hand rests on my cheek, warm and steady. "To defeat Nyoka, you must stop running from your own shadow. It's not the monster outside you that you fear—it's the one inside. The one that tells you you're broken, unworthy. That's where Nyoka's power lies. And only you can take it back."

"I can't," I whisper, trembling. "I'm afraid of failing again."

CHAPTER 49

She leans in closer, her voice gentle but firm. "You haven't failed, my beloved. You've fought battles you never imagined and carried burdens too heavy for anyone to hold. And yet, here you stand. Do you not see your strength? Even now, in your darkest hour, you're still fighting."

Pain wracks my body again, sharp and unrelenting. "It's too much," I gasp. "I can't carry this anymore. I'm not strong enough."

Her gaze softens, filled with both pride and sorrow. She places her hand over my womb, and for a moment, the storm inside me quiets. "Strength isn't about never falling, Gamuchirai. It's about getting back up, even when you think you can't. It's about facing the darkest parts of yourself and refusing to give up. You are not defined by what you've lost, but by what you choose to hold on to."

Tears flood my eyes as I lean into her touch, desperate to believe her, but the fear lingers. "What if I lose him? What if I'm not enough?"

She smiles, sad but loving. "Even if you lose, you are never 'not enough.' Loss does not take away your worth. It's simply part of the journey. But you haven't lost him yet. As long as you keep fighting, as long as you hold on to hope, there's still a chance. For him. For you."

Her words sink into me, grounding me, even as her form begins to fade. "Fight, Gamuchirai," she urges, her voice growing distant, merging with the wind, the rain, and the earth itself. "Fight for him. Fight for the light inside you. Fight for the life still waiting to be lived."

I want to scream, to hold her here, to beg her to stay, but I can't. She's dissolving into the storm, becoming part of the rain, the wind, the very earth beneath me. And I'm left alone, clutching my belly, trembling, my heart breaking for the life I might still lose.

For a moment, I want to crumble. I want to give in. My body is tired, my spirit is shattered, and my hands still shake from the weight of everything I've lost. I feel the pulse of pain in my belly, the fragile life I'm so desperately holding onto slipping further with each breath. How can I face this when everything feels like it's unraveling? How can I fight when there's barely anything left of me to give?

But then I hear her voice, faint and distant, like an echo carried on the wind: "You must reclaim what you've lost."

Something stirs within me, something small but unyielding. I am still here. I am still breathing. And as long as I have breath, I have the will to fight.

Slowly, I rise to my feet, every muscle in my body screaming in protest. The world tilts, the storm raging around me like a violent sea, but I hold my ground. I force myself to turn and face Nyoka, the great serpent spirit coiled in the shadows. Its scales glisten like polished obsidian, reflecting flashes of lightning as its eyes bore into mine—burning, endless, devouring.

CHAPTER 49

For a moment, my fear almost consumes me. Nyoka's presence is overwhelming, a dark abyss that threatens to pull me under, to drown me in all my deepest terrors and failures. I feel its hunger for my pain, its desire to swallow me whole. My heart races, and for a split second, I feel the old familiar pull of surrender.

Is this it? Is this how it all ends? Everything I've ever loved—everything I've fought so desperately to hold onto—has slipped through my fingers like sand, washed away by the relentless tide of darkness. And now, my son, my last piece of hope, is being pulled from me too. I can feel it—his fragile life slipping further away with every beat of my heart. The darkness, always lurking, always hungry, is taking from me again. It just takes and takes, an endless void that devours everything I care about, leaving only emptiness in its wake.

No—*no more.*

A surge of emotion grips me, raw and powerful. My grief, my fear, my helplessness—they collide inside me like waves crashing against rocks. But underneath it all, there is something else, something I had forgotten. It's faint, but it's there: the hum of magic, like a whisper in the back of my mind, a reminder that I am not powerless. I am not just a victim of this darkness.

I am not a failure.

The realization sparks inside me, a quiet flicker at first, but it grows, feeding on the remnants of my will. *I've been here before, haven't I?* Broken, desperate, feeling like I had nothing left to give—and yet I'm still standing. I have stumbled, I have faltered, but I have not fallen. And this darkness—it has stolen so much from me, but it will not take my son. It will not take my soul.

The magic hums louder now, a steady thrum beneath my skin, a force that I had almost forgotten was mine to command. It pulses with the rhythm of my heartbeat, building with every breath I take, growing stronger with each ragged inhale. My hands tremble, but not from fear—from the power gathering within me, begging to be unleashed.

I am not a failure.

No, I am more than that. I am a mother. I am a protector. I am a force that this darkness cannot break. I feel the magic swelling, the energy coursing through my veins like a river, wild and untamed but mine. It is mine to wield, mine to shape, and I will use it to fight for what remains.

The darkness may think it knows me—that it can devour me whole, but it has never seen me like this. It has never felt the weight of my resolve, the strength of my love, the power of my fury. I have given enough, I have lost enough, and I will not lose again.

I close my eyes, focusing inward, gathering every ounce of magic that hums through me. I feel the warmth of it, the steady pulse of power that has been with me all along, buried beneath the weight of my despair. I call it forth now, letting it rise to the surface, letting it fill me from the inside out until it overflows.

I've made mistakes—more than I can count, more than I care to admit. But each one, every misstep, every wrong turn, led me to this moment. Running away when I should have stayed, making choices that broke me, this child—something they might label a *mistake*—they all brought me here. I might've thought that my failures defined me and were a mark of my weakness, but now I see them for what they were: steps on a path I didn't know I was walking.

The darkness shifts. It senses the change in me. Its suffocating weight no longer presses as it did before. It hesitates, its power unsure, wary of the force building in the air around me. And that's when I know—I can fight this. I can win.

I force myself to look up, despite the dread twisting in my chest. Nyoka looms above me, its serpent form massive, scales darker than the abyss, its eyes burning with molten fury. Its presence suffocates, its shadow stretching over me, but I dig deep, pulling from the strength within. I will not falter.

I confront the serpent with a heart battered, bruised, and lined with deep scars. These scars, though painful, have become a map of my life, each one telling the story of battles fought and lessons learned. I think of the sacrifices—of lives lost, of dreams shattered. I think of my ancestors, whose struggles paved the way for this moment, and of my own missteps, each one a step closer to the truth I now hold.

And now, I vow that nothing will be left in vain.

Lifting my hands, I summon my magic, raw and fierce. The energy thrums through me, charged with every sacrifice, every wound. It's no longer fragile or uncertain. It is a force—a living thing born of our collective will, pushing back against the encroaching shadow.

Surrendering to fear means future generations will pay for our failures. I will not let that happen.

Nyoka's roar shakes the sky, its coils twisting with ominous power. Lightning splits the heavens, illuminating its gaping maw lined with razor-sharp teeth. In a blinding flash, it strikes. Its tail crashes into the sea with a force that sends a towering wave over the summit, drenching me in a freezing deluge. I stagger, shivering, but resolve hardens within me like iron.

A single spark of determination flares into a wildfire, pushing me forward. Sometimes, that's all it takes—a single spark. I force myself to my feet, eyes blazing, ready for battle.

"Get out of here!" I shout at Shiwo, her face twisted in terror and confusion. The serpent's eyes flash, and another wave of dark energy crashes toward me. I throw myself aside, the cold bite of its power barely missing me.

CHAPTER 49

Planting my feet, I roar into the storm, "No more! You've had your way with us for long enough!" I pull on my magic, bending the elements around me, drawing on every ounce of strength left in me. I throw my hands out with a cry, and my magic seizes the serpent's form, clashing with its essence, and I wrestle back our fate with every shred of will I have.

Nyoka thrashes, its body writhing in agony as I tighten my grip on its dark heart. I feel its life force pulsing, frantic and desperate, as it fights against me, its massive coils ripping through the sea, sending waves crashing against the rocks. But I hold firm, my magic coiling tighter, forcing the serpent to bend to my will.

The serpent's dark scales shimmer, the unnatural light of its evil flickering as I tear through its flesh. Its roar splits the air, turning into a blood-chilling scream as I rip it apart—sinew and muscle shredding beneath the force of my power. It's body *snaps* in two, each half convulsing in the throes of death.

The seas churn violently, the waves crashing against the rocks with deafening thunder. The air reeks of ozone and dark magic, thick and suffocating. But I do not relent. I gather the last of my strength, my focus sharpening into a blade of pure will.

I weave the energy around each piece of the serpent's body, threads of magic binding and constricting its form, ensuring that no trace of its malevolent power can survive. I pull tighter, forcing every fragment of its dark essence back into the abyss where it belongs. The once-mighty serpent, now stripped of its power, is dragged into the depths with a thunderous crash.

Its halves sink beneath the waves, swallowed by the raging sea, leaving behind only a chaotic froth of water and debris. The overwhelming presence of darkness fades, dissipating into the deep, nothing more than a memory.

Breathless, I stand as the storm rages on around me. My strength finally gives way, and I sink to the ground, utterly spent. The waters still churn and froth, but slowly, they begin to calm, the fury of the sea subsiding. I clutch my stomach, feeling the steady, reassuring rhythm of my baby's heartbeat through my magic, a quiet promise of life. The torrential rain eases into a heavy drizzle as if even the storm acknowledges that the battle has come to an end.

As the first rays of sunlight pierce through the clouds, I sit there, bathed in the growing warmth of dawn. I hold my belly close, taking solace in this fragile peace, feeling the tenderness of a new day rising after the darkness.

With trembling hands, I gently take Sparrow's cold hand and place it on my belly. Tears stream down my face, unbidden but welcome. "He would have loved you," I whisper, my voice thick with emotion. A small bird flutters across the sky, delicate and free, and for a moment, I let myself imagine Sparrow soaring with it, at peace.

Suddenly, I sense a presence behind me. My body tenses,

and I turn, heart racing, only to find Shiwo standing there—drenched, trembling, her face etched with shame and sorrow. We meet each other's gaze for a brief moment, and I can see the weight of her regret mirroring my own.

"Come," I say softly, my voice barely more than a whisper, but it's enough. She hesitates for just a heartbeat, then steps forward and sinks to the ground beside me, her movements slow, tentative.

A heavy silence settles between us, filled with the weight of grief and unspoken words. The storm's remnants fall gently around us, the rain cool on our skin, but we don't move. The ache of our losses lingers in the air, thick and tangible, but so too does the fragile hope for something beyond it.

Shiwo reaches out, taking Sparrow's hand. Her tears flow freely, and for a long while, we sit together in quiet understanding—bound by our grief, and the fragile hope for forgiveness and healing.

Chapter 50

The weight of our reality settles like a stone, heavy and unyielding. With great effort, I push myself to my feet, my legs trembling beneath me, buckling under the exhaustion of battle. Shiwo stands at my side, pale and visibly drained, but steadfast. She sneezes softly, twice, a strange and fragile sound here, between this devastation. Yet she remains a constant presence, her hand on my arm grounding me as we begin the treacherous descent down the slick, rain-slicked rocks. Each step is perilous, the ground beneath us shifting with the remnants of the storm.

Long before we reach the beach, the scent hits us—a nauseating blend of salt, blood, and death that churns my stomach. I try to steel myself, but nothing could prepare me for the sight that greets us. The aftermath of the battle stretches out like a nightmare before us—a landscape of desolation. Bodies are strewn across the sand, lifeless and contorted, the dark smears of blood mingling with the sea foam. The tide washes over them, indifferent, leaving streaks of crimson in its wake before retreating into the foamy waves.

CHAPTER 50

My heart lurches painfully in my chest as I spot her—Six—among the bodies. She lies a few feet away, her form still, her eyes closed as though she might be asleep. But I know better. I feel my breath catch in my throat, and I drop to my knees beside her, my hands trembling as I reach out, the hope of her survival slipping through my fingers like sand.

"Six," I whisper, my voice breaking, but there is no answer. Her skin is cold beneath my touch, her body void of the warmth that once radiated from her so fiercely. The realization strikes like a blade to the heart, and I can't stop the sobs that rip through me. My chest heaves, and I collapse over her, my tears falling freely, soaking into her hair.

Shiwo kneels beside me, her own face twisted with grief and guilt. She hovers, her hand suspended in the air as if afraid to disturb my sorrow. Her hesitation is palpable, and I can see the torment etched into her features—the weight of blame she carries. She wishes it had been her, I can see it in her eyes. It's a feeling I know all too well—the crushing responsibility for a loss that feels too great to bear.

Despite my own anguish, I pull her into an embrace, and together we break. My tears mix with hers, our grief bound together, two souls shattered by the same storm. Losing Six feels like losing a part of myself like a piece of my soul has been torn away. She was my rock, my anchor in the midst of all this chaos. Now, all I want is to make her proud, to somehow honor the faith she placed in me.

I cradle her lifeless body, my fingers threading through her hair as I hum a melody, barely a whisper at first. A memory stirs—an image of an old woman beneath the ancient tree of my ancestors. Her wrinkled hands patted the earth as she hummed a song, a haunting melody that was at once sorrowful and soothing, like a lullaby for the weary soul. The sound returns to me now, shaky but growing stronger, as I pour every ounce of my grief into the tune, hoping it will bring some small measure of peace.

The waves seem to soften, responding to the melody with a gentler rhythm, the air calming around us. The song fills the space between us and the dead, weaving through the air like a fragile thread of solace.

"I'm so sorry, Tari," I whisper through the tears, my voice broken. "I should have protected you. I should have been stronger." I let the silence take hold, the weight of my words heavy, then take a deep, shuddering breath. I will give her the burial she deserves, a proper farewell. She gave me everything, and I owe her at least that.

My thoughts race. "Osi," I murmur, my throat raw with emotion. "Is Osi here?" Frantic now, I begin searching, my eyes scanning the bodies scattered along the shore. And there—only a few feet away—I see him, lying on his side, blood pooling beneath him. His chest rises and falls weakly, the slow rhythm of life still clinging to him.

"Osi!" I cry out, rushing to his side, my heart hammering in my chest. Shiwo helps me turn him over gently, and a surge of relief courses through me when I find a pulse—weak, but there.

"Osi, stay with us," I murmur, my voice trembling with emotion. His eyes flicker open briefly, just long enough for me to see a glimmer of recognition before they close again. Desperation rises in me like a wave, threatening to drown me as I press my hands to his wound, feeling the warmth of his blood seeping between my fingers.

I can't lose him too. Not after everything we've fought for.

I close my eyes and reach deep within myself, summoning the magic that hums beneath my skin, warm and steady. It answers my call, a powerful force responding to the urgency of the moment. I focus it, guiding the energy toward Osi's wound, feeling it wrap around him like a protective cocoon. The magic threads through his body, knitting torn flesh and bone, holding him in the fragile space between life and death. I concentrate on the rhythm of his heartbeat, syncing it with my own pulse, urging it to grow stronger, and more resilient.

The power surges through me, fierce and unrelenting, responding to my desperate need. I will the blood to stop flowing, to clot and seal the wound, to heal what has been broken. Slowly, I feel the wound begin to close beneath my fingers, the blood bending to my will, the magic knitting him back together.

His breathing steadies and his pulse grows stronger. I keep

my focus on him, guiding his body to heal, to fight, to live. Shiwo watches in awe as the bleeding subsides, the wound closing. I continue until I'm sure—until I feel him stabilize, the magic flowing through him, repairing what it can.

"Osi," I whisper, hope trembling in my voice. His eyes flutter open, and this time they linger, a flicker of recognition igniting within their depths.

"Thank you," he whispers, his voice weak but laced with gratitude.

I look at him, my heart aching under the weight of what I have to say. He is so beautiful, so kind—he doesn't deserve any of this. None of us do. The moment threatens to unravel me. "Six..." I begin, my voice shaking, my tears barely held back.

He squeezes my hand, pressing it against his chest, grounding me. "I know," he says softly, a tear slipping from the corner of his eye.

"And Sparrow..." I sob, the words forcing their way out, heavy and jagged, wounding everything between us. I feel the tears mixing with the snot running down my nose, my breath hitching as I fight the overwhelming sorrow.

Osi's eyes close, his own tears flowing freely, choked with emotion. I reach for him, pulling him into an embrace. We break together, our grief spilling out in sobs that shake us both to our core. "I'm so sorry," I whisper, my voice breaking.

CHAPTER 50

"I wish it had been me instead…"

His hand rests on my back, gripping me firmly despite the pain that makes him groan. "You'd just be trading one pain for another," he murmurs through his tears. His voice is rough, but there's a gentleness in it that pierces through the haze of grief.

We hold each other, our tears mingling, the rawness of our shared sorrow almost too much to bear. Each sob feels like a release, as though we're shedding the weight of the world, moment by moment. Slowly, I pull back, giving us both a chance to breathe, to steady ourselves. I help him sit up, my arm a steady presence behind his back, a silent promise that I'll keep him upright for as long as he needs me to.

His eyes drift to Shiwo, who stands apart, her guilt so palpable it's as if she's trying to disappear into herself. She meets his gaze, and for a moment, I see the torment she's trapped in. Osi's expression softens, a mix of confusion and compassion passing over his face. He doesn't fully understand the depth of her regret, but he refuses to place any blame.

"Bring it in," he says gently, his voice filled with a quiet understanding that surprises me.

Shiwo hesitates, uncertainty shadowing her every movement. But slowly, reluctantly, she steps forward and sits beside us. A small, bittersweet smile tugs at my lips as we sit there, fragile and broken, but together.

The moment of solace is shattered by a sound in the distance—an anxious murmur, the rustle of feet approaching. We turn our heads toward the village, where the villagers, once unconscious, now stumble down to the beach. Their faces are pale, eyes wide with horror as they take in the scene before them. Their expressions are a mixture of shock, disbelief, and terror as they confront the reality of what they've just witnessed.

It's their first glimpse of true brutality, the first time they've seen death so close, so vivid. For so long, their lives had been sheltered by the serpent's protection, kept in a bubble of safety and naivety. They had never imagined this—never dreamed that such horrors could exist within their world.

Now, they stand on the threshold of shattered innocence, their eyes filled with fear as they try to comprehend the bodies strewn across the beach, the blood mixing with the tide, the violence that had once seemed so far away now resting at their feet.

It's time for the truth to come to light. As their leader, I must face this responsibility head-on, no matter the cost. Osi looks at me, his eyes knowing. Without a word, he understands what I'm about to do—the promise I made to Six, to return and make things right. No more lies. No more hiding in the shadows of ignorance. We can no longer afford to live divided or oblivious to the darkness that plagues our world. Only together can we confront it—alone, we will be devoured.

CHAPTER 50

The crowd gathers around, their faces a mixture of shock, confusion, and fear. I step onto a raised platform made of uneven cobblestones, elevating myself above the sea of anxious expressions. They search for familiar faces among the fallen, desperate for comfort in a scene filled with horror. But there is none. I steady myself, meet their gazes, and speak with a voice that carries both authority and compassion.

"People of Mvure," I begin, my words cutting through the fearful murmur of the crowd, "it is time to step out of the darkness and into the light."

I pause, letting the weight of my words settle over them. "For generations, we've hidden behind a veil of ignorance, believing that our safety was guaranteed by an ancient and sinister pact with a serpent spirit. This pact, forged by our ancestors, promised us protection from the cruelties of the world. Even I, who left this place, was unaware of the full extent of this dark covenant. But in my time away, I have seen the world. I have witnessed the suffering beyond our borders—the suffering we believed we had escaped."

I let silence fall, watching the realization slowly spread across their faces. Fear transforms into something else—a yearning for answers. "But this protection came at a terrible cost, one we can no longer ignore. Today, we face the reckoning of our denial. The darkness we've kept at bay has finally come for us, and we must confront it."

I gesture toward the fallen bodies strewn across the sand,

the sight of them still raw in my mind. "Look around you. This is the price of isolation. We can no longer afford to live in ignorance, hiding from the world's darkness. If we are to survive, we must face it together, united in our resolve."

I sweep my hand across the beach, toward the devastation that surrounds us. "This is not just a tragedy for our village. This is happening everywhere. We have closed ourselves off from the world, driven by a misguided sense of superiority, believing we were untouchable. But today, we were nearly destroyed. And it wasn't the serpent that saved us—it was the bravery of those who fought for something greater than themselves. It was my friends, my comrades, who rejected segregation and isolation."

I pause, scanning the crowd for that glimmer of recognition, that spark of understanding. "The time for denial is over. My vow as your chiefess is to honor the fallen by confronting this new reality with courage. We must embrace our connection to the world, for we are not alone. We stand together now, not apart."

I let my hands fall to my sides, feeling the weight of my words settle in the air. The crowd stirs, their hushed conversations swirling around me, but I've spoken with conviction. I know the truth has landed, even if they aren't yet ready to accept it.

I step off the platform, and Shiwo, her face weary but determined, helps Osi to his feet. Together, we move through the crowd, the villagers parting to let us pass. Their eyes follow us—wide with fear, curiosity, and hesitation. They've been thrust into a new reality, and I know trust will take time to build. They are grappling with the horror of what they've seen, the truth they've been forced to confront. But there's no turning back. I've made my choice, and I am committed to rebuilding this fractured place into something stronger.

Our next step is to return to Nakuru. I must fulfill the promise I've made—to Six, to myself, and most importantly, to my son. *Tariro Anesu Darare.* That will be his name—a name that carries hope and resilience. He will grow up knowing both kindness and strength, guided by Osi, who will teach him to stand tall and embrace others as his people. He will be a child of both worlds—one who knows that strength comes from unity.

As for Shiwo, the path to forgiveness will not be easy, but I know that it is one I must take. True healing cannot come without it. The journey will be long and fraught with struggle, but I will walk it. For in forgiveness, I believe, lies the possibility of renewal, for all of us.

The future ahead is uncertain, and the path will be difficult, but I face it now with a new sense of purpose. We are bound by the losses we have endured, but it is through those losses that we will find the strength to build something better. Something lasting.

For the generations to come.

Chapter 51

The mine is a sprawling wound carved into the earth; a vast open pit that scars the landscape where lush greenery once thrived. The towering trees that once stood tall here have been felled, their stumps jutting from the ground like broken teeth, and the vibrant undergrowth has been reduced to a layer of choking dust that clings to everything.

The ground is a treacherous maze of loose rocks and jagged edges, each step a gamble. Rickety wooden scaffolding crisscrosses the pit, providing a precarious path between the mine's levels. The planks groan under the weight of the workers, threatening to give way at any moment. At the bottom of the pit, men and boys labor with the desperation of the damned, their bodies gaunt, their movements mechanical. They swing their picks and shovels with exhausted determination, chipping away at the earth in search of the precious *Zambura* ore buried within.

Zambura in its raw form is used by local healers in powerful rituals, believed to hold mystical properties capable of healing or protecting—a resource cruelly denied to its own people, whose villages have thinned, the weak and sick left to die. But Ndambira *craves it* and *demands* it refined, like a vulture, its true value tied to something unknown that makes it a goldmine for his regime. The ore is hauled up the steep paths in baskets, each load heavy and precarious, teetering on the brink of spilling back into the pit.

Above the pit, the processing area is a chaotic mess of frantic activity. Crude smelting furnaces belch thick black smoke into the air, their heat oppressive, turning the air into a blistering haze and the relentless clang of metal against stone echoes through the pit, a grating noise. Men and boys, their bodies reduced to gaunt shadows of their former selves, swing picks and shovels with mechanical precision, their movements driven by fear and desperation more than strength. Their hollow eyes reflect the dim light of a sun that seems to mock them, high in the sky but unreachable, just like their hopes.

Aisha, the overseer, stands at the center of this hellish scene, her figure both commanding and menacing. Her eyes gleam with cruel satisfaction as she surveys the operation, her soldiers fanning out around her, armed and ever-vigilant. The soldiers, bloated with pride and arrogance, mock the villagers with every passing glance, their laughter a discordant melody that grates against the natural harmony of the forest.

Everything I am witnessing stirs something deep within my chest, an anger that claws at my insides, threatening to tear me apart. I've avoided this place—*convinced* myself that I had no business here. But now, standing hidden in the undergrowth with Osi beside me, I know why. Seeing this, feeling this fury, would have only ignited the sense of responsibility I was trying so hard to bury. Osi's expression mirrors my own, his jaw clenched so tight I can almost hear the grind of his teeth.

One of the soldiers, careless in his arrogance, wanders into the woods to relieve himself, his whistle weaving through the trees. He stumbles through the undergrowth, oblivious to the eyes watching him, focused entirely on the mundane task at hand.

I narrow my eyes, feeling the familiar surge of power within me. My blood magic thrums beneath my skin, dark and potent, waiting for my command. As the soldier fumbles with his trousers, I step silently from the shadows. The magic winds around my fingers, invisible yet tangible, snaking forward like a tightening grip around his throat. He stiffens, a strangled gasp escaping his lips as the invisible grip tightens.

I move closer, my steps are as silent as the shadows that cloak me. My voice, a low whisper, drips with the weight of inevitability. I sing the song he was whistling, the notes twisting in the air like the hymns sung at burials, a haunting melody that carries the chill of death itself.

"Tirivakundi, takunda zvatakaona, Tirivakundi, takunda nemweya." — *"We are conquerors, we have overcome what we have seen, We are conquerors, we have triumphed through the*

CHAPTER 51

spirit."

His terror-filled eyes meet mine, but his body is no longer his own. He's under my control now, his will drowned beneath the tide of my magic. I feel his heartbeat quicken, the blood in his veins pulsing in time with my own. With a final, decisive thought, I bend him completely to my will.

His face goes slack, his expression is vacant yet resolute, and his hands drop from his trousers. Wordlessly, he turns and strides back toward the mine, the rifle casually slung over his shoulder. He reenters the clearing and blends seamlessly into the fray, drawing no suspicion from his comrades.

Aisha, still barking commands, doesn't even glance his way, her attention fixed on the next task. But before she can utter another word, the soldier under my control raises his rifle, leveling it at her head. The crack of the gunshot is a brutal, deafening sound that shatters the air. Aisha's body jerks violently, her eyes widening in shock as blood sprays from the wound, splattering the earth in a crimson arc. She crumples to the ground, lifeless.

For a heartbeat, there is only stunned silence—then the forest explodes into chaos. My puppet swings his rifle toward his comrades, opening fire with unerring precision. Bullets tear through flesh and bone, cutting down soldiers who scramble for cover, their faces twisted in terror. He moves with mechanical efficiency, his shots deadly, as if the act of killing is nothing more than a routine.

But his time is limited. Inevitably, he falls, shot down by his panicked comrade. I seize another soldier with my magic, wrenching control of his body, and he turns his weapon on his comrades, mowing them down with merciless efficiency. Bullets continue to fly, and they fall one by one, their confusion turning to frantic terror as they realize the enemy is among them but unseen.

I take control of yet another, and the slaughter continues, their numbers dwindling with every shot. They don't know who will turn against them next, and some attempt to escape, their eyes wide with fear and fleeing their duty. But escape is a mercy I *refuse* to grant.

The men and boys, seeing their captors fall, seize the moment. Armed with nothing but crude tools and the desperation of the oppressed, they rise up, their anger fueling every strike. Picks and shovels become instruments of vengeance, their blows driven by the years of suffering and humiliation they've endured. Blood and sweat mix on the ground as they tear into their tormentors, the air filled with the sickening sound of metal meeting flesh, of bones shattering, of cries for mercy drowned out by the roar of rebellion.

For every puppet that falls, I claim another, and the bullets crack through the air again, cutting down those who remain standing. One soldier, quick on his feet and quicker in his mind, realizes what's happening. He seizes a young boy, dragging him in front of him like a shield. He presses the barrel of his gun to the boy's head, his voice high and frantic.

CHAPTER 51

"Ndichamupfura,"— *"I'll shoot him!"* he screams, desperation leaking into his tone.

His comrades, seeing his command, hesitate, their terror momentarily giving way to a grim resolve. They stand there, their eyes wide with panic, their hands trembling on the triggers. The air grows heavy with tension as if the very atmosphere is bracing itself, every particle suspended in a moment of expectant stillness.

But I am relentless. I seize the fool who dares to use a child as a shield, and with a brutal twist of my magic, his blood spurts from his eyes as his life force is extinguished. He crumples to the ground, lifeless, the boy falling from his grip, unharmed but shaken.

The remaining soldiers are paralyzed, trapped between the urge to seize another hostage and the terror that doing so will bring them the same grisly end. They stand there, their fear stripping them of the power they once held. I take control of another soldier, his body moving with a jerky precision as he turns his weapon on his comrades, mowing them down with merciless efficiency. Osi leaps into the fray beside me, his fists and feet moving with lethal speed as he tears through the remaining soldiers. He is a force of nature, his rage manifesting in every brutal strike. The soldiers fall around him, their once-mighty arrogance crumbling into fear and death.

The men and minors continue tearing into their tormentors, and I step out into the clearing, my presence a specter at the edge of the battlefield. Every soldier who dares to aim at me meets a swift and brutal end, either shot by their own comrades or collapsing as the blood in their veins betrays them, their throats bursting with the force of my will. The forest, once a place of suffering, becomes a battleground of liberation, the mine a hellscape of blood and vengeance. The thick oppressive air is met with the scent of gunpowder, of blood soaking into the earth, of fear and death, and the raw, primal sound of victory.

The last soldier under my control crumples to the ground, drained and lifeless, as I relinquish my grip on his will. I stand there, my chest heaving, my skin burning with the sharp, stifling shards of heat, my heart thundering with the rush of victory and the crushing weight of what I have unleashed. The power surges within me, dark and intoxicating, but I force it down.

The men and boys drop their tools of oppression, tools that had just moments ago transformed into instruments of their liberation. They stand amidst the carnage, blood, and dust settling around them, and for a moment, there is no sound, no movement—just a collective pause. They don't erupt in shouts of victory; there's no jubilant cry to mark the moment. Instead, the weight of their newfound freedom crashes over them like a tidal wave, and they break.

Tears spill down hardened faces, men who have been forced to bury their pain deep within now cry like children, like the human beings they've been denied the right to be. They collapse into each other's arms, shaking with sobs, holding on as if they might disappear if they let go. Tears—tears are how you celebrate when you have suffered beyond endurance. Before there is joy, before there is shouting, there are tears.

And as I watch them, these men and boys who have endured so much, I feel a deep sense of honor. Honor that I was able to give them this, to give them back what was taken from them. They cry, and in their tears, I see the true face of victory.

My thoughts turn to Six, to *Otieno*. He doesn't know it yet, but he is next. His reckoning is coming too. Ndambira remains out of reach, but he will return, convinced that this time the crowd will cower once again at his arrival. This time, however, he will be forced to meet their gaze.

Six Years Later

A little brown boy wanders through the bustling center of Mvure, a caramel-coated apple tightly gripped in one hand. His eyes sparkle with delight as he eagerly licks the sweet treat, savoring every bite. In his other hand, he clutches a few coins, his tiny fingers counting the jingling change with a mix of curiosity and excitement.

Unaware of his surroundings, he meanders along, oblivious to the way people glance at him with admiration. They make way for him, smiles softening their faces as they watch him pass.

But then, his inattentiveness leads to an abrupt halt. He collides with something, stumbling back with a cry of "Ouch!" and rubbing the back of his shorts in discomfort.

In the new Mvure, people from all corners of the world mingle, their varied appearances forming a vibrant blend of shades, textures, and heights. But as the boy lifts his head, his gaze meets someone strikingly different from anyone he has ever seen. The figure before him seems almost angelic, with piercing blue eyes and long white hair tied in a side ponytail that flows gracefully over his chest.

"What is your name, little boy?" the stranger asks, offering him the apple on a stick. The crowd around them tightens, their curiosity unmistakable.

The boy straightens up, his brow furrowing in a mix of stubbornness and surprise. He reaches out to reclaim his apple stick and replies, "Tariro Anesu."

The stranger's smile is barely noticeable. "You look just like your mother," they say, their tone hinting at something more. "But she really shouldn't let you wander around the village alone like this—unless she truly believes I wouldn't come for her."

TO BE CONTINUED.

Made in the USA
Columbia, SC
13 July 2025